onionhead

BY WELDON HILL

onionhead

DAVID McKAY COMPANY, INC.
New York

Contents

PART IV—The Hooligan Navy, Summer, 1942

PART I
The Draft Dodger

CHAPTER 1

Hunger

I T WAS the fashion in those haunted days for a moneyless young
male student to regard himself, publicly and privately, as doomed.
Destined for no good end, slated for nothing but misery and sorrow
and insatiable hungers of the mind and soul, and certainly the body.
But it was required that he accept his gaunt prospects with a degree
of swaggering arrogance, with fatalism, with a jaunty sneer and a
hollow laugh and a deadened eye. Live to the hilt, they told one
another, for tomorrow may never come. But it seemed to Alvin
Woods that about all any of his contemporaries at the University
did was sit around and talk about living to the hilt—and tomorrow,
such as it was, persisted in arriving on schedule.

In America there was the grimly familiar economic depression
which only a convenient war, perhaps, could solve; in Europe there
was a raging and frightening, but horribly convenient war. And
nobody was really neutral. Not America. Not Oklahoma. Not the
laughingly sardonic young men at the University who were at once
intimidated and exhilarated by the thesis that the world, to misquote
somebody they had read, ended with either a bang or a whimper.
But ended soon.

Al Woods was generally in accord with this dismal philosophy,
except that his subconscious mind persisted in associating Death with
Malnutrition, rather than Cold Steel, or Fiery Disintegration. At the
University of Oklahoma, where he misered his way through two
semesters of Freshman courses on money saved from a year in the
Civilian Conservation Corps and a summer on an ice truck, he agreed
with most of his insolvent associates that theirs was The Doomed
Generation, whose best hope was for the least of several evils. They
were not attending the University so much to campaign for degrees
as to kill time while waiting wearily for time to kill them. They were
drifting through a void, with a wary eye cast now and then over the

3

shoulder. Al understood that, like himself, they were stalled, and stalling.

He was nineteen, and then twenty, that year; he had never known anything but hard times as far back as he could remember, and sometimes in one of his more ironic moods he said that he was a charter member of the Lost Weight Generation. Two things obsessed Al: food and sex. He never seemed to have enough of the first, and he never seemed to have *any* of the second. His daydreams were replete with banquets and orgies. When he and his doomed companions sat around drinking ten-cent beer spiked with dollar-a-pint grain alcohol, bemoaning the gruesome and no doubt gory future hovering before their knitted scholar's brows, Al could discuss food as sensually as his transient friends could describe in minute anatomical detail the numberless women they had left sprawled in their wakes. Al was naïve and gullible, and never doubted the legends of brawny lust he was privileged to hear; he only felt a kind of masculine despair and growing inadequacy because he himself wore no trophies at his belt. Sometimes, in order to hold up his end of the discussion, he elaborated on his few adolescent conquests, which had actually been more in the nature of stalemates than victories, but mostly he preferred to recall with hot pleasure the three weeks when he had worked as salad boy in Deacon's Restaurant, and how he had gorged degenerately on shrimp and cream pies and fragile pastries and caviar—until Mr. Deacon caught him with a hand in the premium sturgeon roe.

Al made a B-minus in math that year, but had an awful time balancing his budget. The basic equation had to do with food versus sex. Traditionally, you spent a dollar or so on a coed before you attempted to drag her off into the shrubbery on the less frequented campus precincts; you built her up with caresses and pawings in a movie, or better yet with three or four cans of demoralizing beer in some isolated tavern, and then on the way home you moved in for the kill. More often than not your quarry eluded you, even after you had stalked her cautiously for several evenings in a row, and there was no consolation in the knowledge that you had bought your snares and bait at the expense of your stomach. All in all, that year was about as frustrating as any of the rest of Al's frustrating years, but on the other hand he had some of his best failures as a Frosh at the University of Oklahoma. There were, indeed, some near misses.

On a starry night in early June on that academic safari through the watchman-infested wilds of the campus, Al thought for one dazed, ecstatic moment that he had finally brought down a fine trophy doe, but even as he gloated over the warm, trembling form on the grass, the slender creature bounded to her feet and fled. A toad, seeking insects in Al's Eden, had started to climb over the girl's bare shoulder at that strategic moment, and her weak desire to stay was greatly exceeded by her strong impulse to get the hell out of there. By the time Al caught her and got her quieted down, she had lost all interest in outdoor sex. He took her home, hating toads.

That was how it always happened with him where girls were concerned, and it was almost as bad with food. His idea of paradise was himself reclining among satin cushions beside a steam-heated swimming pool with a phonograph playing Glen Miller records while a squad of lavishly naked girls served him platters of fried chicken and hamburgers and roast pork and assorted desserts, with pitchers of milk and beer and pots of hot black coffee. After he was glutted, he would light an expensive cigar, line up his women, and say, Eenie, meenie, miney, moe ...

Much of the time Al felt stranded and baffled and insecure, with very little hope of improving his situation. Sometimes he had a tendency to feel sorry for himself, and he would adopt an attitude of sulky, hopeless defeatism. Where do I go from here? he would ask himself. He never got any satisfactory answers. He was poor and somewhat shabby and his pipe (using ten-cent tins of tobacco) and his ten-cent-a-pack cigarettes, the simple necessities of a twenty-year-old scholar, were luxuries. He couldn't afford to eat in the campus cafés or boardinghouses, and was often reduced to buying bread and crackers and cheese and potted meats and jelly and instant coffee at grocery stores, from which ingredients he fashioned unsatisfying banquets in his gloomy basement room. And sometimes, when he had squandered his weekly food allowance promoting unsuccessful amours, he prowled the town at night and stole milk from front porches, and fruit from trees (in season), and raided the town gardens for vegetables.

This was, to be sure, a strange and sometimes wonderful period in Al's life, full of hope and despair, gloom and elation, gnawing physical hungers and mental gluttony. Through it all he clung to one wistful ambition: somehow to get through college. Maybe if a man could earn a degree of some kind, he would be less doomed.

A man with a B.A. might get to be straw boss on a WPA ditch-digging job, instead of a mere prop for a shovel. Poverty might be more easily borne by a licensed intellectual. But even in his most optimistic moments he didn't see how he could finance three more years of schooling.

Afterward, half-joking, he liked to say in retrospect that if the draft hadn't come along when it did he would either have starved to death or been shot robbing a grocery store.

Oh, they were conscious of the looming horror of war, and oh, they were sardonic and ironic and sometimes funny about it, too, the young men of Al's acquaintance. "Hello, soldier," they greeted one another, and in parting they said, "See you in the trenches, soldier." Al would laugh without humor and agree that every man should be entitled to one violent and bloody war in his lifetime, just to broaden his experience and understanding—but fundamentally he did not believe it. He did not feel entitled to a war at all, even a mild, unsanguinary war. But there were rare, wild moments when drums would thunder in his mind and he would suddenly long for a war—it would erase everything else, it would be all-consuming. It would, in short, take the strain off a guy who stewed constantly about food and women and shelter and warmth and tobacco. Come on, you kiss of death, Al would think with a grotesque kind of sweet resignation, make my plans for me. Make me an automatic man, fed and oiled and loaded and aimed and fired and wired for sound; and let it happen now, boy, because this old stuff can't go on like this much longer. Then, having accepted death thus easily and even gladly, Al would be filled with a great bursting sense of pity and affection and understanding and brotherhood for his trapped, helpless, haunted, futile, depression-spawned contemporaries; and he would mutely challenge inscrutable fate with reckless abandon. Hold my goddam sword and turn away your face, for I shall run upon it, boys—and they can pour out all the beans and weld iron pants on all the ladies.

He read a lot of Hemingway and a lot of Thomas Wolfe that season, and he was torn between an impulse to sit around drinking whatever came to hand and a powerful urge to go racing across the nocturnal campus uttering poignant goat cries and ropy laughter. And in fact he did a good deal of both.

And always, inevitably, eternally, he was hungry, and by the time June rolled around and the tennis courts were aswarm with nubile girls in maddening shorts, his money had dwindled to nothing and it was time to go try to find some more.

He could have had his ice-truck job again that summer, but it paid only two dollars a day, out of which would come rent and food; and even with the extra income one might derive from a careless accounting of the daily cash receipts, the iceman job would not have enabled him to save the kind of money he would need to scrape through another year of school.

Therefore, logically, Al headed for the wheat harvest. The kindly and obliging landlady, who had attractive legs for all her years, agreed to look after Al's scant belongings, including the portable typewriter he'd foolishly taken as security for a small cash loan in the previous autumn; and Al made a bundle of old clothes and started hitchhiking toward Kansas, secretly suspecting that the land-lady had a yen for him—and wasn't it a shame that a nice-built, well-preserved woman of forty-something like her had such bad teeth?

In the wheat fields they paid a man four dollars a day and fed great staggering dinners at noon—fried chicken, pork chops, ham, sausage, mashed potatoes, potato salad, green beans, buttered beets, candied yams, roasting ears, sliced tomatoes, cole slaw, cantaloupes, milk and iced tea and hot coffee with thick country cream; and they let the harvest hands bathe in the windmill water tanks and sleep in the barn lofts, so that whatever you made in the wheat was all gravy and a guy could really save up some dough in a couple of months. At least this was the way Al had heard it told.

But when he got to the grain country it seemed to him that every other male between twelve and eighty-five had had the same idea, and he suffered severe stomach pangs from missed meals, and chigger and mosquito bites from sleeping on courthouse lawns, be-fore he learned that if you stayed a few days behind the harvest proper you could get jobs plowing the stubble fields for as much as three dollars a day and keep, which might in the long run add up to a better deal than the harvesting—especially in regard to the eating. So Al drove the big Popping Johnnies around and around on the flat sprawling fields of wheat stubble that checkered the rolling bare plains stretching away endlessly under the hot blue, cloud-free skies like a golden ocean, with each scarce tree like a lonely green sail becalmed. From daybreak until noon and from one o'clock until dusk Al stood wide-legged on the decks of the great, roaring tractors, his shirt off and his body browning from sun and wind and dust, his toughened hands sure and firm on the wheel, squinting ahead through the shimmering heat haze like Columbus seeking first sight of the new world. Sometimes there were little cottony puffs of white cloud drifting across the limitless sky, and three or four times there were thunderheads and brief silver rains that stopped the plowing for half a day, or failed to stop the plowing at all, but mostly it was only a hot sun in a deep blue sky, and Al feeling insignificant and important and solitary and at home there below, his ears numb from the deafening racket, feeling good, feeling wonderful, his troubled mind at rest and his heart full of life, full of the world, full of the joy of a man working hard and earning wages.

And there was food. Three banquets each day. And there were no girls to torment him with their unavailable delights. At night his tired body rested, and his libido rested too. He had found true peace.

But it had to end some time, and by the last of July the ocean of stubble was all charted, the sprawling land resting and awaiting the seed and the rains. Al headed back toward the campus with sixty-one dollars in his pocket where he could feel it often and reassure himself and gloat over his well-earned fortune. But there was still August to get through. Wiser this year than last, he meant to be on campus early and seek a meal job washing dishes, so that he need not use his money for his stomach, but there would be no hiring of dishwashers until late August or early September, a month away. So Al set a course for Oklahoma City. He must eat a little in August, although he had gorged himself in June and July, and it seemed to him a man who only wanted modest compensation should have no trouble finding some kind of two-bit stop-gap interim job in the city.

He found a cheap hotel which catered to poor business-college students, and scouted out a café where you could get a huge bowl of macaroni with a scoop of chili for fifteen cents, plus four thick slices of greasy toast and all the grape jelly you wanted. Then he began reading the want ads, and journeying afoot all over the city answering them. Alvin Woods and all the rest of the gaunt recruits in the vast legion of unemployed men.

After a week he was disheartened and eight dollars poorer, and it was a long time until September, and he was hungry again with that hunger that seeps into the mind and heart. In panic he began eating stale doughnuts at ten cents a dozen and Reno Street blue-plate specials at fifteen cents, but by now his approach to potential jobs was hopelessly negative. "I don't guess you're hiring anybody today," he would say with a mixture of resignation and resentment, and the prospective hirer would agree. A few employers, perhaps touched by Al's look and manner, spoke kindly and suggested he leave his phone number, but he was unreceptive to this idea—he wasn't after a job next month, but now, today, this very by God minute. When asked what he had done previously he would say wearily that he had washed dishes, worked as a salad boy, delivered ice, worked in the broom corn and wheat harvests, worked a few days in a flour mill, driven a tractor, and served in a variety of positions in the CCC. Saying it, he knew it sounded unimpressive, and it always seemed that the interrogator was duly unimpressed. Finally Al stopped bothering with the want ads altogether. His feet were sore from pounding the pavement, and he spent much time resting them in his shabby room.

The landlady, a wan, sickly-looking woman who never seemed to go out of the gloomy hotel into the summer sunlight, remarked that if he would let her put somebody in with him she could cut his rent fifty cents a week, and Al agreed reluctantly, prizing his moody solitude but wanting to pare expenses. That same night he awoke some time after twelve to find a hairy stranger in his bed, with one heavy, whiskery, hot leg draped affectionately over Al, snoring and in a state of erotic excitement. Alarmed, Al elbowed him awake and they introduced themselves, and the few nights Al stayed after that he slept on the extreme edge of the bed. This lusty bedfellow was called Grubbs. He was twenty-two, a flabby, pimply, sore-eyed youth who was earnestly and drearily putting himself through business college by hustling newspapers. He took Al over to see the circulation manager one morning at 4 A.M. when he went to work, and the manager said he might have a place for Al in a week or ten days. But Al couldn't wait a week or ten days for a half-promised job that, Grubbs assured him, might pay him as much as ten or eleven dollars a week.

In the back of his mind, Al had been thinking for some time that he ought to go see his father before returning to the campus. When his current week in the hotel terminated, he found that he was down to thirty-nine dollars and sixty cents, and he decided to head back to the University as soon as he had paid a duty visit to his nearest of kin. Maybe he could find some cash jobs in Norman; if not, he might as well be loafing in familiar surroundings. Meanwhile, he hadn't seen his father for a year, or heard from him since Christmas, when a card had come from a small town near Tulsa.

It required three days of hitchhiking for Al to track down his peripatetic father, a cold trail leading through two far-apart shops before he finally located Alvin Woods, Senior, barbering in a small community a few miles from Ardmore, in the southern part of the state. A garrulous, hard-drinking, restless, migrant barber, Alvin "Windy" Woods welcomed his visitor with the customary loud and somehow, Alvin Junior felt, phony cordiality that was his hallmark.

"Well, I'll be a son-of-a-monkey's uncle!" Windy Woods bawled at sight of his only child. "Damned if it ain't old Hotshot!"

And to celebrate, he knocked off work for the day.

CHAPTER 2

Free Haircut and Advice

AL awoke, sick and depressed, on a pallet on the floor of a dingy furnished room, and reconstructed the events leading up to here. There had been, yesterday afternoon and evening, a series of beer joints, in each of which Windy Woods asserted loudly that this was his boy Al who was by way of getting himself a highfalutin education over at the college in Norman, Oklahoma, in order that he wouldn't have to operate a pair of clippers for a living like his ignorant old man. All of which embarrassed Al acutely, and at the same time saddened and irritated him; he was ashamed of his feeling of hot shame for his thick-skinned, thick-tongued father, and tried with some enthusiasm to get drunk enough to lose his inhibitions and develop at least a small feeling of filial pride, or affection, or something, for his father, but it hadn't worked. He only got drowsy and dizzy and ill on the sour 3.2 per cent beverage that had such a potent effect on the barber, and around ten o'clock he had dragged the old man—fifty-two, but an old man just the same—to this awful room where he lived. And Al had slept on the floor by choice, because he was apprehensive that his father would wet the bed after drinking all that beer. He always had, and he did this time, too.

Lying there stiff and sore from the comfortless pallet and with sour cotton in his mouth, Al rejected whatever vague, half-formed ideas he might have had about letting his father support him until September. Being around his old man was a very depressing thing.

After breakfast he had his father go with him to a notary public to fix up a document giving written permission for Al to enlist in the Marines, a contingency Al had remotely entertained for some time. And then, with the paper in his hand, he was abruptly, urgently desirous of getting out of this town.

"Well, good-by, Pop," he said. "Behave yourself."

His father answered his weak grin with his own insincere, automatic grin, and shook his head and squinted sadly down the hot August street of this one more town where he would no doubt soon wear out his welcome. "If you do enlist," Windy Woods said, "you'll come see your old dad before you go hellin' off no tellin' where, I reckon?"

"Sure, Pop," Al said without conviction. He had a feeling, a sad but also strangely relieved feeling, that he might never again see his skinny, long-necked, long-nosed father with his big-toothed grin and sad blue eyes, this blowhard barber with his windy stories and his unenlightened but unshakable political and religious notions, his impossible lies and bragging, his elaborately empty sense of humor, his childish irresponsibility, and his uneasy, self-conscious, clumsy attempts to reveal his vague, mute affection for his only son. Windy Woods, that breezy, loud, comical barber on the back chair (always the back chair and never that for long) who had tried railroading and farming and running a filling station and clerking in a grocery store and being town constable and digging WPA ditches, but always came back in the end to the only thing he was good at, which was operating the back chair in small-town barbershops and, for a while, amusing people.

"Need any dough, Hotshot?" Windy Woods asked, and Al was sorely tempted. Better me than the beer joints, he thought. But a kind of murky and somehow resentful pride made him shake his head quickly.

"I'm loaded, Pop," he said, and his father laughed his brief snorting laugh and said, "I guess we were *both* loaded last night, if we're gonna be honest about the matter." He was always willing to share the blame with others. He was generous to a fault, having so many.

"That's right," Al said uneasily. "Well, I better get going."

"Say, you need a haircut, Hotshot. Come get one on the house."

Al hesitated. He did need a haircut. Shrugging, he accompanied his father to the shop, where he was introduced to the two other barbers for the second time as Windy's son who was getting a high-class education over at the state university so he could be a big shot in industry, or a scientist or something, not just a poor hardworking barber. And then, while he cut Al's hair, Windy Woods carried on a constant, ponderously humorous, and not very intelligent monologue which was in the nature of a conversation with the other barbers and their customers, and Al was hot with his squirmy sense of humiliation, and ashamed for feeling so.

Once, long ago, Al had believed his father was a noble, brave, intelligent, honest, and thoroughly admirable fellow; a sort of minor god. In those days Windy had been a respected and gregarious pillar of the community, a singing man with a fine clear tenor voice, always ready to sing "Rock of Ages" and "Nearer My God to Thee" at the funerals of friends and casual acquaintances, and once the dying wife of an old crony had gasped out her request that Windy Woods should supply the threnody at her final rites. The boy Al had also known his father once as a brave man who killed a mad dog that was terrorizing the small town's main street with only a claw hammer for a weapon. The people used to say, "That Windy Woods, he ain't afraid of the devil himself in person." In Al's mind there were shattered fragments of fine warm memories of his father carrying him high astraddle of his long neck, and sneaking quarters into Al's pockets, memories of surprise gifts and of being awakened in the dark hours before dawn to go squirrel hunting or fishing with his father. But somewhere it had all begun to change, and sickening revelations occurred, doubts and suspicions had elbowed faith and pride aside. Windy Woods had become a man who got drunk, was remorseful, promised, but drank again; a man who wept piteously when he was drunk, or boasted, or became truculent. This different father was angry at a small boy's grief when his dog was mangled under the wheels of a switching railroad engine, and said impatiently, "Goddammit, I'll get you another dog." And he was a man who boasted fiercely around town of how mercilessly he intended to thrash a character assassinator named Sam Haley on sight, and then walked down alleys to avoid sighting his detractor. In time, before the stunned eyes of his child, Windy Woods was stripped of his disguise, laid bare and naked in all his weakness and foolishness and inadequacy. Now, at twenty, Al resented the fragile thread of family affection that still bound them together long after he had judged his father from the critical, disenchanted viewpoint of an adult male; this tenuous sentiment was a source of guilty embarrassment to Al, so that he couldn't stand to be around his father for long, and yet he was ashamed of his desire to be apart from his father and free of the thin shackles of their blood kinship.

The haircut, careful and thorough, and the brassy voice going on and on, solving with idiot ease the great problems of the day, the snorting, nasal laugh, the wheezy breathing above Al's prickling scalp. The perpetual uninterrupted spate of badinage and ponderous, uninformed opinion, as Al lay gratefully hidden under the lather and the hot towel. The brisk scalp massage and application of fragrant tonic, and now the quiet words for Al's ears alone. "You're gettin' to be a good-lookin' man, Hotshot." The hangover breath sour on Al's face. "But you gotta take care of your hair." He ran skeletal fingers through his own thick, graying mane; proudly, ostentatiously. "Never neglected mine," he said, "and you don't see many fellers my age with hair like I've got, I mean to tell you." He had nothing to bequeath his only heir in the coin of pride or honor or self-respect, but only his old man's vanity, his unvanquished hair. And the demonstrated fact that people always *liked* him and were vastly amused by him—at first, for a while, at least. "Son, what you got to do, you got to *stimulate* your scalp; keep it clean an' keep the blood circulatin'. Massage her, like this." He demonstrated, his fingers digging and gouging Al's scalp. "Brush it every day, son, an' keep it clean an' healthy up there, see."

Al felt a vague sense of alarm. What did his father know? Did he see something wrong; were there signs of eventual baldness evident to his trained eyes? Or was this urgency and solemnity a masking of some deeper concern? Did this urgent advice about his son's scalp hide a late-in-life concern for the complete Al?

The object of the worrisome advice glanced surreptitiously at their two images in the mirror. He did not resemble his father much, and was secretly glad he didn't—and ashamed of the feeling. At five feet eleven inches, he was two or three inches taller than his parent; at a hundred and seventy pounds (he had lost a few pounds since his return from festive Kansas) he was twenty or more pounds heavier than his father. They had the same straight nose, only his was not so long, or so thin; the same slightly flaring nostrils, the blue-green eyes, the wavy hair. But Al's was light brown—and not so thick as his father's. Well, okay, so he took after his mother, who had died when he was fourteen. She's had sort of fine silky brown hair and the high forehead and the wider jawline. All in all, Al decided, any resemblance to his father was satisfactorily superficial.

He got out of the chair. "Well," he said awkwardly. "Thanks, Pop."

"My pleasure." His father grinned. "Look, Hotshot, what's your rush? Stick around a few days. Seems like we might find something to do. Go fishin', maybe. Haven't seen much of you lately, son."

"I got to get on back to school and hustle up a part-time job," Al said, avoiding the sad gaze. "I got to be traveling, Pop."

His father looked at him with the sad, distracted, unfocused stare, and suddenly the feeling was very strong in Al that this really was the last time he would see his father; this might well be the final parting, and he believed that his father sensed this too and was groping for some succinct phrase, some eloquent final expression that might bind them closer in the future, although far apart in miles and time. It was a tense moment, threatening mawkish intimacy to Al's rejecting mind, and he wanted to hurry, to get away before his father said something embarrassing. But in the turmoil of his mind there was yet an area that responded to the moment, and he thought he was close to a brief understanding of at least a part of his father's nature: this thing of always moving on, always leaving one place and going on to a new scene, a fresh start; escaping from dissatisfaction into foolish hope, feeling that somewhere else things would be different and better despite the fact that he carried his monster with him wherever he went. The desire to run away from unpleasantness was something else the father had bequeathed the son, so that now Al desperately wanted to run away from the itchy unpleasantness of being the son of a shabby, migrant, back-chair barber named Windy Woods.

He shook his father's thin, soft barber's hand self-consciously, grinned lamely, and his father stared sadly past him and said with a kind of melancholy that had in it overtones of agony, "You gotta take care of your hair, Hotshot." Giving Al the memorable farewell phrase, offering his son all the wisdom he'd accumulated in fifty-two years of futility. Al nodded sheepishly, embarrassed, painfully conscious of the other men in the shop, and took up his hobo bundle of clothes and went out of the shop, hurrying along the dusty sidewalk of the small town toward the open highway that ribboned away forever through the free open land. He felt pursued and literally wanted to run, and behind him his father came to the barbershop door and watched, and called at the very last, "Give 'em hell, Hotshot!"

In the furnace glare of the dry August day Al began to hitchhike back to the campus. He had no definite plan, other than to go back and try to get a dishwashing job. He had no real hope; he knew he was defeated; his little hoard of money wouldn't enable him to pay fees and buy books. But he felt a compelling nostalgia for the campus, as if it were his home, and he would go there and stay there doggedly, as long as he could hold out, waiting for fate to hand him some Big American Opportunity—like a board-and-room job. In the back of his mind he saw military service as a kind of rocky cushion to fall back on when all else failed. As a Marine, he would be fed and housed. But meanwhile, in Norman, Oklahoma, he knew the location of most of the good kitchen gardens around the campus, and tomatoes ought to be ripe and plentiful now. A guy who liked tomatoes could make out for quite a while with little cash; there would be apples and other late vegetables to take up the slack, too. A guy could exist.

Standing beside the highway awaiting a lift, Al counted his money and discovered with a sickening shock that somehow or other he had managed to spend four dollars and twenty cents while roistering with his intemperate father last night. He was now down to thirty-three dollars and eighty-five cents. It looked as if he would be eating a lot of forage unless he came up with some kind of job in a hurry. Thirty-three dollars would pay a few weeks' rent and buy a few weeks' supply of necessary tobacco and soap, but it wouldn't encompass such luxuries as bread and meat.

Al started remembering the locations of the best gardens he'd raided in the past, and the memory made his stomach growl, ruefully. Kansas, he reflected, had probably spoiled his stomach for good.

CHAPTER 3

Woman Trouble

THE landlady was washing clothes in the cool, dark basement when Al arrived. She showed him her ruined teeth in a smile of weary welcome, and he noticed immediately that she was obviously wearing nothing at all under her ragged dress. She had not expected visitors and acted a bit embarrassed. The seam of her threadbare dress was ripped under the arm, so that when she bent over he could see the overripe swelling sag of her breast; and the damp sleekness of the cloth over her hips was unmarred by girdle's edge or waistband of panties. Bad teeth notwithstanding, she made an exciting picture in the dark, untenanted basement; Al's throat was thick and his pulse a bit rapid.

"You want your old room back, Alvin?" she asked him.

"Well," he said, "what I want is to pay a couple months' rent in advance, only not move in until September."

Her expression was puzzled, and in the attempted explanation he made known his poverty and confessed that he'd intended to sort of camp out like a gypsy until September. She scolded him and said he was to move right into his old room and not be silly. "You can do odd jobs for me until school starts," she said. "I've got so much to get done here—I'll be glad to have some help, and your hours worked can go on the rent." She sighed. "I'll be happy to have someone in this empty old house besides myself. It gets awful lonesome, nights."

He gave her a swift glance. What did she mean by that? He read all sorts of subtle nuances into her words. She was a childless woman whose husband was a journeyman construction worker, and his pursuit of a living took him all over the country, so that he was often gone for weeks at a stretch. Al, that keen student of humanity's awful hungers, deduced that the absence of her mate would naturally cause the landlady much restless tossing and erotic frustration at night. The husband was gone again now, it developed, and Al felt that the landlady was probably starved for the warm intimacies of marriage—of which he had heard much comment among his sex-starved fellows. Here, then, was ripe, golden opportunity; here two gnawing hungers meeting in an empty house with no censor around to prevent a solution; here was the rich fruit on the tree of life, eager for the plucking. But Al didn't know quite how to shake the tree. How did anyone tackle a deal like that? With coeds you started out with horseplay, a stolen kiss, and progressed through necking and the exploratory phase of the thing, which either did or did not lead on to the final breathtaking delights. But how did you arrange to steal a kiss from your landlady, especially if she had awful teeth? It seemed to Al this situation called for a very different approach, probably a subtle conversational chess game that would eventually arrive at a question put and an answer given. Then, too, being idealistic as well as lecherous, Al couldn't avoid thinking of the betrayed husband angle—although, obviously, a guy who was always gone from home was sure asking for it.

Al took the whole subject under study, deciding to wait and see if maybe the landlady, to whom sex was a more familiar item, would make the overtures. He moved his gear out of storage and into the same musty, damp, cheerless basement room—six bucks a month for singles, eight for two—and went to work for the landlady, mowing her lawn, painting porch furniture, helping her launder curtains and air bedding and scrub floors and move beds and furniture around in the hot, August-deserted house. And more and more he came to regard the woman as a sultry, seductive, maddeningly desirable creature in her skilled and passionate forties. But though at times the landlady was girlish and coyly playful with him, and sometimes innocently exposed a good deal of her slim, smooth legs to his sly and bothered gaze, and wore old ripped dresses that revealed tantalizing portions of her bare pink anatomy, Al just never could decide whether she was egging him on or was simply unaware of her aggravating effect on him. Perhaps in the busy routine of their shared aloneness it never occurred to her that he was other than a high-minded boy; that he might entertain visions of lusty union with a woman twice his age. At any rate she never clearly invited advances, and he battled his impulse to grapple with her and find out what he needed so wretchedly to know. It was mostly his highly developed sense of self-preservation that dampened his enthusiasm for the showdown—she might be indignant, instead of acquiescent, and boot him out of a pretty good deal. The work he did was light, and each noon the landlady gave him his lunch (forever sandwiches and milk, with an occasional piece of pie, or dish of Jello), and several times a day they stopped their sweaty housekeeping to drink coffee, and the landlady was crediting Al with twenty-five cents an hour against his future rent, and hell fire, things were just breaking too good right now for him to go jeopardizing his economic stability by sexing his disturbing benefactress.

In the cool evenings he poked around the almost deserted campus, reading all the plaques and dates of construction, familiarizing himself with all the statues and pools and nooks and bowers. He always carried one of the landlady's salt shakers with him, and after dark he raided tomato patches. Outside of lunches he had reverted to a strict vegetarian diet consisting mostly of tomatoes and green peppers and new potatoes (usually eaten raw but sometimes baked in the ashes of an open fire), with grapes and other seasonal fruits. He found an orchard whose trees hung heavy with autumn apples, sweet gold-red apples that reminded him of the landlady's breasts (almost anything could remind him of the landlady's breasts), and the insidious similarity somehow robbed them of savor. He needed breasts worse than he needed fruit, and he liked to say to himself wryly, comfort me with love, for I am sick of apples, boy.

He would prowl the town stealthily until late at night, lonely and moody but somehow exhilarated, spying on smugly oblivious, self-centered couples and families, with their insulated domesticity, their gay parties and leisure, their ten o'clock yawns and bedtime snacks—oh, their bedtime snacks!—their vulgar disrobings and their lewd, offensive, distasteful, secretive bedtime glances and leers; their complete, inhumanly selfish total indifference to the tragic fact that a homeless, loveless mortal, a fellow human, was out there wandering restlessly in the black, perfumed night like some ghostly ranging animal.

Al came to regard the spectacle of women and girls getting ready for bed as extremely interesting but no longer astonishing or awesome, but the sight of a bald, potbellied husband hacking away insensitively at a huge, pink, voluptuous ham from the refrigerator, fueling himself for the long, busy, wearyingly delicious night of love and lassitude and sleep, could drive Al to impotent fury. Sometimes he envied the men less their fine shapely women than their foodstuffs. In memory there had been no time when *he* could tease *his* palate with casual bedtime refreshments, and it bruised his sense of justice to see this ugly, jaded, selfish, inequitable munching.

When only he and dogs and policemen and other nocturnal creatures were still awake, Al would run wildly through the dark streets on muffled, sneaker-clad feet, trying to exhaust his terrible, virile energy and empty himself of his excess male vigor, because now came the worst part, the torment of going back to the four-storied house with its lone, luscious occupant. He always dreaded going home and yet anticipated it with excitement, for she always left the door of her apartment open—because of the August heat, surely; with no other thought than to entice an errant breeze through her boudoir; but still Al speculated dizzily, his thoughts running riot in an effort to fathom her *true* reason for that invitingly open door—and he would limp along the hall past the black portal with caught breath, imagining that this time she might suddenly call out softly to him, with plaintive longing, with soft, urgent, anguished desire. But she never did, and he would go down to his bed and lie awake listening with aching hopefulness for the sound of quiet footsteps, imagining that she might yet come stealing down the steps and into his lonely bed. But she never did that, either. And he would see the awful waste of them, man and woman lying awake in the languorous night, each held back no doubt by shyness yet each sleepless with longing. Soon, too soon, the other inhabitants would return to the house-world and Al was positive both he and the landlady would always regret having misused this taut night and all the others.

It always surprised him a little to find no clue to insomnia in her eyes or lining her face at morning, and catch no darkling, sidelong glance of reproach for his obtuseness, for his lack of aggressiveness, for his plain damn foolishness. And the nights were squandered, one after the other, with nothing bought but delirious dreams.

In late August, last year's students began drifting back to the campus, and new ones came, and the molten afternoons rang with music and shouts and laughter, and the landlady's husband came home for a few days, and that was that. Thereafter her door was closed at night, and Al berated himself for having hesitated too long. She didn't need him now. Shrugging, he accepted the new status and got on with his business of continuing to exist in the universe of higher learning without actually being a part of it.

During Rush Week he got a job washing dishes in a fraternity house, and registered for Selective Service, which had become the stern inescapable law of the land. And with a sense of irony he enrolled as a sophomore, although unable to pay his entrance fees. The fees could wait. The Registrar could list Al's fees in the debit column. The hell with the fees. Still, it fretted him, and he decided to sell the typewriter a student had hocked to him almost a year before. The student had long since departed, and surely by now in the eyes of the law, and according to the ethics of hocking, the loan was forfeited. But when Al carried the typewriter to the campus typewriter shop the man said with enormous disinterest that twelve dollars was the best he could do. Twelve dollars! Al snarled. Are you kidding? He was outraged. Of course he had only ten dollars in the machine himself, but it was a good, clean, low-mileage, one-owner Smith-Corona, and easily worth thirty bucks. Anyway, twelve dollars wouldn't begin to pay his fees. Al took the portable typewriter back to his room, smarting with indignation and disappointment. Uncasing it, he gave it a thoughtful scrutiny—and abruptly he felt relieved. Suddenly the idea of parting with the typewriter was repugnant. You take a typewriter, he thought, how many guys have got a typewriter? Never mind about the fees, goddammit.

The frat brother in charge of the kitchen was a large, jovial backslapper with red hair and a booming extrovert's voice; a real swell democratic guy who made Al feel guilty and small-minded because he'd spent his entire Freshman year laboring under the patently ridiculous impression that frat rats were all lousy snobs. Obviously he himself had been an *inverted* snob, as Josephine Hill once accused him. Jo was a sorority girl and very defensive about the "organizations." Actually, as Al could see for himself now, frat men were nice average people, once you got to know them. Take Rusty (the mess treasurer asked the kitchen help to just call him Rusty; hell, fellows, let's not stand on ceremony), old Rusty liked to sing barbershop harmony with the menials, and had once complimented Al on his ability to handle the high tenor part. He said a pure clean natural falsetto like Al's was a rare commodity.

Al formed a liking for Boyd Hinkle, his fellow dishwasher, who was a squat, comical, bushy-browed drama soph from New Jersey;

a mild, shy, nervous, intense boy of nineteen who gnawed interminably on a battered pipe and laughed explosively at Al's mediocre jokes. In time Al invited him to share the basement room, and Hink readily agreed, as it would save him three bucks a month and Al two. Al was pleased to learn that Hink had a battered but serviceable radio, but not happy to discover that his new roommate constantly rehearsed a dozen character parts from famous plays he felt the drama school might decide to produce at any moment. Al also discovered that Hink always wore shabby, baggy tweeds only because he had nothing else to wear. He usually needed a shave and always a haircut; he "feathered" his own nape hair with a safety razor, thus managing to save money and look permanently shaggy. It was soon revealed to Al that his new friend was formidably versed in psychology, being a disciple of Freud and especially interested in abnormal psychology. After he'd been around anybody for a few days, Hink could tell you at length what ailed the poor goof, using very impressive clinical words. It seemed to Al that his roommate was a trifle preoccupied with the abnormal aspects of sex, too; less concerned with women than with the neuter genders, and apparently finding deviation a more challenging subject for study and discussion. Also, it seemed that all he ever *did* about sex was discuss it, and Al was inclined to feel a little scornful and suspicious until it suddenly occurred to him that all he, himself, ever did about sex was discuss it, too. And think about it wistfully.

Actually, Al was eternally alert for the big opportunity, and looked at girls with the rapt fascination tourists give to mountains and lakes and sunsets. He found the female body absorbingly scenic in all its curved, bifurcated, and mammalary grandeur, and he spent a large part of his free time sight-seeing. One afternoon he was standing on the campus corner, leaning on a lamp post, engrossed in the passing phenomena, when a girl spoke to him.

"Why, hello there, Al Woods!" she said, and he turned to meet the shyly smiling glance of a thin, tall girl who wore glasses and had slightly buck teeth and rather prominent eyes and a muddy complexion. He remembered her but couldn't put the name to her, so he grinned and said, "Well, hello. Imagine bumping into *you*."

"I wondered if you'd make it back this year," she said earnestly.

"By the skin of my teeth," Al said. "How've you been?"

"Oh," she shrugged. "Fine. Wrote a book this summer. Lousy."

"I lived a book this summer," Al said. "It was lousy, too."

She smiled uncertainly. "Have you heard from Jo lately?"

Al sobered. "Not since Christmas. She sent me a card. She *here?*"

"No, she's going to Southeastern this year," the girl said. "She says her leg still doesn't feel very good yet."

"Why, I always thought it felt pretty good, myself," Al said, and she giggled, and he began to get interested, the way he always sooner or later got interested in any girl he met. Because after all, maybe she was thin and no raving beauty, but the big important thing was undeniable—she was a girl. "Hey, look," Al said, "let's get together soon and talk about stuff, huh? Reminisce, like."

"I'd love to," she said, and he said, "Tonight, maybe?"

"Why, yes; tonight would be peachy," she said. "Call me, huh?"

"Sure," Al said. Only he didn't know *what* to call her, he still didn't remember her name. "Well," he said, "I'm pearl-diving in a frat for nutrition, and I'm due over there. I gotta be going. See you."

She nodded, beaming. "Al, I'm *glad* you're back this year."

"Ditto," he said, and they parted, and an hour later he finally remembered her name. Beulah Flachtter. Josephine Hill's friend and sorority sister. And then, having remembered Beulah's name, Al spent the rest of his labor period remembering Josephine Hill.

For a few hectic weeks in the previous autumn and winter he had been sick with love for Jo Hill, a democratic and popular sorority girl who was considered—by herself, as well as her acquaintances—to be very wholesome but enigmatic, an Interesting Paradox. As far as Al could discern, she was all that and more. Inscrutable, contradictory, and sometimes a little insane, maybe. She was certainly horse-crazy, maintaining her own private horse at a stable near the campus, and Al had spent some miserable hours shivering on a bale of hay in the dank stable, inhaling the gamy aroma of horse dung (which Jo claimed to find invigorating) while the girl "exercised" her mount. "I'll just take him for a ten-minute canter," she would say. "Be right back, Al." And then she would return an hour later, laughing and exhilarated and unrepentant, and say, "I just got carried away, Alvin." Sometimes he had suspected that her motive in dating him was simply to horrify her stuffy Pan-Hellenic sisters, who were very class-conscious and clung to the tradition that nice sorority girls just simply didn't go around with moneyless, shabby, crude "independent" or "unorganized" male students; it simply wasn't *done*. Unless a girl happened to be a rabid nonconformist, or studying sociology. Al suspected that Jo worked hard at being paradoxical, and enjoyed tormenting her sisters.

She liked to torment Al, too, and was always successful. She was not at all beautiful, yet she fascinated Al and cast a black magic over his mind, and he thought she was the most maddeningly desirable girl in creation. Actually she was somewhat flat-chested and boyishly sturdy of physique, though of small proportions. Her legs were a little bowed—from riding horses all her life, she said—and her head was rather large for her body; she was short of stature and a little awkward, and there were spaces between her teeth, and maybe her mouth was too wide. Al saw these things clearly, accepting them. For she also had a creamy, flawless skin and an enchanting sprinkle of freckles across her cute short nose, and wide gray eyes with thick, tangled black lashes, and crow-black hair which she often wore in thick pigtails, and her grin was wistful and somehow gave the wrong impression of vulnerability and deep sadness, while her throaty, low-pitched voice was apt to break charmingly in mid-sentence. Al never tried to analyze her powers of attraction— she just got under his skin, that's all. She got into his blood and infected his mind and drove him nuts, that's all.

Their courtship had developed into a pretty frustrating routine. Jo would neck with enthusiasm and native skill, and then just when he felt she was going all weak and willing she would push him away abruptly and laugh lightly and say, "Let's not pursue this mad, reckless folly any farther, Alvin my boy, for we are only inviting disaster." She would admit, without prompting, that she liked to kiss him better than any of the other fellows she was kissing those days, and he would be torn between joy and savage anger, because she seemed to be always kissing Greeks when not with him. He'd seen her around with frat rats now and then, guys who wore expensive tuxedos to the hops, and masks of well-bred hauteur at all times. Once, in his agony of spirit, Al demanded a definite, final, once-and-for-all answer—did she or did she not love him, goddammit? "Well," she said gravely, "I ain't asayin' I do, but I ain't asayin' I don't, neither, Alvin." She laughed at his groan of frustration, then snuggled against him and kissed him in a way he was sure she kissed nobody else, her lips warm and sweet and clinging. And he figured, well, she probably did love him, only she was fighting it; afraid of it, for any number of valid reasons.

In December she was riding with a couple of frat ROTC guys, showing off her horsemanship, and her horse slipped on an icy street and fell, breaking her left leg. Al went to the infirmary to see her, picturing himself comforting her in her unbearable pain, but the Greek boys were packed in a solid phalanx around her bed, and he heard her husky laughter floating out of the core of well-dressed admirers, and he slunk away, bitter and full of angry jealousy and self-pity. He never did get to see her alone again—she went home to mend, and didn't return to OU for the second semester. Al wrote her once, but her answering letter was so trite and slap-dash and barren of sentiment—and so short—that it infuriated him, and he renounced the whole silly affair. Because who the hell could compete with ninety-seven tuxedoed frat rats and a goddam horse? When she sent him a Christmas card, he tore it up with cold disdain. He was through, boy. He was cured.

Well, that was all ancient history now, and he sure didn't ever intend to get mushy about any coeds again, especially snooty little sorority girls, and go through all that misery again. Take Beulah now, she was no *femme fatale*, she was safe. A guy could fool around with her and not get involved emotionally. If she intended to be a writer, what she needed was to taste life, and old virile Al Woods, master craftsman, would tutor this thin, unawakened artist in the fine art of living.

He was mulling this generally edifying notion over in his mind, mechanically washing the dishes, when good old Rusty interrupted his euphoria to break the sad news that Rush Week was coming to an end. Somehow Al had got the idea that he could stay on in the frat kitchen indefinitely, and it came as a shock to him to learn that there were chapter members who had been temporarily on detached duty impressing rushees, but whose workaday function was to serve their brothers as scullery knaves. They were men of excellent family but little ready cash, Rusty explained; fellows who would not otherwise be able to live at the house. "It was nice of you to help out while the regular fellows were absent," Rusty said. "Nice knowing you. I mean that, Al."

"You mean I'm fired?" Al asked, a little dazed.

"Let's just say your contract has now expired," Rusty said with a winning grin, slapping Al heartily on the back.

Well, Al thought sardonically, here's where the tomato patches start catching hell again, boys. Here comes old Al Woods again.

CHAPTER 4

September Drift

SOMEHOW Beulah got the impression that Al was hungry and broke, which was not far from the truth, and she kept trying to buy hamburgers for him, but his perverse pride made him refuse to accept anything from her except beer and coffee, neither of which was essential to his survival. Besides, he paid for his beer and coffee by listening politely while she read her short stories to him. She was a rather strange girl, and seemed to have the notion that Al was an astute and sympathetic critic, when in fact he was bored stiff by her witty love stories and her infrequent grimly realistic sketches, and was unable to look her in the eye when he assured her that she got better every day and he only wished he had half her talent.

"You write with authority," he would lie. "I like your style. You are very articulate, Beulah. You're on your way, gal." And she would blush and stammer, tickled to death but rendered inarticulate by his shameless praise—and when she found her tongue again she would nag him to have another beer, and please order something to eat with it this time. Al shrewdly deduced that what any young writer wanted was not so much constructive criticism as praise, and he quieted his conscience with the thought that one should encourage budding genius rather than risk blighting it forever with unforgivable truths. What is a lie? he would ask again. A lie is bearing false witness with the premeditated purpose of injuring somebody. Anyhow, maybe I'm right about Beulah, maybe she's got something on the ball, how the hell should I know?

But he was not much concerned with her literary qualifications. Studying her intently, he would think, How would she be if aroused? Can she *be* aroused? Is she capable of hot-blooded, unrestrained love? You can't judge a woman by surface clues—there may be more to this girl than meets the eye. With her natural

26

potential stimulated and her restraints cast aside, she might be a real wampus cat, boy.

That's how it was with Al Woods. Sex was always loitering in the fringes of his mind, and he sometimes wondered if it was true that malnutrition increased potency—like in China and India where thousands starved to death every year, yet where the highest birth rates in the world prevailed. Well, they had to do *something* to keep from brooding about being hungry, probably.

Lacking a sexual outlet himself, Al brooded about being hungry. Since the fraternity house job expired he'd been unable to find another dishwashing assignment, and after a couple of days of scant pickings in local gardens he'd drifted into the dangerous habit of *buying* food, although he handled the project sensibly. Hinkle had landed a job in a small six-stool greasy spoon just off the campus, and it was here Al took his one real meal a day. This usually consisted of a bowl of chili, padded out with as many crackers as he could stuff in. Hink was loyally generous with the crackers, and tried to see to it there was some meat in the chili. Sometimes Al varied this diet with a bowl of "beef" stew, which was almost as greasy and insubstantial as the chili. And either way, he was bound to end up with heartburn. At more and more frequent moments, he was tempted to splurge on a real dinner—hell, a steak, maybe, or roast beef, or fried chicken. Even oftener he was tempted to let Beulah spend her money on hamburgers for a while and then gradually lead the trend around toward more substantial menus. Like, for instance, ham and eggs. Al dreamed luridly of ham and eggs. Two platters, one heaped with ham, the other with eggs. And biscuits.

Ah, biscuits! Ah biscuits with butter and honey! Ah ham and eggs and T-bone steaks and baked potatoes and butter and biscuits!

"Order a sandwich, silly," Beulah would say, time and time again, and it taxed Al's courage and self-restraint and character to keep on refusing. Goddam, just to stop her constant bickering, he ought to sometime say, O.K., bring me six hamburgers, with French fries...

At this propitious moment Al had the wildest kind of luck, and saved his weakening self-respect. A student at the rooming house had decided to enlist in the Army Air Corps, leaving a vacancy in the dishwater department of a girls' dorm. Al ran frantically all the way over to the dorm, his fingers crossed, praying; breathlessly he applied for the job, and was immediately hired by the plump lady cook, who seemed to appreciate his zeal. The job involved dinner and supper, washing dishes at noon and evening and generally making himself useful to the cook, a jolly widow who was a genuine culinary artist.

The fare was simple, excellent, and bountiful; and the lady was gentle and kindly and motherly, treating her student help well and thereby earning their devotion and stanch loyalty in her eternal war of nerves with the few disgruntled girls whose petty complaints sifted through the swinging door from the dining room. There seemed to be two or three malcontents who were forever displeased with the menu. "Little snips," the cook would snort, "trying to make somebody think they ate better at home." Her eyes would shoot off sparks. "It's always the ones with no breeding or background who complain," she liked to point out. "The refined girls never speak but to praise. Then again, overweight ones without will power generally blame the cook, but they all come out of the same pod. Refined girls don't overeat."

The only times Al ever saw the dorm's inmates was when the dining-room door swung open briefly during meals, and he never got to the point of recognizing by sight the girls who wanted the world to think they had better pheasant and caviar and imported smoked Swiss cheese and marinated snails than anybody in town, back with pater and mater and the fifty servants. But he agreed with the cook, whose art agreed with his digestion, and in later life he was to recognize her statement, although translated into military cant, as a truism about flawed humanity. It was always the bastards from the bread lines who bitched about the chow. Anyway, nobody could fault the lady's cooking, which was a happy cross between Kansas farm food and the frat cuisine.

As September moved away from August's heat, Al began to settle into a fairly contented, lazy, and more or less carefree routine. He was eating better than ever before in his life, except for the total absence of breakfasts. He attended classes when he felt like it, which was less and less often. He was consciously drifting with the tide, afloat on the slow-moving current of time, living from one meal to the next, taking life a day at a whack. He dated Beulah two or three nights a week, stealing a chaste, tight-lipped kiss just often enough to get discouraged about awakening the happy natural animal in her, so that he kept postponing the whole thing. The landlady still bothered him some, but not as much, and there were occasional moments when he would feel a stab of despondency, when for a few minutes he would feel stranded in the world and rudderless, a guy going nowhere, a guy just wasting time, wasting the best days of his life, procrastinating. But for the most part he managed to shut unpleasant thoughts out of his mind, and he knew a sense of sweet peace that was strange to him.

In late September he had a second notice from the Registrar about his delinquent fees, and shrugged it off. Who were they kidding? It was embarrassing to attend classes irregularly, without textbooks, knowing you were unauthorized, a trespasser; this curt dunning notice simply caused Al to stop attending classes entirely. For that matter, he hadn't been making his morning classes anyhow, because he hated to go until noon without food. So all the Registrar's notice did, if you looked at it a certain way, was just to put an end to his feeling guilty about sleeping until noon. Despite strict economies, his nest egg continued to dwindle, since he had to have razor blades and soap and tobacco, and his only plan, if it could be called a plan, was to hang around the University as long as his money held out, and worry about the next step after bankruptcy set in. He couldn't say precisely why he wanted to stay there, being neither student nor native but only a sort of semiemployed tourist, except there wasn't any other place to go, and besides in some indefinite and passive way he kept waiting for something to happen, like with Beulah or somebody. One thing, he hated to leave without at least one campus seduction to recollect with roosterish nostalgia whenever he thought back to his college days. He often was troubled by the feeling that the rest of his life would be in some way marred and robbed of its full flavor unless he utilized the romantic facilities at OU pretty soon now. Things were supposed to happen to a guy at college, and nothing had happened to *him* yet, and that was about as good a reason for lingering longer as any other.

The Draft Board had notified all the men students that they were being deferred until June, but of course this didn't actually apply to Al, since he wasn't technically a student and since he could not support himself until Christmas, let alone until June. In the rare moments when he gave any thought to the matter, he discovered in himself a strong aversion to the prospect of being drafted into the Army. He liked to walk, but not any twenty-odd miles a day with a heavy pack and rifle. He kind of favored the Marine Corps, if it ever came to a choice, but there was no hurry about anything. Somewhere ahead there was an unseen, unplotted deadline, beyond which lay decision, but in the meantime he was eating wonderfully well, living indolently, and still confident that he was apt to seduce a coed almost any night now. And almost any girl would do, too. It was the principle of the thing.

There was another way to look at it, too. Al found it pleasant to read until late at night and sleep late mornings, and he suspected this state of affairs would not be Marine Corps procedure. He just happened thoroughly to enjoy his current mode of living, that's all.

His roommate, Hinkle, did not have Al's ability to relax and slide effortlessly into tomorrow. Hink fretted a lot about the draft. "The Army will coarsen me," he kept saying. "Barracks life will rob me of my innate sensitivity, which makes me such a promising thespian." But Hink had it figured out, he claimed he planned to contract a convenient case of creeping syphilis just before his draft call came. "I'm trepid," he would say, snorting and hiccuping with nervous sly laughter. "I want to be a coward and stay home." And the thing about Hink was his sincerity. He really meant it.

September waned and died, and October began to paint the leaves, and Al sat up late reading and listening to Hinkle's radio, smoking the pipe that was his main solace and luxury outside of food and sleep. Back in August while helping the landlady clean rooms, he had found a mildewed literary anthology in a closet, plainly labeled as property of the University. Inasmuch as it was not checked out in his name, he staked a claim to the thick volume of stories and poems and plays, and at night, propped in bed with his Yello-Bole fired up, he read Keats, Yeats, Eliot, Housman, Masefield, Sassoon, Browning, Hardy, Milburn, Sandburg, O'Neill, Anderson, Cather, and all the others. He liked Milburn's "A Student of Economics" because it could have been written about himself. He read Keats' "To Autumn" pretty regularly, liking it but finding it somehow inadequate, too meager for its subject. He liked "The Eve of St. Agnes" because he knew how it felt to watch a maiden get ready for bed. In fact he liked all of the anthology, finding in it all that he felt anybody might require in the way of great literature, and he would read and ponder and smoke and listen dreamily to "Moon River" on the radio and visualize a utopian world in which it would be strictly illegal for a man or woman to be caught sleeping alone.

Each day he slept until eleven or so and then he would hurry to the dorm and drink some of the strong black coffee the cook always kept hot on the back of the stove. Renewed and stimulated, he would then help her get the noon meal ready. Upon discovering that he had once been a salad boy at Deacon's Restaurant, she had promptly given him the responsibility for producing salads, having, as she said, no genuine feeling for salads herself, being pretty much the cole slaw and sliced tomato and carrot-raisin-celery type. Gradually Al had drifted into doing other things, mashing and seasoning the potatoes, thickening the gravy, slicing the roasts and hams, breading the cutlets. She said he was very handy, and would make some working girl a fine husband. She had, of course, no conception of the true, basic Al.

Afternoons he employed in roaming aimlessly about the campus, or in the cooling countryside. Several times he went fishing down on the river, seining minnows for bait with a gunnysack, and once he brought back eight nice channel catfish—which the landlady converted into a late evening fish fry for Al and Hink and a couple of her other favored roomers. Much of the time during the warm, golden afternoons, Al would just sit quietly on a bench in the wild-honey sunshine, at peace with his immediate world, refusing to consider tomorrow, just loose and comfortable like a worn old man whose ambition and lust had burned down to ashes. Sometimes he watched football practice before going to the dorm to help with supper, and watching would daydream that he was a savage, reckless fullback, crashing through the line, side-stepping, shrugging off would-be tacklers, stiff-arming others, outrunning the rest to the goal line. In high school—in three different high schools—he had always played guard or tackle, and had been a sixty-minute man his Senior year; but he had never come close to realizing his ambition to be a hard-running, high-scoring fullback. Now in this autumn, adrift on the season of life, he accepted with a twinge of pathos and regret the dismal fact that he would *never* be a fullback. His time for glory was gone. At twenty he was an old, erstwhile, washed-up right tackle.

On Sunday afternoons, replete with fried chicken or roast beef, he watched the polo matches on the field south of the ROTC stables, where the action was staged against a backdrop of flaming maples along Jenkins Street. Awed, he watched the men and horses swirling in what seemed wildly reckless tangles and melees, in a confusion of shouts and dust and thundering hoofs and limber mallets whistling through the air. Quite often his attention was distracted by the colorfully dressed girls screaming excitedly along the side lines, and the combination of horses and girls always reminded him again of Jo Hill, and a gust of sadness would blow across his mind.

Autumn, that season of mists and mellow fruitfulness, filled all fruit with ripeness to the core, the way Keats said in "To Autumn," and seemed to do as much or more for girls. Watching them go hurrying along the campus walks through showers of falling leaves, wearing autumn-hued cardigans worn back to front, bright snug skirts hugging their soft, sleek hips and legs, their hair flying and dancing around their shoulders, Al would taste the bittersweet sorrow of loneliness in his throat like tears. He likened himself to a boy with his nose flattened against a candy store window, suffering from a chronic sweet tooth and insolvency. Autumn filled all girls with ripeness.

CHAPTER 5

October Good-by

A ND then one afternoon in the third week of that month when
the trees were aflame and beginning to char a bit, to sear and
shrivel around the edges and spiral earthward on the first sighing
breaths of melancholy winter, Al watched a bright-clad girl coming
toward him under the thinning trees and was abruptly turned to
stone.

It was Jo Hill, or her ghost, sauntering along, boyishly scuffing
and kicking among the windrows of yellow leaves, her manner aimless and dreamily preoccupied. Soft fingers clutched at Al's throat
and he felt a quaking tightness in his chest. Jo, the trick rider,
leisurely afoot in the smoky autumn afternoon, while leaves continued to tumble on a cool west wind and crows cawed in the fields
south of the campus and geese called high and plaintive above the
sandy bed of the river as they hurried south. She seemed a part of
the day, her yellow cardigan reversed in the current mode, her
skirt a plaid of gold and brown and red, her yellow bobby socks,
and scuffed, fringed brown saddle oxfords all blending with the
campus background. He couldn't move. He wanted to turn away,
he wanted to hide, but he was rooted in his tracks. Jo, he thought,
stunned. It's really Jo.

She saw him and faltered and came on, her face lighting up.
"Well, doggone," she said, husky-voiced, grinning her vulnerable
and touching grin. "Hello there!" she said. "Golly, I *hoped* I'd see
you."

"Hello, Jo," he said, feeling clumsy and shabby. "I thought we
got rid of you," he croaked. "What are you doing around this
joint?"

"I hafta visit my dear sorority sisters, don't I?" she said, her voice
breaking in that charming, well-remembered way. "Heck, Alvin,
maybe I even got a little homesick for you, too. Anyway, when

33

Beulah said you were back this year I sorta aimed to track you down."

He was skeptical, not believing she had really hoped to see him. This meeting was sheer accident, but he was achingly glad to see her.

"Still handsome in your brutishly appealing way, I notice," she said with a laugh; he stared at her and saw with a kind of miserable joy that she was even lovelier than he'd remembered. Certainly her black magic was as potent as ever; she could still make his heart ache just by smiling at him, and her crazy voice still could send shivers up his spine. She was an autumn witch, that Josephine, and now she said, "Do you have a class or anything, Alvin?"

"You mean right now?" he asked. "No, I'm just loafing, Jo."

"Me too," she said. "I mean, I'm just being nostalgical, just floating around gawking at the dear remembered scenes. Gee, it's so lovely here now. I've made up my mind to transfer back next semester." She gave him a sudden fierce look. "Why didn't you answer my letter?"

"You call that half-page note a letter?" he said lamely.

"I ain't much of a hand to write," she said. "Besides, I had a broken limb, remember?" She grinned mockingly, and abruptly took his hand and squeezed it. "Well, never mind, I ain't mad any more—I'm too tickled to see you again, I guess," she said. "Golly, I got so homesick for this neck of the woods I could of sat right down and bawled sometimes, despite my cold-natured lack of sentimentality." She wrinkled her cute nose at him. "Remember how we used to go walking in the woods?"

"I remember how I used to go sit on a bale of hay in the barn."

"We strolled midst autumn foliage, too," she reminded him, as if he needed reminding. "You wanta go for a hike, maybe? Huh?"

He was remembering that he'd kissed her in the woods, and he sensed that she was brashly aware of reminding him, and now he was made dizzy by the sight of her mouth, which was red and moist and generously large—and warm and sweet and clinging, he remembered. Her teeth were white and clean and even, with tiny spaces between them; her bosom still wasn't anything to write Robert Ripley about, although less flat than he remembered, and her body was still sturdy and kind of boyish, only maybe more softly accented now, more curved; and her legs were still bowed and her head was a trifle large for her body, but the important things were still most important; her eyes were still gray and alive and blackly lash-fringed, and her skin was still creamy and flawless, with a dusting of freckles across her short, pert nose, and she still had that intangible, magnetic, seductive quality. In short, she was still his cup of hemlock, boy; somehow she just happened to be the most alluring and desirable and unforgettable girl that Alvin Woods had ever met. Goddammit.

They walked across the golf course companionably, Jo briefing him, in her inimitable way, on all that she had done and seen and felt and heard and thought since last they discussed the universe. Al tried to listen but was caught up in dizzy anticipation. She knew he would kiss her if they went to the woods, so she must *want* him to.

They left the campus and walked south on the railroad tracks in the quiet afternoon, and below the right-of-way was the disreputable litter of Shantytown. Jo Hill stared curiously at the junk hovels, her gaze somber. "Golly, Al, do people really *live* down there?"

"If you call that living," he said. "That's Hooverville. That's where the unemployed masses spend their unpaid vacations, Jo."

They walked on a few yards, Jo continuing to stare at the eyesore of Shantytown as they passed the scatter of coops and kennels and shacks built from odds and ends of lumber and tin and tar paper salvaged from the trash heap. "Al, do they *feel* the way we feel?" Jo mused.

"They probably feel gritty," Al said. "They have rougher hides."

"No, I mean do they *feel* things—are they capable of intense emotions? Great joy, terrible grief, religious ecstasy, stuff like that? Ambition. Despair. Spiritual passion. I bet they don't, huh?"

"They may have forgotten by now," Al said through tight lips.

She didn't seem to hear him, or notice his stiffness. She had stopped, beyond the last mean shelter, and was staring back down at the forlorn huddle of pathetic dwellings, with a kind of fascination and revulsion in her manner. She shivered, and laughed, and struck a pose of burlesqued melodrama, and said mockingly, "Do they love on a high, pure, spiritual plane, intellectually, soulfully, madly, forsaking all others, and so forth—or do they know only animal lust and piggish physical passion?"

Al stared at her with grim resentment. Each time he saw the awful shacks of the scabrous settlement he felt a numbing chill creep into his mind; a gray depression would stay with him for hours afterward, and he would think, There, but for my small luck, I might have ended, and might still end. Jo's idle, seemingly amused curiosity had made his gorge rise, and he had got hung up on that insensitive and cruelly mocking tone she used. He felt, in some strange way, defensive about the slum village, and now all at once he felt more than ever that only a narrow margin separated himself from the denizens of this jungle of poverty—while on the other hand he and Josephine Hill were incompatibly far apart in the geography of society. She had never known insecurity; he had never known anything else. The difference between himself and the men of Shacktown was his youth and health and a few dollars, his bachelor status, his eligibility for a twenty-one-dollars-a-month military sinecure. And Jo's bright proximity to the slatterns and undernourished girl children of this village of the damned was a thorny contrast, harsh and irreconcilable, so that he saw clearly the hopelessness of his desire for her. They were an ill-assorted pair, he felt, and he saw the whole goddam doomed unwholesome relationship in the naked light of reality. Her mocking speculation about the loves of the shanty people was like a dagger stabbing him, and the wound spouted a torrent of thick, viscid jealousy and sorrow and rage and resentment, bitter and clotting in his mind.

"Pretty funny, huh?" he said. "A bunch of clowns down there."

Jo looked at him with lifted eyebrows, startled. "Who?"

"Those two-legged animals back there. Real comical."

"Depressing," she said, rather airily, fueling his anger. "But hardly amusing, Alvin, my boy. What dismal lives they must lead."

"Listen," Al said angrily, "for your information, those are people, like you and me, only they got kicked empty, that's all. They don't live there just so smug snobs can sneer at them, and they don't live there because of the view, or the climate. Or because they like it, goddammit. They're broke, that's all. They don't have any jobs or any money, see. They can't buy groceries or pay electric bills and rent and doctor bills and car installments. But if you look at it a certain way, they're free. They have no financial obligations, they pay no taxes. They're free to die any time they choose, without offending any of the nice, well-fed people in the world, because the nice people don't know they exist—or pretend they don't know it."

"Hey . . . whoa!" Jo said. "Don't be gruesome, Alvin."

"Those silly jerks down there," Al raged, "they think you don't care if they live or die. Isn't that a silly attitude for them to take, Josephine Hill?" She was staring at him, shocked and astonished now. "Well, they're right about that," Al went on. "Not a goddam soul in all the goddam world cares if those men and women and kids live or die, except maybe a lot of the respectable citizens wish these bums would either move on or drop dead without any muss or fuss, just so they get the hell away from here and stop lowering the tone of the community." Jo was white-faced from the shocking unexpectedness of his outburst now, and he gloried in it, snarling, "Nobody cares, so they stopped caring, too, see. That's how a person is made. Somebody has to care or they stop caring themselves. They get bruised so bad, so often, and for so long, and the first thing you know they give up, they quit, they stop feeling anything and just quit. And if nobody will give them a job so they can live decent lives, the fools just lie around on their tails loafing."

"Gee," she said weakly, "you sound awful bitter, Al."

"Bitter!" Al snarled. "Why the Christ should I feel bitter? I don't live down there yet. I got no ax to grind, that's not my tribe. But I don't poke fun at those poor devils, or despise them, or doubt for a minute that they're human. I figure they even have feelings, too, maybe deeper feelings than some well-bred little snob who can look at their wrecked world and laugh."

"Please, Al, lay off," Jo said with a stricken look. "Golly, I don't know how we got into this, but I'd like to get out. I'm all bloated with remorse and if it'll make you happy I'll cut my throat or something, only gosh, Alvin, couldn't we just drop the subject?"

"You sneered at them," Al said. "You mocked them."

She sighed. "O.K., O.K. But I *didn't* sneer, I just..."

"You wondered if they know anything about honor or decency or shame or stuff like that," Al said grimly. "Sure they do. You asked jokingly if they are capable of real love. I say they are, or *were*. I'm just trying to tell you they live like rats in a trash pile because the smug nice people who never were cold or hungry or defeated by life don't give a small damn about anything but their own selfish..."

"Oh, shut up!" Jo said. "Alvin, I am bored stiff with the whole silly lecture, or tantrum, or whatever you're having. If you will excuse my rudeness, professor, I'd hardly call you a trained expert on the subject of being cold and hungry and all that junk."

Al jabbed a rigid finger at her. "You're wrong, Miss Smug. I happen to be an authority on the subject. You're goddam right I know about hunger and cold. I've been hungry. And cold, too. I haven't led a soft, sheltered life like you and your frat rat pals." Ignoring the storm warnings in her smoky gray eyes, he blundered on, wanting to smash whatever fragile thing he had once imagined existed in their relationship—it was all over anyway, and had been for nearly a year, hadn't it? "Listen," he grated, "I've lived for weeks right here at OU on vegetables and fruit I swiped out of gardens and orchards, believe it or not. I have been forced to steal in order to live, and I have got a fairly accurate conception of how it feels to be broke. I *know* about those people back there. They were once just like you, baby, only they didn't have rich papas to sponge off of. The difference is money, see."

Jo Hill groaned. "Oh, *hell*, Al! What do you expect me to do, beg your pardon for slurring your dear friends? You slay me, honestly."

She wasn't reacting to his tirade the way he wanted her to react, and Al felt a twinge of disgust with himself. She wasn't taking him very seriously, or something, dammit. "Look," he said coldly, "just don't get the idea I'm feeling sorry for myself, that's all. It's a tough world, all right, but I'm tough, too. I'll survive. Besides, I'm going to enlist in the Marines in a few days, and that will probably take care of the situation." He saw no sudden terror in her eyes, no horrified premonition of his untimely death in battle. "The thing is, I just happen to have a little pity to spare for those poor people, that's all. Do you have any idea how they get food to eat? I'll bet the cook at your sorority magnanimously allows them to claw chicken wings and stale bread and cold mashed spuds out of your garbage. If they can beat the cur dogs to it."

A glassy look of horror was in the girl's eyes. "Oh, Al!" she said, and he thought wildly, Don't you oh Al me, you little snob! And he said wildly and somewhat irrelevantly, "As long as we're on the subject let's clean everything up while we're at it. I used to kid myself about you and me, baby, but I really knew all the time you just dated me to shock your hoity-toity sisters, and also maybe out of curiosity, never having known a lout like me before; and maybe too because you were pretty sick of correct, polite, well-dressed, snooty, soft-skinned frat boys, and because you wanted to be considered a daring nonconformist. I guess it was pretty amusing, bumming around the campus with a tramp student like me, pretending you were pretty warm for me. It didn't hurt your ego to know I was nuts about you, either. Well, O.K. What the hell. It was fun, and I'm not sorry about any of it. While it lasted it was kind of special and wonderful, Hill."

"Alvin Woods, you are really a silly damned idiot, aren't you?" Jo said in a cold, ominously quiet voice. "If you really want to know what I think of you, I honestly, sincerely think you *stink!*"

For some perverse reason Al felt an irresistible urge to laugh, and he laughed, and all of the anger drained out of him. What a way to kill a beautiful October afternoon with a gorgeous coed, he thought. "Well, you got my number all right, kid," he said. "You have got me figured out, for sure. But like I said, it was great while it lasted."

She examined him balefully for a long moment, her lips twisting as if he left a bad taste in her mouth, as if she might decide to spit. Then she whirled away and began to walk furiously along the tracks, her small body stiff and straight. But she was still going south, not back toward the campus, and after a moment's hesitation Al followed. He overtook her and paced beside her without speaking. She ignored him, her head high. But when they came to the bridge where, a year ago, they had always gone down the embankment to the belt of woods along the small creek, she turned down the path. And when he took her hand she didn't try to draw it away.

"Nice day," Al observed wryly. "Real purty."

"It was," she said curtly.

They went on for another minute or so in stony silence, but when they came to the remembered grove of scarlet maples Jo stopped and put her back against a tree trunk and looked at him searchingly, biting her lip, a glitter in her eyes. He thought she was going to take up the cudgel again and exercise her womanly prerogative of having the last word. And so he took her in his arms and held her hard against him, smelling the poignantly familiar fragrance of her hair and skin, remembering all the times when he'd held her in his arms and felt this same melancholy and tender longing for her. Presently Jo sighed and said, "You darned neurotic." But then she said, "Oh, you big lug!" And put her arms around him and murmured, "I hate you, though."

"I hate me too," he said. "I'm sorry I was rude, honey."

"Rude," she said. "Ha, ha." But her arms tightened a little, and then she said against his chest, "Were you hungry sometimes, really?"

"Oh, well," Al said, not wanting to discuss food now, "I guess all growing boys are hungry most of the time. And sometimes it ain't food they're the hungriest for, either, ma'am."

"Al," she said, "I do too feel things deeply. I was shocked when I saw that place. I never really saw it before."

"How long are you going to be around?" Al asked her. She said until the next morning. "How about tonight, then?" he said.

She pulled away and looked up at him. "Oh, gee, there's a formal thing at the house," she said with soft anguish. "I'd rather be with you. Honest. I'm really not a social butterfly. I mean, sometimes I am, but that's not the real me. The real me has been missing you something awful, Alvin; the real me would rather be with you than almost anywhere." That *almost* had rough edges for Al. She always had to qualify things. "Gee, Alvin, I wish . . ." She sighed regretfully and he saw that she really was sorry about it, that she really would rather be with him doing the pleasantly frustrating, tormenting things they used to do together than attend the high-toned sorority shindig. He put his lips against her forehead and said huskily, "You're here now, anyway."

With an impulsive gesture she held him there and twisted her face around and up so that their mouths met, and she kissed him deeply and hungrily and lingeringly. And, he thought, kind of experimentally, too, as if checking her reactions and emotions, as if testing the potency of the kiss and Al's impact on her senses. The impact must have been great, because the slow deliberate kiss stirred them both strongly, and Al dizzily sensed her mood and her response, and crushed her body against him. He felt her fingers digging into his back, and abruptly he lifted her in his arms and knelt, still kissing her, and put her down in a wind-drifted bed of leaves, the kiss uninterrupted, and now she began to respond even more, with a passion and lack of restraint he'd never before awakened in her, sharing and heightening his own urgency. But then, when it was almost too late, she tore her mouth away and said in sudden panic, "Oh, no . . . please! Al, we can't! We mustn't! Oh, please, *no!*"

With a part of his mind that had managed to remain detached, Al realized she was genuinely frightened, terrified of the mindless force of her desire. He knew, too, that she couldn't stop him now and probably wouldn't really try to stop him, for it was her reason that struggled and cried NO, not her soft, yielding flesh or her committed senses. She wanted him as he wanted her, desperately, and he could do as he pleased, the decision was now his alone to make. He didn't want to stop. Let the world come crashing down afterward, let him be hanged for his crime, if this be crime, he *couldn't* stop now. But unreasonably, unbidden, he felt a rush of tender concern that was as strong as his passion, and was enormously aware of a feeling of obligation and responsibility. He was also aware of the possible consequences. It struck him that her ardent response was somehow a direct result of his crazy ranting outburst; he had touched her and jarred her emotions out of balance, so that she had wanted to show him he mattered to her, maybe wanted to console him for the hurt to him she did not understand, solace him for whatever wounds of the spirit she imagined the world had given him, and she had been unwary this time and let down her defenses too far.

The war between conscience and desire raged briefly in Al, and then he groaned and said, "It's all right, Jo baby. Don't worry. This is as far as we go, if that's how you want it to be." But because they had gone a great deal farther than they had ever gone before, he was most reluctant to end it immediately, and so he continued to hold her in sweet, tormenting intimacy there in the golden autumn afternoon, settling for less than enough, Jo trusting him and settling for less than enough, too, but more nearly enough than for him, perhaps.

"I never have," she whispered apologetically. "Not with anybody."

He never had either, not really, not like this would have been. He felt cheated, but he could see her side of it, too. A girl might feel cheapened and guilty afterward, he rationalized. A girl might. He thought he could see how it might change her in a way he wouldn't want to be responsible for, and in some naïve, chivalrous manner he wanted to remember her as a girl innocent and afraid of what came after innocence was gone. People around the campus talked a lot about false inhibitions and obsolete moral standards, but you kept bumping into a thing called conscience, and things called principles, and every guy wanted *his* woman to be virtuous, even if he wasn't. Chastity was all tied up to character and trustworthiness and a lot of other things that were still pretty important in the world. Anyway, Jo wouldn't be remembering him in a guilty, remorseful way, but as the boy who could have possessed her but didn't because she asked him to please stop before it was too late. Goddammit. Talk about hating yourself in the morning, Al thought glumly, I'll bet I hate myself for being such a goddam nice fellow for the next ten years.

The sun was slanting far down in the west when they walked back together, cutting across the fields, very close and affectionate with arms around each other, stopping often to kiss with this new and practiced familiarity, and to kiss with a kind of frustrated, gentle, fierce despair. Once, with her nose against Al's collarbone, Jo said thoughtfully, "I sort of feel like I belong to you now, anyway." Which Al, in his undeceived wisdom, translated to mean: I never did anything quite so wanton as this before with anybody else and I have a closer, warmer, *friendlier* feeling for you than before, and lots and lots of gratitude and respect and admiration and fondness, and we are now and henceforth very *intimate* friends who have a warm private secret between us, and we've had lovely weather for our hike, haven't we, Alvin? What she didn't say, no matter how he tried to read some nebulous, shy admission into her message, was: I love you, Alvin. It had been an exciting and near-disastrous affair, but why get mushy about it? She could have said everything he wanted to know with three well-chosen words, and that would have made him begrudge his chivalry less, but Jo wasn't a girl to use the word "love" carelessly. One thing, if she ever did say it, you could be pretty sure she really meant it.

At the corner of the ROTC stables they kissed for the last time, the forever-after last time maybe, and her hands moved on his back in a kind of inexpressible wishfulness, and Al reflected that this day would probably be a national holiday for both of them the rest of their lives, to be silently observed across the years and the miles that would separate them, remembering themselves as they were now, young and wise beyond their years, having toyed with folly and heroically risen above it. Yes, sir, this was a historical day, but it was a sad day, too. He didn't know quite what they had won, but he was painfully aware of what they had lost.

"I wish you were going to be here next semester, Al," Jo said. Then laughed and added, "Heavens! What are you saying, Josephine? That would surely lead to disaster!"

Al laughed a hollow laugh, feeling frustrated all over again.

"Alvin," Jo said solemnly, "do you know why I first got kind of interested in you?" Al said it had always perplexed him. "That first day in class when the prof called the roll, it just struck me kind of funny. Our names, I mean. Woods and Hill. Like Field and Stream. So I found out which one was Woods, and then of course you were kind of striking. I mean, I guess I was intrigued by your sullen worldliness or something. But I found out you were really a pretty special kind of person. You are, Alvin, and I want you to know I grew terribly, terribly . . . *fond* of you. And I'm glad it was you. Today I mean. I'm so glad it was you, Alvin Woods."

She didn't say anything about love; she was careful not to use that word. Al sighed. "You're damn lucky it *was* me," he said.

"I know it," she said. "But it wouldn't have happened with anybody else, you dog."

She didn't say anything about love. She *avoided* it.

Jo touched his cheek and looked at him for a long, grave moment. "Al, I'd like to just say . . . well, thank you. You're . . . swell." Then she whirled and went racing away from him, so you'd never guess she'd ever had a broken leg, and he watched her go dumbly, with the beginning of desolation in his mind. She slowed to a walk; she turned back.

"Write to me, darn you!" she called.

He nodded, but his mind answered contrarily. Why write? What was there to write about? He remembered the trite, noncommittal note she'd written him *last* year. A few of those would drive him nuts, the way she'd always driven him nuts in person. He wanted her to write him long, emotional love letters, not pen pal notes. And she had been so goddam careful, in her honest fashion, to avoid giving him the wrong impression that she might be in love with him. She was terribly, terribly *fond* of him, for God sakes.

I'm not her type, Al said to himself as he walked toward the dorm. Well, if war came, like a lot of people said it was coming, he might get knocked off, and she'd hear about it and be a little sad for about eight seconds. She wouldn't become a nun or anything like *that*, he thought cynically. She might take it hard, though, and perform some little sacrifice in his honor, like not necking any frat rats that night. "I just heard Alvin Woods, a boy I used to know, died a hero's death in the Marine Corps," she would say. "As a tribute to his memory, Bert, I don't think I'll neck any this evening." Of course it might not be Bert. It could be Bill or Bob or Horace or Sylvester. Just so it was some frat rat, that's all that mattered. Oh hell yes indeed.

That's what Al tried to believe, but he didn't believe it. Jo Hill was a fine, honest, beautiful girl and he loved her, and if he was going to psychoanalyze everybody that came along, he might as well admit one reason he came back to OU this fall, when he knew he couldn't pay his fees or anything and should have gone looking for a job or joined the Army or something, was because subconsciously he figured Jo might be there, sooner or later. Now she'd come back and he was just sorry about the whole thing, because he felt lousier than ever. He was glad, too, of course, in a miserable sort of way; he was desolately pleased that she had turned up today and that they'd had this afternoon together. He never would forget it, goddammit.

Well, then, good-by. Farewell, sweet Jo, little lover of sorts, little almost-mistress. But I'll tell you one thing. If I had it to do over again, I wouldn't do it. You'd be a gone gosling.

CHAPTER 6

Departure: As on a Journey

THAT night he read "The Eve of St. Agnes" again, with new insight, and was racked with anguish and jealousy and despair as he imagined Jo at the formal dance, dressed the way he had seen her once in a low-cut evening gown, her face flushed with pleasure and spiked punch (those frat guys *always* spiked the punch with alcohol, and sometimes even with aphrodisiac, too, as venery was their ultimate intention, naturally), her lecherous frat rat of a partner murmuring subtly suggestive remarks into her delicate porcelain ear. Al envisioned her in the arms of another man as she had been in his that afternoon, murmuring, Oh no we mustn't George! Or Sam or Ralph or Wilbur. But George or Sam or Ralph or Wilbur, being a worldly, sophisticated bastard and experienced with sorority girls, would be deaf to her weak, almost inaudible pleas, and would get on with the thing at hand. Thus Al refuted virtuous love and tried to harden his mind and heart against Jo Hill, play girl. She was an old wound reopened; it would take a long time to heal again, and even then the scar would ache on certain days, in lonely weather, in October. Like an old man's rheumatism, Al thought, groping for a metaphor...

For the rest of his stay on the campus, the very air was haunted by Josephine Hill, and every reversed cardigan, every plaid skirt, every pair of saddle oxfords, hacked and stabbed at him with aching remembrance. He became less and less anxious to cling to that intangible and spurious sense of security the campus represented in his subconscious mind. And for a time he lost interest in his plan to seduce Beulah Flachtter, whose friendship with Jo made her somehow inviolate now; unseducible. Since he had no other candidates lined up, it appeared he might as well start thinking about leaving. As a campus Casanova he was out of work and apparently unemployable.

But in the end he didn't actually *decide* to leave, he was more or less *driven* out of his academic refuge, flushed from his covert by a shocking and appalling discovery. Otherwise he would have stayed longer, since his rent was paid through November and the food was better than ever.

The two notices from the Registrar's office didn't influence his going one way or the other, except inasmuch as they made his status as drifting ex-student official. One notice bluntly informed him that since he had repeatedly ignored previous notices regarding his unpaid fees, he was now being officially dropped from all courses. However, he could request reinstatement, upon payment of the delinquent fees. The other notice stated that he had exceeded the maximum class cuts allowed for one semester, and unless he could show valid reasons for his inattendance immediately, he would be dropped from the class rolls. Al wondered if maybe the same guy wrote both notices, authority's robot mindlessly grinding out two stern ultimatums to the same recipient on the same day. It was kind of insulting, goddammit.

He didn't see Beulah formally for several weeks after Jo's brief return, bumping into her now and then on the campus but not interested enough to make any after-dark appointments. Then one day she telephoned and said she had a new story she'd like him to criticize. So he met her after supper at the beer joint. While he drank Budweiser, she read her story self-consciously, nullifying to a certain extent the benefits of the 3.2 per cent of alcohol in the brew. Al drank four bottles, steadily losing ground, and listened glumly with a minor segment of his attention while the rest of his mind occupied itself with a rumor he'd heard that evening to the effect that if the woman who operated the dorm found out he wasn't a bona fide student she would replace him at the sink with some gaunt and hungry scholar. He brooded and watched Beulah's flushed face as she read her document in a voice so conspiratorial that it would not carry beyond their rear corner booth. She wrote a lot of pseudo-sophisticated love stories replete with stilted dialogue she apparently thought was crisp and succinct; and all of her heroines were elfin creatures with either peaches-and-cream or olive complexions, beautiful teeth, deceptively woolly minds, and bodies that were "tiny but voluptuous"—instead of tall and thin. None of them wore glasses. Her heroes—or protagonists, as she preferred to label them—were all tall brown fascinatingly homely men with

wavy brown hair and flashing eyes and humorous twinkles and compassionate mouths and craggy, characterful faces and rough-hewn
physiques. The nicest thing about them was their solvency; they
were all rich, only that was the snapper, the gimmick, and you were
not supposed to become aware of this fiscal eligibility until the big
anticlimax when the hero whipped out a heavy money belt and
bought the company where the girl worked, so he could discharge
the villainous sub-boss who persecuted the maiden during business
hours and persisted in trying to corrupt her untarnished morals
after sundown. This big monetary revelation always came after the
girl had already said she loved him in spite of his poverty. Generally
the girl managed to convey the sense that she might consider having
an affair with Steve (usually the guy was Steve or Hubert, although
lately Al had detected a blond Latin trend: Alberto, Alfredo, and
once Alvino) just to show how deeply she cared, and also because
she nourished a growing rebelliousness about her hopeless poverty.
But Steve and Hubert and Alberto were a lot like Alvin Woods, too
chivalrous and high-minded to accept the unmistakable invitation.
This particular evening, the story was much the same old plot: The
hero was Arvin Winters; the girl, a tiny, shapely, confused secretary
with snow-white teeth, whose mother suffered from an exotic malady
that could be cured only at great expense, and the girl, Lenora
McQuire, had borrowed a huge sum from the bastard of a black-
haired credit manager, Foster Campbell (who had embezzled the
money from the company till, owned by an absentee millionaire play-
boy named Marvin Summers), who had also tampered with the small
print in the usurious contract, so that little had the poor girl known,
until too late, that she had agreed to work out most of the principal
and some of the interest in the cad's apartment.

Al was glowering at his emptied fourth bottle when Beulah got
around to the surprise ending (Arvin Winters, a third-assistant
clerk, was really Marvin Summers all along, but this story had a
timely double twist, for old Marvin was also Secret Service, and
Campbell's real name was Glutz of the Gestapo, and he was a Nazi
spy, whom Marvin hammered prone with a sockful of money that
Glutz had intended to use in his treacherous assignment, and
Lenora's small but voluptuous body quivered when Arvin-Marvin
swept her into his arms and kissed her passionately, although he was
due to go on a secret mission soon and, Al figured, they had better
not waste time on a lot of talk), and when the authoress lifted her

glance expectantly and humbly to his, Al said it was her best yet, and if the *Saturday Evening Post* didn't buy it they ought to be run out of Philadelphia and lose their mailing privileges. "Why do you waste your time working for a degree in English?" Al said. "You should devote full time to writing. You've *got* it, baby."

Beulah Flachtter startled him by not reacting the way she had always done before. This time she didn't blush and shyly look away and go all mute and giddy. She looked him in the eyes and nodded her head thoughtfully. "I guess I shouldn't say it, but I really think this one is—well, commercial," she said gravely. "I think I have matured, Al, and I owe a lot to you. I can't tell you how much your advice and encouragement have meant to me, and I wish there was some way I could repay you." She took off her glasses and her eyes met his boldly, blinking but unwavering, and he felt a quick kind of hot elation, forgetting that without her glasses she was nearsighted, trying to analyze her last statement and using her somehow nakedly intense gaze for an index to the hidden meaning. To tell the truth, when she read about one of her heroines quivering in the embrace of the hero, it always aroused Al a little, but then she usually nullified his accelerated interest before the walk home afforded him opportunity to follow it up. Now something ambiguous in her attitude, even her languorous posture, quickened his pulse. And she wished there was some way she could repay him, she had said meaningfully. And now, her eyes clinging to his face and her mouth pursed thoughtfully and under the circumstances suggestively, Beulah said, "I feel tonight I'm a new being, Al; I have emerged from the cocoon in my work, and I'm on the threshold of . . . exciting new things. Life. The world." She sighed and smiled a soft smile. "Tonight, at last, I'm a woman."

All right, Al thought. Tonight I'm a man. Let's go.

She wasn't quite ready to go yet, and he impatiently drank a fifth beer and let her talk about how with this last story she had broken through some spiritual husk and emerged from the cocoon and changed from a girl who yearned to write to a woman who wrote, a woman who was ready to grapple with life and meet the world head-on. She sure was different, all right, if you didn't look too closely.

Halfway across the campus there was a sunken garden circled by shrubs and trees, and Al was impatient to get there, and when he reached the inky darkness of the shrubs he wasted no time, not wanting to risk having his aggressive mood dissipate the way it had so often before with Beulah. He stopped her and backed into a shadowed nook and took her stiff, thin body in his arms and began to kiss her, not discouraged by her timid, tight-lipped, passionless acceptance as he would ordinarily have been. Goddammit if necessary he would teach her how to kiss and all the rest of it, if she didn't have any instincts to guide her. He forced her lips to soften and part, and continued to kiss her searchingly and demandingly, so that she was startled and alarmed at first, and struggled against him, and then was passive, and then eager, coming to the kiss helplessly, her arms stealing around his neck. What she didn't know, of course, was that Al wasn't kissing Beulah Flachtter at all, but was in reality kissing all coeds, all the women he'd wanted and couldn't have, the entire total female of the species, and Beulah just happened to have the dubious distinction of being the only available representative of her sex. What Alvin Woods had not yet realized was that he, himself, was many other men named Arvin and Marvin and Steve and Hubert and Alberto, Alfredo, Alvino. So the heroine, Beulah Flachtter Lenora McQuire, quivered in his octopus arms with awakening passion, although she was not tiny and voluptuous and did not have fruitlike skin and straight white teeth and all the other attributes of her creations, and Al made love in hope and urgency and a kind of last-stand desperation to every woman between the ages of twelve and forty-six. Beulah, surprised and delighted, unaware of her role and supposing that Al was kissing *her*, pressed her thin hard body against him and shivered with love and longing, clinging stickily even after Alvino Hubert Stephen Woods had suddenly, without yet being fully aware of it, abandoned this one more seduce-Beulah project, dismayed this time by her too sudden thawing, feeling like a scoundrel, admitting to himself that he had no feeling for her but lust. To some other guy she might feel soft and warm and smooth, to some other guy her mouth might taste sweet and her flesh feel charged with electricity, but not to Al. But the stop message from Al's brain got delayed in transit, and he proceeded mechanically for a few moments, going through the gestures. His hand cupped one of her small breasts with its covering of brassière and sweater, and he tried to convince himself that here, at last, was that conquest he'd almost resigned himself to omitting from his scrapbook of college memories. He pictured himself in a trench, ass-deep in snow, eaten alive by cooties, with the

Germans just there across the barbed wire and ruins of no-man's-
land and zero hour only minutes away and the cold steel of his
bayonet gleaming in the light from his luminous wrist watch—and
he'd be thinking about how he'd had a big, torrid, remarkable
November night of thrilling sexual intercourse with a thin, inexperienced, tasteless, unelectric woman named Beulah Flachtter, back
here in this romantic Alma Mater world. On the other hand, he
had no guarantee that Beulah would be completely acquiescent,
when you came right down to it, and he'd hate to stand there shivering in all that snow and remember that he'd *failed* to make out
with a girl named Beulah Flachtter.

He moved his hand, sliding it under Beulah's sweater, and she
shivered but stood her ground, and he was fumbling with the snap
of her brassière when she began to sob and wailed, "Oh, Al, I love
you so much! Oh, Al, don't you know I'm in love with you?"

Al's deft fingers turned into thumbs and he was paralyzed, all
passion fled, his lukewarm flesh chilled. Jesus Christ! he thought,
appalled. She *means* it!

He could never remember clearly afterward how he had extracted himself from that horribly embarrassing and revolting situation. He had stammered some kind of abject apology and muttered
something about being carried away in the excitement of the
moment, and about how he thought too much of her to slur her
good name and insult her decency and disgust her modesty and
sully her honor and stuff like that. And in despondent silence he
took her on home, wildly trying to think of some eloquent, magic
phrase that would keep her ego from suffering and remove the bad
taste of his own conduct from his mind. And he didn't do too badly,
either.

Across the street from her sorority house he gently took her
shoulder and turned her around. "Let me explain," he pleaded.

She sighed. "Nothing to explain, Al. Skip it."

"Listen, will you? I could be in love with you, Beulah, but I've
been fighting it. It wouldn't be fair to you, because—well, I've
already enlisted in the Marines for six years and I got to leave tomorrow morning, see." She stopped avoiding his glance then, and
he said a pretty thing, although not very original. "I've got a kind
of important appointment with fate, somewhere ahead. And tonight, well, O.K., I wanted you. I wanted something fine to remember, over there. I was falling in love with you, but I didn't know

you . . . I thought you *liked* me, sure, but hell . . . anyway, when you said it, all of a sudden I realized what I was doing, how it was all selfish and wrong. You're a wonderful girl, and I wish . . . well, that fate had been kinder to us. We might have . . ." He sighed regretfully. "Well, for me there isn't any future to plan, it's all planned already, it's in the book. Forget me, Beulah—but allow me to remember you, the sweetest person I ever knew."

"Oh, Al," she said, weeping softly. "You'll come back."

"Maybe," he said, wryly. He wanted a clean break, and he was afraid she would insist on corresponding, but she didn't. She was capable of dramatizing the situation herself, and did. She said she understood everything now, and it was too bad he had to leave so soon, and yet it was best that they part now, because tonight had taught her how dangerous their physical attraction could be. As for herself, she wanted to dedicate her life completely to writing for at least ten years, before she married or anything like that. Someday, perhaps, when he came back . . . but meanwhile, they would both be free. She sent him off to war with a moist, tragic kiss. "Good-by, Al . . . darling," she said shyly.

He ran wildly across the campus, yelling in his mind. It's always like that, goddammit! he thought. Why couldn't it have been Jo? All his life it had been like that, the same old upside-down formula of Al Woods not getting what he wanted and not wanting what he could get, goddammit to hell!

And running insanely across the moonlit November campus, Al snapped the thin strand of false security and empty sentiment that had tethered him to the University. He couldn't stay any longer, not after that goddam lie about joining the Marines for six years. Veering past the stadium and along Lindsay Road past the golf course, he came at last, winded and panting, to the water tower standing high and long-legged and gleaming black in the moonlight. His insane fury sent him climbing up the iron rungs of the ladder, ignoring his aching arms and legs and tortured lungs, until he achieved the railed catwalk high above the sleeping moon-drenched world of the University.

The fury spent itself, and he rested, and grew quiet, and stayed there in the cold high place for an hour or more, smoking his pipe and shivering in the frosty air, filling his mind and heart with all that he was leaving behind tomorrow, storing up sensations, filing away his memories, trying to make a portable bundle of all the fantastic moon-washed world there below him, to take along into his fey exile.

He felt that this was an auspicious occasion, and fumbled in his mind for some apt, debonair words to quote in au revoir. Looking south along the silver ribbons of the railroad tracks, he saw the shadowy clutter of the shanty village, ugly and wretched even at night, with the feeble flicker of kerosene lamps here and there showing that some of the denizens were wakeful, and he remembered Jo Hill wondering if those people were like everybody else. I'm not like them, Al said to himself. I'm not like anybody. I'm probably the most *un*like human being in the goddam world tonight. Those men and women down there are probably all fornicating right this very minute, because that doesn't require any money. And that's the big difference between them and me. I don't do that kind of thing, I'll have you know. Let them have their vulgar fun, I'll cling to my boyish virtue.

It was funny, though—and unfair, by God. Even the lowest forms of Homo sapiens had sex to comfort them in their misery, and all the other levels of society included sex in the recreation program, but there wasn't enough to go around and old Alvin Woods got left out. Who was responsible for this goddam intrigue, this conspiracy to keep Alvin Woods continent, chaste, and reeking with pudicity, anyway? His lack was whose gain? What the hell was going on in the world, anyway?

A night breeze had sprung up and it was growing colder up there, and Al thought, The sculptured dead on each side seem to freeze. St. Agnes. The Eve of. I better get down from here while I can still make it, he thought. Or maybe I oughta just stay up here and freeze to death and let the bastards figure how to get me down. Only they'd probably just shove me over and let me plummet ludicrously planetward. Maybe I should jump and cheat them of the pleasure, huh? That would solve a lot of nasty little mundane problems, boy. But it wouldn't solve the worst one—I can't die yet, I haven't lived. Before I cash in my coupons I have got to sleep with a total of at least six women first. That's mandatory, that's a city ordinance. And I've still got a few to go—six, in fact.

He took one last look at the silvered dreamworld below. Goodby, school, he thought. If you *are* a school. I didn't learn any what you'd call a plethora of stuff here, but Jesus I was a happy boy, wasn't I? About eight seconds of the time. Oh, I admit sometimes

I was sad, in a nice neurotic, depressed, gruesome, haggard, nauseating way, but isn't everybody? Good-by, college. Institute of higher learning. State-supported university, unreal world isolated inside your cocoon of brilliant intellectuality. I learned some precious things from you—I learned how long a guy can attend classes without paying fees, and how many classes he can cut before the Registrar defenestrates him, and how it's always the ones without breeding or background who gripe about the carbohydrates, and how a guy has got to be cruel, in a kind and gentle way, or he'll wind up freezing his butt on a watertank in November without any souvenirs in his biology album.

He climbed down and started home, numb hands in his pockets, shivering, still not satisfied with his valedictory address. The brain new stuffed in youth with triumphs gay of old romance, he snarled to himself. Upon St. Agnes' Eve young virgins might have visions of delight. I'll bet I am one of the very goddam few young virgins left any more, if you want to be technical about it. And soft adorings from their loves receive upon the honeyed middle of the night. Honeyed middle of the night my frost-bitten ass. That Keats, he must have got around, he must of scored heavily in his day. I'll bet he didn't get cold feet when some swooning young virgin said, "Oh Keats I Love You So."

Not a breast affords him any mercy, Alvin Woods recited with profound pessimism. And, warmed by walking, he detoured to a known casement and there did gaze one last time upon a lady's beauty unespied, and when she extinguished her boudoir light he wandered on toward his bare, dank cavern of a room, sighing.

I would of made a lousy fullback anyway, he thought. I stop too easy. A ninety-seven-pound short-story writer can stop me for no gain. A one-hundred-and-ten-pound equestrienne with a broken leg can hurl me for a loss, in the honeyed middle of an October afternoon. Well, I hate to louse up the tradition that a guy never leaves his Alma Mater without knowing a few coeds carnally, without taking with him fond memories of blanket parties and leafy couches in woodland glades and all that crap. Well, what the hell went wrong? There were women all over the goddam place, the goddam campus was overrun with the opposite sex. I didn't try hard enough, maybe. And when I had Jo Hill hanging on the ropes, I went all chickenhearted. Turn backward, O time, in thy flight, and let me have another shot at Jo tonight. And about an hour and ten minutes ago I could have maneuvered Beulah out of her underwear if I hadn't sprouted a mental block or something. What leaf-fringed legend haunts about thy shape, Woods? Jo and the blood-red maple trees, Jo and fruitful autumn. Oh No We Mustn't Hill and Whatever You Say Woods. I wonder what sweet little Jo is doing at this minute, in the honeyed middle of the night. I wonder what *anybody* is doing at this minute, and I wish them luck. Tomorrow I am off to join the Lancers, if they accept young virgins. . . .

When Al walked into the mildewed air of the basement room, he found Hinkle rehearsing a Bund leader role from *Margin for Error*, with his hair combed down over his forehead Hitler style. "*Ach in Himmel*," he said gutturally. "*Heil der Führer. Gestobben der Swinehund.*"

Al looked at him for a moment, bemused, and then he said, "I'm leaving in the morning, so you can have my dishwashing job, Hink."

Hinkle managed to look unhappy and delighted at the same time. He hated to see Al go, if for no other reason than because it would automatically raise his rent two dollars a month, but he was under-standably pleased to swap his chili and stew diet for the nourishing cuisine Al had so often rhapsodized about.

"I'm gonna enlist in the goddam Marines," Al said. "I won't need any clothes, I guess, except socks and underwear and an extra shirt. You can have anything that fits you. Hell, take all my clothes. What doesn't fit, you can swap at the secondhand store for things that you can wear. I got no place to leave anything."

"Al," Hink said, blinking rapidly. "Listen, pal . . . goddammit, what can I say? You're a wonderful sonofabitch and I hate to see you go, and the clothes . . . goddam, Al, what can I say?"

"Sing three choruses of 'After You're Gone,' " Al said, grinning, feeling a big, warm affection for his roommate.

They talked for a long time, and then Al took a shower and went to bed, and the last thing he remembered was Hinkle re-hearsing the Bund leader role in front of the mirror, grimacing and muttering gutturally and gesticulating fiercely. Al never saw him again. When he awoke the next morning, Hink had gone to his morning classes.

The landlady wept a little and blew her nose when Al told her he was going off to join the Marines; she had, she said raggedly, come to regard him almost as if he were the son she'd never had, and she'd never forget him, or the good times they'd had in August when he was such a help and so much company to her.

Now that he was actually leaving, Al was itchily impatient to be on his way, and in his haste he nearly forgot the typewriter. The indispensable typewriter he'd never had out of its case but the one time when he'd thought of hocking it. He was about to board the interurban trolley, known locally as the "toonerville trolley," when he missed the Smith-Corona. He had not intended to bequeath it to Hink, he meant to take it with him into the great unknown. He wasn't very clear in his mind about the typewriter's importance in his life—it seemed a foolish thing to take into the Marines with him, and it would be an extra burden. But, still, he felt he must have it, he couldn't tolerate the thought of parting with it. In high school he had learned to type forty-five words a minute, and he felt capable of doing so at almost any given minute in the future, but the typewriter was more symbolic than useful, a kind of badge.

Anyway, carrying a typewriter marked a man as either an intellectual, a fraud, or a thief, and Al was a little of each. But in a practical sense, he had no real need for a typewriter. For what, letter-writing? An occasional post card would take care of the vital communication with his father, and there was nobody else he might want to write, except maybe Hink, or possibly the landlady who had left her door open last August because she thought of him as a son. To write poems, then? Wellll, maybe poems. Roses are red, violence is blue. There was a man from Boston, who bought himself an Austin. Fools' names like fools' faces are always found in foolish places. O.K., not for poetry, not yet anyhow. Then why the typewriter, where the logic?

Basically, Al was always frank and honest with himself and never made any real effort to deceive himself about his motives, so now he admitted that it was just the principle of the thing. Going off to war carrying a portable typewriter was a gallant and debonair gesture, like if a guy took along his polo mallet. A little like a guy walking to the gallows reading travel folders. It was kind of goddam devil-may-care, even arrogant, even saturnine.

But largely and chiefly the machine was a symbol, like the College Omnibus he had not forgotten to tie up in his hobo bundle of belongings. They were both symbols of his brief matriculation at the University, totems of the tribe of Scholar, and even artifacts of that civilization. They were diplomas of sorts, too, for anybody seeing him using them would at once discern that he could type and he could read.

Goddamit, I *need* it, that's all, he said to himself. And having finally rationalized the thing into clear focus, he left the bus station and trudged back to the rooming house and got it.

He had missed his trolley and there was no hurry about it now, so he made a tour of the campus before he made a second final departure. And it was a sad kind of day to be leaving the campus to go off into the uncertain, ominous future. He sat in the Union Cafeteria and drank coffee and watched the students, and he walked through wind-blown torrents of brown leaves, and Jo was everywhere he looked, and he tried to sponge up all the seeing and feeling and remembering, because he didn't think he'd ever come this way again.

And, goddammit, he'd kind of liked it here, after all.

CHAPTER 7

The Changeling

SOMEWHERE between the interurban station and the post office building in Oklahoma City, Al got cold feet. He dawdled, stopped for coffee, bought a newspaper, intently examined window displays, and eyed the passing women critically. He thought of alternatives—catch a freight south and become a Florida beachcomber; check back into the old dingy hotel he'd stayed in before and eke out his paltry finances while he looked for a job. That about covered it, and neither course appealed to him; in time he reached the post office building and forced himself to enter. He didn't have to *sign* anything. He could say he was just *thinking* about enlisting, shopping around for the best offer. He had one-fourth of a college education, don't forget.

The Marine Corps recruiting office was there, to his right, and he moved along the corridor, his shoes squeaking on the marble floor. When he came to the open doorway he took one quick look and hurried on. It seemed to him there was a whole platoon of oversized, tough-faced Marine noncoms in there, wearing awesome red-white-and-blue dress uniforms—waiting to pounce on him or any other unwary young healthy civilian. Stymied and nervous, Al wandered along the empty hallway, and presently found himself loitering before a recruiting poster showing a small, sleek white ship knifing cleanly through emerald seas under a high blue sky. Studying the picture, he thought, I'll go back there in a minute, but if they start high-pressuring me I'll get the hell outa there fast. I don't *hafta* join. I might take a notion I'd rather get in the Navy or the Air Corps, who knows?

The legend over the white ship read: *Join the U.S. Coast Guard.*

The Coast Guard was not much known in Oklahoma. In fact, Al hadn't the slightest idea what the Coast Guard might be—something like the Border Patrol, he guessed. But he liked the ship in the picture. And he had been thoroughly buffaloed by the large and rugged and kind of hard-bitten men in the Marine Corps office. So he went up several flights of stairs and found the Coast Guard office, and it was staffed by only one man, a kindly looking, middle-aged chief water tender (who introduced himself as such without explanations; Al wondered how one tended water) who was reclining in a swivel chair with his feet on the desk and a pipe in his mouth. He didn't intimidate Al at all; he didn't look tough or especially muscular.

"The Coast Guard," Al said, getting to the point. "Boats, huh?"

"Aye, matey, lots of boats," the old salt assured him amiably, without moving from his comfortable position. "You like boats, matey?"

"Never been on one yet," Al confessed.

"You'd like 'em," the chief said mildly. "The Coast Guard is a good outfit, son. Opportunity to get ahead, plenty of travel. Man ought to make his third-class rating in one hitch easy, nowadays."

"What's the pay?" Al asked cautiously.

"Twenty-one bucks a month, same as the other services."

Al took a deep breath, remembering the big ominous Marines downstairs. "O.K.," he blurted. "I'll enlist in the Coast Guard, then."

The old chief put on his cap and leisurely escorted Al to a doctor's office down the street, and the doctor examined Al and reported him sound of wind and limb and clear of eye. Back again in the chief's homey office, Al signed the papers and the chief got him a room and gave him some meal tickets and said, "Amuse yourself until Saturday afternoon, when the next recruit cadre ships out for Dallas. In Dallas you'll be sworn in and sent on to boot camp in Algiers, Louisiana." Then the chief scowled a good-natured scowl and said gruffly, "Now, matey, you show up here on the dot of thirteen hundred hours—one o'clock to lubbers like you— Saturday afternoon, in prime, seaworthy condition. What I mean is, don't go down on Grand or Reno and pick up a dose of the galloping Chinese yingyang rot in the meantime."

He needn't have worried. Al spent the next two days eating up the meal tickets and his remaining cash, and drinking small beers, and sitting through double-feature movies. The worst malady he contracted was a mild case of Chinese bellyache from eating too much fried rice.

On the train to Dallas with the rest of the twenty-man cadre, the solemnity of the thing hit Al, the finality of it. In all his life he'd been in only two states, Oklahoma and Kansas, and here he was on his way to far-off places and no telling when, if ever, he would return to his native state. He shrugged resignedly; he was no longer in charge of his itinerary; from now on he would go where he was sent. And it was a kind of exciting thing to be riding south on the Santa Fe with these other committed draft dodgers.

A shaggy-haired boy in overalls played a battered guitar and sang mournful hillbilly ballads; and a third-string halfback from the University got tight on a smuggled bottle of whisky and tried to crash the club car, and used abusive language on the conductor, who said coach passengers were not allowed in the lounge car. For a few tense moments it seemed as if the entire cadre of enlistees were about to have their "asses booted off the train—you can *walk* to Dallas." But cooler heads prevailed, the halfback quieted down, and for the rest of the trip the enlistees were more subdued, all except the hillbilly, who seemed to feel he wouldn't be allowed to sing in the Coast Guard and had to get it all done before they reached Dallas.

> I do' want yo' greenback dollah,
> I don't wahnt yo' watch an' chain
> All I wahhhnt is you my darlin'
> Woan't you please come back agin'?

And he droned another which began:

> Way back in the hills, as a boy I did wanduh . . .

and ended:

> . . . moah preshus than di'muns, moah prayyy-shus than gold.

Once, when he struck up "You Are My Sunshine," some of the others joined in halfheartedly for a chorus, then quit self-consciously. They seemed like a pretty crude and motley group to Al, in their assorted civilian garb, and he was melancholy and depressed on much of the trip, not liking the way his life was changing so rapidly, not reconciled to the harsh fact that he had given up his freedom.

They lay over in the Texas city until Monday morning, when they were sworn in with other enlistees from the area. As soon as they had repeated the oath, the swearing-in officer stepped back a pace and scowled fiercely and barked, "You're in the Coast Guard now and in the future you will conduct yourselves as Coast Guards-

men. You will salute superior officers and address them as 'sir.' For
the next three years you will live on a military schedule, you will
learn to instantly obey orders and commands, you will learn seamanship, and some of you will even become competent seamen.
At the moment you are apprentice seamen. You are raw recruits,
which we call boots, and I assure you that you know nothing which
will be of any value to you in this organization. Never forget that,
men. Study hard, listen, learn, observe, and above all obey. Good
luck."

A grizzled chief bosun's mate put them on the train for New
Orleans, still in their civilian clothes, and issued a jackknife to each
member of the group, which now numbered around forty recruits.
Along with the knife went the stern admonition never ever to lose
it. "Mates, you will need them knives many times ever' day you're
in the Coast Guard. Them knives are a part of you. Them knives
might save your life in an emergency, or the life of a shipmate.
Men, never lose them knives, them knives is mighty important
gear from now on."

In the days that followed, Al used his knife several times to
manicure his fingernails. But he came to regard the knife as he did
his typewriter: If he ever *did* need it, he had it.

The boot camp in Algiers, he was delighted to discover, was
across the river from New Orleans. It was raining when the truck
hauled them from the railroad terminal to the camp through dripping rows of dark green waxen magnolia trees, and whenever they
passed old tars who had already been in training a week or so, the
veterans would howl, "Fresh meat!" And, "You'll be sorreeee!"
And, "Draft dodgers!" All in all, the arrival was pretty dishearten-
ing, and was followed by a hungry waiting in the cold dusty supply
warehouse, a hurried short-arm inspection, the issuing of sea bags
and clothing, the long rainy itchy sweaty slogging march with
their ammonia-smelling burdens, and the awkward, self-conscious
settling into bunks and stowing of gear. Al decided, when he finally
had time to relax, that he was unhappy and wished he had stayed at
OU. He had been foolish as hell to sign away his personal liberty
for twenty-one bucks a month. The succeeding days were not
calculated to change his mind.

The master-at-arms in charge of the barracks to which Al was
assigned turned out to be, in boot camp patois, a "chicken bastard."
An arrogant petty tyrant with a hateful, supercilious expression and

a whiplash voice, the chicken bastard awakened his nervous charges in the morning by hurrying down the aisles between the rows of double-decker bunks blowing a bosun's pipe and waving a paddle and bawling threats. On his second rapid tour of the big sleeping room he used the paddle on the bare thighs or buttocks of tardy risers and taunted them with his cocky, scornful laugh. He was instantly and heartily despised by all the new men, and it became their pleasant pastime to plan horrible methods of exacting revenge if they ever caught the chicken bastard off the precincts of the base.

The second day they stenciled names on their gear and learned about swabbing decks and soogying bulkheads and sweeping down fore and aft, how to make bunks and how to wear the white hats square on their heads. Also they were given their first taste of calisthenics, and short, unbecoming haircuts at the base barbershop. Al found himself an anonymous member of a marching group known as Company Q, which had the distinction of being last in line for chow. And the ordeal began to settle into a barely tolerable pattern. Each foggy morning he was jarred out of his restless dreams by the shrilling bosun's pipe and managed to hit the deck in time to avoid the laggard's stinging rump. Still groggy, and suffering from a head cold, he was given an insufficient time in which to dress, wash up, tidy his bunk, and fall in on the street. Then with his ninety-nine Company Q mates he plodded in a semblance of regimented orderliness to the parade ground, where the next hungry eternity was spent in calisthenics, after which all hands ran around the perimeter of the drill field three or four times before marching to breakfast in the huge warehouse of a mess hall. The running, and possibly the fact that he hadn't been a breakfast eater for quite a while, caused Al to suffer considerable nausea of a morning, and a loss of appetite. He drank coffee and skipped most of the gelid stuff that Company Q found by the time it got inside the building (once they were offered pickled pigs' feet for breakfast when the cooks underestimated, or ran short of the scheduled chow) and then became famished long before noon. And every time he performed one of the mechanical mass functions of boot camp, he yearned for the good old days, those carefree, indolent days when he was a free soul.

And all day there was the marching. Hup toop thrip forp, hup tup three four, walk down yonder and to the rear march and come back up here and left oblique over that way and company halt about face, while the assistant company commander, a seaman, second class, who was obviously striking for admiral, contemptuously asked if anybody knew which was his left foot. Huttenshun! Right face! *Marsh!* And the sun beat down and the sudden rains came and the ground was slippery and the grass too wet to sit on when a guy had a rare opportunity to sit on anything, and there were inspections, insults, semaphore drill, threats, Morse code, slurs, seamanship classes, abuse, knot-tying instructions and dry-land boat drills and humiliations and embarrassments, and every time they started to get rid of some of the tension and stiffness there was more close-order drill hup toop hup toop t'rip march.

Also for those first few days there were periodic needles in the arm, and sniffles, and the scalding misery of sunburned necks from the unaccustomed semitropical sunshine. There were scarce moments of humor, brief bursts of laughter, but there was *always* the goddam sore weariness and blistered heels and dull, mute resentment and timid fear of authority and the growing certainty of having made a disastrous mistake up there in Oklahoma City. And once Al had an acute attack of stomach-ache, or appendicitis, or maybe just a general psychosomatic transference of his mental woe to his alimentary system, so that when sick call break came he got permission and went to the sick bay, feeling better every step he took away from the indignity of being 1 per cent of a thing called Company Q, wanting desperately a few sweet moments of privacy and freedom more than anything else in the goddam world. "My stomach hurts," he told the pharmacist's mate with convincing agony, hoping to be excused from the goddam constant endless marching for a couple of hours maybe, but the petty officer wordlessly gave him a shot glass full of liquid salts and, when Al hesitated, shuddering, the P.O. said with stern authority, "Down the hatch, mack." And Al returned to Company Q, gagging and retching, and the rest of the morning his stomach really hurt. He avoided the sick bay thereafter; any ailment was easier to bear than the harsh remedy of salts.

Al liked the chief quartermaster who was company commander, a quietly efficient and patient instructor with a friendly manner. But Al grew to hate the assistant company commander, who seemed to feel he had learned everything in the six weeks he'd been a Coast Guardsman and was incomparably superior to the stumblebums of

Company Q. Six hours a day he shouted and bullied and insulted and infuriated his charges, and between times he was hopeless and wearily resigned and baffled and disgusted and maddeningly condescending. He was number two on the company's blacklist, right behind the master-at-arms.

A fat ex-Marine was made platoon leader of Al's half of the company and tried to emulate the assistant C.O., but he looked a great deal like a toad and had absolutely no sense of rhythm. Even with the entire platoon singing out in cadence, hup toop thrip forp, hun doo three four, the ex-Marine couldn't keep the beat, and was forever getting out of step and then angrily denouncing the platoon for being out of step. After several days of this the men had become mutinous, and finally the chief permitted the ex-leatherneck to slip back into the obscurity of the ranks, where his faulty metronome wouldn't be so noticeable. And it was here that Alvin Woods fumbled his only opportunity to become base personnel, or ship's company, at Algiers. The soft-spoken company commander looked the platoon over and thumbed Al out of ranks and said, "Woods, you want to be platoon leader?" Al begged off in panic, stricken with stage fright. He would feel like a goddam fool marching out there by himself hollering hup toop thrip forp t'rip march. His voice wasn't right for it, having a slightly nasal southwest twang to it—he'd rather sing "The Star-Spangled Banner" than go strutting around yelling the marching cadences. So the chief chose a pleasant-faced blond youth who played the saxophone, and Al wondered if he'd missed the brass ring again.

While he learned to march and tie bowlines and feather an oar and wigwag a few simple one-syllable words, Al absorbed various bits of information about the Coast Guard. It was America's oldest seagoing military outfit, starting out originally as the Revenue Cutter Service, and had absorbed a couple of other services along the way, including its recent annexation of the Lighthouse Service, and it now operated patrol cutters, ice breakers, buoy tenders, picket boats, troop-transport ships, stationary lightships, weather ships, lighthouses, and a great number of shore stations. Al had no particular preference, but rumor had it that the transports were rugged duty, especially during landing maneuvers. And he didn't particularly want shore duty. But he figured, pessimistically, that he would get what he got, and he didn't think he would like it.

One morning during a brief respite his platoon was sprawled in the shade of a magnolia, and a squat, tough-talking, ugly fellow named Berger leered at him and snarled, "How long you been inna Coast Guard, guy?" Al, although somewhat repelled by Berger, added in his mind and replied, "Eleven goddam long miserable days."

"I outrank yuh," Berger said scornfully. "I'm in *twelve* days."

"Listen," Al said wearily, "*everybody* outranks me, buddy."

That was the monstrous indignity of military life. There were about sixteen or seventeen plateaus of authority in the Coast Guard, and everybody on every goddam level above apprentice seaman was his boss, it seemed. He was the very lowest form of military life.

"I wanna go home, fellows," someone said plaintively, and Al recognized the voice of a slender, handsome, too-amiable guy named O'Neal, who treated everything as a joke. O'Neal, Al opined, was one of those smart alecks who always wanted to be the life of the party. Also he was conceited. Somehow O'Neal had bribed or cajoled the barbers into letting him keep his hair longer than the other boots, and he was always combing it and roaching it in front. A real ego type, and a drugstore comedian, this O'Neal. Al didn't care for him at all.

"What they oughta do," O'Neal said humorously, "is let a guy sign up for a sixty-day trial and then if he don't like it, they tear up his contract and let him go back to Cincinnati."

"I wouldn't go back to Cincinnati," Berger snarled. "I'd go back to Cicero, yuh dumb jerk." He turned to Al. "Where would you go back to, guy?" He sure was an insolent bastard, that Berger.

"I'd gladly go back to Oklahoma," Al said morosely.

Berger gave him a stupefied stare. "You one of them Okies?"

"Yeah," Al said.

"I didn't know they took Okies in the Coast Guard," Berger said, pretending to be astonished, and the rest of the platoon laughed.

"I was shanghaied," Al said. "What I can't figure out is how you passed the physical, not to mention the I.Q. test, buddy."

"Whatta yuh, a wise guy?" Berger snarled. "You want a fat lip or somethin', Okie? Whatta yuh want from me, trouble?"

Al rolled over and got to his knees and squinted at Berger, "Yeah," he said. "Give me some trouble, boy. That's what I want."

And the saxophone player yelled, "Fall in! Let's go, gang!"

"Don't go away, Okie," Berger said ominously.

"I won't," Al said, and he felt a little like laughing. Don't go away my ass, he thought. Nobody leaves this prison camp. I got on the wrong train, I got mixed in with a batch of convicts. What I hate most about this humiliating, undignified, brutalizing situation is the low class of crummy bastards you have to mingle with socially. I wonder what old Hinkle is doing back there in Norman. I wonder what all the people *outside* are doing. I wonder what the *Marines* are doing, boy.

CHAPTER 8

Neko Soap

WHEN the quarantine period ended, Al's company was allowed to make its initial reconnaissance trip to New Orleans. He was roused out of his dissatisfaction with the course of his life by the prospect of visiting the city, which he had heard referred to as the "Queen City of the Exotic Southland." In his pocket he had half a month's pay, amounting to the munificent sum of nine dollars and fifty cents after deductions for having his uniforms altered to a near fit, and the price of the crock haircut he hadn't wanted in the first place. He would not be able to sample many of the rich tourist attractions of Canal Street, but he could see the sights and feel a brief sense of freedom. And in the back of his mind was always the thought that conceivably, he might be able to remedy the exiguousness of his love life. He had heard the boys mention a place called Baronne Street, which was alleged to abound in two-dollar cat houses.

He had elected to explore New Orleans alone. By now he knew a good many of the men in his company by name, but as yet he had not formed any friendships. As he saw it, there hadn't been anything to be friends about. Some of the men from the original cadre had gone into another company, and the rest had become lost in the anonymity of the company, where everybody wore the same costume and nearly everybody had a peeling nose and an unflattering haircut. Sometimes at night he would hear a twanging guitar and a nasal lament in a distant corner of the sprawling barracks, but the hillbilly musician wasn't in Q, and although Al had rather liked his looks and manner—despite his singing—and thought he might make a good buddy, he'd already begun to sense the impermanence of service friendships. Other men of the company had begun to form attachments and buddy up, like Berger and O'Neal, for instance—as unlikely a duo as Al could imagine, offhand—and shear off into small groups and cliques as they found interests in common, but Al was in a passive frame of mind and made no effort to be gregarious with those barracks neighbors and company mates who aroused his interest. And those who made tentative overtures were not the ones he would particularly have liked to know better.

Especially cocky, conceited O'Neal and arrogant, offensive Berger. *Especially* those two. But on the ferry heading for New Orleans, unaccountably he found himself in the company of these two for whom he had no fondness. From almost the first day, they had been persistently gravitating into Al's orbit; squat, tough-mannered Berger with his cynical eyes and mockingly sarcastic voice, which grated on the ear, and the handsome, comical, too-amiable Harry O'Neal, who laughed when the situation was un-funny, and who combed his hair too often and too painstakingly. Now they seemed determined to join him on this first liberty as Coast Guardsmen, and he was too diffident, or too goddam innately courteous, to let them know how he felt.

"Ain't yuh seasick yet, Okie?" Berger wanted to know.

"Not yet," Al said.

"Some of that New Orleans rum will cure *my* seasickness," O'Neal said, licking his lips. "Rum with beer chasers, yum, yum."

"I'll be too busy layin' dames to do any drinkin' fuh a coupla hours," Berger said, leering. He elbowed Al in the ribs. "You wid me, Okie? How bout it, kid?" Since the day when he and Al had almost come to blows during the rest break, Berger had managed somehow to convey the impression that he forgave Al's rude conduct, only don't let it happen again. He confused Al by being at once very crude and very subtle, and you never could be certain if he was being earnest or slyly insulting your intelligence.

Right now he made Al feel irritated, and Al shrugged and said, "How far will nine bucks go in a town like New Orleans?"

"Hey, yuh jerk, don't worry about dough," Berger snarled. "Me brudder in Cicero sent me a bale of lettuce. When ya wid me yuh don't need to worry bout money, Okie. Be my guest, ya jerk."

Maybe I had this guy wrong, Al thought wonderingly.

They walked up Canal Street purposefully, anxious to get out of the lower section that was off limits to boots. They came to a bar and O'Neal said, "Let's just step into this here s'loon, men, and oil up the old artillery. I'm spittin' cotton."

"Tote that bale," Berger said. "I'm right behind ya, pal."

In the bar, O'Neal ordered rum-coke, and Al, not wishing to appear ignorant although from a prohibition state, followed suit.

"Double rye," Berger snarled. "I ain't no goddam sissy."

I'll have this drink, then I'll excuse myself, Al decided. It was pleasant in the bar, especially in contrast to boot camp and the graceless barracks, and he thought his reflection in the mirror behind the bar was fairly jaunty, all in all. The drink tasted fine and warmed his guts, and the music was nice, and it was only the middle of the afternoon. Time unlimited, he thought. No hurry. I ought to let that Cicero gangster pay for a couple more drinks.

"Okie," O'Neal said loudly, "as soon as we bankrupt this tenement dweller from the Chicago slum district, let's you an' me go find us a brace of them quadroons I read so much about."

"Watch ya langwidge, yuh Cincinnati punk," Berger said darkly. "I got contacts in dis boig—I'm liable to have yuh scragged." He dug an elbow into Al's ribs. "Youse is wid a big-time operator, kid, don't listen to dat penny-ante bum. He's so cheap he cuts his own hair."

"Bartender, I believe I'll have a whiskey sour," O'Neal said.

Al tried his first whiskey sour. It was sour. "I'm paying," he said, digging his money out of his pocket. But Berger was indignant, even bellicose. "Don't insult me," he said. "I told ya, I'm loaded. Dis is my party, see. Put ya dough away, Okie, ya jerk."

Al put his money away. He felt rather good. Rather good, boy.

"At's it, cop wise fer a change," Berger said. "Hey, bud, give us a round of dem double ryes," he snarled at the barman.

"Hamburger, what did you used to do?" O'Neal asked. "Pimp?"

"Go ahead, get nosy, jerk," Berger said dangerously. "I'll have me mob bump ya off. Ya might get ya juggler vein split." He bellowed with laughter and dug an elbow into Al's ribs. He went back to the nickelodeon and fed it a handful of coins and came waltzing clumsily back, snapping his fingers. "Hot dog," he said. "Drink up, ya jerks. We gotta hit Baronne Street before the six o'clock rush." He stared at Al balefully. "Wanta know wot I done in de old days, kid?"

"Not especially," Al said. "I mean, I ain't nosy."

"Ever'body's nosy," Berger snarled. "I drove a goddam truck. Beer truck. I had it good, but dat goddam draft board was fixin' to louse me up so I'm down here for me health."

"I'm a barber by trade, myself," O'Neal said absently.

"A barber!" Al said.

Berger laughed cynically. "A lousy wig trimmer. How bout dat?"

A barber, Al thought. Always combing his goddam hair.

As the afternoon wore on into evening, Al somehow couldn't get over his disappointment in O'Neal's choice of profession. He tried his first sauterne wine, his first Tom Collins, his first brandy. The conversation revolved around the subject of whores, and Berger seemed well informed. Al listened, learning, and stared at the spectroscope that kept flashing before his unfocused eyes. "Berger," he said heavily, "if that is your name, which I doubt, tell me something—do you talk like that on purpose, like a dead-end kid?"

Berger looked hurt. "Wot's wrong wid how I talk, ya crum?"

"You got a strange accent," Al said. "It sounds phony."

"Lay off, Okie, he can't help it, he's from Cicero," O'Neal said.

Al studied O'Neal intently, not seeing him clearly. "Got a few questions I'd like to ask you, too, you cute barber you."

"If you ast me, you don't talk so hot yuhself," Berger snarled.

"Barber," Al said thickly, "how come you're a goddam barber?"

O'Neal bristled. "Wait just a minute, now, you Oklahoma bastard. Anything wrong with being a barber? You got any objections maybe?"

Al felt an unreasonable antipathy for barbers which he couldn't quite elucidate. "It doesn't take *intelligence* to be a goddam barber," he said. He hiccuped. "You don't have to know much about very much."

"I talk *American*," Berger said, nursing his injury.

"I'm as intelligent as you are, that's for goddam sure, Okie."

Al laughed scornfully. "Ever hear of Edna St. Vincent Millay?" O'Neal glared at him resentfully. "Tell me, barber, who wrote— 'What lips my lips have kissed'? Who wrote, 'Who have turned me at midnight with a sigh,' you brilliant barber, that's all I want to know from you."

"Ole Vincent wrote it so shut yuh goddam yap, Okie," Berger snarled. "Who ast you to butt into de conversation anyway, ya jerk?"

"If, as you claim, you are an intellectual shampooer of scalps," Al said to O'Neal, "just tell me who wrote the 'Prusong of J.

Alfred Lovefrock,' if that is not asking too much of your enormous brain cells."

"I wrote it," Berger said. "I admit it, so shut ya goddam yap."

"Get out of my hair, Okie," O'Neal said coldly. "I don't hafta talk to you an' I don't hafta listen to that crap either."

Al laughed scornfully. "You're not so smart, boy. Admit it."

"I never claimed to be a brain," O'Neal said wearily. "And I'm not ashamed of being a barber. What the hell were you, you bastard?"

"I was a college student," Al said. He had the hiccups now.

"Jesus!" Berger groaned. "Ya never know wot ya gonna run into in a goddam saloon any more. A college student, fa chrissakes!"

"Look, you stuck-up bastard," O'Neal muttered, "I happen to be a good barber, with a license. I know all about barbering. I can look at a swell-headed jerk like you and predict if he's gonna get bald in the future or not, which is more than you can do."

Berger looked interested. "Is he?" he asked. "Is he gonna?"

O'Neal nodded triumphantly. "He is, I am happy to report."

Berger chortled, then looked worried. "Hey, how 'bout me, pal?"

"Not you, pal," O'Neal said tenderly. "Not you. Just *him*."

Berger inspected Al with hard-eyed scorn. "One t'ing I can't stand it's a ball-headed college boy. Blow, Okie, ya got dandruff."

"Yeah, take a walk," O'Neal said coldly. "You bore us."

Al frowned at the spectroscope swirling in his vision, and hiccuped. "I happen to be a customer in here. I got a right to stay."

"We don't wanta catch ya dandruff, ya jerk. Ain't I right, pal?"

"Anybody says I got dandruff is a goddam liar," Al said, and for a moment he had a tendency to weep, but he quickly regained control and ordered a Martini. "Heavy on the olive," he said. He did not like the taste. Not enough olive, he thought. Maybe I shoulda told him to make it extra dry, then they'd know. He glanced scornfully at the others, who were ignoring him, and laughed knowingly to himself. I told *them*, he said to himself. I corked *their* pistol, boy.

"I once got a haircut in a cat house," Berger remarked, and the barber laughed, and Al gave them a baleful but wavering stare.

"Who wrote 'With rue my heart is laden,' wise guy?" he demanded. They ignored him. "Housman, just for your goddam information." He studied the bartender. "Sir, am I being obnoxious?" he asked.

"You're trying to be," the barman said. "You'll make it yet."

"What is your personal opinion of Cincinnati barbers, sir?"

"I like everybody," the bartender said patiently. "Even you."

"If I get obnoxious," Al said earnestly, "let me know, will you?"

"I'll send you a post card," the barman said wearily.

"I apologize for my friends," Al hiccuped. "They are drunk, but I will restrain them, sir. I am looking after them, don't worry."

"Okie, ya bastard, take a stroll downtown," Berger snarled.

Hiccuping, Al studied this suggestion for a while, and finally said thickly, "Oh. I get it. I can take a hint." He fell into a brooding silence except for the steady hiccups, staring with deep melancholy at the blurry bottles behind the bar. He didn't feel well at all. He had a sensation of going up and down rapidly in an elevator. "The thing is," he said to nobody in particular, "I am from Oklahoma, which is a dry state. I'm not used to drinking this kind of stuff. I think I am going to vomit or something." He got off his stool carefully and put a hand over his mouth and stared at the bartender in distress, his insides heaving and churning.

Berger grabbed his arm. "Come on, ya bastard," he snarled disgustedly, and he led Al back to the men's room and stood by while Al unloaded the incompatible contents of his stomach. Afterward his belly was sore and his throat raw, and he had a sour puckery taste in his mouth, but all in all he felt much better. Back at the bar he leaned his head on his propped hands and tried to sober up.

Presently O'Neal said to the bartender, "Where is Baronne Street?"

"Eight blocks down," the barman said.

"That street is out of bounds for us boots," Al reminded.

"At's wot makes it innerestin', ya dumb jerk," Berger snorted. "At's where all de cat houses is at."

Al found himself on Canal Street with Berger and O'Neal, and he walked very carefully like a man on stilts, the problem less a matter of equilibrium than of merely staying vertical.

"I'd like to try a quadroon," O'Neal said. "I heard they're hot."

Women, Al said to himself. The idea of women took root in his reeling brain, it appealed to him, it grasped his interest. The idea of women had *always* grasped his interest. Berger was addressing him.

"Ever been in a cat house, Okie, ya rum-dum bastard?"

"Cat house?" Al inquired gravely. "Yessir, men. Millions of 'em."

They were on another street and it was dark and furtive here, and Al stared blearily around, wondering if his two bitter enemies had lured him into this black, deserted street in order to attack him. He decided to interrogate them cleverly. "Where are we goin', boys?"

"To the YWCA, naturally," O'Neal replied, laughing softly, "Young Women's Cathouse Association." He laughed less softly now.

Al was dissecting this suspicious, clearly evasive answer when the voice came out of the shadows, through the shutters of a dark window on the street. "We're in here, boys," the soft feminine voice cooed. "Come in, boys. Come have a good good time." The siren call of the carnal flesh stopped the trio in its tracks, and Berger nudged his companions and spat insolently on the sidewalk.

"Wot ya sellin' in dere, sister?" he asked coyly.

"A good good *good* time," the girl squealed softly.

"Open 'at goddam door, baby, here we come," Berger said lustily.

The next few minutes in fabulous New Orleans were fantastic and dreamily astounding for Alvin Woods, a drunk young virgin from Company Q, by way of Oklahoma. He found himself sitting in a shabby, garish, amber-lit parlor staring dazedly and incredulously at a dozen young prostitutes, all wearing the uniform of their trade: dainty panties and snug brassières and high-heeled pumps— and the empty, false, fixed smiles of presumed seductiveness. Crouching in a chair, Al examined them with fascination and shock and a kind of solemn dismay, for they looked just like ordinary, pretty girls and women, and there was nothing visible about any of them that would mark her for a whore away from her place of business. They had no distinguishing marks or characteristics, they could have been college girls, schoolteachers, waitresses, secretaries for all a man who passed them on the street might know. Maybe they all looked tired and pretty bored, but it amazed Al that they did not look evil or vicious or depraved or venal. They didn't even look especially sexy, somehow; only two or three of them could be described as voluptuous.

On the other hand, the boss man looked like evil incarnate. The whoremaster, or pimp, or panderer, or white-slaver, or manager, or whatever the hell you called him, sat like an evil, gray-fleshed toad in a rocking chair looking obscenely indifferent and smoking an obscene black cigar and scowling with dull, bleary eyes at the threadbare rug. Every now and then he received some tainted money from a despoiled virgin when she came wearily downstairs, and put it in an evil cigar box on his lap, and wrote some terse evil data in a cheap tablet with a stub of pencil. "You keepin' score?" Al wondered aloud, but the bleak-faced proprietor just gave him a sour stare and spat into a coffee can he kept under his chair. "O.K., *get* sore," Al said.

There was a constant restless movement of hungering masculinity and the dubious entrees they selected: sailors and soldiers and a few civilians were in and out of the parlor and up and down the stairs, and Al watched it all in mute and baffled horrification. It was all so goddam casual and businesslike—unashamed and brazenly routine for the girls, and the men all acting as if they were buying a loaf of bread in a bakery. It seemed grotesque to Al, and somehow revolting; as it probably seemed to every man who came here for the first time.

Berger had been lasciviously eying all the merchandise, joking with the girls in his tough Ciceronian fashion, boldly fondling them, pinching the fruit. He finally made his selection—a tall slender girl with long black hair, who was slightly knock-kneed. As he led her away, Berger looked back at Al and grinned wolfishly. "Wot ya waitin' on, ya jerk?" he snarled. "Don't be picky, grab a bag an' come on up."

"Any minute now," Al said. But the trouble with him was that he felt bashful and reluctant and mighty nervous about the idea of going upstairs with one of these matter-of-fact beauties. He was physically shaky from the effects of his indiscriminate drinking, but his mind was clearing rapidly, unfortunately. He rather enjoyed watching the girls and feeling disillusioned about the female gender in general, and he indulged in prurient speculation about their glistening bodies and eyed them with the critical and measured scrutiny of a connoisseur, but he hadn't the courage to single one out and engage her services. Evidently his procrastination was nothing new to the girls, they knew how to handle reluctance, and presently one of the tired-eyed inmates got out of her chair (she had been upstairs twice in the short time Al had been there, which may have accounted for her sigh of patient resignation as she arose) and gave him her attention.

"Don't you see anything you like, sailor?" she smiled. She had a sweet face, considering everything, and Al approved of her plumpish hips and thighs, her long legs and short torso, and her large breasts that shivered as she walked, spilling richly over the top of her tight brassière. She slid onto Al's lap with the casual ease of long practice and began to fiddle with his neckerchief, pouting prettily. "What is it about me you don't like, honey?" she asked softly.

"Nothing; I like you fine," Al said. "I always did like you."

"Well, why don't you ask me to go upstairs, then, sweetie?"

"I figured you were tired," Al said, feeling nervous and itchy. "Anyway I'm a poor man, I can't afford these luxuries."

"Pooh, it's only two dollars," she said.

Al squirmed restlessly. "I just ain't in the mood, and besides it's against my religion to pay for my romancing."

She laughed gently. "I can *put* you in the mood, honey. And the money is just for the room rent, the overhead. Anyway, you never got any for free as good as me. Those little old give-it-away girls are amateurs. They don't know how to be a *real* woman, sailor boy. I *do*."

She seemed real enough to Al, and she certainly knew how to rout reluctance in a balky customer. After a little more flattering and squirmy sales talk, Al went staggering self-consciously up the stairs with the girl, whose name was Annabelle.

In the squalid room with its dirty antiseptic smell, she dropped her girlish coyness and became appallingly businesslike, giving Al a brusque physical examination as brutally efficient as any crude pharmacist's mate might give him. "I know you sailors are safe," she explained, "but we have to be careful anyhow. You're supposed to give me the money now, sweetie." Al gave her the two dollars, which she put on the cheap dresser, and then she outraged his romantic soul further by introducing him to the argyrol rinse. By now he was hot with embarrassment. There sure wasn't any soft, sentimental nonsense about Annabelle, once you got to know her better. And as if to remove any lingering doubts about it, Annabelle stripped off her scanty garments and sprawled immodestly on the bed and gazed wearily at the stained ceiling and sighed, "Come on, sailor. Make it snappy, honey."

I can't do it, Al thought. He stood there half-undressed in the uninviting room and stared with growing repugnance at the girl on the mussed bed. "Aren't you gonna turn out the light?" he asked.

She yawned. "Uh-unh, we're not allowed to. Come *on*, sweetie."

If she had once been attractive to him, she was no longer. Her animal magnetism was a little too animal now, and her glamour had been destroyed by her rude efficiency and by the ugly cubicle in which she performed her duties as a *real* woman. Her breasts had flattened loosely on her chest like melting suet and her stomach looked slack and flabby and repulsive to a boy whose ideal of womanly beauty in the nude ran more to firmness and sleekness and daintiness. Annabelle was a slob of a woman, a tired aging professional female, and he wanted out of there badly now. He stood holding his trousers and staring at her sickly, and she shot him an impatient glance and wriggled lewdly.

"What are you waiting for, big boy? We haven't got all night."

"I'm sorry," Al said gruffly. Boy, if this was sex he was going to hang onto his amateur status. He felt drearily disillusioned. A girl like Annabelle ought to learn to keep her goddam clothes on. "I am sick to my stomach from drinking," he said, putting on his pants. "I need to get some fresh air."

She got off the bed and walked toward him, swaying her hips seductively, smiling indulgently. She looked a lot better on her feet, but not enough better to change his mind. "What happened, baby?" she inquired. "Did you get scared? I'm clean, honest I am, honey lamb."

"I can't make the grade," Al muttered, and she laughed and pushed her nakedness against him, squirming and bumping horribly. "Little Annabelle can help you," she cooed. "Let me show you, honey."

Al grabbed his hat and jammed it on his head. "It's not your fault," he said hurriedly. "I'm engaged to a nice girl back home, a preacher's daughter—it's my conscience, see. I just can't do it."

"Oh, pooh, she's probably in bed with some other man right now," Annabelle said. "You know I have to give Leo the money, sailor."

"Give Leo the money," Al said, backing away from her nakedness. He had a sudden mental picture of all the men she had brought to this room, and he turned and stumbled out, disgusted and ashamed of himself. Sex was beautiful, huh? If that was sex, then the hell with it.

In the parlor Berger leered at him. "How was it, Okie?"

"Marvelous," Al said. "Astonishing. You wouldn't believe me."

"No, hey; it was somethin' special, huh?" Berger asked alertly.

"Sensational," Al snarled. "I mean it was *mammoth*, boy." He laughed bitterly. "Best deal I've run across in a coon's age, buddy."

When Annabelle came downstairs, Berger waited impatiently until she turned in her earnings to the flaccid old toad of a whoremaster (who, Al thought with a shudder, probably laid every girl he employed whenever he felt like it), and then the tough, cynical, worldly truck driver from Illinois clutched the girl's plump arm and hurried her back upstairs.

Wondering what had become of O'Neal, Al leaned against the wall, wanting to leave the brothel but also reluctant to go, wanting to look at the girls some more, thinking incredulously of the dreadful lives they must lead and wondering how they ever got into such a sordid racket in the first place. How many times a night did they go up and down the stairs? Did they enjoy it? (Remembering Annabelle sprawled indifferently on the bed, he doubted that they enjoyed it.) How many rutting stags did they ordinarily accommodate in the course of an average evening—if accommodate was the right word? Night after night, he thought. Up and down. On and off. So this is a cat house. Just what the hell, would somebody kindly explain, was it all about, anyway?

Is every woman a potential whore? Alvin Woods asked himself. The question depressed him; he wished he hadn't asked it.

Time passed and girls solicited him and he shook his head and wondered if every woman had a price.

"Let's go, Okie," Berger snarled. "I'm caught up on my sex life."

"What happened to the goddam barber?" Al wondered.

"Ahhh! He took a powder. Hey, ya jerk, ya give me a right steer about that Annabelle. She was O.K., I mean. She had *talent*, kid."

In spite of himself, Al began to feel cheated. You should never judge a whore by the way she looked. He was too squeamish, probably. He was a goddam prude, too goddam fastidious. Twenty years old and nothing to show for it. I paid two bucks to be revolted. But goddam it, sex ought to mean a little more than that business back there. I'd rather neck a girl and not make out than make out with a girl I wouldn't want to kiss. I've got some pretty peculiar ideas, I guess. Or else I'm suffering from a vitamin deficiency or something.

When they got to the foot of Canal Street, O'Neal was there

waiting for the ferry. "Where'd ya go, fa chrissakes?" Berger snarled.

"I got sick," O'Neal said. "I hadda go toss my cookies."

"Me an' Okie, we hadda party," Berger said with relish. "Ah, dat Annabelle. Dere's a goil wid real talent. How bout it, Okie?"

"You goddam right," Al said wryly. "You said it, boy."

When they got to the barracks, Berger, the cautious man of the world, suggested they had better take an all-over shower bath with some of that medical soap the pharmacist had issued to all the boots. Al agreed, wishing to maintain the fiction of his worldliness, and O'Neal joined them. "Just to be sociable," he grinned. "Not that I need it."

"Hey, Okie, did she kiss you like she done me?" Berger asked.

Before he could frame an answer, O'Neal laughed. "You better brush your teeth with that Neko soap, too, Hamburger," he said, turning on the shower next to Al. And presently he asked curiously, "What you got against barbers, Okie?"

"Not a thing," Al said. "My father is a barber. And listen, what I did before I joined the Coast Guard, I washed dishes."

O'Neal grinned, and Al grinned, and on the other side Berger laughed appreciatively. "Hey, barber, ya know somethin'—dis goddam student ain't such a bad guy. Okie, I like ya. Ya my buddy, see."

Al grunted under the spray of lukewarm water. He wasn't sure he wanted to be Hamburger's buddy. He'd never seen anybody like him before, except in gangster movies. It made him pretty uneasy to know that the crude, loud, insulting, insensitive, uncouth Berger liked him. I attract the goddamnedest kind of people, he thought.

Scrubbing his hide furiously with the Neko soap, trying to wash away the memory of the Baronne Street fiasco and the hangover he was beginning to develop, Al thought about the University. Who was Beulah Flachtter reading her love sonnets to nowadays? Maybe she had already found some better critic, some guy who bought his own beer and honestly liked her short stories, some guy who even liked the way she tasted and felt in his arms. And how about Jo Hill, by the way? Was she shoving some panting frat rat away and laughing lightly and saying, "Let's not pursue this mad folly any further, Elmo, for it can only lead to disaster." Or was she, perhaps, at this very moment in time, writhing helplessly on some couch of fallen leaves and gasping without conviction, "Oh, no,

Elmo, we mustn't!" Assuming which, was Elmo so goddam stupid he believed she really *wanted* him to stop?

Women, Al thought morbidly. What's the complete story on the female sex, anyway, men? What are the true, hitherto-unrevealed facts about all the whores and prospective whores and potential whores of the world? I am getting to be an expert at the fine art of futility, he told himself somberly. And he said aloud, "Boys, I'll tell you what else I used to be, in the days of yore. I used to be a vegetable thief and a shiftless bum. And I used to be a gentleman."

He had crossed the line. Gentlemen didn't need Neko soap.

CHAPTER 9

Chicago Pool

THE Monday Al's company had been scheduled to get bayonets for their rifles and, it was hoped, learn to perform intricate close-order drills without puncturing, slashing, or stabbing one another, they were abruptly assigned to duty in the mess hall instead, without explanations. Some of them were chagrined, and most of them griped in the traditional recruit fashion, but they knew that this was a speeding-up of their training and meant they would be shipped out sooner than they had expected; all the preceding companies had drawn mess-cook duty the last week of their stay at Algiers. In a time of world tension and war scares the Coast Guard was expanding rapidly, and it was apparent the top gold braids were anxious to hurry recruits through basic training and assign them to permanent stations.

Al felt that mess-cook duties were vastly preferable to the interminable dry-throated sore-footed marching and the boring classes in knots, signals, regulations, and nautical idiom. Mess cooks ate better, and there were lazy breaks between meals.

The commissary steward, no doubt impressed by Charley Berger's belligerent cockiness, put him in charge of the dishwashing machine, and he immediately selected Al and O'Neal as members of his crew. "I always take care of me buddies, ya jerks," he snarled. "But ya bums gotta do wot I say or I'll stomp ya brains out, see."

Al and O'Neal exchanged wry grins; they knew Berger well enough by now to discount much of his tough, threatening manner. They knew each other better now, too, and Al was amazed that he'd ever thought of Harry O'Neal as either conceited or smart-alecky. O'Neal was a good guy and an amusing character who could always cheer you up. As for Berger—well, he was Charley Berger, whatever *that* was.

When the company rated liberty, the three of them went to

79

New Orleans together without discussing the matter; it was tacitly understood that they were now a team. But after that first liberty, a disgusted Berger made the trek to Baronne Street alone. Harry O'Neal, it turned out, was a married man with in-law troubles, not sure of his marital status but not yet ready to start philandering. He confessed to Al that he'd bolted the cat house that first night because he was afraid he would succumb to the allure of a joy girl in spite of his noble intention just to window shop. On the subsequent liberties, Berger would drink with the other two for an hour or so, growing increasingly fidgety, and eventually begin nagging his friends to go with him to the flesh markets.

"I'm a clean-livin' married man," O'Neal would say, and Al would say ominously, "You keep on going down there, Hamburger, and you'll wind up with a severe dose of lingering leprosy."

Al wasn't tempted by visions of delight in the honeyed middle of the night. His customary excuse was that he was all caught up, as far as commercial romance was concerned, and was now being faithful to his sweetheart back in Oklahoma. When he said this he always thought of Josephine Hill, whom he never expected to see again, and at times he even believed he was actually honoring her sweet memory in renouncing any cheapening, ignoble transactions with the Baronne Street girls. His real reasons were a little less simple and commendable. Partly it was the expense—two dollars for a few minutes of dubious fun seemed an undue extravagance for a man earning twenty-one bucks a month. Partly he remembered his vulgar fiasco with Annabelle and felt he was likely to react the same way with any other whore. And if he needed any further reason, there was always the nagging fear of venereal disease—which would mean loss of pay and privilege, and a blot on his service record that would dog him throughout his term of enlistment; there was also the injury it might do to a man's self-respect.

So Charley Berger would sneer and snarl and register massive contempt and say, "O.K., ya bums, here's where we supperate de men from de sissies. See ya in camp, chumps."

With the libidinous Berger gone, Al and O'Neal would settle down to a leisurely and economical evening ashore, drinking beer and strolling down Canal Street on the alert for pickup girls. For although Harry was too considerate of his wife to patronize bawdy houses, he had no real objections to casual romance with nice clean noncommercial ladies. And he had a knack for it. Al lacked the boldness to accost strange girls on the streets, but O'Neal had enough boyish impudence and brash charm for both of them. It was probably this unique social facility, as much as anything else, that endeared him to Alvin Woods. But there were, inevitably, flaws in the arrangement. Usually, when they found two girls together, one would be very pretty while her companion would compliment her by being utterly plain, if not downright dowdy, and it was tacitly understood that the guy who effected the introductions had first choice. So it usually transpired that O'Neal acquired a handsome companion, while Al too often found himself stuck with a drab creature of the Beulah Flachtter type, who stilled his lust and aroused his martyr complex. At times he brooded about the manifest inequity of the system; after all, Harry was supposed to be a happily married man who loved his wife if not his mother-in-law, and it struck Al that in order to lend verisimilitude to his pious protestations of fidelity, O'Neal might occasionally choose the homelier and therefore less tempting and morally dangerous girl for himself. But if he was living recklessly, O'Neal seemed to relish doing so, and Al went on being seen with girls who were almost no threat to his moral purity. He always got the culls. . . .

Working at the hot, sweaty, greasy dishwashing machine that last week in boot camp, the three friends often wondered aloud about their future, and O'Neal always expressed the wish that they could stick together. Al agreed, but with the mental qualification that if he didn't start getting slightly more ravishing women, this stagnant old custom of double-dating would have to cease, boy.

It was the custom for departing companies to buy their good old company commander and good old assistant company commander simple and inexpensive tokens of esteem. It was not mandatory, and in this case the company felt almost no esteem for Seaman Leggas, who had insulted and goaded and abused them for weeks under a blazing sun or in the sudden brief rains. But everyone liked the chief quartermaster, and so there was an unofficial muster during a rest break and a two-man committee (Berger and a quiet boy named Gillihan) was elected to handle the selection and purchase of a suitable going-away gift. It was decided that some insultingly cheap present would be tendered Leggas, so that he would not feel left out, and each man of Company Q contributed a sum commensurate with his fondness for the chief on one hand and his dislike of Leggas on the other. Eighty-one dollars and sixty cents

was vouchsafed to Berger and Gillihan, with the instructions to buy
something practical, something useful. The presentations would be
made at the final muster, just prior to their departure from Algiers.

On Sunday evening the company was relieved of mess-hall duty
and given liberty until Monday morning muster, and since it was
to be their last visit to fabulous New Orleans, Al and O'Neal and
Berger had a farewell banquet and went on a seafood binge, consuming dozens of oysters, boiled Mississippi crayfish, fried shrimp,
gumbo, and other dishes native to the region. Berger tried to persuade his buddies to cap this feast by glutting themselves on the
delights of Baronne Street, but, as O'Neal said, there would probably be better cat houses wherever they were sent. Berger said that
by now Annabelle, quite understandably, was crazy about him,
and he was sure he could get her to service his buddies for free.
"Which," he said, "there ain't nothin' better than, take it from me,
ya jerks." But they maintained a steadfast and resolute attitude of
moral rectitude, and finally he said contemptuously that they were
just dumb, hopeless bastards, and he hurried off to enjoy his moral
turpitude.

Shortly thereafter, Al and Harry encountered a pair of dusky
Cajun girls of tender age who looked like sisters and spoke a delightful patois and were enthusiastic about dancing, drinking, and
necking, but were unfortunately no give-it-away girls. It was a
pleasant evening, if frustrating, and they all got a little drunk, and
Al, wanting her at any cost, proposed to his girl six or seven times,
and was very melancholy about leaving New Orleans now that he
had finally found the one big overwhelming love of his life. Around
three o'clock in the morning he kissed Simone good night and good-
by, and got on the ferry for Algiers, and accompanied a silent
O'Neal back to camp in wordless sorrow. Walking from the gate
to the barracks, Al said glumly, "Keep moving. All I ever do is
shove off for somewhere else. Just when I start feeling at home I
hafta pull up stakes and move on, boy. But anyway, tonight I
finally got a good-looking girl in the raffle."

It seemed to his groggy brain that he'd barely dozed off when
the master-at-arms came tootling down the aisle. The weight of his
weariness pinned him down and slowed his reactions, and he was
still abed when the scowling M.A. came hurrying on his punitive
second round.

Whack! The paddle descended on Al's bare thigh, shocking him completely awake. Crack! the paddle said a second time as Al contorted himself violently, causing the board to land on his shin-bone. It was the first time this debasing discipline had caught up with Al, and he was enraged. Reacting without thought, he vaulted off the bed and launched himself at the leering M.A. His shoulder smashed into the paddler's chest and drove him into a tier of steel lockers with a loud crash, and the M.A. flopped to the deck. Al ripped the paddle from his grasp and yanked him into a prone position and wielded it with all his strength, whacking the as-tounded, shocked petty officer on his lean bottom and his skinny legs. Then Al smashed the paddle into splinters against the lockers and dropped the fragments to the deck. But he wasn't thoroughly satisfied yet, and he stood over the cowering petty martinet threat-eningly, breathing rapidly. "You sonofabitch!" Al said hoarsely. "You dirty sonofabitch! I oughta kill you!" He clutched the M.A. suddenly by the collar of his blouse and half-dragged, half-swung him in an arc and let him go sliding across the linoleum deck, and the M.A. bawled frantically, "Grab him, you guys, he's nuts!"

Al watched him through slitted eyes, his face twisted with fury, as the P.O. scrambled shakily to his feet.

"O.K.," the M.A. gasped. "You're in trouble, boot."

"*I'm* in trouble!" Al snorted, and went pacing slowly toward the fellow, who promptly began retreating down the aisle—until he bumped into Charley Berger, who shoved him toward Al.

"Come on, ya ain't quittin', are ya, pal?" Berger asked with snarling solicitude. "Show us how tough ya are, pal. You wouldn't run from no *boot*, pal—hell, ya a big man around here, M.A.; ya don't hafta take nothin' off us boots. Go on, M.A., show us ya muscles."

And O'Neal was there, too, grinning. "Hell, fellows, let's just kill the creepy sonofabitch," he said.

"Yeah, leave us t'row him out duh goddam window," Berger said.

"O.K.," the M.A. whined. "All you three guys is in trouble, now. I'm puttin' you three guys on report." He pointed an un-steady finger at Al. "You gonna draw some brig time for hittin' *me*, boot."

"It's worth it," Al said through gritted teeth.

O'Neal laughed merrily. "Hell, let's *all* do brig time," he said, and he gently slapped the M.A.'s face. "That's for all the mornings you came strutting in here with that silly paddle, M.A., thinking you were safe because you had a little authority. *Now* report me, you penny-ante dictator. My name is Harry O'Neal. I'm an apprentice seaman."

Berger caught the M.A. by the shoulder, whirled him around, and twisted his nose. "At's fer bein' such a jerk, ya jerk," Berger snarled. "Me name is Charley Berger. Ya want me to spell it fer ya?"

"You can go now, M.A.," Al said. "Go tell the C.O. you made the mistake of hitting a dumb boot named Alvin Woods with your paddle."

Every man in the barracks was there now, encircling the four principals, eyes avid, grinning with delight. The M.A. looked around at his erstwhile victims, his sick eyes blinking, and then he went scuttling toward the door. He didn't look back.

Al sighed. "O.K., you dumb jerks, you had to buy in."

"We'll beat duh rap," Berger said scornfully. But he refused to meet Al's glance, and O'Neal's expression was rueful and contemplative. Cooling off, Al was worried and apprehensive, but he couldn't worry away a warm triumphant feeling and a strong sense of affection and comradeship for Berger and O'Neal. They had deliberately assumed part of the trouble he'd got himself into—and it was undeniably a serious thing to lay hands on a petty officer, no matter how great the provocation. Al sighed, shrugged, and resigned himself to whatever came, and thought, Those two wonderful, stupid characters. Goddam!

He went through the motions of washing up and dressing and tidying his bunk, and then it was time for calisthenics and loping around the drill field, and then it was time to march to the mess hall. As senior company, Al's bunch were first in line and got good hot French toast and generous portions of bacon, and dry cereal and pints of milk and coffee and grapefruit juice. But Al wasn't very hungry. Any minute, any second now, the summons would come, he thought; he wondered if whoever came would be armed, if they would handcuff him. Looking down the table he noted that O'Neal and Berger were also men of delicate appetite. They shoulda stayed out of it, the chumps.

Nothing happened during breakfast, or after breakfast. At the signal to muster they fell in at the drill field and waited, the entire company silent and expectant. The chief quartermaster and Seaman Leggas appeared. Under a bright morning sun the grass sparkled with dew and the magnolia trees looked richly green, and all the other companies were beginning their regular daily routines. Al felt a little lonesome for yesterday, and for civilian life, and peace.

"Men," the chief said in his friendly baritone, "you're shipping out today. You have four choices of assignment. Some of you will go to Philadelphia, some to Boston, some to Chicago, and some to Hawaii. As far as it's possible, you'll be allowed to pick your assignment. I'd suggest you pick an alternative preference. Leggas has four rosters; the company is dismissed for thirty minutes, so you can think about it and discuss it with your buddies. When you decide, Leggas will be at the mess hall with the lists. Go there and sign up. Dismissed."

Al and Berger and O'Neal walked along in moody silence until Berger said, "Well, where ya wanta go, youse guys?" As if they were going anywhere but the brig, Al thought; he shrugged and said in a desultory way that Hawaii sounded all right. "Aw, I mighta figured ya'd say that, ya sap," Berger growled. "Look, t'ree fort's of dis company's gonna sign up for Hi-wah-ya, an' already dere's millions of soljers an' sailors already in dem islands— dey already got all de dames sacked up. Go where dere ain't so much goddam competition."

"Philly is where they crew up the transports," O'Neal said. "Hell with *that*. Boston's a Navy town. So what's left—I'm afraid?"

Berger leered. "Chicago, me old home town, dat's what's left. At'sa first choice wid me an' any other dumb bastard wid any brains."

Al and Harry looked at each other, shrugged. And signed up for Chicago, although Al, who was a bit fuzzy on geography, thought of the windy city as a prairie metropolis surrounded by stockyards, and couldn't imagine what the Coast Guard would be doing there.

No tough brig attendants came for Al during the decision break, and when the company assembled again, Berger and Gillihan carried the going-away presents for the chief and Leggas. For the company commander they had a wrist watch, a chronometer impervious to water. The chief spoke a few sincere words of thanks, and said it was a good company, in many ways the best he'd ever worked with. He wished them luck in their careers. Then Gillihan stepped forward with the large package for Seaman Leggas, the ambitious, sarcastic, and aloof assistant C.C., and Company Q watched with sly interest, not knowing the nature of the gift but knowing Berger, suspecting that it would be some ridiculous article Leggas wouldn't be able to use, wanting to see him embarrassed in public, let him by God know how they felt about him. But as it turned out, there were two presents for Leggas. The one that came out of the box first was a tissue-wrapped officer's dress hat. Leggas inspected it impassively in the hushed silence, and then he slapped it on his head. It was much too large and came down over his ears, giving him a comical appearance; the company roared with glee and Leggas accepted the practical joke with a wry smile. Then he got the other gift from the box, and Al heard mutters of surprise around him. It was an electric coffee maker, about as practical and useful as anything could have been—and Seaman Leggas stared at it, blinking, and held it as if it were fragile.

"Well," he said at last, "you guys crossed me up. The hat I expected. But this . . . !" He held the coffee maker tenderly. "This is a swell surprise. I'm a coffee fiend, I'll get a lot of service out of this beautiful thing, and I can't express my . . . my gratitude. I know I've seemed like a real hardnose, and I couldn't blame you guys for resenting it, but that's basic training—a drill sergeant or drill instructor hasta act tough and hard to please. You guys never were as bad as I *said* you were, and you worked hard, you learned fast. And I just want to say I've come to like and admire you, individually and as a group, and if our paths ever cross again I'd be damn proud to buy you a drink . . . and . . . well, thanks, you *ex-*boots."

The men looked a little stunned, somewhat emotional. Why, goddam. Old Leggas, why, he wasn't such a bad guy after all. Hadn't he whipped them into shape, turned them into a hell of a good outfit, maybe the best-drilled company ever to pass through Algiers. They stared at Leggas, and suddenly the too-large hat wasn't funny at all.

Alvin Woods shared this abrupt reversal of feeling, this sudden epidemic of respect and fondness for Leggas that swept the company. But he was jittery, too, and kept scanning the horizon for the hard-cases he expected at any moment. He was pretty resigned to his fate; sorry he had messed up his budding career, but also stubbornly sure he had been morally right. In a narrow military sense he'd been wrong; as a man of honor and self-respect he'd done the only thing possible. So the hell with it. Come on, throw me in your dirty old brig, he thought bitterly. I can take what you dish out, Coast Guard.

But they weren't swift in administering harsh discipline, it seemed; they procrastinated, they stalled, and the chief dismissed the company until after noon chow, elaborately consulting his shiny new wrist chronometer and grinning proudly, and the men went to barracks to pack sea bags and roll their mattresses. With his gear secured, Al lay on the bare springs of his bunk and waited for the M.A.'s threat to become a reality. The injured party was in and out of the huge room, directing the cleaning details, his voice noticeably less loud and domineering than usual. He threw Al one bitter and vengeful and disturbingly sinister glance and then ignored him pointedly.

Al sighed and wondered if they would let him take his portable typewriter with him into durance vile. A guy in the brig, just sitting on his butt marking time, might get to where he'd need to *write* something, like Oscar Wilde wrote "Ballad of Something Jail." Or who knows, maybe a letter to Jo Hill. Or an essay on how the Coast Guard tried to destroy something fine in a man and reduce him to a servile, pickle-headed automaton, a zombie. Suddenly Al sat up.

Hey, where the hell *is* my typewriter? he thought, and got off the bunk to go hunt for it. He'd loaned it to a guy named Nickelson, who wanted to write his parents. Al found the boy sitting on his bunk. "Where's my typewriter?" Al asked. Nickelson looked blank. I thought you got it, he said. Somebody took it off of my bunk. Al ground his teeth, scowling. "All right all right don't just sit there, let's locate that typewriter, boy," he said. They looked all over the big room, but none of the company or base personnel who bunked there had any recent knowledge of the typewriter. One of the ship's company men suggested Al check with the M.A. Maybe he'd seen the Smith-Corona.

The M.A. shared a small room at the head of the stairs with three other petty officers, and Al stood grimly by while Nickelson timidly inquired of the forbidding M.A., who was now in skivvy shorts getting dressed in undress blues. Maybe he's just getting around to going over there and tattling on me and O'Neal and Berger, Al thought. The M.A. coldly ignored Al's presence and said to Nickelson that, yes, he had seen the machine, and as a matter of fact, for anybody's goddam information, he had impounded that machine, as it had no business in the berth deck in the first place, it was nonregulation equipment.

Al broke his grim silence. "It happens to be *my* typewriter."

The M.A. stared stonily past Al's left ear. "So what, boot?"

"So give it back or I'll finish the job I started this morning," Al said, his voice breaking with his sudden torrent of anger.

"Ain't gonna need no typewriter in the tank," the M.A. growled.

"Don't worry about what I'm gonna need," Al said hotly. But in spite of his indignant wrath he suddenly felt sad and hopeless, seeing with clairvoyant simplicity that this was undoubtedly going to be the fouled pattern of his military future—a series of nasty little run-ins with lower-echelon egos, sickening collisions with petty authority, and Alvin Woods felt the stark futility of being an apprentice seaman pitted against the tyranny, unfairness, indifference, vindictiveness, and overwhelming, mindless, demeaning authority of *any* goddam service branch, where a guy was nothing—where a guy could be a college man, a thinker, a reader, a sensitive intellectual, but they would still regard him as an adaptable animal to be herded around with whittled boards wielded by vain idiots, and constantly abused and insulted and sneered at and shouted at like a balky mule. Al felt like bawling. Ah, fair patriotism, sweet love of country, go to hell, you treacherous unworthy deceitful emotion. This was the last time anybody was going to find Alvin Woods voluntarily entering a soulless servitude where a guy had to let some sonofabitch impound his typewriter like this.

"I want my typewriter, you sonofabitch," he moaned drunkenly, and the M.A., who may have mistaken Al's weak moment of self-pity for the symptoms of acute mental deterioration or the mumbling of an established manic depressive, went to a locker against the wall, extracted the cased typewriter, set it on the floor, and circled around Al to the door. From which safe vantage point he gave Al a cocky smirk and said, "I'll see you at the skipper's office later, boot." Al took a deep, shuddering breath, picked up his typewriter, and told Nickelson with bitterness that this was the last goddam time he would ever loan anybody his goddam typewriter. And of all the vows he would make under pressure during the next five years and three days, this was one he would adhere to with inflexible stubbornness.

After noon chow the chief read off the lists of men assigned to each of the four travel pools. Only six men were going to Chicago, but three of these were Al, Harry O'Neal, and Charley Berger.

"Cicero, get excited, here I come," Berger snarled happily. "Chi, ya wunnerful boig ya, I'm comin' home!" He said this at least fifty times while the three of them sat on their mattress rolls waiting for the trucks to come for them, and each moment, as Al continually scanned the vicinity for belated S.P.'s to come drag them off to a general court-martial, he edged closer to believing that Berger might be right. The trucks arrived, and they loaded their gear and clambered aboard, and Al couldn't bear the eternity of dangerous waiting until the truck began to move. Berger grabbed him, grinning hideously, and snarled, "Awright, ya jerk, youse didn't treat me good an' now ya in trouble, see. Wen we hit ole Shy, me mob will fix youse, ya rat." But Al expected trouble at the gate. They want us to think we're escaping, he thought bleakly. That'll make the thing more dramatic.

But they got through the gate unchallenged, and they achieved the train unapprehended and headed north, away from cruel justice, and Charley Berger sighed, his tough, ugly face twisting into a grimace of cynical rapture, and snarled, "We made it, fa chrissakes—I been sweatin' like a chain gang. Don't tell nobody else, ya jerks, but I figured we was gonna wind up in Portsmouth, not ole Shy." And O'Neal gave a shaky laugh and wiped imaginary perspiration from his brow and said, "Somebody musta lost the subpoena, but we're sprung. What happened, I bet, they just didn't have time to do anything because it only happened this morning."

Al thought that was a fairly close guess, but he had a better one. Since it *was* the last day, and the M.A. would have fresh boots in the barracks as of tomorrow, the M.A. had been reluctant to spread the news that he'd been spanked by his own paddle. The cold, pitiless machinery of Coast Guard discipline hadn't got started because it had a weak spark plug. So Alvin Woods got on a train with five other grads of boot camp and left this one more home, this strange campus that specialized in dehydrated courses in seamanship, and he felt nostalgia flutter against his throat. Here he had eventually known a kind of happiness, the joy of sharing misery with ninety-nine other men, the pleasures of wanton New Orleans, where beautiful, ravishing women had hurled themselves seductively at his lap, and onto fetid couches, for no less noble reason than two dollars paid in advance; given funds and a stronger stomach, he could have made

up for the paucity of love in his past life. In Algiers, La., he had
been shown the jealously guarded secrets of centuries—how to tie a
sheepshank, a running bowline, a square knot; how to signal SOS
with his arms; how to feather an oar; how to do a right-face, right-
oblique, to-the-rear; and how to operate a dishwashing machine
capable of cleansing unbelievable quantities of soiled cups, plates,
and stainless steel side arms. Why, goddam, boys, a month ago Al
Woods hadn't even known how to box a compass.

I'm a sailor, he thought with pleased astonishment. A tar, boy.
And Chicago ahead. O.K., Chicago then. But after New Orleans,
what had Chicago to offer a lusty, brawny sailor like Al Woods?
Well, perhaps love on cleaner couches at only *one* dollar a session,
he thought, and grinned lewdly to himself as he watched the glistening magnolias speed past the train windows.

Berger produced a new ditty bag and, like a magician, pulled a
bottle of whisky out of it. Winking elaborately, he said that he'd
bought the whisky for the chief and Leggas, only he'd forgotten to
give it to them. "Ya jerks better help me get rid of it," he snarled.

"I am repelled by your dishonesty, but edified by your taste in
whisky and your cunning foresight," Al said, liking the sound of
the educated words. And for the rest of the trip north the three of
them stayed cheerful and optimistic, because there were two other
fifths of smooth and ardent spirits in the ditty bag, and they felt
gallant and heroic and a little doomed in their snug-fitting dress
blues, and O'Neal even managed to look well tailored, having the
build for sailor suits. The trip was marred by only one minor detail.
In New Orleans' semitropic clime they had somehow forgotten
that it was now December, and they were a bit stunned to see the
landscape changed from sunny and green and springlike to bare,
bleak, and winterish. But it was December, and 1940, when they de-
trained in Chicago, and they were welcomed by the numbing, whiplash blasts from Lake Michigan.

Al didn't believe Lake Michigan. The bitter wind howled in from
a huge tossing gray wilderness of water, and he said, astonished,
"What the hell is that?" Berger regarded him with disgust and
incredulity, and said Lake Michigan, ya dumb college student. He
said it pityingly, and Al shrugged and mumbled that he'd forgotten
it was so close to Chicago, and the six newly minted sailors were
hustled into a waiting truck and taken to the District Office.

And then, with stunning suddenness, they were split into pairs and reassigned, and before he had a chance to say good-by or shake hands with O'Neal, Al was whisked away with Berger, destination unknown. Shivering and depressed, Al sat stiffly in the truck cab and listened to Berger interrogate the driver. "Surf station," Berger said, elbowing Al. What's a surf station? Al wondered, weighing Berger against O'Neal and feeling guilty because, when you came right down to it, he'd much rather have been paired off with O'Neal. Being sent anywhere with Berger and without O'Neal was an unsatisfactory arrangement.

"I got a brother runs a saloon in Cicero," Berger announced.

"Who the hell cares?" Al snarled.

"I had a uncle dat was a surfman one time," Berger told the truck driver. "Always savin' people's lives. Drownin' dopes, ya know. Sometimes dey dragged fer bodies, an' sometimes dey got bloaters outa de river an' places." Al shivered; the subject seemed macabre for such a day as this. "My uncle, he says dey always picked a stiff's pockets, lookin' fer dough, or jools or watches, anyt'ing dey could find."

The truck driver laughed appreciatively. "No kiddin'?" he said.

"No kiddin'," Berger snarled earnestly. "One time dey find a guy floatin' around, all swelled up an' stinkin', wow! See, dis bastard, he had a ring on his finner, a big diamon', my uncle tole me. On his middle finner dat was all puffed up. So my uncle, he's a no good bastard anyway, he breaks off de finner. To git de diamon' ring, see. An' he *wears* it alla time, ain't dat a laugh? Hey, Okie, ya dumb jerk, maybe me an' youse will hit it lucky sometime like dat, huh?"

Al stared at the squat, ugly, brutal fellow and was repelled, and wondered if here in his native habitat, which was also the native habitat and haunt of hoodlums and sadistic killers and gangsters, in some subtle fashion Berger was reverting to a previous savagery. Al kept shivering, from the cold that had seeped into his mind.

"Where you reckon Harry got sent to?" he asked.

"Who knows?" Berger said indifferently, shoving his flat hat lower over his right eye. "Wotta hell, Okie, we're inna goddam Coast Guard now. Ya gotta take it like de dice rolls an' like it, ya bum."

"I love it," Al sighed. "Is Chicago always this damn cold?"

"Cold!" Berger snarled. "Jesus, ya call *dis* cold?"

Shivering, Al thought dismally, Why the hell did I pick Chicago? I just got here and already I hate the damn place.

PART II
Lake Michigan

✝✝

CHAPTER 10

Christmas

A YEOMAN, third class, was in the station office singing "Jingle Bells" when the two new men reported in. "Hmmm," he said gravely, and hummed another chorus, and said, "Rooms all full up, guess you'll have to bunk in the attic. That's upstairs, all the way. I'll show you."

He showed them to the dusty, cluttered attic room that held four empty cots, a litter of lines and ropes and bales of rags, buckets of paint and wax, stacks of lye soap, brushes, mops, brooms, and an assortment of boxes and crates. It was a cold, uninviting garret of a place. "On a clear day you can see Lake Michigan," the yeoman said.

Al tied his sea bag to the foot of one iron cot, unrolled his mattress, and made up the bed. He shoved his typewriter under the bunk and sat down, feeling weary and lost and forlorn, and watched Berger finish his chores and then stretch out on his bunk, and scowl at the low slanting ceiling. "Wot a crummy joint," Berger remarked.

Feet pounded on the stairs and a middle-aged, bleak-faced man came stumping into the attic, his pale eyes hard and unfriendly. "I'm the C.O. here," he snapped. "Get on your feet!" They scrambled to their feet and watched him warily. He gave an impression of leashed violence. "There will be no lying on your tails around here," the C.O. bawled. "Get into dungarees and get topside to the lookout tower and start learning your duties around here. Nobody loafs during work watch. I put in fourteen to sixteen hours a day myself and by God so will you. This is not a beach resort and you are not fat millionaires on vacation; try to pull the wool over me and I guarantee I'll make you wish you had friends in Washington!" He had grown red of face and his voice had climbed to an almost incoherent shriek, and his hands shook noticeably. Al was appalled and frightened by this unprovoked outburst. "Catch me letting you fellows gold-brick off around here and I'll...I'll..." the C.O. sputtered. "I'll...goddam it hit the deck!" And abruptly he went stomping angrily across the floor and down the stairs, leaving Al and Berger frozen in their tracks, eying each other with consternation.

"What the hell did *we* do?" Al quavered.

"We jerned de goddam Coast Guard," Berger snarled. "Okie, dat jerk musta not knowed who he was talkin' to. I better wise him up." He grinned toughly. "Me mob'll make him some cement underwear, pal."

They changed into dungarees and turtleneck sweaters and found the lookout tower, and the seaman on duty up there showed them the routine, the clock-punching, the alarm button to be used when somebody phoned in a drowning or boat trouble that required the Coast Guard's assistance. "Be sure you get the location right or the old man will rip your ears off, he's a ravin' maniac, what I mean," their tutor said gloomily. "After you sound the alarm you yell down to the guys where an' what's the matter. Ever' fifteen minutes you make a round on the catwalk an' check the lake for sailboats or fishin' boats in trouble, only there ain't hardly no boats out there now on account of the ice. The main important thing is punch that goddam clock or the old man will boil you in oil the rest of your goddam enlistment."

"Nuts," Berger said toughly. "How's de chow here, bud?"

"Lousy," their informant replied bitterly. "It's garbage."

They soon learned that he had lied—the food wasn't that good. In boot camp Al hadn't been very preoccupied with food, but he had noted that the cuisine, while it left something to be desired (like those pickled pigs' feet for breakfast), was at least nourishing. Now, thrown into a new and ominous situation, his old lonely insecurity came flooding back and he sought comfort in food, and found none there. The cook was a seaman, second class; the job was either a form of punishment or a sinecure handed out to favorites, Al wasn't sure which. But he was certain that the seaman was an atrociously bad cook whose offerings were either half-done or burned, tasteless and soggy and greasy and indigestible. I wish they'd either shoot him or me, Al thought, and he spent a cold, lonely, heartsick night in the attic, listening to Berger's crude, insensitive snoring.

The next morning, after a breakfast of scorched eggs, cold limp toast, and awful coffee, Al was put to soogying line by himself in the cold and drafty boathouse. He had a bucket of cold soapy water, a stiff brush, and what seemed a mile of dirty one-inch hemp rope, and stern orders to make the rope look like new. The Lake Michigan winter whined through cracks around the loose-hung doors and turned his wet hands fiery red and the rest of him goose-pimple blue, and he shivered and ground his teeth and cursed under his breath and hated the goddam world and all the so-called human beings who inhabited it, with a special emphasis on the Coast Guard and everybody in it with enough authority to make an apprentice seaman's life miserable, raw agony of body, mind, soul, stomach, and spirit. Which included nearly everybody.

I don't hafta stand for this kind of stuff, he thought over and over. I'll desert, goddammit; I'll go over the hill. I'll jump ship.

There had been times in the CCC when he'd felt maltreated, but nothing like this. It did not occur to him that he was probably being tested and that his reaction to this inhuman assignment might have a big influence on his future in the Coast Guard—and if it had occurred to him, he would have been wrong. The Coast Guard was in a state of flux; it had growing pains. Old-timers resented this invasion of clumsy, ignorant landlubbers who could not handle boats or throw heaving lines or scull a skiff or even paint a ladder properly. To the Coast Guard, as represented by the surf station, Alvin Woods was a big pain in the neck, a misfit. It did not occur to him, either, that he might be free to go inside the warm building and thaw out. He assumed he must stay where he was until somebody came along and released him from this bone-chilling, tooth-chattering, burningly cold assignment; he felt he'd been stripped of all initiative, all decision. He tried to warm his numb mind at the thinly guttering fire of self-pity, imagining himself getting pneumonia, or dying from exposure (turn away your face, somebody, for I shall run upon my sword), and the C.O. getting his ass in a jam because of it, maybe losing his commission (the C.O. was a warrant officer, not a commissioned one), and everybody standing around in shocked, even tearful silence, paying grateful tribute to this purple corpse from Oklahoma who, in dying at his post, elbow-deep in a bucket of soapy slush-ice, had rid them of the tyrannical near-lunatic master they feared. The whole world would know remorse.

Self-pity flickered out, to be replaced by the hotter fire of anger, which warmed only his brain, searing it to revolt. He had about

twenty feet of rope renovated when his agony and fury reached
the limit of endurance and he arose shivering from his cramped
position and cast a baleful look around the arctic boathouse. The
hell with this crap! he snarled to himself, and he abandoned his
bucket and brush and went shivering up to the attic. He got a
blanket off his bunk and found a secluded nook behind a pile of
ladders and paint cans in a nest of coiled ropes, and snuggled down
in his shroud, teeth chattering.

He hadn't been there two minutes when the C.O. came upstairs
and made a beeline for Al's covert like a bloodhound on a hot
spoor. The C.O. was looking for something else, but he forgot that
when he saw Al cowering there in the gloom. He grabbed Al, his
face flooding with wrath, and yanked the culprit from his hideout,
howling a shrill torrent of invective. For one horrible moment Al
thought the man was going to hit him with the fist he waved under
Al's nose. The C.O. had his yellow fangs bared in a savage snarl,
and Al thought, with dread and a kind of eager resignation, If he
hits me I shall *kill* him. But the C.O. had a shred of control left, and
checked that impulse. He'd *wanted* to, all right. Anybody could see
he *ached* to hit Al.

"You gold-brick, what do you think the hell you are doing?"
he shouted, and Al said he was trying to get warm—the sound of
his own timid voice sickening and angering him so that he added
harshly, "I was freezing to death washing that damn rope."

"Nobody ever froze to death if he was working," shrieked the
warrant officer. "Get your worthless ass below and turn to and don't
ever catch me letting you pull a stunt like this again or I'll kick
you all the way up the District Office, you liver-lilied milksop.
Next time I'll throw you in the goddam brig on piss and punk for
thirty days, you...you...!" He shoved Al toward the stairs. "On
the double!" he howled, but Al showed *him;* he *trudged* back to
the boathouse, hating the C.O. but hating himself worse for joining
this lousy outfit in the stinking first place. Piss and punk, he'd been
told, meant bread and water. Why didn't they just *say* bread and
water, goddam them all? But in the midst of his raging misery he
kept being vaguely troubled by something the C.O. had said, by
the continuity of his words, and finally he put his finger on the dis-
crepancy. The C.O. had said, Don't ever catch me letting you do it
again. And he had called Al a liver-lilied milksop. Al had to grin
a little, a stiff, ghastly, frozen grimace. Why, that old bastard was

crazy as a loon—no wonder he ran this station like a prehistoric insane asylum.

Again that night Al huddled forlornly under his blankets in the attic, shivering, cold of body and mind, listening to the lusty snores of Charley Berger, who took everything in stride imperviously. Al wanted to weep a little just for the pleasure of it, because he was trapped in this hell and there was no escape, no alleviation, no hope. But tears were unmanly, and if a twenty-year-old chump who'd never been further from Oklahoma than the Kansas wheat country until the Coast Guard got its sinister, squeezing hands on him could be *treated* like a backward, delinquent child, he couldn't act like one. Crying in bed wouldn't solve anything, he thought, and anyway he'd probably just freeze his eyeballs if he tried it. So he lay shivering and dry-eyed, listening to the wind off the lake and the slapping sloshing eternal voice of the lake and the callous, arrogant snoring of Berger, and something began to harden in him, a cold and steely resentment began to replace his self-pity and rebellion stirred in him and he said to himself, I'll show them; I can take it. And the way it looks to me, I'll *get* it, all right.

For several days Al mistook the three surfmen for ominously powerful men only slightly less sinister than the C.O., but finally one of them put him straight about that. Surfman Mahoney was a pleasantly stolid, shy-mannered fellow who went about his duties silently, and when he found it necessary to give an order to Al, he always winced at Al's automatic "yessir." "You don't hafta call me sir," he said. "I'm only a surfman." Later Al learned that "only a surfman" could have been translated to: one of the most courageous, highly skilled, and underpaid small-boat sailors in the world, rare master of the specialized craft of the service, picket boats, lifeboats, and on down to skiffs. (And, in time, landing barges and other invasion craft.) In the foulest weather imaginable, the surfmen unhesitatingly leaped into their puny boats and went out onto the ice-choked, storm-lashed lake to rescue foolish yachtsmen and fishermen, or survivors of bigger boats in trouble. Despite this ability and courage and responsibility, the surfman's authority was sometimes ambiguous, his rank ill defined, his work and worth unrecognized and taken for granted by his own service, and his pay that of a third-class petty officer. "Don't call me sir," the surfman said mildly. "Call me Norvil, or just Mahoney."

Al liked Mahoney and wished he knew half as much about boats and seamanship, and realized that Mahoney and the other surfmen were somewhat intimidated by the C.O. Once, when Al stormed that in his opinion the C.O. was paranoid and apt to slip his mooring at any moment, Mahoney grinned his bashful grin and murmured, "I wouldn't say that—but I'm glad somebody did." Al liked Mahoney, all right; he had great respect and admiration for all surfmen. But he hated the C.O., avoiding him when possible and retreating into a shell of sullen, stiff-spined silence when in the C.O.'s volatile presence. If the C.O. spoke to him, he froze into wooden-Indian rigidity, eyes bleakly straight ahead, the epitome of sloppy but thorough regimentation. He never uttered a sound in the C.O.'s hearing unless forced into it, and therefore he became, in a peculiar way, at once inconspicuous and impressive. More important, it worked, as if the C.O. felt that with this particular liver-lilied gold-brick he had been successful in achieving at least an external semblance of military efficiency, and could now concentrate his acid attentions on others. There were times in fact when he almost beamed at Al, with the pride of authorship. But Al did not beam back. He just ducked into his shell like a turtle, wary and on guard. It was his strategy of survival, his defense.

As the Christmas season approached, the C.O.'s bright and chipper little wife put up decorations around the station, and Al thought about his father, and about Jo Hill. Christmas had never meant much to him. At the University it had been a lonelier time than usual, an outcast sort of time, with nobody left on the campus but himself and a few local people, and he had roamed aimlessly the streets after dark, looking with sad, wistful eyes at the cheery lighted windows, seeing families gathered in snug living rooms around the traditional yule tree. He was of the opinion that Christmas was an enormous fraud, a dishonest, mercenary season of emotional blackmail during which merchants waxed rich selling overpriced love tokens to fools whose sales resistance was destroyed by mawkish sentiment. Al had sneered at Christmas, a season whose purpose had long since been corrupted, but in his heart he had grieved because it could mean nothing to him, who had no family but a father who would honor Christ's birthday by getting drunk and maudlin and awaken in a sodden bed with a bad hangover, because you simply couldn't mix eggnogs with 3.2 beer. Christmas in the CCC had been pretty nice, with only a third of the men present and a program of carols by the foremen's wives and kids, and a wonder-fully lavish turkey dinner. But except for that one Christmas, Al could not recall another since childhood he would want to live through again.

Last year, Jo Hill had sent him a card, which he had torn up in a jealous tantrum. He decided that he would send her a nice costly yuletide greeting this time, and a card of some kind to his father, just to let the old boy know his whereabouts. The novel idea per-sisted, and when he got liberty he brought it to fruition. He sent a card to his father, one he felt suitably noncommittal, and was shopping for something frilly for Jo Hill when he was electrified by a momentous impulse—why not send her a real Christmas pres-ent? He went scouting in the gift departments and located a magnificent box of candy with a plush heart on the cover. It was not expensive, but it gave the impression of being expensive, so he bought it. Then it struck him that Beulah Flachtter might learn of the gift, since she would be seeing Jo after the holidays when Jo transferred back to her old sorority house, and he hated like the devil to wound Beulah's sensitive writer's soul. She'd feel that he'd lied about how he felt toward her, that last night, unless he sent her a present too—and after all she had bought him a lot of beer. Al sighed, checked his resources, and bought a second box of candy exactly like the first. Me and my big fat ideas, he thought ruefully. Al the splurger. Woods the reckless spender.

Several days before Christmas the mail brought a modest card from his father, with a postmark indicating the barber had made one more futile transfer in his perpetual flight from himself, and a day later there was a large envelope from the same town with nothing inside but a folded pamphlet entitled "Hair Care." The old boy must have been drunk when he sent that, Al said to himself, grinning.

But there was no word from Jo, or Beulah either, for that matter. Christmas Eve came and the C.O. and his wife joined the men in the dining room and they had eggnog and sang carols, Al over-coming his stiff reserve around the C.O. sufficiently to toss in a little tenor on "Silent Night." Everything was going fine when the alarm started squawking and the C.O. and surfmen took off in the picket boat to rescue a foolhardy small boat trapped in grinding floe ice somewhere in the black cold night. They had not returned when Al fell asleep, and in fact the picket boat didn't get back until daylight. Such was the life of a surfman, and there were treacherous times when Al felt a small flicker of pride in being a part of the Coast Guard. Not, of course, like the hard, arrogant, virile pride of a Marine, with his tradition of fighting guts and durability, but a *sort* of pride anyhow. While the Army and Marines rehearsed their deadly destructive roles, the Coast Guard saved lives and property, and patiently removed the horrible swollen corpses of drowning victims and suicides from lakes and rivers and oceans. On Christmas Eve Al weakened in his grim resolve to hate the Coast Guard forever, and captured for a moment a feeling of admiration and affection for this nonmilitant, unbelligerent outfit into which he had stumbled because of ignorance and timidity.

And on Christmas Day he had trouble remembering how brutish and psychopathically tyrannical the C.O. really was, for the warrant sat with his men and ate heartily of the turkey and trimmings fixed by his cheerfully sharp-tongued wife; he even engaged in clumsy banter with Mahoney and Berger and others who weren't scared to open their mouths. But the *pièce de résistance* came later, after the table had been cleared except for bowls of candy and nuts and fruit, when with no fanfare or warning the C.O. sat down at the battered old upright piano some philanthropist had donated to the station and began to bang out creditable ragtime jazz. Al was astounded. The C.O. grinned almost becomingly as he tickled the ivory, and a warm sense of fellowship invaded the room and penetrated even Al's tough defensive armor.

Why, Al decided with Christmas insight, that violent old bastard wasn't such a violent old bastard after all, when he relaxed and let his hair down. Maybe he just had such heavy official burdens, such terrific administrative and executive responsibilities, that it kept him edgy and nervous and prone to explosive angers most of the time.

For several days after Christmas, Al continued to feel a kind of indulgent tolerance toward the C.O., extending the season somewhat. Then one night Al was reading a book in the recreation room when the C.O. came in silently on cat feet like Sandburg's fog, restlessly on the prowl for somebody to chew out. Al happened to be convenient, and the C.O. said testily, "Have you got a lookout watch tonight?"

"Nossir," Al said. "Had it last night, eight to twelve."

The C.O. squinted suspiciously. "What are you doing in here?"

"Reading," Al said. The C.O. demanded to know why. This

stumped Al, he was at a loss to say exactly why he read. It seemed evasive just to say he *liked* to read; beside the point, too, since the C.O. didn't care what he liked, or what anybody else of low rank liked. His mind fumbled with a file of ready answers, none of which seemed to fit the occasion, and the C.O. snorted with discouraged disgust and rolled his eyes upward as if calling on Providence to witness this one more infuriating example of the unreasonable burdens of his command, a dumb, tongueless, apprentice seaman who, reading, knew not why he read.

"Go ashore, what's-your-name," he said patiently.

"Sir?" Al said.

"Go ashore, you've got liberty," the C.O. said sternly.

"Well," Al said carefully, "I'd just as soon stay here and read, if it's O.K.—I kind of planned to hit the sack early, anyway." The C.O.'s face began to flood with color.

"Hit the sack, hit the sack," he said sarcastically. "That's all you gold-bricks ever think about, hit the sack. If I didn't watch you people you'd lay in your sacks twenty-four hours a day and spend the rest of your time eating. Dammit, when I tell a man to go on liberty, I want no arguments, he'd better *want* to go on liberty."

"Yessir," Al said, sighing. It was a black, cold night out, and the sheeted dead were probably squeaking and gibbering in the streets. He didn't want to venture outside. It was not a fit night to turn out a pregnant daughter. He closed the anthology—he'd been re-reading "The Eve of St. Agnes," with its preoccupation with bitter cold, with frozen grass and frosted breaths and numbed fingers and the owl who, for all his normally adequate feathers, was acold. Ah, bitter chill it was, and outside the Coast Guard station the lake pushed its grinding ice against the sea wall, and the wind sobbed. "Yessir," Al said regretfully.

"All I ask," the C.O. said with agitation, "is that you men act like normal human people, not a bunch of sulky sea lawyers. Is that asking too much? Is that so damned unreasonable, what's-your-name?"

Al removed himself stiffly from the abrasive presence of his commander; in the chill attic he changed slowly into his dress uniform, dawdling. Dressed, he felt his chin and realized he must shave, and he undressed, stumped below to the bathroom, shaved in a leisurely, procrastinating way, limped aloft again, and resumed his dress. Outside, he was greeted by storm; sleet and freezing rain slashed at his bowed head. He lifted his face to peer through the darkness and a fugitive flake of dry snow exploded against his left eyeball; his eyes watered and his breath hung cloudy in the polar atmosphere. The hell with this old crap, he said to himself, and turned back. Ten minutes later he was drinking coffee in the galley when the C.O. came in, his rubber soles making soft kissing sounds on the waxed linoleum.

"How's the coffee?" he said amiably. Al said it wasn't very good, but it was hot. Pouring himself a cup, the C.O. glanced at Al several times with knitted brow. "Back from liberty already, are you?" he wanted to know. Hesitant and apprehensive, Al said, yessir, he was. "What's the matter, short on money?" the C.O. demanded. Al clutched at this prefabricated alibi. Christmas had hit him a big lick, he said, and the C.O. nodded sympathetically. "That's the Coast Guard," he said, wryly. "We're overworked, underpaid, underfed, and underrated."

"Yessir," Al said, grinning lamely. "Well, guess I'll turn in."

"Good idea," the C.O. said approvingly. "Some of these birds around here go helling around all night, lose sleep, drag anchor all day, and then wonder why they stay seamen all their lives. Nothing like a good night's sleep to make a man efficient. Some of these gold-bricks think I'm too blind to know what's going on around here. I'm not blind."

"Nossir," Al said. "Good night, sir." And he went grinning up to the attic. There wasn't anything wrong with the skipper's eyes, it was his brain. There wasn't really anything complicated about that comical old bastard. He was just nuts, that was all.

If I stay here long enough, figure out why the hell I read, don't ask for too many liberties, take liberties I don't want, work sixteen hours a day but get a good night's sleep, stay out of my sack, and keep him thinking I'm coming back when I haven't been anywhere yet, I might get so I could stand that old coot, Al said to himself.

He was beginning to fit into the Coast Guard pattern.

CHAPTER 11

A Cook for the *Skedeelia*

I T WAS the middle of January when the C.O. established the cooking school at the station. The Cooks and Bakers School at New London, Connecticut, could no longer turn out chefs fast enough to fill the increasing needs of the mushrooming Coast Guard, and to meet this emergency the various districts were beginning to train their own cooks in small groups at permanent stations. When the officer from the district came to the station and explained about the cook-striker classes and asked for volunteers, Al had just spent a miserable morning scraping paint in the full blast of the winter winds. He knew that it was warm in the kitchen, and a cook had ready access to choice morsels in the pantry. He liked to pamper his palate and he hated to scrape paint. So he volunteered for the cooking school, little knowing as he stepped forward that he was walking toward his natural and inevitable destiny. It did not occur to him that he had spent most of his young life establishing a wistful affinity for food.

Berger volunteered, too. He was a creature of impulse, and his impulse was to stay warm and well fed, and earn better wages.

The following day a fat, pasty-faced, pompous man arrived in a truck and unloaded his gear and announced in a rich Teutonic accent that he was Adolph Wollager, toid-class cook, come to tutor the strikers. He was, it turned out, the entire staff and faculty. Also he was not a very good cook himself. His pies were soggy and he wanted to fry everything, and he was overly fond of garlic, sage, and sauerkraut. He was an improvement over the seaman who had been in charge of the station's diet—who now became second in command to Wollager—but he was no Escoffier. Furthermore, his methods of teaching the culinary art struck Al as being a little too painstakingly basic. Wollager believed a man must learn to crawl before he could learn to walk, and must become an expert pot-washer before learning the rudiments of using the pot. "Ve stard at de boddom and vork hop vun ting at a time," he announced the first day. "Virst koms zanitation. Iss necessary to have alvays a glean, spick-span galley, you zee."

What Wollager actually taught, in fractured English, was how to be a cook's helper—galley hygiene, the delicate skill of washing utensils, the knack of swabbing a deck and waxing it to a high sheen, the flair for polishing brasswork and buffing pots and pans with steel wool. "Still vool" was more important than soap, he emphasized. And he made Al increasingly impatient and a little sick at the stomach.

"Everybody knows cleanliness is next to godliness, Wollager," Al said. "Fine, leave us be neat. But when do we start *cooking?*"

Wollager gave him a look of moist reproach. "You shut pee obserffing vot I do all de time, Alfin. Vatch effery ting, memorice —den zomday you vill pee able to do it too. You learn like me, zee."

That was his theory of teaching. If you're not busy waxing a deck or washing pots, glance occasionally my way. Catch me in the act of performing a secret culinary rite and store it away in memory, poys.

Al had a different theory: You learned by doing. "Why the hell don't you let us *cook* something sometime?" he would snarl impatiently, and Wollager would be deeply hurt. Cruel infidel Alvin Woods, who would destroy the beautiful subtlety of Adolph's progressive cookery tutory. Teacher and pupil were from opposite schools of theory, they were not compatible, and daily the rift between them widened.

"Vy you ain't gleaning off de table, Alfin?" Wollager said.

"Goddamit I'm observing," Al said. "I'm watching you, teacher."

"I'm not doink anyting ride now, Alfin. Off de table glean, so?"

"I noticed you wasn't doing anything, professor," Al said. "But I figured you were about to begin to start to commence to do somedings."

Along toward the second week of matriculation, a brand-spanking-new third-class cook was bunked at the station temporarily while awaiting orders, and he elected to monitor the course. His name was Ralph Wildoe, but he said everybody called him Red. He was short, pudgy, pink-haired, pompous, scornful, and infuriatingly superior. He had just come from New London, where he had spent several months in the Cooks and Bakers School. He knew the whole works about cooking, and then some; he stood around the galley drinking coffee, a cigarette dangling casually from his faintly leering lips, watching with arrogant amusement this pitiful imitation of a cooking school. He talked without moving his lips, without agitating the cigarette, without displacing a single muscle of his face, and he would make remarks like, "You teach 'em how to fry water yet, Wollager?" He knew the professor from other days, it seemed. And he stood around flashing his bright-new rating badge and the hash mark on his sleeve indicating he'd been in service longer than one hitch. And he made the students terribly nervous, especially Berger.

"Yuh inna goddam road, mack," Berger said.

"At's interestin'," Wildoe sneered. "You wanta try movin' me?"

"Youse is beggin' for a fat lip, ya crum," Berger said ominously.

Wildoe's eyes glittered. He brandished his new rating badge. "You happen to be talkin' to a man with a crow on his arm, boot," he said, referring to the eagle patch. "Come on, buy yourself some misery."

"Ahhh, ya crummy jerk," Berger muttered, intimidated by the badge. And Al observing, always observing, reflected ironically that here it was again, that thing of petty authority. A seaman, first class, bullied seamen, seconds, or apprentices. A petty officer, third class, spoke only to the Cabots. Everywhere you looked, there crouched new, heady, dangerous Power and Influence, waiting to crush and destroy you. Every rank lorded it over every next rank down and all the subordinate levels. A little authority was a dangerous thing; it corrupted; it offered a snug harbor for conceit; it represented safety from below, although it offered no guarantee against avalanches from above. Touch a man with a crow on his arm and your ass was in the sling, boys.

Teacher and pupils were mutually relieved when Wildoe got orders to go to Milwaukee and join the *Skedeelia*, a buoy tender. He came to say good-by and scatter a few derisive taunts in parting. "*Bon voyage*, you scholars," he said, the words emerging flat and narrow from his slot-machine mouth. "I sure hate to leave, just when I was beginnin' to pick up all this new stuff Wollager's teachin'. You experts better hope you don't git sent to a ship. You wouldn't last a week on a ship." He stalked majestically to the door in his penguin walk, a man with a ship, a man with a crow on his arm, reeking with power and knowledge. He stopped for one last remark. "If they send one of you geniuses to *my* ship, you won't last long enough to unpack your sea bag."

"Aw, blow it, ya crummy jerk," Berger said, but Al sighed and scowled and said, "Hell, the guy's right, Charley, we're sure not learning a goddam thing about cooking." And Wollager, over-hearing this deprecatory aside, looked at Al with moist, pink re-sentment, his eyes albuminous. "*You* don't learn someding, dot's ride, Alfin Voods—you tink you alretty know efferyting, py Gott."

"Aw contrar, as we French are always saying," Al snarled. "It ain't that I know anything about cooking, professor, it's just that you and me neither one of us know anything much about cooking."

Wollager seemed about to weep. "Voods," he grieved, "I haff been a toid-glass gook now tree years yet, I haff you onnerstan'."

"Dot's vot I am meanink, Adolph," Al said unkindly. "So vot vas hoppenink? How come you never got promoted no higher, Schickelgruber?"

It was inevitable that anybody of German extraction with Adolph for a front name would now and then be called Schickelgruber, and Al had not been the first student to do so in this case, but now Wollager's doughy body began to shiver with outrage and his mouth worked with a kind of helpless fury, and he said, "I don' vorget dot, Alfin Voods."

"Boy, are you sensitive," Al said, shrugging. Crazy Adolph.

On Tuesday in the second week of February the C.O. came pussyfooting into the galley, looking fiercely upon the busy anti-septic scene, and asked in his usual harassed howl, "Who's ready to ship out?"

"Surr?" Wollager said with his customary humility in the pres-ence of the high and the mighty. He was one of those little men who genuflected to superiors and was jealous of his own dignity and authority, and wished his inferiors would kowtow to him but wasn't quite able to bring them to heel, somehow. This was not un-characteristic of cooks, Al was to discover. Nobody considered a cook either powerful or dangerous.

"I say," the C.O. snarled, "who's ready to ship out, Wollager?"

"Ass a shib's gook, surr?" Wollager asked, astonished. The C.O. said that was the gist of his meaning, and something ugly happened to Wollager's eyes. They slid around to Al like raw eggs on a cold griddle. Alfin Voods, the rebel, the know-it-all, the dissident fac-tion, loud critic of the curriculum, malcontent, general pain in the ass. "Voods," Wollager said unctuously. "Dot Alfin Voods, he iss retty, surr." He giggled triumphantly. "My gootness, soch a smard stootend—alretty he iss almost so goot I don' belief my eyes. Voods, he is *retty*, surr."

This was praising with loud damns, and Al felt trapped, and he lifted his voice in prompt protest. "Hell, *I* can't cook," he said with alarm. Stoobid head wice guy, Wollager had called him once—correctly. "Cap'n, I can't *cook*," he said frantically. "I *can't* cook, sir."

Wollager chuckled obscenely. "He iss yust modest, surr. Voods iss vonderfully intellichent and enerchettic, vit orichinal ideas how efferting shood be done. He iss my *most* retty stootend, dot's ride."

Al knew he was trapped. He looked at the glazed pink spite on Wollager's face and shrugged. "I fried an egg once," he said wryly.

"Pack your sea bag, Woods," the C.O. said. "You're going aboard the *Skedeelia*. They need another cook." And Al's spirits plummeted even lower, achieving new depths, for that was Red Wildoe's ship—Red, who had spent six months earning his rate.

Berger helped him pack. "Ya lucky creep," he kept saying with sneering envy. "From twenny-one rocks per month alla way up to sixty. Youse wouldn't even of been a lousy second-class seaman till March. How lucky can ya git, ya lucky stiff ya?"

"You may call it luck," Al said somberly. "I call it madness." He looked at his tough-faced friend. "One time when I was eleven I made a mulligan stew. When me and my old man were batching I used to make my own fried eggs and toast and coffee for breakfast. That covers my cooking ability, that is the sum total of my culinary accomplishments, except for the salads I made when I worked in one of the girls' dorms."

By the time his gear was packed, his promotion had been cleared through the District Office and his travel orders cut and on their way to the station. Whether he liked the distinction or not, he was now a petty officer, a SC3/c. A man with a goddam crow on his arm.

In the confusion and shock of his sudden graduation and departure he forgot his typewriter, which had been gathering dust under his bunk, unused and neglected. Several times it had occurred to him that when he became a cook he would need to type up menus and copy recipes from magazines and stuff like that, but now the portable slipped his mind. This station, the galley, in spite of

the C.O.'s unpredictable temper, represented safety. Beyond the
station was uncertainty, disaster, disgrace, embarrassment, failure,
and ruin.

When he left, the C.O. shook hands, twisted his face into a
fierce smile, and said some damn nice things about Al. "I knew you
would go far," he said. "I get a lot of hopeless cases here and most of
them stay that way, but I've watched you, what's-your-name, and
I've seen you turn to and batten down and get squared away and
take up the slack. You had the right mental attitude, you made
yourself shipshape. I've had to harpoon you a couple of times to
keep you on course but that's how the wind blows in this outfit,
we don't pamper anybody, a man worth his salt won't sound deep
and sulk if you step on his tail now and then. You'll admit I've been
fair and impartial on this cruise, I chew every manjack out the same,
and by God you can tell Orlando I'm sending him my best man."
He beamed ferociously at Al. "Now, good luck to you, uh, what's-
your-name," he said.

"Voods," Al said dully. "Alfin Voods, sir."

He was halfway to Milwaukee before he missed the typewriter,
and all he did was shrug. He could pick it up or send for it. In
fact, he'd probably be back in a day or two—they wouldn't let him
stay on the ship when his stupidity was revealed. Boy, he said to
himself, at last I'm up here with the big shots, two dollars a day,
board and room, teeth checked twice a year, tonsils extracted free,
bowed to by low vulgar seamen on every hand, having made a
niche for myself in this so-called Coast Guard by dint of hard work,
supernatural effort, study, and congenital brilliance—and all I need
to *stay* up here is a miracle, a rare fluke of fate, or a miscarriage of
social justice.

In Milwaukee he was met and trucked through gray wintry
streets by a stolid, laconic Coast Guardsman in filthy dungarees,
turtleneck sweater, and knit watch cap. "What's it like on the
Skedeelia?" Al asked.

"Oh, so-so," the man said phlegmatically.

"You on it?" Al asked, and the guy gave him a horrified stare and
said, "Hell no!"

The last part of the trip they seemed to be lost in a wasteland
of railroad tracks, soot-blackened warehouses, and tall mountains of
coal. The ship was a dirty, disreputable-looking old tender with
grimy black paint on her hull and sallow, sooty yellow-white on her

superstructure. She was moored at a narrow splintery wharf by a long low building in a dirty, ice-choked creek. The day was misty and gray-blue with a dank, penetrating, knife-edged wind whining monotonously, and as Al carried his rolled mattress and sea bag across a weathered gangplank onto the gritty, deserted well deck, a foghorn bawled somewhere nearby in the swirling mist, a hoarse and mournful sound. Off yonder Al sensed the winter-locked lake in all its icy endlessness, and the foghorn was answered by his forlorn soul.

There was no welcoming committee, no quartermaster around to log him aboard, no side boys and bosun's pipe. For several indecisive minutes he hesitated on the dirty arena of the well deck, staring bleakly around at the depressing water front, feeling utterly lonely, timid, uncertain, alien, and wretched, wanting to turn and flee this cold unfriendly strange ship before it was too late. But he knew it was already too late. This was his new home. Goody, he thought dismally.

Forward, the foc'sle (at the time he thought of it as the *front end* of the vessel) offered one area of exploration. He could hear mocking, sepulchral laughter and weird music coming muted and indistinct from there, apparently from below decks. Downstairs, he thought. In the other direction, aft, there were two doors, one on either side of the well deck; above the deck, behind the long angled arm of the boom, a row of windows indicated a living compartment of some sort, and Al had a crawly, itchy feeling that saturnine, sardonic, gloating eyes watched him up there, but no face peered out at his lost and lonely figure, the stranger come to this foreign shore and stranded down there in the gelid oil-and-fish-and-coal smell and the icy wind. Above the row of windows was what he guessed must be the bridge, but no life stirred there either. It was a ghost ship, a derelict abandoned to the grinding ice and frozen blasts of air, and the music and ghostly laughter were only hallucination.

Feeling a little spooky and very cold, he moved toward the near hatchway, the starboard entrance to the covered part of the main deck. Inside the door a passageway stretched down the side of the ship toward a door far aft, with closed doors at intervals along the inner bulkhead and portholes in the hull. Also at regular intervals, the foghorn moaned its dolorous warning, which Al felt was probably meant for himself. What would happen if I yelled *yoohoo* real loud? he wondered, moving warily along the passage-way on the gritty steel deck. He peeked through the first door and saw a small empty mess compartment with its door shut. He tried the next passageway portal and abruptly felt less lost, for he was looking into the galley.

Moving fully into the open doorway, he saw Red Wildoe lean-ing on the meat block, sourly studying the *Navy Cookbook*, a cigarette drooping from his taut lips and a cup of coffee in his right hand. He made a familiar, homey picture, and Al was almost happy to see a known face. He dumped his heavy gear against the bulkhead and stepped inside.

"Hello, Red," he said diffidently, and Wildoe gave him a sour glance. "Whatta ya want?" he asked, stiff-lipped, like a man with his face injected full of novocaine. Al said, "Uh... I'm the new ... I've got orders transferring me aboard this ship. I'm..." He sighed. "A cook."

Recognition blazed in Wildoe's eyes and his face went violently astonished and outraged and incredulous; he seemed in a state of shock. He pointed a finger at Al. "Chicago! Wollager's pot-walloper school!" Al nodded, embarrassed. "You were a goddam apprentice seaman," Red said huskily. Al nodded, grinned feebly. "I... uh... just got my crow."

With careful deliberation Wildoe poured the coffee out of his cup, watching it splash on the tiled deck, and then he hurled the empty cup against the bulkhead, his mouth gaping cavernously as if he wanted to scream and couldn't. The *Navy Cookbook* followed the cup, but still the scream hung fire, tongueless, mute. Wildoe turned and put his head down on his arms on the meat block, like a man offering himself to the guillotine. There now ensued a long, awful silence. Then Wildoe said softly, "I knew it. I knew they'd send one of them stupid bastards. I *knew* they would."

Knowing better than anyone else his shortcomings, Al winced and kept quiet. Wildoe was right—except, of course, about that bastard part, and that was only a justified figure of speech.

A shaggy youth in dungarees and a filthy turtleneck sweater and knit cap stuck his head into the galley, stared with interest from the disconsolate Wildoe to Al. "You the new cook?" he asked, and Al shrugged and said he was supposed to be, and the fellow stared at him unblinkingly. "I *knew* they would," Wildoe whispered, and the guy in the doorway began to worry and twist a strand of long, lank hair that hung over his forehead. "Well," he said to Al, "I better show you where you bunk at, cookie. I'm the quartermaster on duty."

Without raising his head Wildoe said, "Not in *my* stateroom!"

Twisting his forelock, the guy said, "Where the hell at then?"

"I do not give a goddam where," Wildoe said bitterly. "Anywhere but in with me. Up forward or back aft, but not in my cabin, Salter."

Salter took off his knitted cap and stared into it, grinning with bewilderment and worry, exposing ugly tooth snags and gaps in between—reminding Al, for all his painful humiliation, of the landlady back at OU. Salter put his watch cap on the back of his head again and checked to be sure the strand of hair was handily left dangling. "Well, there's a couple empties in the black-gang quarters. Come on, cookie."

Al gathered up his gear and looked back into the galley in time to see Wildoe pick up a huge iron spider and begin to bang it on the meat block while he muttered hoarse obscenities. Feeling miserable and unworthy, feeling despicable, dishonest, unattractive, and unacceptable, Al trudged aft and below. I'm a fake and a fraud, he said to himself. I don't blame Red. Me, a cook? **Don't** make me laugh. Who *wouldn't* be sore?

"What's eatin' old Wildman Wildoe?" Salter asked.

"I'm not his type," Al said, wishing he'd trip on the ladder and break a leg so they would transfer him off the ship real fast. At the foot of the iron steps he found himself in a gloomy, odorous metal cave, where five men sat around a table, with a single shaded bulb hanging low over it, playing cards and arguing. They were tough, baleful, ominous, sinister types who eyed Al thoughtfully and returned to their game. "It's the new cook," Salter said, and the gamblers turned as one man to give Al a careful second scrutiny. "We *need* a cook," one said, and another said, "Not like 'at muckin' Red, though."

Bunks lined three bulkheads of the square compartment, with lockers in the corners; the deck was bare, grimy steel plates, and the ceiling was the same except that there were pipes and conduits and wiring squirming and crawling across it. The bunks and bulkheads were in shadow; the single harsh light fell on the faces of the men with a sickly whiteness that revealed their pimples and blemishes and turned their eye sockets into secretive, shadowed caverns.

"Hey, you s'pose to sack in with Red in the after cabin," one of the men said. Al shook his head. No, he said. Down here, he said. They looked at one another quizzically, they shrugged indifferently. "Who opened?" the man said. Nobody opened yet, another said. Well, whose bid is it then, goddammit? Yours goddammit. Play goddammit. Goddammit goddammit goddammit everybody and everything goddammit as Al spread his mattress on an empty top bunk, found an empty locker, goddammit, stuffed gear into it you sonofabitch, changed into cook whites, two cents ya bastard, cancha hear nothin—Al heard ice grating and grinding along the side of the ship as he climbed into the bunk and turned his face to the rough cold steel bulkhead.

"Hey," a gambler growled, "someone ain't in."

Me, Al thought with deep sorrow. I'm the one. I ain't in. I never am in, I never will be in. If I get to be an admiral I'll always be the one that ain't in, boys. I'm strictly an outside man.

CHAPTER 12

The Invisible Man

THE word got around. The ship was a small world, isolated from the outside, trapped in the ice and the winter, and news traveled fast. The new cook couldn't cook; the new cook was a phony.

Almost nobody spoke to Al. A water tender named Brownie spoke to him the first night, then got the word and joined the silent ranks. Salter, the snaggle-toothed, hair-braiding quartermaster, third class, at first took a proprietary interest in Al, but Al's own guilty, self-effacing sense of inaptitude made him defensively aloof and curt, and Salter left him alone. That first week nobody spoke to the new cook, a screwball who spent most of his time in his bunk in the dark after berth deck with its stink of sweat and dirty socks and stale cigarette smoke and unaired bedding and winter mildew. The ice-locked routine of the ship went on around him, but Al hid in his bunk.

The first morning he had reported to the galley in whites and apron, ready to do whatever Wildoe ordered him to do. Wildoe ordered him to stay the hell out of the galley. "Go hit the sack, take it easy," Wildoe said with bitter sarcasm. "You gonna git your sixty bucks a month, but you ain't gonna ruin no chow in *my* galley, mack. Just blow."

A dark-eyed, sharp-faced, muscular boy in the uniform of the ship, with his sweater sleeves pushed up over knotty biceps, was washing pots and pans in the galley sink. He grinned with sly, insolent scorn, and Al formed an instant dislike for the pot-walloper.

"I hadda go to New London an' sweat my ass off for six months to earn my rate," Wildoe said bitterly. "I hadda be inna Coast Guard four goddam years before *I* got a chance to go for a rate. So now they give guys like you a rate when you ain't been in four *months*, yet."

"Don't blame me," Al muttered. "I didn't ask for it."

"What the hell you know about cookin', anyway?"

"Not much," Al said humbly, "but I could learn."

"Not on my time!" Wildoe bawled, the words erupting from his frozen mask of a face. "This ain't no goddam cookin' school, mack."

"I told them I couldn't cook. They shipped me out anyway."

"What are you, braggin' or complainin'?" Wildoe said nastily.

Al's pride had been trampled all he could stand. "Aw, go to hell!" he said in a voice that shook. "Is it my fault you're so dumb it took you four years to earn a rating? Listen, when you get all done pouting, let me know." And he stalked out of the galley, to retire to his bunk and curl up like a possum, and Wildoe's squalling voice pursued him below. "Stay outa my galley, goddam you!"

Al studied the bulkhead for a week. Except for meals, which he took in the deck gang's messroom in grim silence, with downcast eyes, he barricaded himself in the emotional fortress of his bunk. The ship lay imprisoned at the depot wharf, and the men came and went, cursing and bickering and laughing. Al saw no officers around; maybe there were no officers. Maybe Red Wildoe was in charge of the ship. Al studied the bulkhead and slept and hibernated in his bunk, and stopped worrying about what was going to happen to him. Just let it happen *soon*, because he'd had about enough of this old crap, this persecution and ig*nor*ance and contempt. He was about ready to slug a few snotty characters.

He daydreamed, losing himself in fantasies of revenge. He imagined **himself** going through the ship like a tornado, his brutal fists wreaking bloody havoc, winning respect and admiration. And he would say to Wildoe, From now on I'm taking every other watch and you will kindly stay out of the galley when I've got the duty, or else.

This is what I'll do, he daydreamed. This is what I'll say. Then he'll say . . . then I'll say . . . then he'll, then I'll . . . then they'll all realize . . . then they'll say, then I'll laugh coldly and say . . .

Nobody helped ease Al's debut as a cook. Nobody told him the score about liberty, and he refused to ask. He was in a prison of his own fashioning. The others came and went, going eagerly ashore, dragging in late at night, happy, half-drunk, noisy, satisfied. He yearned to get off the ship, but nobody told him what his privileges were and he was too proud to ask. To hell with them. To hell with everybody. He addressed nobody, and the men accepted him as an eccentric screwball and left him to his own devices. Except that he had no devices.

He had been there a week when Salter shook him awake one cold morning at five-thirty. "Wildoe's dog-drunk," Salter said. "He jist come aboard an' hit his sack an' I can't git him up. He's out cold."

Al got out of his bunk, shivering, and put on his cook whites and apron, and went to the frigid galley. Give me the old football, fellows, he thought shakily. I'll win this old ball game. Let me pinch-hit, coach, I'll bring in that winning run. Like hell I will! But I used to be able to make toast, fried eggs, and coffee. He looked at the stove with dismay—he'd never seen such a stove before. "How do you start the stove?" he asked of Salter, who hovered anxiously by.

"It's simple," Salter said. "I'll show you." He got a twist of newspaper and lit the end of it. "This here's an oil-blower range," he said. "Up here onna bulkhead's the oil tank. You turn this valve to start the oil goin'. This here on the front of the stove, it's a blower. It's got hinges and pulls out like this." He pushed the blower back into place. "This here button, you push it to start the blower. It's electrical." He pushed the button, meanwhile casually holding his blazing torch. "This little lid here on top," he said, as the blower began whirring noisily, "it's the fire hole. You take it out like this." He removed the fire hole lid. "Now," he said with *sang-froid*, "all you do is drop the burnin' paper inna hole like this, an' at's—"

WHUMP! the stove said tersely, and greasy smoke vomited from the fire hole and all the cracks and joints and seams, and the blower was blown out of its hole, swinging around on its hinges, and all the pots and pans in the galley rattled and winced, and Al's eardrums popped. The blower continued to throw a fine spray of oil all over the front of the stove and on the tiled deck, but there was no fire in the stove. Salter sighed and kicked the blower back in place. "Sometimes it does that," he said, and began busily twisting his forelock. "Better turn off the oil," he said thoughtfully.

Al turned off the oil at the tank, Salter turned off the blower, and they stood there looking at the black and ominous galley range. Salter removed his knit cap and examined the inside of it carefully and returned it to his shaggy head. "Well, that's how you do it," he said, and turned and sauntered out of the galley, leaving Al alone with the infernal machine and his mechanical inaptitude.

Salter stuck his head back inside the galley. "Keys to the icebox and everything is on the desk inside the door of Red's room." He left again, hurriedly, and Al lit a cigarette with numb fingers and glowered nervously at the stove, and it glowered balefully back. Presently he stirred. He found a wad of newspaper, lit it, dropped it into the fire hole, and leaped back. Nothing happened. He put the lid in the hole and reached a cautious foot toward the switch on the blower and kicked it on. The blower whirred, there was a gentle *pouf,* and fire glowed brightly through the numerous cracks and crevices of the stove. Remembering the oil, he turned the valve, and the fire began to hum and purr prettily. The galley range was lit, and warmth began to fill the world and drive away the numbing cold.

He went along the cold port passageway to the last cabin and timidly knocked. No answer. He knocked again, louder. No answer. He pushed the door open. Hey! he said. No answer but strangling snores, the sodden, drunken snores he remembered from somewhere else in time. He found the switch and flooded the cabin with light. Wildoe lay on his back in the lower of two fine spacious bunks, fully dressed even including his peacoat and flat hat and shoes, sleeping the sleep of the dead-drunk. It was a very nice, snug cabin. Roomy, with huge built-in lockers, a big wide desk with drawers and a leather-bottomed chair with armrests, a fine reading lamp, a sink in the corner, a mirror. And an empty top bunk. My bunk, Al said to himself. I oughta be sleeping there right now. The keys were on the desk, and he got them and looked at Wildoe again. "Pleasant dreams, you poor drunken excuse for a cook," he said, and went back to the galley, feeling better.

He filled the big three-gallon coffeepot with water and put it on the stove, feeling unsure and clumsy and self-conscious. O.K., a little touch of stage fright, he told himself. It's to be expected. Now, where does he keep the coffee? Boy, do I need me a cup of coffee!

The fragrance of boiling coffee lured Salter back into the cozy galley, and Al was glad to see him. "Is there a menu?" he asked, and the quartermaster braided his forelock distractedly and said, hell, Red just fixed whatever he taken a notion to fix. And he added hopefully, "How's for givin' us some bacon an' eggs for a change, cookie?"

"Why not?" Al said. "Bacon and eggs with crunchy buttered toast."

"I generally eat before the crew does," Salter hinted.

So a nervous, fidgety quartermaster named Salter had the great distinction of eating the first breakfast ever officially prepared by Al Woods, ship's cook. It consisted of three fried eggs, over easy, six slices of bacon, five pieces of bread toasted on top of the range, three mugs of coffee generously laced with "canned cow" and sugar, and about half a bottle of catchup, known locally as "red lead," which the quartermaster poured generously over the contents of his plate.

"How was it?" Al asked anxiously, and Salter said, "O.K." Al relaxed a little. Well, I'm in business. I'm cooking with oil, boy.

The two surly, sleepy mess cooks came straggling in, unshaven, untidy, uncommunicative. They registered blank astonishment at the sight of Al on duty, but said nothing. The dark, tough-acting pot-walloper went about his chores with a reeking insolence that made Al want to slap his silly face. The other mess cook was a big, dumb ox with small eyes and bushy yellow hair and a negative personality.

Al broiled bacon in the oven, as he'd seen the fraternity cook do, during Rush Week. He put grease in all the skillets he could find and set them on the stove to heat, and made a pile of buttered toast. When the crew began arriving he lost himself in the business of frying eggs. He knew how to fry eggs and there was no mental strain, and suddenly breakfast was over, the ordeal of his maiden effort was ended, and nobody had uttered one unkind word about the food or the coffee.

The mess cooks hurried through their postbreakfast chores and vanished. Al noticed a few odds and ends neglected by the pot-washer and shrugged them off. The guy knew his duties. Al had pondered some on the matter and decided, early in his student days, that he would not be one of those loud, overbearing, dictatorial cooks. He was going to be a kindly, tolerant, democratic, paternal cook, the kind mess cooks liked and considered nice guys. But still, this pot-walloper . . .

Al finished a cigarette and faced the facts of life. Breakfast had been easy. Anybody could do breakfast. But now he had to start worrying about the noon chow, the big meal of the day. He looked in the big walk-in reefer. It was bare except for a hind quarter of beef and some salami and bologna. He stared at the beef with frustration—he hadn't the haziest idea of how you cut up a hind quarter of beef. But he had to do it, so he lifted the meat off its hook and wrestled it onto the meat block. The knives and saw and cleaver were all arranged handily on the bulkhead, and he got to work. As a starter, he sawed off the shinbone and laid it aside. Soup bone, he said to himself knowingly. But the crisis hadn't been passed yet. There was a right way and a wrong way to cut up this meat, and he didn't know *either* way. The hell with it, he said to himself with sudden recklessness, I'll do it the *new* way, the Alvin Woods method of dismembering a bull's drumstick. And with a total disregard for the ethics of the butcher's trade, he attacked the offending member, cutting and sawing and hacking off four-inch slabs right across the whole leg. He had three big roasts cut off when the officers' steward, a thin, bald, middle-aged, walnut-colored, very wrinkled Filipino named Angel Santiago, came into the galley and stared at him with oriental inscrutability, curiosity, disbelief, and astonishment. "Where ees Red?" he asked.

"In his sack," Al said gruffly. "Drunk as a skunk." Angel laughed heartily. "How many guys in the crew?" Al asked, and Angel stopped laughing and looked inscrutable again. Thirty, maybe forty, he said. "I navver count heem," he said. "Maybe feefty, who knows?"

"Well, let's put it this way," Al said. "How much of this cow should I scorch for lunch? Reckon this'll be enough?"

Angel squinted at the three huge hunks of meat. "That ees planty," he said, and got himself a cup of coffee and crouched on a stool in a corner like an overgrown rhesus monkey, watching Al. Presently he said, "Hey, somebody tal me you no cook, I theenk. He say you no cook."

"At's right," Al said. "At's the truth, friend."

Angel laughed uncertainly, and Al got a pan and dumped the three roasts in it and hung the remains of the quarter in the meat box, and started operating from memory. He had watched hungrily, fascinated, as the frat cook prepared prime beef for roasting several mornings during Rush Week; now he tried to recall the details, as an eyewitness. Lots of salt and pepper, rubbed into the meat. Three or four chopped onions and a double handful of chopped celery. Bay leaves—and while hunting bay leaves he found the paprika. By golly yes, paprika. What else? Garlic, but of a certainty. He slivered half a dozen fat cloves of garlic and tucked the slivers here and there on the meat. And all the while, Angel Santiago watched him with oriental inscrutability.

Al checked the clock. Almost nine. Three hours until chow down. How long should the meat cook? Well, it was better to have it done too soon than not soon enough, although he liked it a little rare himself. He shoved the pan into the oven and banged the door shut emphatically. Spuds. Mashed potatoes. No strain there, boy. He'd mashed plenty of spuds for the lady cook at the girls' dormitory. But the peeling—was that not a mess cook's obligation? He shrugged; no use being hard to live with the first day. He started peeling potatoes, and Angel said with shocked disapproval, "The mess cook do thees stoff."

"Got no time to hunt those guys," Al said. "Do it myself."

Angel studied for a moment and nodded, as if Al had a certain logic on his side. When Al finished the spuds and put cold water and salt on them, as he'd seen *real* cooks do, he put the pot on the back of the range and worried some more about the menu. He found green beans in the store locker. A guy couldn't go wrong with green beans, not if he remembered a certain high-class frat cook adding that little cultured Greek touch. Al grated part of an onion and half a carrot into the beans and added a liberal amount of black pepper, a dash of vinegar, and a big glob of butter. He put the beans aside for future reference.

"Meester," Angel said, "somebody tal me you no cook."

"Never touch the stuff," Al said. "I'm a noncooker by birth." Angel grinned uncertainly and retreated into inscrutability, and Al thought, Salad. Now he was really on familiar ground. He'd been a salad boy in Deacon's Restaurant, he'd fixed a ton of salads for the dorm cook. Whistling, he selected vegetables from the reefer and began chopping and grating. Lettuce, celery, carrots, cabbage, onions, green peppers. He mixed it with salad dressing and vinegar and seasonings and sampled it. Right on the nose, boy. Maddeningly delicious.

Angel Santiago came prowling across the galley and tested the salad. "Wan beeg liar tal me you no cook, meester," he chuckled.

"Listen," Al said solemnly, "I don't know what I'm doing." He put the salad in the reefer. "I'm sleepwalking, that's all," Al said.

A big, fat, heavy-eyed man came padding into the galley, wearing a bathrobe and slippers. His thin hair was awry and he had a ruddy face and large nose. He looked hungover and moody, Al thought.

The officer got some coffee and stared at Al disagreeably, curiously.

"Well, well," he said. "The invisible man. I was beginning to think they lied about having another cook. Where have you been?"

"Well, I was sort of sick, sir," Al said. "I been in my sack."

The officer looked at him a little longer, eyes skeptical, and then told Santiago he wanted three soft-boiled eggs and some orange juice, and went out through the seamen's messroom.

Al looked at Santiago. "Which one was that?"

"Kretlow," the steward said. "Ongine-room boss." Al asked who was Orlando, then, and Angel said, "Orlando ees skeeper." Al said how was he, O.K., or hard to live with? Santiago shrugged. "Leetle both."

Al began browsing among the supplies, getting oriented. He noticed a recipe for muffins on a bag of cornmeal, and got a brilliant idea. He had to learn how to cook, so he ought to practice, learn by experience, trial and error. He would make some goddam muffins.

He greased some pans, mixed the batter according to the recipe, and checked the meat. It was sizzling nicely and smelled good, so he put some water in the pan as he'd often seen bona fide cooks do. I'll even make some brown gravy, he thought recklessly. As many times as I saw it made, and helped stir it and season it, I believe I can do it.

All of a sudden he felt pretty good. It scared hell out of him to *think* about cooking, but shucks, *doing* it wasn't so rough. Why, goddammit, cooking was fun, when you got your teeth into it, boy.

A few minutes after eleven one of the yeomen came into the galley for coffee, a man who was so homely as to be striking. Al had heard him called Blanket-ass. He had black curly hair and a broad big nose and full lips and black eyes and a dark complexion. Blanket-ass got his coffee and looked around the galley. "Where are the mess cooks?" he demanded suddenly.

Al shrugged. "I don't know," he said. "Why?"

The yeoman consulted his wrist watch. "They're layin' out on you. They're trying to see how much they can get away with, bub."

Al shrugged. "How come they call you Blanket-ass?" he said.

"I'm one-eighth Choctaw. If you don't start out on the right foot with those mess cooks, show 'em you're boss, they'll sure take advantage of you, bub. You oughta go rack them out."

"All right," Al said. "Thanks for the advice, Blanket-ass, but I'll make a deal with you. You let me run the galley when I got the duty here and I won't interfere with your department. Suit you?"

He had come to the conclusion that he didn't much like this yeoman. A feather merchant. A seagoing stenographer. This one was
just a little bit too goddam officious, throwing his weight around
like this.

"Maybe you're scared of Gutsell," Blanket-ass suggested.

Gutsell was the tough-acting, insolent pot-walloper, and Al
laughed scornfully. "You tickle me, feather merchant," he said.

The yeoman shrugged. "Well, it ain't no skin off my butt, boy."
He finished his coffee and went out, and Al put the potatoes and
green beans over the hottest part of the stove and checked the meat
and started fretting and brooding about the mess cooks. They *should*
be here before this. They oughta be getting ready for chow. Maybe
they *were* dogging it to see how much he'd put up with. Al started
getting angry. He'd never thought of this aspect of being a petty
officer. He'd always been on the other side of the problem until a
week ago. They wanted him to prove he could handle the kitchen
help, was that it? I'll give those wise guys five minutes, just five
minutes to show up, he thought.

Five minutes later he was damn good and mad, and he went out
across the windy well deck and descended into the foul-smelling
hold that was the crew's quarters. At the foot of the ladder he stared
angrily around the crowded compartment and listened to it suddenly
go quiet and expectant. "Where the hell are the mess cooks?" he
bawled. He was furious now, fighting mad, ready to explode. He
looked at the half-dozen men sprawled on bunks. One of them was
Gutsell, lying comfortably on his back with hands behind his head,
watching Al from the corner of his eye with smirking insolence.
"All right, Gutsell," Al snarled. "Hit the deck. Climb outa that sack
and make it fast."

"Who's gonna make me?" Gutsell asked archly. "You, cooksy-
wooksy?"

Somebody should have told that kid about terrible-tempered Al
Woods; they should have warned him about the way fate had been
pushing Al into a dangerous psychological corner lately. Al hadn't
had a fight since his CCC days, but he'd had some good ones then,
and he hadn't ever lost one yet. And now he lunged across the deck
and, without further ado, grabbed Gutsell by his turtleneck sweater
and savagely dumped him out of the bunk. Then he stepped back
with his left shoulder hunched forward and his fists cocked, ready.

"Come on," he invited. "Let's go to knuckle junction, boy. By way of fist city. Come on."

Gutsell stared at Al with shock, with indignation, but also with cautious speculation and wary surprise. "You're a petty officer."

"Don't let that crowd you out," Al said through his teeth.

Gutsell shrugged. "I can't touch ya. You got a crow on ya arm."

"Don't let the crow stop you," Al grated. "You thought you were really pulling something smart, didn't you? You give me some guff and I'll knock your goddam head off, Gutsell. You know when you're supposed to be in that galley. Where's that other gold-bricking jerk?"

"Who, Poznicki?" Gutsell asked loudly, something sly and eager in his swift sidelong glance. "Ya better not call Poznicki a jerk, he's not scared of your goddam crow."

Al turned to find the dull-eyed Poznicki watching him from an upper bunk. "Come outa there, you ape!" Al bellowed. Poznicki blinked and climbed down awkwardly. "Get your lazy ass up to that galley fast!" Al bellowed. Poznicki blinked, hesitated, frowned, and then went lumbering up the ladder, stolidly, unoffended, almost meekly. Al swung back to the disappointed Gutsell. "Now," Al said. "You, Gutsell, you're the one I yearn for, you smart punk. Let's give it a whirl, boy."

"Not here onna ship," Gutsell evaded smoothly. "I'll see ya up the street some night, cookie. Ya can't hide behind ya rate badge ashore." He spat on the deck and sauntered to the ladder and began to climb, and over his shoulder he said, "You just scare a person to death." And he laughed scornfully. But he went.

Al looked around at the others in the berth deck and grinned. "Excuse my loud voice," he said. "I got all worked up."

"At's O.K., pal," somebody said. "We enjoyed it, we got a honk outa seein' somebody take the starch outa Gutsell. What's for chow?"

"Roast beef," Al said, and he went on up the ladder feeling like a petty officer, feeling like a ship's cook. He'd done a pretty convincing job of exercising his authority, if anybody asked him, boy.

In the galley he ignored the busy mess cooks and proceeded, with no misgivings, to manufacture some excellent gravy. The beef was done and he removed it from the pan and dumped a gallon of the potato water in the roasting pan and set it on top of the stove. He thickened it with flour-and-water paste and used soy sauce to season and give it that nutritious brown color. He let it come to a boil and pushed it to the side and sampled it. Fit for a Greek. He put the muffins in the oven and mashed the spuds, using lots of butter and canned milk, and whipped them into a smooth froth, as he had learned to do for the widow who cooked at the girls' dormitory. For dessert he decided canned peaches would suffice. And suddenly dinner was ready, the chow was accomplished. I didn't know I had it in me, he gloated. And it struck him then—he'd done it all from memory, from watching hungrily while *other* cooks cooked. Maybe Wollager had the right theory after all. What Wollager had was the wrong teacher.

He put a pan in the sink and curtly instructed Gutsell to wash it. Gutsell saluted him sarcastically and bowed from the waist and said, "Aye, aye, your royal highness." But the sarcasm was wasted, it didn't bother Alvin Woods. He had a crow on his arm and confidence in his mind and noon chow ready to cast before the crew.

Whistling lightheartedly, he sliced the beef across the grain as the dorm cook had taught him to do, and it was tender and delicious, with just a sigh of garlic in the flavor. Hell, *everything* was tender and delicious, including the gravy and cornbread muffins, and Al's day was complete when, during the course of the festivities, he overheard somebody remark that it was sure a welcome relief to eat a *decent* chow for a change, by God. And his auditor agreed. This is *chow!* he said. And along toward the end of the meal, Red Wildoe came out of hibernation and appeared in the galley with bloodshot eyes and a woebegone, headachy scowl. Wordlessly he heaped a plate and took it to the black gang's mess table and ate it, and Al noted that he cleaned his plate. But when the senior cook came again into the galley, walking in his peculiar way like a fat man learning to skate, he only said sulkily, "The goddam gravy was too salty."

"I'll watch that in the future," Al said politely.

Poznicki, overhearing, muttered, "*I* never thought it was salty."

Wildoe wheeled on him. "Whatta hell do *you* know about gravy?"

"I know if it's salty or not," Poznicki said stolidly.

"Get them tables cleaned off!" Wildoe snarled, and turned back to Al. "Where the hell did you learn to cut meat?"

"I didn't learn yet," Al said. "How was the *rest* of the chow?"

Wildoe scowled sourly. "Muffins was doughy. It wasn't no banquet." They ate it, Al thought smugly, and Wildoe said gruffly, "As

long as you're gettin' paid for cookin' you're gonna hafta stand your
regular watch from now on, mack. You're off now until noon tomorrow."

Al nodded. "Listen, could I use your cookbook sometimes?"

"I'll leave it in the galley," Wildoe said grudgingly. "There will
be a menu here, too, an' you better cook what it says."

"Look," Al said earnestly, "I was lucky today, at's all. Anybody
can fix a chow like roast beef. But I still ain't a cook, and I wish
you'd kind of keep that in mind when you write up the menus,
huh?"

"A third-class cook is s'pose to be able to handle any menu I make
up, mack, git that straight," Wildoe said coldly. "An' don't ever forget who's the head cook here. I'm in charge, what I say goes. *You*
take orders from *me*, mack." He turned and started away, taking
long strides with short legs, reminding Al of a penguin. "And don't
forget it, mack," Wildoe snarled over his shoulders, for the benefit
of the dawdling diners. And Al said, for the benefit of the same
people, "Aw, go to hell."

Al was eating some of his own cooking when Santiago came
from the wardroom, which was topside aft. Santiago looked
cheerful.

"*They* like the chow?" Al inquired hopefully, and Angel said
they liked it very moch, meester. "The skeeper, he say eet wonner-
ful theeng not hafta eat Rad's cookeeng alla time any more," Angel
said. He chuckled. "Anybody say you no cook, hee ees goddam
liar, meester."

"Aw," Al said modestly, "I was just lucky today." But it had
been a pretty auspicious debut at that, marred only by Wildoe's
bad manners. That academy cook. A goddam sorehead, that Wildoe.

Ho hum, Al said to himself smugly. Another day, another two
dollars. Who was that sonofagun tal me I no cook? I cook fine.

CHAPTER 13

That Empty Sack

BETWEEN the seventeenth day of February and the fifth day of April, many interesting and tragic and important things happened in the world. In that forty-seven-day period, Spain's government decreed that only Castilian could henceforth be written and spoken there; a truckload of ice cutters crossing the St. Lawrence River at Montreal broke through the ice, drowning eleven men; Greece had earthquakes; President Roosevelt began his ninth year in office with a head cold; New York City had an eleven-and-one-half-inch snowstorm; the United States Court in Milwaukee, Wisconsin, fined ASCAP five thousand dollars for violating antitrust laws; high winds and extreme cold weather caused twenty-eight deaths in western Wisconsin; the state of Georgia went on Eastern Standard Time; work was begun on the third set of locks for the Panama Canal; and four hundred thousand soft coal miners struck.

None of these things except the Wisconsin weather had any immediate effect on the life of Alvin Woods, ship's cook, third class. But this stretch of days was significant to him because his superior, Ralph Wildoe, also SC3/c, did not speak to him in all that time. And the end of Red's stony silence on the night of Saturday, April fifth, coincided, on account of another of those enigmatic twists of fate, with the crashing termination of a cold but steamy love affair Al ran through with an impulsive girl named Stella Pappharonis.

Several times during this interim phase, Al made up his mind to go to Chicago and get his typewriter, but each time something came up. And early in these forty-seven days, Al came to realize that for all his culinary education, Wildoe was at best a very mediocre cook, a stubbornly opinionated man who resisted, if he ever felt, the impulse to experiment. A chary user of herbs and seasonings, a doggedly mechanical chef, Wildoe lacked that intangible quality of instinctive artistry which elevates a cook above the multitude of common cooks. On the other hand, it soon became evident that Al had that gift, that touch of mild genius. Prone to gamble, never satisfied to leave well enough alone, an experimenter and inventor with herbs and spices, Al incorporated a great deal of imagination into his mundane chores, and forever sought elusive perfection. Lacking knowledge, he relied on a *sense* of how to do, he *imagined* how things should be concocted, he mixed various tastes and flavors in his mind and developed elastic formulas and theories. But perhaps his greatest gift in the galley was his phenomenal memory regarding matters of nutrition and diet, which enabled him to shut his eyes and recall step by step, as if seen on a slow-moving microfilm stored in his head, kitchen tricks and lore and secrets and basic hypotheses he'd audited during endless hours of dishwashing in other kitchens and other times. For his sudsy labors he had been paid in the coin of succulent viands, and he had watched its minting with the slavering intentness of a starving dog, and now he ran off a kind of counterfeit so good as to be undetectable.

In moments of philosophical meditation, he sometimes felt very grateful for his impoverished youth—his perpetual hunger had turned out to be a strange investment that now paid surprising dividends. The University of Oklahoma would be startled to learn that it had conducted a course in dietetics, and graduated a bachelor of cuisine.

Up to a point, he and Wildoe made a pot of vegetable soup exactly the same. But at that point where Wildoe called it finished, Al began to get in his best licks, adding a cheesecloth bag containing garlic, bay leaves, and any other spices that nudged his fancy at the time, which invested the brew with a certain graceful authority the senior cook could never achieve. And Al would give it texture and rich body with a thickening paste he made of hot, strong-flavored grease and flour. The result would elicit praise from the clientele, which Red resented bitterly, but all the more sullenly he refused to engage in such trickery. He seemed to feel that, technically, it was no longer soup. Once, in fact, when Red was eating supper in the black gang's messroom, Al overheard him say disgustedly, "Whatta hell is it s'pose to be, gravy or soup?" And Al had the keen pleasure of hearing someone reply, "1 dunno wot it is but I want another bowl of it, boy."

When Red's chows turned out somewhat less than good, he always blamed the goddam stove. Can't regulate the goddam heat, he would mutter. But it was the same stove Al used.

Al's genius really cropped up in sauces and gravies. He made brown gravy, country style gravy, red gravy, white gravy, and gravies he didn't bother to label, all of them given zest by a use of horseradish or grated cheese or tomato puree or mustard or Worcestershire sauce or soy sauce. Once he made a peanut-butter gravy; once he found a brown gravy wanting in *savoir-faire* and struck the right note by adding half a cup of molasses. Al tasted; forever tasting and testing, adding, subtracting, blending, sampling. I'm an average guy, he said to himself. If I like it, so will everybody else. Except that sorehead Wildoe.

Wildoe had one basic gravy, and made only indifferent attempts to refurbish it now and then. He would put a clean roasting pan on top of the range, add a dab of shortening, and scorch some flour in it—to which he added water or milk, or both, plus salt and pepper. At rare times, struck a glancing blow by inspiration, he would red it up with a dash of catchup, without altering its drab personality. Alvin Woods recognized no specific limitations; he was a master gravy maker.

But it had to be admitted that Red was a good baker. He could do some pretty amazing things with "basic sweet dough," the jumping-off place for most of the Navy and Coast Guard's yeast-rising goodies. His cinnamon rolls were succulent, his Parker House rolls a delight, his raisin bread just like mom used to make. He salvaged his sorry main courses with an endless assortment of rolls, pies, and pastries. And if his tossed salads were usually tossed into the garbage can, there were never any leftovers in the bakery department.

And this was his ultimate triumph over Al Woods; this was Red's victory and his revenge. For Al simply could not master the mechanics of baking, the knack of kneading—which was nine-tenths of the secret of bakery skill. Al had no feeling for dough, it bored him, and his results with it were always near-failures. These were the times when glee illumined Wildoe's alabaster features. He had found Al's Achilles' heel and he was relentless. The menus for Al's watches listed doughy desserts and hot breads regularly, inevitably. Since never once, in forty-seven days, did he direct so much as a grunt Al's way, Wildoe became of necessity a prolific writer; his orders were always well documented and footnoted. Each time Al donned apron and entered the galley, there would be a concise page of carefully written instructions on the meat block, and the *Navy Cookbook* would be prominently displayed—with its every recipe ending in the frustrating notation: "Serves one hundred men." Al had to divide all the menus by three and then add a little, and it was no simple matter to guess at a third of an ounce of some vital ingredient, since there were no scales delicate enough to weigh it on. Al always approached the galley with trepidation, with foreboding, and his worst fears were always justified. Al chafed and smoldered under Wildoe's basic-sweet-dough tyranny, and while kneading the stuff he would picture a time and a place ashore, and a violent scene in which Al Woods battered a wooden-faced villain into cringing repentance.

It never occurred to either of them that in trying to make life miserable for Al, the head cook was throwing a boomerang. He was forcing Al to become a competent all-around cook and baker, he was strengthening the foe. A cleverer man would have given Al insultingly simple menus to prepare, thus stunting his growth as a cook and retarding his career. But Wildoe cherished the small daily triumphs and went on winning every battle while losing the war.

Sometimes the humor of the situation struck Al's funny bone and he would have to laugh about it. They were both acting like morons, except, of course, Wildoe wasn't acting. And all Al needed to do to stop laughing was think about that luxurious bunk back in the cooks' cabin. Red had unlimited seclusion and privacy, yet he used the stateroom only for sleeping. When not on watch, Wildoe was either up the street or gassing in the CPO's messroom above the galley or playing cards in one of the two mess compartments off the galley. On extremely rare occasions he might be seen studying a *True Detective* magazine or a picture magazine, but he was not a reader. In direct contrast, Al, who valued privacy and yearned for solitude and a good reading light, was stuck in the noisy, smelly, dirty, ill-lighted after berth deck, where the dim light and the eternal profanity and bickering made it impossible to do much reading, or otherwise improve his mind. But, still, even if Captain Orlando (a chief warrant officer) should order Wildoe to share the cabin with his colleague, it would be intolerable under the circumstances. Al didn't want to room with anybody named Ralph Wildoe, but he resented being cheated out of the privilege of *refusing* to room with Ralph Wildoe.

It was largely this domestic strife that drove him into the clinging arms of Stella Pappharonis, for he would have been content to stay aboard ship on those bitter cold nights and read and listen to the radio, given light and quiet and a little peace of mind. It was Blanket-ass, the part-Choctaw feather merchant, who got him started in the habit of going ashore to be free of the racket and tension.

"You never go ashore," the yeoman noticed. "What's wrong, you broke or something? If so, I'll loan you some lettuce, Woods."

"I got money," Al said. "What's Milwaukee got to offer a boy?"

"Get dressed and I'll show you," Blanket-ass suggested, and Al took him up on it, suddenly enthusiastic about the idea.

Thus Al was introduced to the Oval Bar, on Wisconsin Avenue, and that same night he met Stella, a passion flower who bloomed in the glacial snows. She immediately became two or three of the half-dozen reasons why his good intentions to run down to Chicago after his typewriter always ran aground between ship and railroad station. He couldn't stay away from Stella.

The Oval Bar was a large, congenial, soft-lit saloon with its long oval bar in the center of the room, booths down both sides, and tables fringing a small, slippery dance floor in the back. The first time Al saw Stella she was sitting at a table with a girl friend, and he was instantly fascinated by her dainty size, dark lustrous hair, flashing gypsy eyes, and the way her breasts pushed her sweater out tight and full. "Would you be interested in dancing with me?" he asked, and she said rather coyly that she *might*, so they danced and she was fragrant and dainty and soft and warm in his arms, and pressed snugly against him in an unself-conscious manner that intrigued and aroused him. He moved his glass of beer to her table and met her friend, whose name was Gailla, and that was how it started. He was ripe for romance that winter's end, and he always had responded powerfully to girls who were small, shapely, dark, and vivacious, and who had one minor flaw. With Stella it was the nose. She was a beautiful girl with a homely nose, large and slightly curved; it made her somehow *human*, he felt.

The Oval was headquarters ashore for Al's shipmates, who were a cocky, jovial group in their dark matching costumes of flat hats, turtleneck sweaters, and dress blue trousers, but Al was still new enough in his rating to prefer wearing the blouse, with its glossy symbol of red stripe, white crescent, and white eagle.

"What does the moon mean?" Gailla asked, and he told her it meant he was a celestial navigator, and wished she would go away. Who needed a chaperone? But she was Stella's chum, and although any chum of Stella's still made it a crowd, he didn't want to antagonize her—because Stella danced bonelessly and adhesively, warming him to the marrow, and she seemed pretty interested in one Alvin Woods, boy.

"You got funny eyes," she said softly. "I don't know . . . green."

"I'm part Irish," he told her. "I'm jealous. Green with envy."

"You got nice teeth," she said admiringly. "Gee . . . so *regular*."

"The better to bite you with," he said wittily. "You mind?"

"I don't know," she said, and shivered. "I never was bit."

"You haven't lived, girl," he said. "I'd *like* to bite you."

"Gee," she said dreamily, "you talk crazy. You're . . . *interes*ting."

Even with Gailla in constant attendance, the budding romance was inexpensive to finance. The girls both drank plain cokes, being under the legal age for alcoholic drinks. Al danced with Gailla once, out of a sense of duty, and she acted as if she were terrified that her stomach might touch his, which eliminated her from possible consideration. Stella was the one, all right. She *liked* to have her stomach touching his. But the first and second nights he was unable to separate the wheat from the chaff, and found himself buying Coca-Colas for seemingly inseparable childhood chums. ("Her name is really Gail, but she changed it to Gailla because I'm Stella, only she wanted me to change *my* name to match *hers—Stell*, can you *imagine?* See, we went to school together all our lives. We're . . . you know, *close*. Like sisters or something.") They were close, all right, and twice Stella refused to let him take her home. But she wasn't pushing her luck with that hard-to-get routine, and the third time he asked, she said yes.

"I about decided you didn't like me much," Al said.

"Maybe I like you too much," she said. "You *do* something to me."

That's my goal in life, madam, Al said to himself humorously. That is precisely why I am here, Miss Pappharonis.

She refused to let him hire a cab, saying it was only a few blocks and she liked to walk. It was a brittle cold night with a thin wet wind that got down the back of Al's collar, chilling his spine. They walked six or seven blocks and then Stella stopped before an apartment house. "Here's where I live," she said. He put his arms around her, saying he was cold; he was cold, all right. "Gailla lives just next door," Stella said nervously. "All her life." Great, Al told her. Nothing like having next-door neighbors, he said, and kissed her with a certain amount of clumsiness, being out of practice. She seemed to like it, though, and he said, "It's awfully public here."

She was acute, she got what he was hinting about, and led him around the corner of the building into a shadowy alleyway between her house and Gailla's house, and he kissed her again. This time Stella's response was nothing if not eager; she was obviously hotter than a three-dollar pistol, he thought happily, and he unbuttoned her coat and his peacoat and pulled her yielding small body against him with his arms under her coat, and she said, "Gee, you're so big."

"Yeah," Al said.

"Gee, I'll bet you're real strong, Al," she said.

"Yeah," he said, wishing she were a little taller, or standing on something.

"You certainly have a nice pair of shoulders," she said very nervously.

And Al said, "You have a nice pair of *several* things."

She giggled and pinched his back, and he clutched her masterfully, lifting her off the concrete, kissing her with controlled violence, and she began to squirm a little, and writhe against him, making soft moaning sounds. Al was delighted—she was a real woman, boy. He was made bold by her immediate response, and he got his hands under her sweater and unsnapped her brassière and fondled her firm, vibrant round breasts. She liked that, too, although she whispered ruefully that his h-hands were c-cold. This will warm them, Al said happily. She was passionate and sensual, she was what the doctor had ordered, all right. He hadn't expected to get so far so fast, but he wasn't complaining, boy.

"You make me feel all weak and funny," Stella moaned.

Al wasn't much of a guy for talking about it, he was more the man of action. He fondled her breasts and stroked her warm silken back, kissing her urgently, and her lips clung and her body rolled and squirmed against him in a kind of agonized pleasure, and she moaned, "Oh, I'm so weak and you're so strong, please don't take advantage. When you do me like this I couldn't stop you from having your way, so please be nice, don't take advantage of my passionate nature, darling."

"I won't," Al said unsteadily. "Where can we go?"

"What do you mean?" she sighed against his lips, her breath warm and Coca-Colaish and cigarettish.

He said, "We can't do anything here, let's go where it's more secluded like."

"Oh, darling, I want to so terribly, but we can't do it," she moaned, digging her large nose into his neck and squirming helplessly. She reminded Al of another girl, another place, another time; he seemed to hear someone wailing, Oh, No, Please, We Mustn't. Well, he would never play dead for *that* line again, boy.

"Why the hell can't we?" he said tersely.

And Stella said wildly, "When spring comes, darling. We can find someplace. Some real private place. Oh, you're so strong and I'm so weak and everything. But it's almost spring . . ."

"That's too long to wait," Al said hoarsely, but his mind raced ahead to warm nights when you could at least crawl under the bushes somewhere and have a little private seclusion. Ah, private seclusion, he thought. Ah, springtime without this cold wind freezing my ankles and making my ears ache. "I need you now, tonight," he groaned.

"Don't *say* things like that, I can't *stannnnd* it!" she wailed.

Well, what could a guy do? Standing up in a cold alleyway with the street lights reflecting back in there and dirty cold concrete instead of a nest of autumn leaves or a bed or something. So they just stood there groaning with frustration and tormenting each other, crazy with desire, Al's mind thrashing around like a trapped animal, trying to solve young love's eternal cruel problem of nowhere to go to be alone. She couldn't take him upstairs and he damn sure couldn't take her to the ship. The Coast Guard had strict rules about that.

Passion denied loses its white heat, desire thwarted loses its fine edge; soon the cold crept into Al's bones and made goose-bumps on Stella's satiny skin, and she said unhappily that she had to go upstairs now. Her teeth were chattering and she wasn't so much squirming any more as shaking with a chill. So he helped her with the brassière and sweater, regretting her loss but also feeling exhausted and numb from the futility of it all. Next time, he thought. I'll figure out something. He kissed her one last time and she began to make those noises again and wriggle again, and he thought, Now don't start *that* again for chrissakes! So he broke it up. "Good night, baby," he said.

"Good night, big strong wonderful you," Stella said fatuously.

"Yeah . . . well, see you tomorrow night," Al said wearily.

She went upstairs and he walked back to the Oval Bar feeling tense and feverish and disappointed, but elated too, a little delirious because if this was only the beginning, no telling where it would end. If it ever *did* end. Goddam, who'd want to end a thing like this? I never knew anybody like Stella before, he thought. But then he added, except Jo Hill. Jo was kind of like Stella, only not so . . . well, a little more *restrained*, but just as *responsive*. Jo, he thought with nostalgia. To be honest about it, I'd still rather have Jo.

By the time he got to the bar and had a drink to thaw out his bones and steady his nerves, he was no longer quite so happy about Stella, somehow. Thinking about Josephine Hill had taken the edge off this deal in some inexplicable fashion. It hadn't revised his program in regard to Stella, it had only somehow eliminated the risk that he might ever foolishly think he was in *love* with Stella. This was physical, not spiritual. This was strictly sex without sentiment.

After that he never entertained the notion of staying aboard ship at night, no matter what the weather, and if Stella didn't show up at the Oval Bar he would feel frustrated and miserable and restless. And when she did come, and they made impotent love in their dark, air-conditioned, brick-and-concrete trysting place later, he invariably ended feeling more frustrated and miserable than ever.

One unforgettable night during a considerable snowfall they stood knee-deep in a drift in a narrow windswept place and Al got Stella half-undressed under her coat, and she was clawing at him and writhing and moaning, and she said, "Oh, darling, even though I want you insanely and cannot prevent you, do not take advantage, don't let me do something I'll regret tomorrow."

And Al simply had to laugh, because it struck him funny. "Now how the hell could I take advantage of you when we're rump deep in snow in the middle of a howling arctic blizzard?" he asked, half-annoyed with her but bending down to kiss her cold bare ice-goddesslike breast. Nobody but an oversexed Eskimo would want to seduce anybody outdoors in this weather, he said, but Stella was offended because he had laughed. She covered her bosom and arranged her attire in a frigid silence, and he said, alarmed, "Hey, what's the matter? You sore . . . or just cold?"

"You made fun of me," she said aloofly.

"Aw, no baby," he said earnestly, trying to pull her into his arms again, but she resisted and backed away from him, buttoning her coat with icy finality, her face grown haughty.

"Good night," she said. "In fact, good-by."

She walked away and he followed and caught her at the steps and kissed her, but her lips were cold and she didn't start moaning or act like her old self in any way. "See you tomorrow night?" Al said.

"Not tomorrow night," she said quietly.

And he said anxiously, "Well, when, then?"

And she said dramatically, "Never again. You laughed." And she left him standing there shivering in the howling blizzard.

He spent a bad night and day, worrying, fearing that he had laughed away this great opportunity to know at last, come spring-time's balm and glade's grass, a full sex life. But when he hurried to the Oval Bar the next night she was already there, and alone. He didn't even sit down, just pulled her to her feet and walked out with her into the glittering cold night. Neither of them spoke until they found a dark doorway, where he drew her into his embrace. That night was the best-worst yet, and Stella quavered, "Oh, summer, hurry up!"

Summer, hell, Al thought. This business will ruin me long before summer comes. And that was the night his frustration-honed mind came up with the originally obvious idea of renting floor space for their torrid romance. He tentatively mentioned the subject of hotels, and when she failed to register shock or indignation, he waxed eloquent. She was silent, but clearly in favor of the plan. Still, they got nothing settled definitely, they only voted unanimously that they couldn't go on like this much longer, torturing themselves. "We're driving me crazy," Stella said.

And Al said firmly, "We've got to have each other or else just stop seeing each other, one of the two."

"Oh, I know it, lover," Stella said tragically. But nevertheless she wouldn't quite commit herself about renting a hotel room.

Not until the last Saturday in March did Stella Pappharonis agree to effect the illicit rendezvous, and even then she insisted on post-poning the final surrender an entire week, an eternity. She had her reasons; she would need to prepare her parents for her all-night absence, for Al insisted it would be an all-night affair. "Gee, I hope they don't ask me why I look so sleepy the next day," Stella said, and Al groaned, his imagination inflamed, and kissed her hungrily. So they went into *that* again, but stayed clearheaded enough to make plans. Al would arrange for the room and they would meet as usual at eight o'clock in the Oval Bar on Saturday, April fifth.

The week of waiting that followed was pure agony for Al, worse than anything he had gone through before. The weather stayed cold and the hours seemed treacherously to walk backward. His nerves grew tauter and he began to suffer from insomnia in the afternoons when he had always done his best sleeping. The week was interminable, but April came, and then Saturday came, and Al hurried through supper and dressed and loped to the streetcar line and fidgeted all the way downtown. Goddam, boy, this is *it!* he kept saying to himself.

He no longer envied guys like Brownie and Pelliteri and Agnelli and Horse Flanders, shipmates who were reputed to be the most successful Casanovas in town, and who employed four different techniques in their nocturnal campaigns. Brownie was of the quietly blunt, calmly cold-turkey school. Buy a girl a drink, kiss her, feel her leg, and say, Let's go to a hotel. It wasn't supposed to work, but for Brownie it did. Pelliteri just sat around with his big liquid brown bedroom eyes and his dramatic, intense silence and his thick, inky-black hair, and his guilty Catholic conscience, and the girls—especially big buxom Nordic types—made all the advances. Agnelli was a slight boy with blond curly hair and a baby face and very blue eyes, whose gimmick was to sneer at some girl until he had her full attention and then ignore her until she couldn't stand it any longer, and would come flouncing haughtily over to give him a piece of her mind, only then he would feign a charmingly boyish shyness, and the girl usually ended up giving him whatever it was he wanted. Horse Flanders, a big, homely, loud, comical guy, used no subtlety, but only his braying laugh and uninhibited brashness and earthy persistence, and although Al didn't envy Horse the shopworn, aging conquests he generally made, nobody could deny that Horse always made them. Meat's meat, Horse would say. I like it aged a little, cured out . . . wot I mean is *experienced.*

But you take old Alvin Woods, now, he had a better system than anybody. He only picked on gorgeous little gals, and then he just kissed them until they didn't know which way was south. Let's be frank about this matter, Al said to himself. I just happen to be a guy that when I kiss a girl I really jolt her. I'm dynamite in the clinches.

Al had made cautious inquiries, and Brownie had recommended a discreet hotel where license and liaison were condoned, and Al bought matching toothbrushes at a drugstore and then checked into the hotel with his ditty bag, registering as Mr. and Mrs. Ralph Smith. "My wife is arriving on a late train," he said, and the clerk winked solemnly and nodded. Al inspected the room, testing the mattress and springs, imagining Stella lying there stark naked, her skin warm and honey-colored, her body supple, slender, shapely, maddeningly seductive. And ready, too, boy. Short of breath. Excited. Anxious.

Al was anxious too. He left the room and explored the hallway running to the rear. He hated to bring Stella past that leering wise guy at the desk, that lewdly leering lecher. Maybe there was a rear entrance to this place, he thought. What he found was a rear exit at the foot of the back stairs, the outside of the door smooth, flush with the jamb, and minus handles so that it couldn't be pulled open from the dark side street, but only pushed open from inside. They're not dealing with any amateur here tonight, Al thought scornfully, and he put a book of matches in the crack and let the door ease against it. He checked and found that he could easily open the door from outside with the matchbook in the crack. He closed the door carefully again and headed for the Oval Bar, almost running.

Stella wasn't there, but he was a little early, an eager beaver. He had a couple of beers to drown the butterflies in his stomach and listened restlessly to the juke box and watched the door. The clock said Stella was tardy now. Men from the ship came in and said hello, and he talked to them distractedly, his eyes wearing a path in the air between clock and door, his head spinning with visions of delight on the honeyed middle of a leased mattress. Eight-thirty, and he was worried now, he was very tense. Goddammit, you guys, go away, can't you see I'm sweating out a big deal here? I don't wanta carry on no goddam idle conversation. Can't you see I'm dying by the minute?

At two minutes of nine Stella and Gailla came into the bar and walked back to their customary table, and if she saw Al there across the oval she gave no indication. He followed them, furious.

"Hello, Gailla," he said tersely, and to Stella, "Let's dance." She acted odd, peculiar, funny, bashful, maybe even unfriendly. He took her onto the crowded floor and crushed her hungrily in his arms and said huskily, "You're way late. Let's get going, honey."

She looked at him blankly. "Go where?" she asked innocently.

"It's Saturday," he said. "You know where. Everything's ready."

"I'm sure I haven't the slightest idea what you're talking about," Stella Pappharonis said archly, uttering a short laugh.

"I'm talking about a hotel room," he said fiercely. "Where you and me are supposed to go and be together for the night, baby doll."

"Well, don't be ridiculous," she said, avoiding his eyes.

"Hey, *listen!*" Al snarled. "What cooks here? You trying to rat out on me? You're acting pretty gruesome, if you want my opinion."

She tossed her head. "That's right, go ahead and insult me."

"Who's insulting anybody?" he said tensely. "I just want to know what's the score here, that's all. What's the deal, baby?"

She sighed. "A girl can change her mind, can't she?"

"Oh, no, baby," he said frantically. "Don't *say* that."

"It's a girl's purrogative to change her mind," she said weakly.

"Now listen," Al said grimly, "you're not pulling that stuff. You're not gonna bail out on me at the last minute like this, baby."

"*Well*, after *all!*" Stella said. "Just *what* do you think I *am?*"

Brownie, or Pelliteri, or Agnelli, or even Horse Flanders—in fact almost anybody you'd care to name—would probably have seen right off the bat that Stella was just a frightened girl who had got cold feet, a virgin who had thought too much about being an *ex-virgin*, about the immorality and dangerous finality of the project, and had developed a bad case of jitters and qualms. Even Al sensed all this. But those other guys would have also remembered how easy it was to addle her wits with kisses, so that none of that other stuff would matter any more and her wantonly sensual flesh and nerves would take charge. Al should have babied her a little, starting this night like all the others, applying his high-voltage kisses to her un-insulated lips and generating a white-hot passion. But he was a rookie lover who had suffered insomnia and drum-taut anticipation all week, and whose powers of diagnosis and therapy had been drugged by a riotous imagination and by the irritable waiting for her tardy appearance. And now Stella's natural feminine procras-tination and need to be reconvinced seemed to him nothing in the world but deceit and treachery, the old double-cross. He forgot all about his ability to make this hot-blooded girl squirm and gasp in helpless recapitulation; he got angry as hell.

"I *know* what you are, all right!" he snarled. "A lousy little tease, that's what! A double-crossing little barfly! A cheap..."

Her eyes glazed with shock and she slapped him, and he finished the sentence and stalked off the dance floor, leaving her standing there blinking and wounded in the wreckage of their wintry romance, probably thinking that Alvin Woods was the world's callowest oaf not to understand that when a woman said no she really meant yes.

Al drank a double-bourbon with a beer chaser and tamped it down with another double-shot, and sat staring balefully and lugubriously at the bottles back of the bar. Little bitch, he thought bitterly. Little Wisconsin Avenue bitch. Women! I am through with the whole tribe. Show me a woman a man can trust and I'll call you a goddam liar.

He was working on his fifth double-bourbon when Red Wildoe lurched out of a booth up front and came staggering pompously toward him in that short-legged, long-striding, overbalanced pace. Red had been doing some drinking himself, and now he climbed unsteadily onto the stool next to Al and pulled Al halfway around and tapped him on the chest, right over a huge, cold lump of lead that had once been a trusting heart.

"Wennever I givva goddam order I speckit to be essacuted, see?" Red Wildoe said thickly, and Al peered at him with eyes that wouldn't focus and said, "Aw, havva drink, you academy cook you." And he told the bartender to give his ole buddy and boss, who jus' happen to be the bes' baker inna Coast Guard, although *not* the bes' cook, a drink. "You ole tough-ackin' basstard," he said to Wildoe. "I jush wish I could hannel at ole basick sweet dough like you can. Downa hatch, buddy."

Looking a bit confused, Red tossed off his drink. "Now," he said, "about them cimmanon rolls. Wen I tella guy make cimmanon rolls..."

"Nobody," Al said, "can make cimmon rolls like you, Ralph."

Wildoe stuck a finger under Al's nose. "Skip 'at Ralph crap, we're talkin' bout wen I say make cimmanon rolls, mack."

"Bartenner," Al said, his head rolling, "filler up."

"I'll drink with yuh, but at don't make no differns," Red said.

"Wen I put cimmanon rolls onna menu, I don't mean punkin pie, mack."

"See at swee' lookin' lil bish sennovert at table witha big nose?" Al said emotionally. "Lemmee tell you bout at lil bish, Ralph."

"Way minnut, now," Wildoe snarled. "Jusha goddam secon', now. Wot I wanna know, ya read at menu I leffis saffernoon or dincha?"

"I reddit," Al said. "Ralph, I even renda room an' bod at lil bish *tooshbrush*. Madgin' at. Bodder tooshbrush, nice soff bed."

"*Shove* at toofbrutch," Wildoe mumbled. "F'yuh reddit, yuh cook por'chop, fried taders, ficks gree beans. O.K." He hiccuped. "I ben enna Coast Guard five years an' wennever I fixxa goddam menu . . ."

"Oh, *she* was willin'," Al said bitterly. "She wannit O.K. Ben stanna roun in snowdriffs ass-deep to tall Indian all winner, thinkin', figurin', plannin'. Go head, she tole me. Renna room, ged all ready for Satty ni', we gonna have wunnerful time, lil bish said." He gazed sorrowfully at his boss. "Happen t'me hunner times m'life. Las' goddam mint sum always hampen foul zup the deal. S'awful."

"Fi' years I ben Coast Guard," Red said thickly, hiccuping. "So *did* yuh, or *din* juh, fick cimmanon rose seevenin's chow?"

"Changer mind, las' goddam mint," Al said bitterly.

"Askiff you fick cinnamull rones for seevening chow. Didya?"

Al rolled his head around on a limp neck and peered at Wildoe. "Smatter fack, no, I *din'* fick snow cimmon rose. Hadda buy tooshbrush an' renna room, gever thing ready. Then bish changer mine las' mint."

"Din' fick snow cimrose, huh?" Wildoe inquired, solemnly.

"I *swear* I din'," Al protested. "Honest I din', Ralph."

Wildoe frowned thoughtfully. "Sawl I wanda know, mack."

"Sicken tired cimmon rose," Al complained. "*Hate* cimmon rose."

"Do' blay mew," Red muttered. "Savva drink."

They had another drink, and Al kept mourning the tragedy of an empty hotel room, and Red suggested they ought to take some bag up there and sack in for the night. Know any *other* bags? he asked thickly, and Al shook his wobbly head and said he was a one-bag man but she done him wrong. You know any? he asked, and Red pondered drowsily for a time and announced that he knew a bag in Chicago, but she wouldn't come to Milwaukee, he always had to go sleep in *her* room.

The evening grew very hazy and kaleidoscopic for Al. Vaguely, he realized that he and Wildoe walked down a rocking crazy street, and Wildoe kept asking him who was in charge of the galley, and he kept saying, You're in charge, buddy. Foggily he was aware that they went to the hotel room and Wildoe had a bottle and they sat against the wall solemnly watching the bed that was haunted by the naked ghost of a passionate, big-nosed girl with cold feet. Al kept shaking his head at the bed and saying sadly, "Nobody home at *this* bed, Ralph."

Wildoe remarked that it looked comfortable, and asked if Al minded if he tried it out. Cerny not, Al said. Go ride a head, mack. Red stretched out, sighed, and said one time he and a girl in Sheboygan ... Al passed out lying on the dingy rug, trying to get the bottle open.

It was after nine the next morning when a taxi dumped them at the depot gate and they marched carefully and sleepily aboard ship, where a harassed Angel Santiago had coped with breakfast. They relieved the steward of the duty, and without changing from his dress blues Al proceeded to turn out the worst meal of his entire career, while Red went back to sleep on the black gang's mess table with the bottle balanced precariously on his portly chest.

Al was badly hungover. Whisky, stay way from my door, he said to himself. Boy, if you ever see me hobnobbing with a shot glass again, it'll be my spittin' image but it won't be abstemious Alvin. I won't take another drink until I'm safe in my coffin.

But the whimsy of his still-drunk mind didn't amuse his heavy heart; he wore misery and melancholy like a wet overcoat. I shouldn't have blown my top at Stella, he thought. Oh, he had it all figured out, now that it was too late. He should have wooed her some more, that's all. He should have overcome her scruples with tender persuasion. Well, it was all over now. A figment of the past, forever lost.

When he turned the watch over to Wildoe at noon, Red looked at the inch of whisky left in the bottle and offered it to Al, who shuddered and gagged and said, "You drink it, Ralph."

"Stow that Ralph crap," Wildoe said gruffly. "Lissen, you move your gear, mack. That's a order, see. Move into the cooks' cabin."

"Well, gee," Al said, touched. "I don't wanta cramp your style."

"My style don't cramp easy," Red said without moving a muscle of his face. "You're entitle to that empty bunk, so take it, mack."

"Well, thanks," Al said, yearning for unguent sleep.

"Sure you don't want any more of this whisky?" Red insisted.
Al's throat constricted. "Hell no," he said, shivering.

"Then I'll kill it," Red growled.

"Go ahead, kill it," Al groaned. "Murder the goddam stuff."

Al stumbled back to the cooks' cabin, undressed, and climbed
into the top bunk. It was a fine, roomy, comfortable bunk, the kind
he'd always wanted, and he quickly escaped into the pleasant
world of slumber, where nobody ever heard of a headache and a
girl almost never got cold feet after you'd gone to the trouble of
buying her a toothbrush and registering her as Mrs. Ralph Smith.

While he slept, his new-found buddy proceeded to turn out
what was undoubtedly the magnum opus of *his* culinary career, or
at least the tastiest supper he'd ever produced aboard the *Skedeelia*.

And everywhere in the world the ice was rotting and dissolving
in the zephyrs of early spring. It was Sunday, April 6, 1941. There
was death in the world, and fear, and misery, worry, unrest, gloom.
The ore freighters and car ferries and pleasure boats were ready to
start using Lake Michigan again, and the skipper of the *Skedeelia*
had sailing orders, and the lonely sound of bell buoys would soon
be heard in the fog. But the center of the universe was occupied by
a sleeping ship's cook from Oklahoma who had just lost a lover,
found a friend, and acquired a better bunk—in a spacious, luxurious
cabin that had a fine reading lamp and a sink and a splendid desk
on which a man could type up menus; if he ever got his typewriter
from Chicago.

PART III
Summer and Autumn, 1941

✠✠✠

CHAPTER 14

Hair in the Chow

WITH her well deck laden with bell buoys and channel markers, the *Skedeelia* left Milwaukee and steamed uplake through slush ice, and Al Woods was seasick and spent a day in his sack, and was never seasick again on Lake Michigan, even at its churning worst.

The first ore freighter from Duluth came downlake to the steel mills of Gary, Indiana, and the lake was officially open for the summer's commerce. A bartender in Manitowoc told Al the lake was 310 miles long, 75 to 80 miles wide, with a maximum depth of 870 feet, and was the only one of the five Great Lakes located entirely within the borders of the United States. Al thanked the bartender and ordered another rum-coke (he hadn't sworn off rum, only whisky) and eyed the girls in the place, which was known to some as The Passion Pit and to others as Gonorrhea Gardens. He hadn't sworn off *looking* at girls and it was, after all, springtime.

Each day the cutter traced the trails and roadways of the lake, placing the channel markers, setting buoys to mark ledges and reefs and hidden dangers, hauling equipment and machinery to isolated stations and lighthouses on islands that sunned themselves after winter's exile from the mainland world. "Hold what you got, boys," the bosun's mate would tell the galley crew. "We're gonna lay way over to port." And the boom swung the heavy potbellied buoys over the side and the ship leaned far over, and Al cursed the pots and pans that skidded and slid and sometimes crashed to the deck.

"The skipper is in a quandary," Blanket-ass reported one day. "He always located this reef by takin' bearings on an outdoor john and they put in plumbin' on him this winter an' tore it down, so now he's got to use the sound lines an' start from scratch again."

The skipper was O.K., he never rode the crew, he didn't go in much for discipline or inflexible routines. But some of the CPO's took themselves pretty seriously. "You shouldn't be so friendly with seamen, Woods," a fat, bald chief machinist's mate advised Al, peering disapprovingly through his smudged glasses. "Someday you'll have to decide whether you prefer your own kind, or the *unrated* men."

"I already have, Chief," Al said. "Or hadn't you noticed?"

It was April and the ship went to Chicago and moored just inside the locks at Old Chicago Lifeboat Station, and Al went ashore and rode a streetcar to his old address, wanting to get his typewriter and visit with Charley Berger. The C.O. did not remember Al. "What are you doing in dress uniform this time of day?" he growled, and when Al told him, the C.O. beamed fiercely and said he always liked to see one of the old boys again. In the galley they told Al that Berger had shipped out on the *Algomotoc* as a third-class cook and the ship was now in the Manitowoc shipyards being fitted out for duty as a convoy cutter in the Atlantic. Al had missed him there by only a day or two; Berger could have been depended upon to log in at The Passion Pit.

Al found his typewriter untouched in the attic, the case deep-coated with dust, and suddenly he was anxious to be on his way, the station depressed him. Adolph Wollager, who was now, at long last, a ship's cook, *second* class, smirked pinkly at Al with the tenderness of maestro for protégé. "So? How goes it vit de cookink, Alfin?"

"Great," Al said. "You was right, professor. All I know I kind of inhaled from watching." But not watching you, Schickelgruber, he added mentally, and departed. On the way back to the ship he bought a new ribbon for the Smith-Corona. In the stateroom he uncased it and put it on the desk, handy if he should suddenly need it.

"What's that thing?" Red asked stiffly, pretending ignorance.

"A lineograph machine," Al said. "I'm starting a newspaper."

"Blow that!" Red snarled. "What's it *for?*"

"It's for us," Al said. "Is for you an' me, buddy."

"I'll sell yuh my innerest in it for a stale beer," Red said gruffly. But several times after that Al caught him self-consciously typing letters to his mother in Menominee, with one rigid finger.

As for Al, he often felt like a motherless child. But in April he got a terse communiqué from Josephine Hill, an OU sorority girl.

"What's this?????" she wrote. "Coast Guard!!! I thought you were enlisting in the Marines. What happened???" And she wrote, "Spring is tippy-toeing onto the campus and I miss you when the sap begins to rise and the birds make nests and all that stuff. I have no new love, Alvin, I just play the field dating multitudes of Greeks, but they are pale by comparison. I must take some sulphur and molasses. I am rooming with Beulah, who sends her love. She got a handwritten rejection slip from *Ladies' Home Journal* and is beside herself with joy. *Both* of her send their love. What *were* you two *doing* behind my back??? In fact, Alvin, what *are* you doing behind my back??? Write verbosely. Yours with high esteem and *fond memories*, Jo."

"Oh, No, Please, We Mustn't," Al said ruefully aloud, but it kind of excited him to hear from her, and he wrote her a witty letter on his typewriter—all about being a cook.

In April the man who had informed the Dies Committee that Italian Fascist secret police had infiltrated American defense industries was found shot to death in Chicago, and the *Skedeelia* returned to the Milwaukee depot twice for buoys and supplies, but Al did not go to the Oval Bar either time. He didn't want to see Stella.

The first time, Wildoe said, "I seen your ex-pig at the Oval last night. She was asking about you."

"Don't tell her *nothin'*," Al said, shrugging irritably.

"She ain't hard to look at," Red said. "Except the nose."

"You can have her, nose and all," Al said indifferently.

The second time, Wildoe said, "I seen Stella last night. She never ask about you. She never mentioned your name, mack."

"All right," Al said. "So what, Ralph?"

"Watch that Ralph stuff," Red said threateningly. "So I walked her home. You got any goddam objections, mack?"

"Nary a one," Al said. "Help yourself. She's not my type, boy."

"I figure she kinda goes for me," Red said modestly.

"Why not?" Al grinned. "She never tasted your lousy cooking."

"Make cinnamon rolls for chow," Red snarled. "At's an order."

It was still April, and the sun shone brilliantly on the blue water and Al felt more at home on the ship than he'd felt anywhere for a long, long time. He guessed it was being a petty officer who had a semiprivate stateroom and earned sixty dollars a month, mostly. Mostly that. But it was also a sense of belonging, of fitting in. And it was the guys, too, the nice friendly guys on the ship. In April Al decided he liked being in the Coast Guard after all.

It was May, and the bones of a dinosaur one hundred feet long and approximately six million years old were found near Edmonton, Canada; a two-day Japanese air raid on Chungking, China, killed 230 persons and indiscriminately damaged foreign embassies; in Florida a lynch mob shot to death a Negro charged with raping a twelve-year-old white girl; and in May, Alvin Woods reached voting age and celebrated his twenty-first birthday by getting drunk with his roommate.

"Whatta you want to be when you grow up?" he joshed, and Wildoe stared at him coldly and said without moving his lips, "Alive, mack."

"What I wanta be," Al said, "is test pilot for a white slave ring. That is my consuming ambition in life, Ralph."

"You got no respect for women," Wildoe said coldly, and stared into his drink. "I'm twenty-six years old an' a goddam bachelor."

"Yeah," Al sympathized. "Every guy needs a wife and family."

"There you go, readin' my goddam mind again," Red smirked.

It was May in Waukegan, Kenosha, Benton Harbor, Muskegon, Grand Haven, Holland, Ludington, Charlevoix, Sheboygan, Winnetka; on Little Sable Point, Sleeping Bear Point, on Manitou and Fox Islands, on Hog Island. The ship was always going to some new place to chart the depths and shallows and set the markers and haul machinery and supplies, and every place had at least one bar where a man could sit idly over a drink and ponder the riddles of being a member of the human race. Sailboats and speedboats and sleek yachts skimmed and skidded over the shimmering blue water that was sometimes like a mirror and sometimes shrouded in mists and fogs and sometimes dappled with whitecaps and sometimes gray and mean and dangerous; but always the *Skedeelia* plodded about her workaday chores, and always the gulls shrilled and wheeled, and always the girls wore as little as the law would allow. Fish were jumping and the cooking was plumb easy. You didn't fix a menu, Al would say. What should I fix for chow? And Wildoe would gaze at him blankly and say absently, negligently, Fix anything you want, just don't bore me with your stupid little problems. It was May and Wildoe was a smitten man.

The ship returned to Milwaukee and Al invested twelve dollars in books and bought himself a bait-casting rod and rigged up a fan in the stateroom. I'm gonna read, fish, eat, and loaf, he said to himself. I'm a hard-working man of leisure, and I hate women.

He was awake with Saroyan at two o'clock one night when Ralph Wildoe came reeling in drunk and belligerent.

"I wanna know the goddam truth, mack," he said miserably.

"The truth shall make men free," Al said humorously.

"Nevermin' at smart stuff," Red snarled. "I got to know, did you or din't you ever sleep with her? Don' lie to me, mack."

"Who, Stella?" Al asked. "No, buddy, I never came close."

"Could you if yuh'd *wanted* to?" Wildoe said through gritted teeth, and Al looked at the taut suffering face, the sick jealous suspicion in Red's eyes, and he said evenly, "No, Red, I couldn't. I tried to make her, but she was strictly no sale. That's the truth."

Wildoe glowered at him for a full minute, the sick worry slowly dissipating; he nodded curtly. "O.K., I b'lieve yuh. O.K."

Red was lovesick. Somehow it astonished Al, he couldn't imagine stiff, wooden-faced, pompous Red in an emotional scene with a woman; he seemed incapable of tenderness. Red and Stella, Al thought. Well, I'm glad I didn't hafta lie to the poor chump; I guess.

In May, Jo wrote that her social butterfly night life made it difficult to maintain a high scholastic standing. She said Beulah Flachtter was going with an elderly student in the Creative Writing course who had sold a whole bunch of stories to the pulp westerns. "He's almost thirty!!!" Jo wrote. "Horrors, what is this young generation coming to??? Do you ever miss me, or can you spare the time from all your *new* conquests in Chicago???" (Al's address was c/o The District Office, Chicago, and Jo apparently had the impression he spent most of his time there.) "Sometimes I miss you something awful," Jo wrote. "There'll never be another Alvin Woods in my young life—which is just as well, for it would lead to sheer disaster, no doubt! ! Do you suppose we'll ever cross trails again?"

There was a little more, but that last sentence caught his attention and held it. He was dubious about the likelihood of ever seeing Jo again, and it made him a little melancholy.

Suddenly it was June, and the skipper got drunk and went to three cat houses in a certain broad-minded community and executed a successful one-man raid. "I'm from the FBI," he announced at each house, very courteous and mannerly about it, they said later. "Due to the great number of young, innocent boys now entering all branches of the military," the skipper said with dignity, "the FBI is checking all girls in this branch of the entertainment world. Please line up here in the street and follow me—and do not be alarmed, this is not an arrest, technically. We merely wish to examine you young ladies and issue certificates and identification cards."

These were all girls who long since had forgotten how to veto any reasonable proposition; unquestioningly, obediently, they assembled in the street, draped in expensive winter coats, starchy frocks, and sleazy kimonos. "Please try to keep in step," the skipper said courteously, and when he had collected the inmates of all three brothels, he paraded twenty-six assorted whores down the town's main thoroughfare and into the town's toniest cocktail lounge. "Ladies, please seat yourselves," the skipper said with old-world dignity and charm. "We will wait here for the medical authorities."

Whereupon he marched out again and went to his favorite bar and ordered another drink. As the story went the rounds later, the astounded, chagrined management of the cocktail lounge was speechless for the time it required his respectable customers to drink up and make an exodus. Halting inquiries elicited only the information that the prostitutes had been told to stay there by a high government mucky-muck and stay they would, despite the management's anguished protests. But after some twenty minutes they grew very restless—"We're not making a dime in *here*," one of them complained—and then suspicious and indignant. Another ten minutes and they had all gone back to their brothels.

In June Al's scalp itched in the hot galley and he stopped wearing a white hat on duty, and one day an indignant CPO, whom Al rather disliked anyhow, came lumbering down from the chief's mess room with his plate rampant on a field of purple turkey wattles and flaring white eyeballs. "Goddamit this has gotta stop!" he squalled.

"What are you screaming about, lard bucket?" Al said wearily.

"This is the second time I find a hair in the goddam chow!"

"We don't charge no extra for hairs," Al said. "They're free."

"Oh, a smart guy! A comic, are you? We'll see about this, Woods!" And the tattle-tale went panting aft to lay his complaint before higher authority. An hour later the executive officer, who was also the engineering officer, came into the galley and eyed Al's bare head.

"Why aren't you wearing a hat on duty, Woods?" he wondered.

"It's too hot, sir," Al said. "Head gets sweaty and itchy."

"Woods," Kretlow said benignly, "if you insist on going bald, do so on your own time, don't molt in the goulash. Wear a hat."

"Yessir," Al said. Bald, he thought. Don't make me laugh, boy. But after that, sometimes, he worried about losing his hair. Harry O'Neal, the barber buddy in boot camp, had predicted it. And his own father's parting admonition had been to take care of his hair. But they couldn't *prove* that was his hair in the CPO's lunch. Anyway, he'd read somewhere that each little hair reaches maturity someday, dies, falls, and is replaced by a new one. Relax, nobody was going bald.

In June he went again to the Oval Bar in Milwaukee, and saw Wildoe and Stella huddled over a table, gazing into each other's eyes, holding hands. It was a disgusting spectacle, it saddened Al a little. There was a hot article, that Stella, a real steamy dish, and he could have had her for himself if he'd been wiser, calmer, less anxious.

He spotted Gailla at another table, looking lonely, and on impulse he approached her. "Hi, beautiful," he said. She smiled at him, a strained shy smile, but she was pathetically glad to have somebody notice her—especially a sailor. Maybe particularly me, he said to himself, and noticed her with shrewd, critical eyes. She was built a little thicker than Stella, bigger in every department except the nose, but she wasn't bad looking at all. Kind of appealing. So he danced with her, gradually forcing the stiffness out of her spine, the nervous self-conscious trembling out of her back muscles, soothing and disarming her with words, kidding her, flattering her, and at last she allowed her stomach to touch his. Nothing terrible resulted, and she limbered up and became more graceful; she wasn't a bad dancer at all. And she smelled nice, like cherry blossoms or something.

He took her home and kissed her. She was tight-lipped, but he expected that and gentled her out of that, too, making her loosen up and relax and enter into the spirit of the thing. But it was really no use, no use at all. There was only one Stella, soft and squirmy, moaning and clawing and wonderfully responsive. Gailla merely allowed herself to be kissed. Apparently it did nothing to her, awakened no dormant nerves and senses. Al debated, Was it worth-while to try to awaken the sleeping glands in this statue? She isn't ripe for romance yet, that's all, he decided. She isn't a keeper, I'll throw her back.

There was only one Stella, and now Wildoe had her all wrapped up. Old butter-fingered Al Woods had let her slip through his fingers.

So in June, being no statue himself, Al went prowling for a new love, a lupine sailor on the trail of tender quarry. Not that he found any. All the girls were tender in June, but there were none for Al Woods. Life was bittersweet in June with the lake a sparkling blue and the islands green and the beaches white and the girls brown from the sun, and all the beer cold and benevolent to a parched throat. And Wildoe was benevolent with that mellowness that en-riches men who are host to the nesting instinct, and he would say in his gruff, stiff, but kindly fashion, "Too hot to cook, afternoons. Give 'em cold cuts."

That last June of peace, the colleges and universities spewed forth freed students, and Jo Hill wrote that she was going to be a counselor in a girls' camp in Arkansas for the rest of the summer. "I will warn the gullible little maidens never to go for a walk in the woods with anyone like you, Alvin," she wrote. "For that would be folly, but such fun!!! I almost hate to counsel them, every girl is entitled to her share of the dangers of osculation, I always say. Since you are far away I don't mind admitting that I'd kinda like to let you scare me out of my wits again sometime. Now don't desert, or come rushing down to Arkansas on leave or anything. I will just deny writing this letter. All my love, though, as I have just renounced all my Greek suitors. What are you doing? Do you ever think of—yours truly, Josephine."

Over all the distance between Milwaukee and the Ozarks her mortal ghost came again to haunt him, and irritate him. Women just naturally can't help being teases, he thought. They must get these animal urges like everybody else. And he wrote her that if he ever got her alone again, he would ignore her pleas for mercy.

In June the ship worked hard servicing buoys and acting as a tugboat and freighter and passenger boat for island-bound Coast Guard people, and when they came in time to a small town they had not visited before, a kind of magnificent insanity infected the entire crew and the officers, and they went on a binge. The skipper was very happy and found a loose toilet seat that would slip down over his head; he wore the bizarre collar with pride and charm and jauntiness all evening. He joined Al's table for a while and bought a round of drinks and said his great ambition, his secret yearning, was to be a lighthouse keeper somewhere on Lake Michigan. He was a wonderful, wry, dignified man, and a peerless seaman who navigated in dense fogs (with vast unconcern) by dead reckoning and an extrasensory perception not unlike that which permits bats to fly freely in total darkness. In a pea-soup fog he would sail across the lake and into the narrow, sea-walled channel of a river without slackening speed, hitting it right on the nose, apparently judging his position from the mournful-braying foghorns on the breakwaters. Al was proud to be seen with Captain Orlando, toilet seat and all, for he was a kindly man, a nautical expert, and a very rare character.

Life was good in June, and life was agony, capriciousness, laughter, anguish, tranquillity; in June the wives of crew members lucky enough to have mates seemed always eagerly waiting at all the docks around the lake where the ship's work took her—they drove ahead in pooled autos, preceding their men to new ports, wanting to be there for their men, or wanting to be sure no other woman waited there; in June 700 Chinese died in Chungking's largest bomb shelter—not from Jap bombs but hysteria, trampled to death; and 33 men perished aboard a reconditioned U.S. submarine that sank off Maine during diving tests; and California union members ended a 49-day strike against Alameda and Oakland shipyards.

A sight-seeing boat carrying vacationing office girls skimmed past a dirty old ship which their guide called a buoy tender, hardly glancing at the sweaty, lonely cook on the well deck to escape for a few minutes the furnace heat of the oil-blower range; they dismissed him with an indifferent glance, not knowing or caring how much he loved them each and every one. And the cook followed them with hungry eyes and hungry mind and tried to placate his famished heart.

I'm too impatient, that's all, he told himself. I want it all now, this minute. I'm too impatient, that's the main trouble with me.

CHAPTER 15

Promotion

ON THE Fourth of July, 629 people died accidentally in the United States, and one of them was a five-year-old boy who fell into Lake Michigan while running along a wall excitedly pacing a dirty old buoy tender. The skipper saw it happen and stopped the ship and put a boat over, and several men who had been sun-bathing on deck swam to the spot and tried to find the child in the dark, deep water. One of these was Al Woods. It was necessary to drag for the body, and when the hooks found the child and brought him to the surface, one barb tore cruelly at the small, waxen face, pulling the mouth into a ghastly half-grin. The victim wore sandals and shorts, and had curly yellow hair, and they spent twelve frantic minutes locating him and getting him out of the water, and tried for thirty-seven minutes to revive him. A doctor administered insulin shock, and the parents prayed and screamed to God for mercy, but the child was dead.

"He was racing the boat," the mother pleaded. "I yelled at him but he wouldn't stop." And she screamed at the men who had tried to give him back to her, with terrible shrill accusation, "He was racing *your* boat. Oh, God, why did *you* let him die?" And then, mercifully, she fainted, and the men from the guilty *Skedeelia*, which had excited a child into racing to his death, rowed back to the ship in silence, their faces frozen, their eyes dark with hurt, grieving heavyhearted for the child who had been robbed of all but five years of living, and for the parents who had been robbed of the joy of living forever.

For a week Al had bad dreams at night, and in sunlight he looked at the terrible, treacherous beauty of the placid lake and accused himself of a terrible and tragic blunder—he hadn't dived in the right place, he hadn't considered the sluggish current that tumbled a small body away from the spot where the exuberant race ended.

It's all my fault, Al thought at times, and he was sick with thinking how it might have been if he'd only *used his goddam head*. For a week he relived with haunting horror the twelve minutes of sense-less blundering and the thirty-seven minutes of trying uselessly to undo the blunder. He knew that he would never forget how the little kid had felt under his hands when he took his turn—in the rotating five-man resuscitation method practiced by the Coast Guard—kneeling astraddle the small cold limp body, compressing the small cold clammy chest with his big hands. One two three press, one two three release—afraid of injuring the fragile body, staring with desperate hope at the dead face, wanting to see a sign, a flicker, a twitching eyelid, wanting the mouth to move and cry out, but seeing only the brutal dirty forefinger and thumb of Bosun's Mate Becker holding the dead boy's tongue so that it could not be sucked into the throat. One two three, press gently but firmly, one two three, one two three—a futile human attempt to restore something that was no longer human, to revive a heart that would never thump excitedly again at sight of a dirty old Lake Michigan cutter.

It was the first time Al had felt death in his hands, or seen the stark gracelessness of a new-made corpse, and it was something he would never forget. He vowed that he would never again be present when anyone dragged for a drowning victim, or voluntarily go to look upon death in any form, or be morbidly curious about death.

It oppressed him intolerably, coming at him suddenly from no-where—"Why did *you* let him die?"—and he could not discuss it with his shipmates who shared the innocent guilt with him; he couldn't know that they felt, in varying degrees of self-accusation, as he felt. And in the end he found some ease and self-forgiveness by writing about it to Jo Hill. It was the first time he had revealed his naked heart to anyone, and when the letter had been mailed he wished he had not sent it. He felt it had been unmanly.

But it was unmanly to weep, too, and he wept publicly after he read in the newspaper that the man and the woman and the child had been tourists from Kansas, and the child had never seen a ship before. The parents had planned an excursion cruise of the Great Lakes, the story said, but they had cut short their vacation and were taking the body back to Kansas for burial. And later that day, drinking to forget, Al remembered vividly and wept drunkenly and told a hard-faced waitress why he wept, so that her face was no longer hard. And then he went back to the ship, staggering and ashamed, and wondered if he would ever grow up and stop acting like a goddam kid all his life.

But the letter and the weeping and the telling helped. He had unloaded some of the grief and the guilt, and it now belonged to Jo and to a hard-faced waitress in a saloon. And time's panacea pulled off layers of the tragic remembering like leaves from a calendar, until only the permanent residue remained, to haunt him less and less. The ship moved farther away from the scene of its crime and lumbered across the lake, and it was hot July and the sun shone and the lake was ever sparkling blue and innocent by day (although black and sinister at night, when a kind of atavistic terror of the deeps would prickle Al's scalp and he would shudder, seeing, like watchful eyes, glittering stars mirrored in the endless blackness that lapped and murmured against the ship's flank) and the saloons were cool, and laughter grew less self-conscious, and in time Al was able to put death out of his mind.

In July there was horror and guilt and weeping, but there was also laughter and much living to be done, and in July the skipper summoned his cooks to the wardroom and offered them opportunity —with strings to it. "I've got the word from the D.O. that all capable third-class rates, all you ultracompetent petty officers, may put in for promotion if they have held their present ratings for as much as four months. You guys have been rated longer than that, and I'm willing to perjure myself and endorse your competence. However, there may be a hidden reef here, gents. Becoming second-class might make you pretty susceptible to sudden transfers to salt-water duty, probably the Atlantic and possibly rugged convoy duty, or troop-transport duty. So it's up to you. Shall I kick you up the ladder or not?"

"I'd like to make second," Wildoe said woodenly.

"He wants to get married," Al grinned. "I don't, and I'm not anxious to get transferred, but I'd sure like to have the extra dough."

The skipper looked thoughtful. "Frankly, Woods, I imagine you're apt to get transferred without warning either way. The Coast Guard is growing so fast, and men with seniority will be sent wherever needed."

"Then I'd like to go for second-class, sir," Al said.

The skipper nodded. "I'll recommend you both."

That was also the week of July when he got a letter from Jo Hill, a girls' camp counselor in Arkansas. "Your letter made me cry a little," she said. "I don't know why. Life is kind of tragic and glum sometimes, isn't it?" Then the mood changed. "This is a very very very wholesome life—the only men around are *old* men!! Early to bed and early to rise. Say, I heard from Beulah, and she has sold a story at long last!!! To a western-type love pulp, for fifty-seven dollars and thirty-five cents. I don't know how to break it to you gently, but I fear Beulah no longer loves you, she is all agog about her thirty-year-old cowboy-story writer. They plan to live on a ranch and write shoot-em-ups together and raise kids and longhorn cattle or some such animals. Ain't it a scream? Well, I must go now, my little nuisances are due for a dunking." And then the switch back again. "Al, I never supervise their splashing now but what I remember your terrible experience, and I guess it makes me more alert and careful. Please, Alvin, don't blame yourself, you were only an innocent bystander. It seems things like that happen as often as they do just to keep us from being smug and taking anything for granted, to sort of remind us how feeble and destructible people are or something. I'm kind of a fatalist, I guess, I sort of think it's all arranged long in advance for us poor puny people. I wonder if there's anything about *us* in the future plans of fate???? Gosh, this dump is dead—sorry, I mean dismal. Wish you were around to liven things up, you scoundrel. Love and kisses, Jo."

Her letters always depressed Al a little. They were so short, and too buddy-buddy. Not sentimental enough. Too damn *noncommittal*.

There were storms in July, and rain pocked the gray-green surface of the lake, but most of the time there was only sunshine and high white clouds idling in an immensity of blue sky. On such a day the ship was moored in the narrow passageway between Lake Charlevoix and the town harbor, and the cooks were fishing off the wharf with Blanket-ass, the yeoman, and Al wearing only swim trunks, but Wildoe, who burned easily, dressed in pants and denim shirt and a baseball cap pulled low to keep his nose from blistering. It was a peacefully disturbing summer afternoon and they discussed idly those vagrant matters that occupy the minds of most young men in July, notably fishing and women. Al divided his attention between the fish visible in the clear water of the creek and the girls in sleek bathing suits and summer frocks yonder across the harbor. Scornfully tossing another dinky lake perch into the bucket, he pinched off a chunk from a ten-inch night-crawler (using monsters for bait to catch midgets, he called it) and disgustedly dropped his hook into the water again.

"Ralph," he said, "I've been fishing with you on and off all summer, and all we ever catch are these sardine-sized perch. Back in Oklahoma, little kids catch these things on bent pins and throw them back. You got the biggest fishworms and tiniest fish in the world."

Red grunted tersely. He had been a little sulky lately, partly because Stella was clear to hell and gone across Lake Michigan, but mostly because he resented Al going for second-class the same time he did. It stuck in his craw, and he'd made some sarcastic references to the subject—a little butt-kissing sure speeded up some people's careers, he'd hinted. Which was grossly inapplicable, in this case, although one of the undeniable truisms of military life. Al was not obsequious; if he had a fault it was his *lack* of humility.

Now Red said, "We catch perch because we're perch-fishin', mack."

"I know that," Al agreed. "Up here you even have a season on these itty-bitty boogers and people sit all crammed up on the docks catching them on wet bread and think they're having fun. And in the spring everybody goes crazy sacking up smelt, that's even ittsy-*bitsier*."

"Nobody give you an order to fish," Wildoe snarled. "You got my permission to quit any time you like, mack." And then, as if his voice had sounded unnecessarily harsh even to his own ears, he jeered, "Tell us about Oklahoma, the fisherman's paradise, mack."

Al swallowed his rancor and told about Oklahoma fishing. Black perch the size of your hand, pumpkin seed perch, bluegills, crappies as big as horse blankets, black bass up to maybe ten pounds, and catfish that often went close to a hundred pounds. Touched by summer nostalgia, he bored his audience with his self-centered reminiscences, and after a while, during a breathing stop, Blanket-ass took the floor.

"Speakin' of sex," he said dreamily, "you take guys like Brownie and Pelliteri, I bet they just make up most of their hairy old sex stories. I got a hunch they don't do any better than the normal, average guy—like me—only they just *talk* a better game."

Red nodded, poker-faced. "If they do make out, you notice how it's always some gorgeous movie-actress-type hot too-molly."

Blanket snorted. "Yeah, I've seen some of the beauty queens they talk about. Hell, if I wasn't fastidious, I could shack up with some rusty old tomato too, and come back aboard ship braggin' what a truly scrumptiously gorgeous young teen-aged pig went an' seduced me."

Al stared at the water. "Everybody makes out better than I do."

"What makes you so goddam sure?" Wildoe snarled.

"Yeah," Blanket said glumly. "Stop that goddam braggin', Al."

"I wasn't bragging, I was complaining," Al said, and the three of them gazed wistfully off across the harbor for a lingering moment, three young bucks in July sharing a common poignant hunger. But Al was thinking, Red's probably lying—I'll bet whenever we get back to Milwaukee he shacks up with Stella. Like I could have been doing if I wasn't such a pork chop. And, sighing resignedly, he said, "Well, getting back to the subject of fishing . . ."

It was hot, voluptuous, indolent July, a time of sorrow and dumb misery and laughter and a sense of expectation, and the fish were too small but the beer was cold and the swimming was invigorating and a man could live vicariously in the literature of mankind. And there was a kind of quiet and affable pleasure in seeing the beautiful summer homes and the yachts and cruisers and catboats on the water, and the dark mysterious forests of evergreen trees. And anyhow July was really too languorous a time to knock yourself out seeking erotic diversions, so Al drank beer with his shipmates and fished and swam and read anything he could get his hands on—including a post card from his father.

"Dear Hotshot," his father wrote. "Why not drop your old man a line sometimes? I am as well as can be expected. How's it going with you? Hoping this finds you well, I remain. Your old man." And it was from the same town as the Christmas card had been, which was amazing. Staying so long in one place was a record of some kind.

Al wrote his father a letter, a stiffly self-conscious letter, a dull letter. But at least it was a letter. A letter to a stranger.

Toward the end of the month Al became a ship's cook, *second*, but the occasion had its unfortunate aspect. For some reason his promotion came through two days before Wildoe's did, and this flagrant, unjust favoritism froze Red's wooden-Indian face into rigid bitterness, and he coldly ignored Al until his own upgrading notice arrived.

"I'm still senior cook here," he told Al belligerently. Al, wanting to salve Red's injured pride, agreed meekly. "I'm still runnin' this goddam galley," Wildoe said threateningly.

"Sure," Al said. "You bet. Who said any different, buddy? You're the boss around this joint."

"Just don't forget it, that's all," Red muttered, and slowly he began to thaw toward his subordinate cook, his assistant in the galley.

In a drugstore in Michigan in late July, Al bought a bottle of Lucky Tiger for his dandruff, or whatever. He didn't really need it, of course, but it made his hair smell nice. And if the tiger was lucky, maybe he would be lucky too. About *time* he was lucky, goddammit.

And Wildoe, his scornfully friendly, stiffly affable self again, said, "I'll miss you after you're gone, mack. Them feather merchants in Chicago are prob'ly cuttin' orders on you right now."

Al grinned. "Maybe I won't be the one to get shipped, Ralph."

"You don't stop callin' me Ralph you'll transfer in a box," Red said without moving a muscle of his chiseled features. "And don't worry about me, mack. I'm an old Lighthouse Service boy, they'll leave *us* here on the lakes where we always been."

Al wasn't fretting about it. He was fatalistic—what comes, it just by God comes. He liked the *Skedeelia* fine, but he was romantic enough to crave adventure, to want to see foreign ports. Anyway, hell, maybe they'd both stay where they were. The ship was big enough for both of them—only just barely. Any cook wanted his *own* galley. A guy got fed up, always being reminded he was the *vice*-president.

And suddenly July was gone, and the ship returned to Milwaukee in time for Labor Day; and suddenly old inscrutable, poker-faced, stiff-legged, portly, pompous Ralph "Red" Wildoe decided that the month of September was a good season to quit fooling around and get married. All over the world thousands of individuals, and even entire towns and villages, were living on borrowed time in September of 1941, but Red Wildoe, who seemed to have been born with a stiff upper lip, had been pierced fatally by Cupid's arrow and believed that he was so madly in love with Stella Pappharonis that marriage was the only solution. Or maybe he just wanted so badly to get married, in a world askew and insecure, that he'd decided Stella was good enough for him.

Somehow, Al felt in a nagging, troubled way, Red was making a big mistake. He felt he knew Red as well as anybody could—he had a faint inkling of Wildoe's fundamental nature and character— and he kept wanting to say to Red, "You don't have to *marry* Stella." *You* don't have to marry Stella. You don't *have* to marry Stella. Or maybe you don't have to marry STELLA! For chrissakes, didn't Ralph know by now that he could have all of that hot-natured eighteen-year-old Coca-Cola drinker he wanted, without any legal entanglements?

"*Why* do you suddenly want to get married?" he asked Red.

The cold eyes regarded him. "I ain't gettin' no younger, mack," he said. "Any guy wants a home an' family, don't he?"

"You want kids?" Al asked incredulously, unable somehow to feature Red as the father of a child. "I mean . . . now, in *this* world?" he added lamely. "The way things are nowadays?"

Red shook his head. "This ain't no time to be havin' kids." It was not an original remark. Many a grim parent had uttered the phrase to an unwed daughter; many a lover had spoken it in urgent protest.

Then why the hell get married at all right now? Al wondered, but did not ask, seeing Red's cold eyes rebuff any further interrogation.

The thing was, Red probably didn't know himself why he had made up his mind to get married. Perhaps the deep-rooted insecurity that made him a caricature of a tough, phlegmatic, hard-bitten *man.* Perhaps the humorless fellow believed that marriage would somehow teach him the secret of laughter, of taking himself less seriously. But more likely, Ralph Wildoe was nature's pawn, being moved by incomprehensible destiny; being urged by his chemistry and biology, his ancestral mating instinct which was not the same as his libido, to accept a social responsibility he had hitherto declined. All over the world life was being snuffed out, flesh shriven and scorched and rended, eyes glazed and voices silenced, pulses stopped and lungs collapsed forever; the books had to be balanced, and Wildoe, seeking chiefly some perplexing justification instead of rapture and contentment, was instinctively going to wed a girl who manifested all the more recognizable symptoms of being a very poor marriage risk for a ship's cook, or a traveling salesman.

"I'm free, white, and over twenty-one," Red said belligerently. "I got a right to get married if I want to, an' it happens I want to."

But still, Al had a feeling of prescience about the thing, and somehow the stateroom was awfully crowded when they were both in it at once, and the galley just wasn't quite big enough any more for both of them; he felt restless and uneasy around Red.

What he didn't know yet was that Milwaukee wasn't big enough for himself and Red Wildoe, either. Something had to give.

CHAPTER 16

Everybody Kissed the Bride

A L COULDN'T leave the subject alone. Some baffling compulsion kept prompting him to try, in a roundabout way, to warn Red that he was getting into very deep water. But at the same time Al suspected his own motives. What am I, consumed with envy? Am I jealous? Old dog in the manger Alvin Woods—is that it? And he would remember cold March nights when Stella moaned and squirmed passionately in his arms. So maybe he secretly, subconsciously, couldn't stand the idea of Red getting something he couldn't have himself, was that it?

I'm just trying to give him a right steer, that's all, he would decide. This is just one hell of a bad time for any second-class cook to marry a lusty wench like Stella, that's all. Maybe he's just a noble chump that wants to do the right thing, which is the wrong thing. So he hinted, in his subtle, intellectual fashion, that Red's chosen course could only lead to disaster.

"September is a helluva month to get married," he said.

"One month like any other," Wildoe growled.

"Yeah, but look, suppose there's a war? You might get shipped out to hell and gone, be away from home a *year*."

Wildoe eyed him bleakly. "So what?"

"Well, hell! That's putting a strain on *any* marriage, Red."

Red switched from sternness to horsy coyness. "What's a little strain between a boy and a girl?"

"Yeah," Al said doggedly, "but what's *she* doing all that time?"

"Waitin'," Red said with bleak confidence. "Waitin', mack."

Al gave it up, shrugging. "O.K.," he said. "It's your business."

But now Red was eying him thoughtfully, suspiciously—maybe pondering Al's peculiar status as ex-member of a nonexistent triangle. "How come this worries you so much, mack?" he demanded gruffly.

"You're my buddy, much as I hate your guts," Al grinned. "I just wanta be sure you know what you're doing, that's all."

But Red's look of chilly speculation didn't alter. "I'm not so goddam sure," he said. "I'm beginnin' to wonder about you, Woods. You know what I think, I think you're hurtin' with the green envies."

Al laughed hollowly. "Maybe you're right, buddy. Or maybe I keep seeing them poor little kids with red hair and big noses." He saw the glitter in Red's eyes and added, "Well, let's drop it. Like I keep telling the boys down at the office, it's none of my goddam business."

"That," Red said icily, "was gonna be my next remark, mack."

So Al dropped the subject and silently wished the fools a long, happy marriage and a long, deliriously wonderful honeymoon and money in the bank and twins every spring. But he didn't have any influence with fate, and the honeymoon lasted less than two weeks —because Wildoe got orders to replace the first-class cook on the *Algomotoc*, who had an attack of acute appendicitis less than a week before the remodeled cutter was to start the long voyage around through the lakes and down the St. Lawrence to the Atlantic. Counting just the nights, Wildoe got to sleep with his bride thirteen times.

Although Al didn't attend the wedding, which was a civil affair, he was able to give Red the best wedding gift of all. He volunteered to take over both cook watches for three days so the happy couple could go visit Red's parents in Menominee. What the hell, Al thought, I sponsored this romance in the first place—Red wouldn't ever have got to know her, probably, if she hadn't accosted him to make inquiries about that *other Skedeelia* cook, the one with the empty hotel room.

The days passed and there was a chill in the air that made the galley's warmth pleasant again, and autumn began coloring the shores and islands of Lake Michigan with pinks and golds and tawny browns, and Red came back from visiting his folks. To Al's critical eyes, the boss cook looked a little drawn and haggard and pleased with himself.

"How you like the responsibilities of married life?" Al asked. Red shrugged and calmly said he liked them O.K. "You look tired," Al said. "You look like you been having insomnia or something, Ralph."

"Go to hell," Red snarled. Marriage hadn't mellowed him *yet*.

Orders came from the District Office assigning Water Tender Brown, Quartermaster Salter, Seaman Flanders, and Coxswain Pelliteri to the converted 165-foot *Algomotoc*. They were to report aboard in the shipyards at Manitowoc. Wildoe had fun ribbing them about it.

"In Boston there is twelve sailors and eight gyrenes for every dame," he said. "But you won't care 'cause you'll be at sea alla time vomitin' your landlubber guts out over the goddam railin'."

"Knock wood, Red," Flanders said. "We'll save you a spot downwind." But Wildoe laughed scornfully and said, "Not me, mack—I got suction with the D.O. in Chicago. They need me here, boys."

Pelliteri said he kind of hated to leave the *Skedeelia* now that his stomach had got hardened to the chow Red turned out, and Al butted in to request that both Pelliteri and Brownie leave him a list of their old cast-off mistresses, but they demurred. "Gonna have mine all come to Boston," Brownie said. "They'll live in one apartment, like a harem."

"At's right, you better take some Milwaukee talent along," Red leered, "for there won't be none available out there, boys."

And then, stunningly, the D.O. *radioed* the ship two days later that the captain should send Ralph Elmer Wildoe, SC2/c, to Manitowoc immediately to replace the stricken first-class cook of the *Algomotoc*. They were getting another stricken cook, in case they didn't know it; Red went about his packing in bitterly stunned silence. Once he cried out in poignant and futile wrath against this manifest injustice—"Goddammit to hell anyway, of alla lousy stinkin' breaks!"—but after that he maintained a stoic silence, although gritting his teeth.

"Well, mack," he said to Al, "it's all yours now."

"This is a helluva note," Al said mournfully. "I wish to hell they'd picked me instead of you, Red." He meant it sincerely.

"So do I," Red said. "But I guess they wanted a *cook*, mack."

He stayed in character to the bitter end, and then he left, walking in that peculiar short-legged, long-striding way of his, like a small boy trying to step on the cracks of a sidewalk, or every other railroad crosstie. And watching him go, Al felt a great affection for the gruff, sarcastic, pompous, wooden-faced Wildoe.

As he stepped onto the dock, Red turned back for a last look at the ship and saw Al watching. "Give the bastards cinnamon rolls for supper," he said. "I'm still boss until the five o'clock whistle blows."

And, Al learned at a later date, old Red followed his own advice about taking some Milwaukee talent along, as far as it was applicable in his case. Stella went with him to Manitowoc and stayed until the *Algomotoc* started her journey to the ocean, three days later.

There was a letter from Jo Hill the next day, one of those nutty, noncommittal, irritating letters she knew so well how to write. This one was almost formal. She sure don't try very hard, Al thought with dissatisfaction. She could at least try to be entertaining.

Jo said she was bored with college and didn't think she would ever finish. She was not attending OU now but had got herself a job in a news-clipping service in Oklahoma City. She explained that she read newspapers from all over the Southwest and cut out items about clients of the service—mostly notoriously wealthy types, she said. "Who knows, maybe I'll trap me a handsome millionaire," she said. But it didn't sound like much of a job to Al. And she signed the letter simply, "Yours, Josephine," instead of, "Love, Jo." Al had a feeling that she was about ready to stop writing him letters at all.

Pulling both cook watches made a stay-at-home of Al, but he went ashore on September 28 to buy some razor blades and Lucky Tiger, and decided a couple of fast ones wouldn't hurt him. And so he went to the Oval Bar, out of loyalty to the management. If he'd had any vague notion of seeing Stella there, he wouldn't have been so surprised to see her there, *would* he? He'd have gone elsewhere, *wouldn't* he?

Mrs. Stella Wildoe (nee Pappharonis) sat at her customary table with Miss Gailla Ginetto, a local spinster with atrophied nerves. It was the third or fourth time Al had seen Stella since the night she left him stranded beside a cold and lonely couch, and he wasn't even going to nod or anything—why should he, for chrissakes?— but all at once she saw him and smiled hugely and waved and called, "Hello, Al—come here a minute." Well I'll be goddam, he thought.

He walked over, nodded at Gailla, and looked at Stella. She was smiling at him in what he suspected was a mocking manner, so he grinned and asked mildly, "How do you like being a sailor's wife, Stella?"

She flicked her eyes at him, pursed her cute mouth, and said ruefully, "Oh, it's all right . . . I guess." Then she explained why she had called him over. When she was in Manitowoc with Elmer, she said, an old friend of Al's had asked her to relay his greetings. (Elmer! Al thought, wincing.) She said it was the other cook on the *Algomotoc*, Chuck . . . what was his name? Chuck Berger. (Charley Berger, Al thought.) "So," Stella said with vivacity, "hello, Al, from Chuck Berger."

"Hello," Al said. "Well . . . can I buy you ladies a drink?"

The ladies thought that would be nice, and Gailla ordered her usual Coca-Cola, but Mrs. Wildoe, with a wicked smile, asked for Schenley's Seven-Crown and seltzer. (Elmer, you *fool!* Al thought.) Stella laughed at his astonished reaction and explained that her husband had taught her to like that particular drink, while they were on their honeymoon. Then she said, "Al, for old times' sake . . . one dance?"

So Al was dancing with Mrs. Red Wildoe, trying to keep it impersonal, when a couple of the guys from the ship who were dancing nearby spotted them and said, Hey, there's the gal that married ole Red. And they came over and impeded Al and Stella's progress, laughing and being charmingly impertinent about it, and one of them, a nice sort of kid named Gelborn, said, "Do we get to kiss the bride or not?"

Al felt annoyed. "How should I know?" he said. "Ask her."

"Well, my goodness, why not?" Stella said with that new wicked gleam in her eyes. "It's traditional, isn't it?" So Gelborn—who maybe wasn't such a nice kid as Al thought—yelled at some more *Skedeelia* crewmen at a table, and the first thing Al knew there were about a dozen sailors passing Mrs. Ralph Elmer Wildoe around, kissing her. She was flushed and laughing, having a hell of a time, and it just made him sick. It made him angry, too. She was the wife of his old friend and ex-colleague who had just got shipped out to brinier waters, and here she was giddily passing out free samples. It shocked Al's sense of propriety—that sort of thing wasn't done in Oklahoma.

Along in the middle of the queue was Seaman Gutsell, the cocky, muscular, insubordinate guy who had been pot-washer when Al first stood a cook watch on the ship, the one who said insolently that someday he'd catch Al up the street where the crow on his sleeve wouldn't protect him. Al had seen Gutsell any number of times in any number of places, but nothing had ever been done about that unfinished business.

Now Gutsell took Stella into his muscular arms and bent her over backward, like a movie villain, and kissed her much too long and experimentally. It enraged Al, and he moved to intercept Gutsell as he strutted arrogantly away, pretending to be half-swooning. In a tight, low voice, Al said, "You sonofabitch!" Gutsell looked at him with surprise. "What's gnawin' *you*, cooksie?" he demanded.

"Embarrassin' her in public like that!" Al said furiously.

"Embarrassin' her hell, she *liked* it," Gutsell leered. "Wot's it to you, anyways? It ain't no skin offa *your* ass if I smooch Red's wife, cooksie-wooksie. Wot's your main trouble, you jealous?"

Al hit him, surprising both of them, and Gutsell staggered, and Al hit him again, and Gutsell went plunging against the railing that enclosed the dance floor, and when he righted himself Al was waiting and hit him a final time, not because he was that angry now but simply because he was afraid Gutsell would recover and give him a bad time of it. This time Gutsell went down, shielding his face in his arms.

"O.K.," he muttered shakenly. "At's enough. At's enough."

Al was stricken with remorse, and a little nervous about having struck a subordinate. "Hell," he said. "You O.K., Gutsell?" Gutsell mumbled that he was O.K. "I'm sorry," Al said gruffly, "but that's been brewing a long time—since the first day I had the cook duty. I guess that kissing stuff was just an excuse to choose up sides."

The sardonic glitter in Gutsell's eyes showed he wasn't buying that excuse angle, but he only said oddly, "I never knowed you was nursin' a grudge all this time. Hell, I thought we was buddies now."

"We are, if you still want to be," Al said, ashamed of himself.

"Then we are," Gutsell shrugged. "You never hurt me anyways."

"No hard feelings?" Al asked. No hard feelin's, Gutsell said.

So the kissing, which had been interrupted by the sudden flare-up of violence, continued until Al was thoroughly disgusted. Stella must have decided, belatedly, that it was getting silly, and she broke it up, laughing, and came back to Al with her lipstick smeared all over her face. She looked rumpled and rakish and wanton—like a whore, Al thought. The music was going, and she moved into his arms unbidden, and they danced, Al stiffly and sullenly but Stella, who just couldn't help it, dancing bonelessly, intimately close. And she said wickedly, "I don't recall seeing you in the stag line, Al."

"That's right," he said. "I didn't get to kiss the bride."

"You were too busy fighting," she said. "What was the trouble?"

"It started long ago," Al said, and saw by her wicked, mocking smile that she knew what the trouble was, all right. But she said mock-reproachfully, "I'll bet it was just to keep from kissing me."

"Not at all, my dear young lady," Al said. "Not at all. On the contrary, I feel pretty melancholy about missing my turn."

"We can't just ignore that oversight, can we, Al?" she smiled.

"No, I guess we can't," he said, and he started to kiss her lightly, just to get it over with, just so as not to make a big burning issue of the unkissed kiss, not even interrupting the dance to kiss her quickly like a brother. Only Stella Wildoe wasn't having any of that, thank you; she refused to be kissed negligently, and presently he stopped dancing, feeling the blood pounding in his ears, and crushed her in his arms. Her warm lips clung in the old way and her body stirred subtly against him, arousing him, and finally he tore his mouth free and wished he'd had sense enough, or razor blades enough, to have stayed aboard ship.

With her nose in his collar, Stella said, "Whew! That kind of got out of control, didn't it? We'd better watch ourselves." And she threw back her head and gave him that bold, wicked smile again.

"Yeah," Al said. "So you like the life of a sailor's wife, huh?"

He'd had to say something, but he hadn't been required to say just that at just this moment. It sounded like *double-entendre*.

And Stella said, "I liked it . . . while it lasted, Al."

And he started fighting the big fight in his mind. Decency versus temptation; friendship versus desire; conscience versus passion; sensuality versus principles. It was going to be a tight fight with a short stick, he thought. Already he had that guilty feeling.

I tried to warn him, Al thought sadly.

CHAPTER 17

The Defeated

THE *Skedeelia* left temptation behind in Milwaukee and crossed
the lake to Holland, Michigan, a town of festival and frolic,
and tied up at a filthy coal dock. It was October and Al thought
there was no pageant to match October around Lake Michigan, but
he wished to hell they would send him a galley partner so he would
have some time for gazing upon the autumnal splendor. He was
mixing a dishpan full of biscuit dough for evening chow when
Blanket-ass appeared in the door.

"So long, old hoss," the yeoman said with forced humor. "Don't
move, I want to remember you just as you are, sloppy and untidy."

"What are you chippin' your teeth about, Hiawatha?" Al asked,
assuming from Blanket's dressy appearance that he was headed
ashore for a jolly evening of recreation.

"Radio orders from the D.O.—me an' Gutsell gettin' the boot."

"You can't do this to me," Al said. "Where to, buddy?"

"Detroit, to go aboard the *Algomotoc*," Blanket said. "She's laid
up in River Rouge with condenser trouble an' the senior feather
merchant fell down the bridge ladder an' busted his short hand arm
in two places. And one of the seamen turned up with Wisconsin
clap. So they are sendin' Guts to assist with my luggage an'
protect me."

Al shook his head lugubriously. "Goddam," he said. "I don't mind
seeing *you* leave, but I'm sure gonna miss that Gutsell."

"I'll sure miss them buffalo stews an' horse biscuits you fix," said
the part-Choctaw. "You'd make some warrior a good squaw, Al."

Then suddenly there was nothing more to be said, and they looked
at each other and were speechless, until Al said there was a pot of
fresh coffee. Coffee got them past the moment of self-consciousness,
and Al said, "Now, Sittin' Bull, you're just an innocent country boy,
so I got to give you a little worldly advice. When you get among

them coarse salt-water types, be careful. Like if you drop your soap in the shower, don't bend over to get it, kick it over to the bulkhead and *crouch* down after it, see."

Blanket-ass laughed sadly. "I won't even use no soap, dad."

"And if any of them officers start pattin' you on your pink little cheek, you better jump over the side an' swim for it."

And he wiped flour from his hands and shook good-by in October, knowing that winter and ice and the foghorn's lonely anguish would soon fill the world. All the good guys were leaving, going down to the sea in ships, migrating like salmon. Al got a lonely pang.

"Well, cooksie," Gutsell said from the doorway, "this is it, buddy." Since their fight he had been warily friendly. "I'm coppin' a fast sneak to Deetroit, takin' my seckaterry along. They want me to take over a new battleship they got there. They need a guy with brains."

"You got enough for everybody, Guts," Al said, grinning. "With a little charm and diplomacy tossed in, you will go far."

"Yeah, far," Gutsell said. "Alla way to Deetroit."

"Maybe all the way to Boston, even," Al said. But he was worried. He kind of liked Guts, but he didn't trust the seaman's discretion; he was too cocky and too garrulous. So Al said, "Look, Guts, when you see Red Wildoe, I don't hafta tell you this, but for chrissakes don't cheer him up by mentioning how his wife was kissin' everybody that night. Let him be unhappily ignorant about that little orgy, huh?"

"I never even *seen* his wife," Guts said. "Don't *know* the broad."

"Anyway, be careful," Al advised. "And if you can't be careful, be sanitary, be chic. Good luck in your new command, Captain Gutsell."

"Commodore," Guts corrected, and sighed. "Old lake sure is pretty this time of year—I almost nearly hate to leave, cooksie."

And then they were gone, trudging across the gangplank under their burdens of sea bag and mattress rolls, going to join a hard-luck ship called the *Algomotoc*, which had a fast personnel turnover.

The *Skedeelia* worked around the north end of the lake without losing any more of her crew, and Al thought about Stella Wildoe with a yearning akin to love, and he thought about her husband with a feeling akin to guilt. I got to stay away from her, that's all, he told himself firmly. If she was going to make a cuckold out of a cook, let her do it with somebody else—if she hadn't already done it. Nobody ever questioned my honor, Al thought. Except me. I question it, boy.

In October the islands emerged from the deep blue water like flaming rafts, all gold and scarlet and amber and wine-colored except for the noninflammable evergreens, and the lighthouses stood white and clean against the background of flamboyant autumn, reflected in the smooth, sparkling, sun-dappled coves and bays. I'd like to live in a lighthouse on an island, Al told himself. Away from the madding throng. Away from the scarlet temptations of the venally demented cities. And if anybody happens to want to know, I happen to mean Milwaukee.

The mornings were frosty and the evenings were chill in October, and it was good to be a cook, but it wasn't good in October or any other month to be the only cook aboard, and Al decided he wasn't going to fool around with the D.O. much longer. They better send him a cook in a hurry—or else, boy. And they damn sure better not send him a cook as dumb as *he* was when *he* came aboard this ship, either, by God.

So they came down the lake again to Milwaukee, and there was a cook waiting at the depot, and when the mail came there was a letter from Jo Hill—and the cook and the letter were both terrible. But Al found out about the terrible letter immediately, and it took a few days to get the complete lowdown on the counterfeit cook.

The letter wasn't long. Jo liked her new job, she said. And she was unofficially engaged to a boy named Richard O'Brien whom she had met in Arkansas during the summer, who was soon going into the Army. (She said all the men in Arkansas were *old*, Al remembered.) He was, Jo said, a really swell guy, and reminded her of Al in some ways, and she wished Al could meet him and see what a really swell guy Richard really was. (Oh hell yes, I'm dying to meet Richard.) Jo closed by saying, "Now for heaven sakes don't let this affect our friendship, Alvin. I want to know where you go and what you do, I've *got* to know."

Friendship! Al snarled to himself. Pen pals! Maybe good old Richard will write me some letters because Jesus Christ I dearly long to be dear friends with Dicky boy like I have been with his fiancée!

Al laughed hollowly, mocking himself. Somewhere in the back of his mind he had carried a hope for the future, a silly, illogical kind of daydream. Bang! Now it was gone. Jo Hill was nothing to him, just a girl he used to know. A girl with bowlegs and picket-fence teeth and a head too big for her small, sturdy, boyish body. And freckles. She wasn't even pretty, let's face it. Or very interesting. To be quite utterly frank about it, she was pretty dull, pretty shallow. And one goddam thing for sure, she was deceitful. No men in Arkansas, ha ha. All women were fickle, treacherous, capricious, insincere. Duplicity, thy name is female, any way you spell it.

Well, that's that, Al said to himself, tearing up the letter.

He was in his cabin at the time, feeling restless and lonely and strangely uprooted in October, and a knock came at the door. A hesitant, timid knock. Al opened the door to a delicate stranger in dress blues. "This where I'm suppose to live?" the stranger asked.

"You a cook?" Al asked wearily. The stranger nodded without much conviction. "This is the place," Al said, and held open the door while the new cook moved in his gear. Al should have felt elated; now he would have more leisure time for reading and getting tight on beer and fighting temptation. But somehow he couldn't work up any elation. This cook was so new his uniform smelled of mothballs, and his face was young and callow despite Latin sideburns and a dinky mustache; he had slicked-down black hair and girlishly delicate lips and scared eyes.

"I'm Woods," Al said. "Just call me Al."

"Clark here," the newcomer said. "Whew," he said, and took off his peacoat, and Al saw with relief that he was a second-class cook.

"I'm glad to see you," Al said. "I been pullin' both watches for the last month. I'm dog-tired, and tonight I aim to get dog-drunk. So it's all yours tomorrow, starting at five-thirty."

The new cook frowned, bit his lip. "Uh, is there a menu?"

Al shook his head and began to get dressed to go get drunk. "Buddy, just fix whatever you want to fix. I'm weary and thirsty, and you're a second-class cook. Expect me back when you see me."

A guy named Richard O'Brien, Al lamented. Oh, Yes, Richard, You Must! And outside, down the creek on the breakwater, the foghorn moaned a heart-wrenched moan, like a lover grieving for his lost love, sobbing into the shrouding night fog, and the chill of the coming ice-locked winter sifted and seeped into the dismayed heart of Alvin Woods. It would take a lot of whisky to thaw the frost of woman's faithlessness out of a ship's cook's aorta. But there were other ways, more vengefully satisfying ways, to strike back at the trustless gender. Al knew that all the time, but it had slipped his mind for the moment.

He remembered when he saw Stella Wildoe at the table in the

Oval Bar, alone and toying with her Schenley's and seltzer and gazing into space with a softly wicked, anguished smile. And the whisky spoke for Al's wounded pride and anesthetized conscience: All women are tramps at heart, and it might as well be me as some unworthy stranger. Let's keep this hot apple pie in the family, fellows.

And he said fiercely, "Ah, Stella, my love, my lost lovely."

And she smiled a welcome with her wicked eyes and her wicked, voluptuous mouth. She would have made such a fine whore, he thought cynically—in fact she may yet.

"I'm celebrating," he said. "I finally got a night off."

"You must be happy then," she commented, as if she *weren't*.

"No, Stella," he said. "You oughta know I'm not happy."

"I want to dance, Al," she said plaintively. "I'm lonesome."

"We'll be lonesome together," he said, and they danced, and then they drank, and then they danced some more. And she pushed her soft smooth body against him, giving herself to him on the dance floor as she had always done, and he told his conscience to mind its own damn business. Stay out of this, he said to his conscience. This league is too fast for you. This is just collecting an old debt; she is going to pay for a cruel April Fool's joke. Go away, conscience.

"Let's try another saloon," he said. "Where we're not known."

"That's a good idea," Stella agreed. "I hate gossips, don't you?"

"Can't stomach gossips at all," Al said. He'd noticed before how any anatomical reference (even Naval Reserve) would draw a wicked glance from her, and when he said stomach her smile was almost lewd. My God, he thought. Cohabitation has coarsened her something awful.

Outside, he pulled her into a darkened doorway and kissed her and she came to him hungrily, demandingly, squirming and moaning; it scared him a little, horrified him a little, but excited him even more. It was like old times, except tonight there would be no empty bed, no cold feet. He tore his mouth away from her and put it as bluntly as he knew how. "Let's go to a hotel, baby, I've got to have you *now*."

She answered with a groan, and with her body and wicked eyes.

He knew the hotel, all right. He hoped he would get the same room, where he'd been left holding the bag. He walked to the desk with Stella brazenly and the desk clerk looked at them without expression and pushed the register toward them, and Al signed it

Mr. and Mrs. Albert Smith. He paid two dollars for the room and took the key and got in the elevator, the shabby dumb-waiter to heaven, and the empty-faced old Negro took them to the fourth floor without looking at them, having seen the stiff masks and dazed eyes of lust too many times before. Al tipped him a quarter and hurried Stella along the dingy hall, looking for a door with 410 on it. Fumbling shakily, he got the door open and went inside and shut the door behind them. He locked the door and snapped on the light and saw the room. It was a dismal room and he was suddenly afraid it would offend Stella, or the light would scare her, or something; he snapped the light off. *He* wanted it dark, too. He would like to see her naked beauty, but still he wanted it to be dark. He tossed the key where he'd seen a bureau and heard it clink on the glass top, and he pulled off his flat hat and peacoat and dropped them where he'd seen a chair, and undid his neckerchief, feeling rushed and terribly impatient. He was afraid Stella would change her mind, and he got out of his tight jumper and scuffed his shoes off without untying them and fumbled with the thirteen buttons of his flap-front trousers and got them off, and finished undressing down to his feverish skin. He could hear Stella's rapid breathing nearby in the dark room, and reached for her in the darkness and found her struggling out of her sweater, her arms over her head and her breasts pulled high and taut. He drew her hard against him and helped with the sweater and fumbled with the brassière, unsnapping it. She shrugged out of it and he felt her warm smooth breasts lifting and nudging elastically against his chest, and he got his fingers twined in her hair and bent her head back and kissed her deeply and demandingly as she unzipped her skirt and let it fall; he heard it slide whispering down her legs onto the floor and heard the silken sound of her thighs brushing together as she stepped out of the skirt, and he couldn't wait any longer. He picked her up and got on the bed with her and tore off the last flimsy garment, Stella lifting herself warmly against him to help, drawing her knees up to free her feet and ankles of the silken manacles, and whispering over and over, "Hurry hurry hurry hurry..."

He felt no compunction yet, no qualms. They might come later, but now all he knew was unthinking, mindless desire and careening senses and the tumult of his blood and nerves and flesh. Neither had spoken since he suggested the hotel room, and neither spoke now, for there was no need for words, and there was only the gasping breaths and Stella's incoherent moaning. Al's brain was reeling and he wanted to prolong it, to make it last forever, but Stella's supple body was frantic and urgent and it seemed to end almost as soon as it began, and the fury and violence and intensity died slowly and they were relaxed and spent. But they stayed as they were, Stella's mouth clinging with soft insistence to his, and he felt very strong and thought that the night was young yet, they had only rippled the surface of passion and would drown themselves before this night was over.

But Stella kind of spoiled it by talking during intermission. "Is it wrong, what we're doing, darling?" she whispered, and he said gruffly, "This doesn't concern anybody but you and me." He didn't want to moralize about it now. Later, perhaps. Later surely. But not now. "That's how I feel, too," Stella said eagerly. "I know it's wrong, in a way—technically it's wrong, but I don't care, I love you, Al." Oh, sure, Al thought. That made them blameless, of course—if she loved him she wasn't responsible, she couldn't help it, and God would forgive her even if nobody else did. "I don't care," Stella said softly, and kissed his chin and snuggled bonelessly against him. "I made a mistake when I got married—I wish it had been you, dearest. Al, why wasn't it you? We belong together; I wish it had been *you*, Al."

"So do I," Al said, having nothing to lose by the lie, and she said kiss me *here*, and he kissed her warm yielding breast, and she shivered against him and caught her breath and said, "Oh, Al, nobody can drive me crazy like you." Al felt strong and virile and supremely confident of his ability as a lover—some people just had a knack for sex—but he wished the ghost of Red Wildoe would go out of the cheap room and quit looking so sad and reproachful. It would be very cozy and delightful and richly satisfying, lying naked in the dark with Stella, investigating Stella, giving Stella little tentative promissory samples of his knack as a natural-born man and hearing her gasps and feeling her little lazy squirmings—if only she would let Red's indignant ghost depart in peace. Yakkity yakkity, Al thought, and she said drunkenly, "It can't be wrong for us, it's so wonderful." Um-hmmm, Al murmured, tracing the softly firm curve of her hip. "Even if it *is* wrong," Stella quarreled with herself, "I simply don't *care*. I can't help it with you, Al, you were the one I really wanted, and I'm not made of stone or ice, I'm flesh and blood." And hair, Al said, kissing her breasts to get her mind off the moral pros and cons, and was pleased with her prompt reaction and the way she whispered wildly, "Oh darling you're so wonderful sooo wonderful." On a caught breath, biting her lip. And Al thought, I know it, baby doll. I won't deny it.

"Nobody can help how they are," Stella said quietly. "I know I'm too passionate, but I can't help it. I was born that way. I can't help how I was born, can I?" That's true, Al said, and exercised a privilege as her conqueror, and she gasped and clutched at him spasmodically and arched her warm silken body against him straining, and he wondered how he happened to be so lucky all of a sudden and how he managed to exist for so long without this most natural, most astonishing, most exciting, most available luxury and necessity that the world afforded the human race. "Oh make love to me darling," Stella begged tearfully, sniffing. "Don't ever stop, I know it's bad, it's adultery, but I don't care, I *want* to, I *have* to." And she said poignantly, "He shouldn't have gone away and left me so soon, just when it was . . . so wonderful."

That was the whole story right there, Al reflected. Wildoe shouldn't have gone away so soon. Just got her all hot and bothered and accustomed to passion's rapture, then left her hurting for more. The ghost of Red Wildoe tried again to intrude itself between Al and the naked girl in his arms, and he felt the first pang of remorse, tainted with guilt and shame, but only a very small one. Because if it wasn't me, Al thought self-righteously, it would be some other guy. And if you look at it a certain way I'm entitled to this, it's no more than I deserve. I saw her first and I worked on her for a long time, I got her all aroused and thinking about sex, I was to blame for her wanting so bad to get married in the first place. If I'm guilty of anything, it's of driving this hot-blooded little woman into a hasty, ill-advised wedding. And I *warned* the chump.

But if he could easily justify himself at the moment, Stella could take the keen edge off his well-deserved pleasure by continuing to debate the ethics of illicit love-making. Al took her again, and her response was even more urgent this time, but her lack of restraint was countered by his restraint, and it lasted for an eternity of numbing, dizzying sensation. And yet it was not complete, somehow, it fell short of the ultimate rapture. Lying quietly, inert, utterly relaxed, with the cat-napping Stella snuggled against his side, he tried to analyze the failure. Some part of him had held back, aloof from the clamorous, unreasoning passion. All that talking, partly;

reminding him that she was an adulteress and he a betrayer of friendship. But it was something else that had robbed him of the full sweet consummation of this first real affair of his lusty young life.

And as he tried to pin it down, he remembered the letter from Jo, remembered that he was here with Stella because he wanted, through her, to express his cynical attitude toward all deceitful womankind. Somewhere along the way he'd become so engrossed in the action that he'd forgotten it was not for joy but vindication. And now, suddenly, he understood why this bountiful feast of passion had not quite matched his famished appetite, why he was still hungry. And why he hadn't wanted the light on, too. Since the moment he'd come inside this room he'd been trying to pretend it was Jo and not Stella. Not consciously; just *wishing* it were Jo and trying to make the wish *seem* true. In the dark Stella might have passed for almost any beautiful and passionate woman, but talking had made her nobody in the world but guilt-ridden Stella Wildoe, lust's willing but uneasy pawn. With Jo there would have been no mental barriers, no nagging thoughts, but only mutual fulfillment; only a wild singing tenderness and urgent compassion.

Or so he'd once believed, he thought sourly, resenting this trick he had been trying to play on his imagination. Hell, Stella was more desirable than Josephine Hill. Bowlegged Jo with her boyish body (Stella was all woman, utterly feminine) and her Oh No We Mustn't inhibitedness. Stella wasn't afraid of passion (he forgot her Please Don't Take Advantage routine), even if she did worry about a bunch of phony, obsolete moral standards. She was no phony puritan, like Jo.

Thus, instead of thinking how fine at last it was to be here with delicious Stella, how astonishingly rewarding this had been and would be again, Al preoccupied himself with a tormenting image of Jo Hill lying nude and love-weary like Stella—beside a dark sinister shape labeled "Richard, a Swell Guy."

The hell with Richard, Al thought, stroking the substitute woman-nakedness in his arms. To hell with Jo, too, incidentally—her with the cowpuncher legs and big mouth and peculiar teeth and freckles and flat chest and boy's body. I'll bet she's a big disappointment to that dumb jerk of a Richard. I'll bet she's about as hot-blooded as a cigar-store Indian in January, Al lied to himself.

Stroking warm, velvet-skinned Stella. This is Stella, the *best*. Nibbling Stella's breast, stroking her satiny softly firm belly with a growing sense of urgency now, his own pulse quickening, and Stella coming softly eagerly awake sighing with pleasure and desire, gasping and murmuring, her mouth seeking his. And there was nobody, especially nobody named Richard Whozis, as virile and strong and instinctively knowing in the art of love as Alvin Woods, on the night when he learned that Jo Hill planned to wed another and wreck a wistful love story Al had been daydreaming, off and on, for quite a long time.

Going back to the ship in the morning, sleepy and pleasantly exhausted—but not very happy, not very proud of himself—Al thought, How can I ever get married when I know so much disillusioning truth about women? Women just aren't built to be faithful and true.

He had barely closed his eyes when the new cook awakened him, and he fought up through the smothering weight of sleep and got his eyes open and said, "What's the trouble? What's all the panic about?"

"Say," the new cook said worriedly. "Uh . . . excuse me . . ."

"What's the *matter?*" Al snarled groggily.

"Well," the cook said embarrassedly, "I'm kinda messed up."

"Get your thumb out and talk plain words," Al said thickly.

The cook looked scared. "I . . . guess I lost my nerve. I don't know what to fix for dinner, or where to start or anything . . ."

Groaning, Al dragged himself out of the bunk and splashed cold water on his face and blinked haggardly at his reflection. Can't a man get any sleep any more? he wondered, and turned to scowl at the worried, miserable face of the new cook. "Now tell it simple, Clark."

"Well . . . I'll level with you, I . . . well, I just never cooked what you'd call a *regular* meal before, and that's the truth."

"Then how come you're sportin' two stripes on your sleeve?"

"Aw, *they* give 'em to me," Clark said nervously, shifting the blame. "The recruitin' guys. I *enlisted* as a cook."

"Holy jesus h. johnson!" Al exploded. "You mean to stand there and tell me they give you that rate to sign up in the Coast Guard?"

The new cook hung his head. "They said they needed cooks bad."

"Maybe," Al said. "But we don't need *bad* cooks. What *are* you?"

"I was a short-order cook in a drugstore," the boy mumbled. "I fixed hamburgers, grilled steaks, French fries, ham an' eggs." He sighed. "That's about all I know how to cook, I guess."

Al glared at him bitterly, wanting to say nasty things to him, but also remembering how he himself had come aboard the *Skedeelia* under false colors. He'd been a fraud, too, and looking at the new boy so humble and meek and lonely, he knew just how Clark must feel.

"Lissen," he said suddenly, "you go back to the galley and you'll find fifteen pounds of hamburger in the reefer—the refrigerator. Give 'em hamburger steaks and French fries for chow. Open some vegetables and heat 'em up. Open some canned fruit for dessert. Try to whip up some kind of salad, just chop a lot of lettuce and stuff and douse it with some of that salad dressing. And relax, when I came aboard this vessel I couldn't boil water, but I learned—by trying. If you get stuck, don't be bashful, ask Santiago, the steward. He'll help you out in a bind. You got nothin' to worry about, kid."

Clark sighed and gave Al a grateful grin. "Man, I been feelin' like a convict ever since I enlisted. Jeez. I feel better now. I was scared you'd have me demoted or something. Whew! Well, one thing I *know* I can do, I can sure as hell make good French fries."

"The guys will appreciate French fries," Al said. "It'll be the first French fries they had on this ship." And he climbed back into his sack and fell asleep, to dream of betrayal and dark sins.

He awoke in midafternoon to feel the vibration of the engines and the rolling of the ship, and knew with quick despair that he would not see Stella that night. They were leaving Milwaukee far behind. But after the first disappointment, he felt kind of relieved. Yes, sir, it was sure a big relief, not being compelled to stand the duty again for Ralph Elmer Wildoe, SC2/c, who was on leave from marriage. By the time we get back, Al thought, I'll probably be able to stay away from her.

It was November, and there wasn't a ship on the Great Lakes that had French-fried potatoes as often as the *Skedeelia*, and Al pushed prurient hankerings to the back of his mind by great effort of will, and concentrated on teaching Clark a few rudimentary tricks of the cooking trade. Clark was earnest and willing and energetic, and Al was pleased to discover that his colleague had that feeling for food which marks the true-born cook. Meanwhile, most men would eat fried food seven days a week and never complain.

But the lake in November was a melancholy environment, and Al was always sensitive to environment. Under lowering leaden skies when the lake threw its notorious short, jolting waves against the ship, Al would suddenly think of Jo Hill and feel desolate. Sex and love, he philosophized, are two interlocking parts of a whole, and one without the other is only half-happy. I would be half-happy if I went on with Stella, maybe, even feeling like a louse. But I would be half-happy too if Jo wrote she'd changed her mind and was mine all mine someday.

But it always came back to which was likelier, and the ship would go back to Milwaukee someday, but never to Oklahoma City. And Al did a lot of troubled thinking about human nature, about life and the hungers of youth, and love and honor; idealism versus realism; fact versus fancy; life in conflict with the dream. Nobody was all good or all bad; most people were a complicated blend of godliness and evil. And even wrong had many facets, many degrees of wrongness. Like, if Stella had to have a lover, wasn't it somehow less wrong if it was Alvin Woods, instead of some evil stranger? Some *responsible* party had to keep her from winding up in the gutter, or a cat house. Some friend of Red's ought to look after his interests in his absence. And if Red had to choose (or some proxy had to choose *for* Red) between having his wife made love to by clean, conscientious Al Woods or a dozen sinister, dirty, haphazard strangers —well? The thing to do, Al said, shifting responsibility, is to leave it up to Stella herself.

But conscience was alive in gray November, and conscience said, Stay away from that woman, it's not your problem.

Conscience was wrong. It *was* Al's problem. But just when a guy finally developed a chain of intellectual, scientific, psychologically sound, philosophically admirable, *indisputable* proof that marriage in 1941 was an outmoded, obsolete custom based on primitive ignorance and too-rigid rules of conduct intended in the first place to be just general and not specific—well, here came old Moral Scruples like a goddam policeman carrying a sign that said: No trespassing.

Then the sophisticated part of Al's being would stroll around the corner of his mind, wink roguishly, and say, She's waiting for you, but you're not indispensable, boy. Plenty men around Milwaukee. So don't be a chump. Do everybody involved a favor and sleep with her.

You live once and you're a long time dead, chump.

And conscience said grimly, Thou Shalt Not!

In November poor Al Woods was very unstable—angrily perplexed, firmly convinced, prudish, sophisticated, cynical, idealistic, uncommitted, rational, foolish, sensible, a very troubled young man. And always the face of Josephine Hill swam mistily in the background, and whenever he was haunted by Jo he would transfer his sick longing to Stella and want her worse than ever.

The ship went to Beaver Island and Hog Island, to Green Bay, to Escanaba, but not Milwaukee. And the new cook asked anxiously, "What I do wrong *this* time, Al?"

"You cooked all the juice out of it," Al said.

"What should I done that I didn't do?" Clark groaned.

And Al said, "A roast, you got to baste it, keep it moist, see. But don't worry, pal, you're doing all right. Stay in there, boy."

The wind was wet and stinging in November, and there was mail for the buoy tender in Charlevoix. Al drew a battered package and a letter from Oklahoma. When he saw the tidy feminine script on the envelope, he dropped it into the fire hole of the galley range. He didn't want Jo for a pen pal, he didn't want to read about any guys named Richard. Why did women always hate so much to relinquish all claims to a man? Why couldn't they say, I'm going to marry another guy, so drop dead. He tore open the package, which was from his father, and from the same town as before, and it contained a set of military hairbrushes and a scribbled note that read: "It strikes me you had yourself a birthday some time or other lately, Hotshot. I hope these fit your head, I didn't know the hat size, ha, ha. Drop your old man a line once in a while." Al thought, I ought to write him. But he was not thinking of his father, he was regretting the impulse that had caused him to burn Jo's letter without reading it first, and wondering uselessly what was in it. Probably a wedding announcement, he thought sourly. And then he felt the powerful longing for Stella blaze high, like a letter dropped unread into the stove.

The ship dawdled, going to Sheboygan and Benton Harbor, and Al had it whipped now. He had steeled himself. He wasn't going to mess around with somebody else's wife, thank you. He'd find him another girl, the world was full of beautiful women.

But when at last the ship headed across the lake to Milwaukee, his blood came alive and grew turbulent, and hot anticipatory thoughts fevered his brain. He was too restless to read a book, or play cards, or listen to the radio; he stood bundled against the cold in the bow of the ship and watched the gray waves shatter and split against the heavy ice-breaker nose, and saw the little patches of slush ice on the lake, and thought that nothing was as agonizingly slow as a ship.

He was the first man ashore in Milwaukee in the dusk of a gray November day. I'll have a few drinks, he thought. I'll take in a movie. I'll get me a T-bone steak.

But Stella wasn't in the Oval Bar. He waited impatiently for an hour, and went to several other nearby bars, and returned again and again to her usual haunt, but Stella didn't come that night. And he prowled Milwaukee like a hired assassin looking for a man he was to kill, staring at all the people on the streets, checking the theater crowds, even looking in the drugstores. He walked past Stella's house a dozen times but could not summon the courage to go inside and find out if she was home or not. He did not see her that night.

But he saw her on the second night. She was going into the hotel with a tall, slim soldier. The same hotel where she had gone with Al, consuming his strength with her wild sweetness. It was Stella, all right, with her long black hair and tan polo coat and her nose. Al was stunned and sickened and enraged, feeling deeply betrayed and insanely jealous. He began to drink like a demented alcoholic, staring bleakly into his glass, torturing himself with his vivid, lacerating imagination, seeing Stella hot-naked and moaning in the arms of a slim soldier. Oh I know it's wrong but I don't care, dear soldier boy.

Some time in that calamitous night Al stumbled blindly into the Oval Bar, led there by instinct, and passed out in a booth. His shipmates found him there and fetched him home to the ship and stowed his limp body in his bunk. And being young, he recovered quickly from the incredible amount of alcohol he had poured on his wounded male pride. But being young, he did not recover from the wound.

He did not go ashore for two days, but it was almost as bad to stay on the cramped ship, and on the third day he went ashore to see if a few beers would restore the chemical balance of his blood. He did not mean to go to the Oval Bar and was chagrined when he went there anyway. She wouldn't be in *there*, he thought, and went glumly inside. Talk to the guys, he thought moodily. Hoist a few.

And Stella was at her accustomed table, looking bland and innocent and horrible. Seeing her jarred and sickened Al, seeing her at once sitting at a table and lying with a soldier, but because he despised her so tremendously, he was able to approach her with false friendliness and an insolent grin.

"One drink," he said, sitting down and ravishing her with his bold, bitter eyes. She drank with him, adoring him wickedly with her own treacherous dark evil eyes, and he gulped his drink and pushed back his chair and said harshly, "Let's go, baby." And she arose eagerly, she of the round heels, and accompanied the lover she had betrayed. This time Al registered them as Mr. and Mrs. Richard O'Brien, and the discreet Negro elevator man averted his gaze and took them topside. Al led her to Room 307 without touching her and unlocked the door and they went inside. But this time he left the light on, and undressed her slowly and with appreciation before he even took off his hat, hating her and conscious of her wicked, wanton, helpless, puzzled, pleading gaze all the while. Then he pushed her down on the bed and undressed himself, taking his time and staring at her nude loveliness, her vicious beauty. She was sure a lovely woman to be so rotten. And he meant to use her contemptuously, without sentiment, until he had his fill of her evil lewd beauty, and then tell her brutally how he really felt about her, how she *really* looked to his disenchanted eyes. Cheap, disgusting, indecent, without honor, shameless, depraved—a contemptible animal. For not only had she been unfaithful to her husband, she had committed the deadly, unforgivable sin of betraying her lover as well.

He was going to avenge himself, strip her of any scraps of pride and self-respect and hope she might have left. But something went wrong.

The instant he kissed her and felt her moist warm mouth fasten greedily on his and felt her cunning body mold itself hungrily against his own hard body, all his vengeance and hatred drained suddenly out of him, and he was stricken with a kind of passionate pity and sad tenderness for Stella. He sensed clearly in that instant that the world was a sordid and treacherous prison where all normal and abnormal men and women were helpless victims of overwhelming forces, compulsions, and emotions, slaves to hungers and yearnings and irresistible impulses, driven by passions they did not understand and might fear and despair of, but could not deny. In each man and woman the flame of life burned, but in Stella it raged out of control. Poor lovely burning Stella. But Al did not dwell

long on this sad, newly acquired compassion and wisdom and understanding of the human tragedy, for he was himself engulfed by the
flames that seared Stella, he was falling down and down into the
hot swirling depths of sensation. But when the flame burned low
he still felt pity and tenderness for fiery Stella Wildoe, who was
born that way.

She lay sniffling in his arms and he said, "You're crying." She
nodded against him. "Why?" he asked gently. "Why, baby?"

"I don't know," she moaned. "I don't know."

But Al knew, he was wise now. He knew that she wept because
she was doomed. And he sensed that any man who got too involved
with her would be doomed, too. He had felt the touch of that
destructive force the night when he saw helpless, will-less Stella
coming into this hotel with a slim soldier. And poor old Red Wildoe
was doomed, too; he was certain to reap a terrible harvest of heart-
ache and betrayal. Red was bound to find out about her sooner or
later. She couldn't help it.

"Don't cry, baby," Al said, looking down at her wonderful, flawless body and thinking, It's a shame. It's a goddam lousy shame.

"Al," she quavered. "Al, I love you."

"Sure baby," he said.

"Al," she whispered, her wet face against his neck, "darling, turn
out the light and love me. Love me to death."

"Sure, baby," he said. He got off the bed and turned out the light.
And as he moved back to Stella he thought with sudden panic, I've
got to break this up, I got to call it quits with Stella. She's dangerous
as hell. She's beautiful and deadly.

She was waiting to take him with her to that doom, waiting in
the dark demandingly, and her mouth and arms and legs drew him
down into the endless devouring flames of her passion, and as he
moved over her, victim of this burning hunger, slave to his own
demanding flesh, he thought helplessly, But how can I ever stay
away from her?

He should have had more faith in Providence. Al Woods, an
admitted fatalist, should have trusted fate. It was growing late for
November, and down in Chicago the mysterious, inscrutable finger
of fickle fate was prodding through personnel rosters, looking for
a competent ship's cook who needed a change of scenery, who
needed to escape from a doomed but overwhelming, irresistible
madness. They had a hot-new seagoing buoy tender ready for com-

missioning in Toledo, Ohio, and there was a vacancy in the commissary department. But not for long. Even while Al lay spent and guilt-ridden and resigned to the fact that he could never leave Mrs. R. E. Wildoe alone, his orders had been cut. Fate was rescuing him from the flames of illicit love.

The hot-new Coast Guard cutter was called the *Legume*.

CHAPTER 18

Reunion in Toledo

IT WAS Sunday morning in Toledo and there was nobody there
to meet him. Everybody has gone to church, he thought wryly,
and decided to take a cab to the shipyard. He told the driver he
didn't know exactly where he wanted to go, he was supposed to
go aboard a brand-new ship that hadn't been commissioned yet.
The cabbie asked what was the ship's name, and Al told him reluctantly, remembering that servicemen were supposed to be wary
about giving vital information to strangers. But the cabbie grunted
and said he knew where the *Legume* was. He should give *Al* some
vital information, maybe.

The first glimpse of the ship thrilled and awed him. She looked
enormous and rugged and warlike, her superstructure rising above
the sprawling sheds of the yard; she was dark gray and mean-
looking, long and broad and towering, with guns on her upper
decks. Al felt like a raw boot again, a little scared and nervous
and lost.

Boy, he said, that don't look much like a buoy tender. Compared
to the *Skedeelia*, and the other Lake Michigan tenders, *Hollyhock*
and the other ship that sometimes had been at the Milwaukee depot
but whose name Al never could remember. Goldenrod or Dogwood
or something. But none of them compared to this big powerful-
looking gray ship with the guns on her upper decks. Boy, this was
a seagoing ship, all right.

Al paid his fare at the gate and unloaded his gear and showed his
orders to the guard at the gate and walked toward his new ship
with a kind of sinking feeling, a kind of stage fright. Suddenly he
didn't know whether he could cook or not. He didn't know
anything.

Under his cumbersome load of gear, carrying his typewriter in
his left hand, he started up the new gray-painted gangplank, and a

189

harsh voice snapped, "Halt, there, you!" Al bent his head and looked under his mattress roll that was wrapped around his sea bag, and saw a young, red-faced officer standing at the head of the plank. "Where do you think you're going, fellow?" the officer snapped.

"This is the *Legume*, isn't it?" Al asked worriedly.

"It is," the ensign said. He had a very sour, sarcastic face.

"Well," Al explained, "I'm assigned to the *Legume*, Ensign."

"That may be," the ensign admitted vinegarishly. "But there is a proper boarding procedure, or hadn't you heard? How long have you been in the Coast Guard?" Al said roughly a year, saying it meekly. "Then you should know how to come aboard a ship, fellow," the ensign said with thin scorn, but Al had to admit that he'd remained ignorant of boarding-ship protocol, somehow. "Haven't you ever been on a ship?" the ensign demanded impatiently, and Al had him there. He was getting sick and tired of standing on the slanting gangplank under his aching load, and he backed down to the wharf and off-loaded his gear and said, "It happens I have been cooking on a ship for about nine months." He didn't say it any too politely. He was feeling pretty annoyed.

"What's your name and rate?" the ensign barked.

"Alvin Woods, ship's cook, second class," Al said wearily.

"Well, you must have been on a pretty sloppy vessel," the ensign said condescendingly. "Otherwise you'd know enough to address an officer as 'sir,' and you'd know enough to request permission before coming aboard a ship. You request permission of the O.D. I am the O.D."

That don't mean old dear, Al thought. It might mean officer of the deck, officer of the day, officer of the duty. Maybe it means Oddly Deficient. Obscurely Dismal. "O.K.," he said. "Can I come aboard?"

The ensign scowled. "You say, 'Permission to come aboard, sir?' "

"Permission to come aboard, sir," Al droned with exasperation.

"Permission granted," said the ensign.

Al studied him warily. It couldn't be that simple. It wasn't.

"However," said the ensign sourly, "there is the small matter of saluting. You are required to salute the O.D.—or any other officer you happen to encounter. *Then* you request permission to come aboard."

"You already gave me permission, I thought," Al said gruffly.

"Let's run through it again, Woods. So you'll remember."

Al was getting hot under the collar. "Where would you like me to start? Should I go back to the gate and make a new entrance, sir?"

"Don't be insolent, Woods. I shouldn't advise it at all."

Shrugging grimly, Al gave a salute. He hadn't saluted anybody since his boot camp days. "Permission to come aboard, sir?"

"Permission granted," the ensign said bleakly, saluting back.

"Now," Al said tiredly, "as I understand it, I actually come aboard ship, sir? Or is there more to the procedure?"

The ensign didn't like him, any fool could see that. But he said curtly, "Once the ship is commissioned you will be required to salute the bridge and the colors before coming aboard, but for now you just do this humiliating business with the O.D., although it's clear you feel that it is a lot of foolish, unimportant nonsense."

Al withdrew into his protective shell. He picked up his gear and went aboard the *Legume* and asked politely if the ensign could tell him how to get to the cooks' cabin. The ensign stared at him for a moment and then laughed, which startled Al. The guy could laugh.

"Well, now, Woods," the ensign said, like a man talking to an idiot, "I'm afraid somebody made a bad mistake when they drafted up the plans for this vessel. They omitted a most important detail, it would seem. They forgot to include cabins for the cooks."

Al wondered what would happen to him if he slapped this ruddy, pickle-complected, supercilious sonofabitch; anything short of a firing squad would be a small price to pay for the pleasure.

If he is an example of the kind of goddam officers they got on this ship, then I don't believe I would care to stay here, Al said to himself. I believe I will resign from this vessel immediately. And he was thinking with nostalgia of Captain Orlando and Warrant Officer Kretlow when somebody shouted, "*Okie!*"

Al looked around, startled, and saw a familiar swaggeringly graceful figure, a familiar face, a well-remembered cocky grin.

"The barber!" he said. "Harry O'Neal, from Cincinnati!"

"You ole whoremongerin' drunkard," O'Neal said delightedly.

"You ole Baronne Street whore hound," Al said, and saw the left-arm rating on O'Neal's undress blue jumper. "A pharmacist's mate!"

"Just call me Doctor O'Neal," Harry grinned. "Any time you need a short-arm, laxative, urinalysis, or blue ointment, ole Doc

O'Neal is here to serve you, Okie. This week we are featurin' a special on circumcisions, all the latest styles. Where you *been?*"

"Lake Michigan, on a buoy tender," Al said. "Well, goddam."

The ensign cleared his throat noisily. "Since it appears you know Woods, perhaps you would help him get his bearings, O'Neal."

"Sure, I'll take care of him," O'Neal said. "C'mon, Okie." He picked up Al's typewriter and led the way through a watertight door into a passageway and into a spacious mess deck, where Al dumped his mattress roll and stopped to make an inspection. "C'mon, turn your orders in at the office," Doc said. "They'll call you when it's time to eat, Okie. You'll know it's chow time when you see everybody headin' ashore to the nearest restaurant."

But Al was hanging over the lower half of a double door gazing raptly at a shining new galley. "Hey," he said to a dark-eyed boy in cook whites, "it's all electric, isn't it?" The cook nodded. "Wow!" Al said delightedly. "No more oil-blower ranges for me." And then, belatedly, "I'm Al Woods, ship's cook, second."

"Curly Matoli, *third* class." The dark boy grinned.

"How many cooks does she carry?" Al asked.

"Me an' you." Curly grinned. "Looks like you the head stud around this kitchen," he said. "Except," he amended, "for Chief Miller, commissary steward."

"How many guys we hafta feed?" Al inquired.

"Around a hundred all told," Curly said, and Al winced. He'd never fixed for any hundred guys before.

Behind him O'Neal said, "Okie, I must be dreamin'. I'm shocked. I want a transfer. Don't kid me, you ain't *really* a gut robber?"

"I happen to be the new dietitian on this here vessel," Al said with a lightness he didn't feel. He was scared, his stomach felt loose and empty. A hundred guys to feed and him the head cook. He took a deep breath. "Well, let's go make it official," he said.

Much to his chagrin and disenchantment, Al learned that he was expected—in fact required—to bunk below decks in the crew's berth compartment. Given his choice of half a dozen empty bunks, he picked the middle sack in a triple tier in the after-port corner of the crowded quarters. There were bunks and lockers everywhere, and a man could touch the overhead where pipes and conduits seemed to grow like monster vines. There was a strong smell of fresh paint and newness about the place, but already the smell of men living in cramped space was trying to vanquish all other odors and winning. Standing in the narrow aisle, Al estimated there were at least sixty bunks in there, and it rankled that he should be stuffed into this seagoing flophouse with all the common people. He was the head cook, wasn't he?

He felt a terrible homesickness for the *Skedeelia*, where a cook was important enough to rate the luxury and privacy of a state-room.

"Where's your bunk?" he asked Doctor O'Neal.

"Up in the CPO quarters, where else?" O'Neal grinned smugly. "I'm head of the medical department on this luxury liner. In fact, I happen to be the whole cheese, the only surgeon aboard."

After Al got his bunk made up and his gear stowed away, O'Neal took him on a guided tour of the ship. "You got to see this wonderful, marvelous, magnificent ship we got the honor of bein' allowed to live on, Okie," Doc insisted, and Al thought, I better look now, when I start cooking for a hundred guts I won't have time to go sight-seeing.

The *Legume* was two hundred feet long and had a reinforced, cutaway bow for ice-breaking. Her high foc'sle dropped sheer to the huge well deck, or buoy deck, which was about twice as spacious as the *Skedeelia's* had been. There was a long cargo boom powered by electricity as compared to the erstwhile Lighthouse Service tender's wildcat-engine boom. In some respects the two ships were constructed similarly, but the *Legume* was much bigger, with Diesel engines instead of oil-burning steam turbines. Doc took Al up the steep ladder to the high flying bridge, and it made him dizzy to look down at the well deck. It also made him a bit dizzy to look at the two 20-millimeter antiaircraft guns mounted on either side of the flying bridge. And when they had descended and gone aft to the big gun tub with its sinister-looking 3-inch weapon, Al began to feel queasy. Was this a buoy tender or a goddam battleship? There were even depth-charge racks on the stern, and a curious-looking device on the quarter-deck that Doc called a Y-gun. "Shoots depth charges into the air two ways at once," Doc said with proprietary pride, and it was very obvious to anybody that this ship had not been designed for duty on the Great Lakes.

That night Al lay staring at the canvas bunk above him, in which slept a Negro mess steward, and wished he were somewhere else. The ship had too many crewmen, too many CPO's, and es-

pecially too damn many officers. They were bound to get underfoot. Only two cooks, he thought. Take a lot of pork chops to
feed a hundred guys.

And he thought with longing of Stella Wildoe for a while, and
then put her out of his mind. He would never see Milwaukee again
and she was out of his life now, permanently. Just as Jo Hill was
now out of his life for good, for all time. This was a new ship, and
Al was starting a clean slate. Let the dead past bury its dead lusts
and dreams. I'm a man without a history, Al thought.

On December 2, after the commissioning ceremonies, all hands
laid aft to the quarter-deck and the skipper addressed them. He
was a thin, grim-faced, hard-bitten man crowding fifty, and he bit
off his words like a man eating celery.

"Our home port will be Boston," he said. "That could mean we
will do a considerable amount of convoy work. It is also possible
that we might see some rough action before long. I do not antici-
pate an actual war with Germany, despite all the scare propa-
ganda, but the fact remains that we cannot honestly be called a
neutral nation. We are escorting convoys to England all the time,
and that is an open invitation to the German U-boats. So it may be
rugged out there, men, but we've got a rugged ship here—and I
intend to have a rugged crew."

There was more, a great deal more, but Al did not listen very
attentively. He was studying the seven officers, trying to see behind their carefully blank faces, trying to guess what sort of men
they were. The ensign who had given him a bad time when he
came aboard was Higgins, and Doc had labeled him as a real horse's
rectum, but Al had not run afoul of any of the others yet. So he
stared at the closed faces and registered only the more pertinent
passages of the long and somewhat redundant lecture. But when
the skipper strained for a laugh, Al heard it good. "It has come to
my attention," the C.O. said, "that some of you men are not too
happy with the accommodations aboard this vessel. It seems one of
our cooks is indignant because there are no private staterooms for
second-class petty officers." And Al thought with shock and embarrassment, That old bastard is talking about *me!*

There was a general murmur of careful laughter, and Al felt a
multitude of eyes on him, but he did not smile—he glowered at the
smirking face of Ensign Higgins, who must have spread the funny
word.

The skipper had enjoyed his little joke so much that now he decided to pursue it further, and he trained his grim, piercing stare on Al, prominent in the front rank in his cook whites, and Al was self-conscious, resenting being singled out, but unflinching.

"If I was misinformed, Woods, please correct me," the C.O. said.

"You weren't misinformed, sir," Al said tightly. "I just figured what the hell, if there were private cabins for ensigns . . ."

This time the laughter was full-throated, although not general among the officers, and Al stared brazenly at Ensign Higgins and decided the disdain in the ensign's eyes was somewhat nullified by the deeper brick red of his face. Al was further rewarded by a grin and a wink from the big, black-browed lieutenant beside Higgins, who was Bennett, the executive officer. And although he couldn't be certain, Al thought the skipper's thin trap of a mouth twitched a little before he went on with his get-acquainted speech.

There were always problems and strains in adjusting to a new ship, the skipper said. It took a while to settle into new patterns and routines, learning to co-operate and perform duties competently, et cetera, et cetera. A taut ship, he said, was invariably a good ship, and a good ship was generally a happy ship, but happy or not he had every intention of knitting his crew and officers into an efficient and rugged, taut organization, ready for any exigencies that came.

While the skipper talked grimly of taut ships and exigencies, it was December 2 all across the continent, including Milwaukee, Wis., and Norman, Okla., and Boston, Mass. There was bitter fighting in Libya. On the Rostov front Russian troops were pursuing Germans. Off the coast of Australia the German auxiliary cruiser *Kormoran* engaged and sank the Australian cruiser *Sydney* with her entire crew of 42 officers and 603 men, the badly damaged *Kormoran* later being abandoned by her crew. It was December, and who should know whether, in Milwaukee, a beautiful girl with an ugly nose wondered sadly why a virile, sympathetic cook came no more to the Oval Bar; who could say if a pretty, wistful-faced girl in Oklahoma City wondered why Alvin didn't answer her last letter? It was bleak, fateful December.

And the skipper, whose name was Thomas Fox and whose rank was lieutenant, senior grade, and who was not a regular Coast Guardsman but only a very competent ex-merchant mariner with a colorful past and a painful duodenal ulcer and a reserve officer status in the nation's oldest seagoing outfit, faced the difficult job of welding his human complement into a cohesive, adequate, functioning crew, of attempting to instill in them a feeling of pride and dedication to the service in general and the *Legume* in particular. And so he talked longer than was necessary or desirable, much longer than he would ever find it necessary to talk again. He was groping, searching, trying to find the magic words, and not sure, being a man of action and not a man of words, which were the magic ones. Therefore he used all the words he knew, it seemed, because it was only December 2 and his men, for the most part, wondered what the hell they were doing in the Coast Guard in the first place, and why they were assigned to this ship in the second, and why it was necessary to have all this long-winded crud about taut ships and efficiency. The skipper seemed unable to explain himself.

In the end it was all made brutally clear to the men, and to the skipper himself, in six simple and hideous words.

THE JAPS HAVE BOMBED PEARL HARBOR!

PART IV
The Hooligan Navy, Summer, 1942

✠✠

CHAPTER 19

The Recluse

AL WOODS awoke with a fragment of his mind while the rest of his brain continued to wallow in the suffocating stupor that he knew, on alternate mornings, as sleep. But suffocating or not it was sweet and insufficient, and he bitterly resented the way Quartermaster Jenkins was slapping and pawing familiarly about his person.

"Come on, Onionhead, hit the deck," Jenkins snarled.

Like thawing mud, a little more of Al's brain came awake and he realized he was bone-weary and stiff and sore—as if he'd only been asleep for a few minutes, when it had really been a good three hours. The worst thing about being a cook, aside from exceptional hazards like Lt. Higgins and deficient budgets, was the loused-up duty schedule. Yesterday it had been luxurious to sleep until noon, but it kept you from being able to sleep last night when you needed to.

"You awake, you balastridge?" Jenkins demanded belligerently.

"You know what you are?" Al mumbled. His eyelids were like inch-thick slabs of lead and his eyeballs felt as though somebody had used sandpaper on them, or maybe sautéed them for a while. His mouth was dry and his throat was parched and sore, and he thought woefully, Man, I got to get my sleeping program organized better, it's killing me. "What you are," he told Jenkins thickly, "is a horse turd unless you call me again in five minutes. Just five minutes, buddy."

Jenkins sighed. It was such a familiar routine. "I gotta go call a couple other bassids," he said. "Flake out till I come back."

Al returned to sleep immediately, but now the sleep was restless and disturbed and nervous, dreading the return of Jenkins. His subconscious kept sounding alarms and warnings, ringing bells, blowing whistles, sticking needles in him, so that his extra few minutes of stolen sleep only deceived and tormented him. When Jenkins came clattering down the steel ladder again, Al snapped wide-awake and crawled guiltily out of his bunk and stood teetering drunkenly between the bank of lockers and his alluring mattress. Ah sleep, O lovely sleep, O illegal prohibited sleep. Sack time is the best time of all.

"You alive?" Jenkins asked skeptically.

"I'm breathin'," Al said. "Do me a favor, shoot me."

"Not me, I hate ya too much," Jenkins said. "You the guy starvin' me to a dyin' skeleton of my former fat self."

Bitter reminder of the mess deficit. Was there anything good about morning? Morning is mourning, Al said to himself. My eyes are raw, my tonsils are sore again, there will be the customary hotcakes without eggs or bacon for breakfast, and I am a sick man. He yawned and rubbed his eyes and scratched his scalp and vigorously massaged the back of his neck, trying to bring life to his bloodstream. I ought to swap my tonsils for a few happy days in bed at the hospital, he thought. What am I saving them babies for? He shivered and yawned hugely again and stood there slack and without volition or purpose in the murky, stale, hot gloom of the berth deck, dilating his eyes.

"You look like Gypsy Rose Lee at the end of her ack," Jenkins said, waiting around to be sure Al didn't sneak back to bed. "You about the most entirely naked person I ever saw, boy. *Totally* nude."

Al scowled at him. "O.K., Milton. How's the war comin'?"

"Just dandy," Jenkins said. "The Germans is still winnin' all the marbles, far as I can tell. Them an' the Japs."

Al grunted and fumbled a pair of clean white pants out of his locker and got into them, adding clean socks and a clean skivvy shirt to his costume. Then he took out the same apron he'd worn for days. He had a system. Most cooks wiped their hands on their aprons and looked untidy and had to change aprons every watch, but he always lifted his apron and wiped on his pants. This kept the apron tidy and the apron concealed the condition of his pants, and he got a lot more mileage out of both. "You clean out the urn?" he asked dully, groping under the bunks for his shoes.

"What a nasty thing to ast a quartermaster. Hell no I didn't."

Al expected that answer. Aristocratic bastridges. "Afraid of a little manual labor?" he complained, and Jenkins said, "Cleanin' out urns ain't very manual, if you ast me. It's dirty degradin' toil."

Every other day at this hour Al felt persecuted and adopted a very jaundiced attitude toward everything. All over the ship men were sleeping, and even Jenkins and the other watch-standers who were now awake would soon be climbing into their sacks. But Al would be prowling the almost silent ship like a tired embalmer treading through a lonely morgue full of cadavers. This is the graveyard shift, he thought, and I am the sick and sexless sexton. "We'd have coffee sooner," he griped.

"Oh I don't mind waitin', rilly I don't, Onions."

Al felt he was quirting a dead horse, and dropped the subject. He sniffed the air delicately. "No wonder I wake up feelin' so lousy. Who is it turns off the ventilator, anyway? The air is so thick in here you could slice it with a dull knife." Jenkins said go ahead and slice up some for breakfast, it beat a steady diet of pancakes or French toast. Ignoring him, Al thought, Oh, man, I need some coffee! If I can't have sleep I got to have coffee.

"My theory is Higgins does it," Jenkins said thoughtfully, still not trusting Al to stay vertical. "Turns off the vennilater, I mean."

"Don't say that word before breakfast," Al complained, and he brooded about Higgins a while. After today only Higgins and the C.O. would be left of the original seven officers; today Lieutenant Theron Bennett, the exec, was leaving the *Legume*. For some time there had been hopeful speculation among the men that maybe the skipper, whose ulcer made him most difficult to love, would be transferred to a shore station near a drugstore well stocked with pills, in which happy event the logical choice to succeed him as skipper would be Bennett, who was big and bluff and hearty and assured and did not use his rank as a shield to hide behind. Bennett wasn't afraid to fraternize with the lowly enlisted people—somehow he seemed to sense that they, too, were human, and not really scheming to become grossly intimate with him if he showed them some occasional affability. But Higgins lived strictly by the stern doctrine that enlisted men were only awaiting a faint show of friendliness so that they could exploit it and undermine discipline; smile at an enlisted man and the next thing you know he would be familiarly slapping you on the back and calling you buddy. Anyway, today Bennett was being transferred elsewhere, and by a horrible process of elimination which made him second in seniority to the C.O., Higgins of the catchup-red, sneering face would become exec officer.

A lot of things had happened to Al in the seven months since he joined the ship in Toledo; for one, he'd developed a weary and cynical resignation which was covered succinctly by the phrase: That's the Coast Guard for you. Now he silently spoke the words in his mind as he got his towel and soap and toothbrush out of the locker. Before he remembered that it was not necessary, he also reached for his comb. Remembering, he sighed and closed the locker. For no good reason he remembered how, as a child in grade school, they had always begun the classroom day by singing, "Good morning to you, good morning to you, we're all in our places with sunshiny faces..." The things a guy's mind dredged up at five-thirty in the morning in July! He started up the ladder and behind him Jenkins sang softly, "Did ya ever see a corpse walkin', well I did." Al told him to go to hell, and stumbled on up to the main deck and turned left along the passageway toward the crew's head. The light hurt his eyes and he felt rebellious and irritable, and when he came abreast of the CPO head he stopped abruptly. Gilt lettering on the door read: Chief Petty Officers Only.

Every time he looked at that door he felt like checking in his certificate of citizenship. It irritated him almost beyond enduring that CPO's should have a private bathroom. There were only eight chiefs as compared to eighty-odd other enlisted men on the ship, including a dozen first-class ratings like Al who were only one thin pay grade lower than the chiefs, yet the CPO's had more deck space allotted them—including sleeping quarters, private mess compartment, and the goddam exclusive head—than all the others had. Al seethed inwardly. Was this America, or some feudal kingdom where oleaginous dukes stared haughtily down from their moated crappers upon the peasants scurrying about in urgent search of a little john space? Oh, those dainty fastidious princelings, Al thought sourly. I'll be guillotined if caught, but I am going to violate the sacred precincts of the royal can, boys.

He shoved the door open and went in, and he was disappointed. The fixtures were just fixtures—no monograms, no gold leaf or chrome inlays, no mother-of-pearl handles on the spigot, no champagne in the stools. And he learned to his vast dismay there was absolutely nothing thrillingly different about using the CPO's urinal. I tell you, he said to himself, I am melancholy and blue. I am disenchanted, boy. Why should I knock myself out trying to become a chief if they haven't got any better plumbing than us common folks?

He looked in the chiefs' mirror and winced. It was larger than the mirror up forward in the slum area and the lighting was better, but it wasn't magic. I still look gruesome, he thought, and as he stared at his reflection he felt the old familiar sadness, the quick touch of woe and horror. Good morning, cueball, he said to himself. Did anybody ever tell you that you look pretty goddam bizarre, kid? But you don't look quite as bad as you did, at that. You're leafing out a little.

The first time he had seen his shaven head reflected in a glass it had shaken him badly. That had been the middle of May, when he had begun in earnest to worry about losing his hair. His head itched too chronically and he'd been raking out too much dead timber with his comb, and he kept remembering with sinking heart the admonition of his father to take *care* of his hair. Haunted by the grisly specter of premature baldness, he had wondered how the hell you took care of your hair, and had gone to the only available medical authority at the time, one Doc O'Neal who had been a barber and who was widely informed.

"You say ya goin' bald?" Doc asked like a pitchman. "You say ya losin' ya lovely locks, friend? Tell ya what I'm gonna do."

What he did was persuade Al that his only hope was to shave his head, with an eloquent harangue that rose to hortatory heights. Doc related half a dozen allegedly similar cases wherein miraculous cures had been accomplished with a razor, and offered Al this sure-fire panacea for incipient baldness. "I calls it the nude noggin method," he said. "Fightin' fire with fire, like. It's ya scalp that's sick, not ya hair. You got to cure ya scurvy epidermis. This is what we refer to in the trade as a nonfollicle, or strictly cutaneous, situation."

"Nuts," Al scoffed. "How do I know it'd work, boy?"

"Lookit me," Doc offered. "Lookit my hair, Al pal." He had offensively thick, wavy, deeply roached hair; he didn't wear a white hat, he just hung it on the back of his head. "Would you believe I once had thin, undernourished, sickly hair? Why, people laughed when I took out my comb, them days. It was pitiful, Al. To be frank about the matter I was gonna kill myself. Then my old grandpappy, a veteran practitioner of the tonsorial art an' a gay horny old codger with more hair than a litter of collies, he saved my life by givin' me an ancient secret recipe that had been in the family for generations, an' rubbed this herb mixture into my scalp an' massaged her a few times an' . . . well, hell, look at me now, my worried Okie companion."

Al looked, half-convinced. "Do you *hafta* shave it?"

"Shaving," Doc said solemnly, "is obligatory. Also mandatory."

Better I should be bald on purpose for a while than helplessly bald permanently someday, Al rationalized. And twenty minutes later Doc rinsed his razor and studied Al for a moment and began to laugh up an attack of hysterics. "Look inna mirror, Frankenstein," he said, and when Al confronted his image he was shaken to the core, stunned and horrified. The ravished skull was slick and white and shiny and ghastly. But that was only the first time. Having gone so far, he allowed Doc to shave his skull twice more after that, the last time now only three weeks in the past. At first Doc had been conscientious about getting Al in the mess compartment at night—where there was always a ribald and appreciative audience—and rubbing the gooey secret family formula into his scalp. This herb preparation ran heavily to egg yolks and salad oil, with salt and pepper and paprika and mustard and catchup and nutmeg and, Al suspected, garlic powder, plus those several mysterious key ingredients from the dispensary. There had been times, midst the gales of laughter, when Al suspected that he was the goat of a gruesome and messy practical joke. But he *wanted* to believe and managed most of the time to believe that Doc was sincere about growing thick curly hair on what he called his "victory garden plot." Also, Al figured if he played along, the massages would do more good than harm, even if the magic formula was a fraud. Lately, however, Doc had tired of the game and insisted his part of the great master plan was finished. "Keep workin', Al, massage an' stimulate it good," he urged.

Except for half a dozen self-conscious excursions to the nearest beer joint or movie house, Al hadn't left the ship since the middle of May, being painfully bashful about his odd appearance. And he had acquired the habit of wearing a white hat at all times except when he went to bed. Now on a stuffy July morning with the ship tied up at the Chelsea depot, he glowered at himself in the forbidden CPO mirror. It grew back so slowly, goddammit. And everybody had taken to calling him Onionhead, partly because his head resembled an onion, but mostly because Doc had once

sneaked half an onion into the treatment routine. I am an object of
ridicule, Al told his reflection. I am scorned by my shipmates. But
I scorn right back at the bastridges.

Onionhead the poet, some called him, because during his volun-
tary incarceration aboard ship he had whiled away some of the
endless hours entering limerick contests, with no success. Lately
they had taken to calling him Onionhead the Malnutrition Expert.

With just cause, boy, he thought. But when he reflected upon
the screwed-up finances of the general mess, he felt baffled. He
couldn't figure out what the trouble was. They just kept going in
the hole a little more each month no matter how he and Curly
economized, and Higgins, who had unfortunately been commissary
officer from the beginning, kept jumping on Chief Ed Miller, the
commissary steward, and old Ed kept passing the word on to the
cooks.

Sighing, he began to massage his scalp. Hit her a few licks three
or four times a day, Doc had prescribed. So Al did, and leaned
close to the mirror to examine his skull. It was at that stage now
where the sharp ridges and cornices were blurred and softened by
the short fuzzy growth, but it was such a pale brown that he was
not yet able to say definitely whether it was thicker or not. It
never had been what you'd call thin, actually. He shrugged; wait
and see. At least it didn't itch like before—or fall in the chow.

The big concern was just to keep what he had until after he
got married, he thought. After a guy got married it didn't matter
if he did go bald. Hell, it was about halfway expected of him,
even. Take old Red Wildoe, for instance. The last time Al saw him,
Red's pink hair was noticeably thinner. And Stella, when he saw
her that time with Red, was noticeably thinner too, kind of worn
down. She had come to live in Boston, and she managed to let Al
know that her husband was gone much of the time, and had even
slipped Al her phone number. Which Al had been afraid to keep,
not trusting himself. His libido was living a pretty austere life
lately, but he didn't want to mess around with Stella any more.
Somehow there was something vastly different about cuckolding
Red when he was halfway across the country, and just sneaking
around to avoid Red in order to sleep with his wife. Besides, you
never knew when Red's ship was apt to come in. The old *Algomotoc*
was pretty erratic in her comings and goings.

Sometimes, plumbing his innermost mind, Al admitted to himself that one reason he'd stayed so close to the ship for nearly two months was a fear of bumping into Stella and getting involved again. And maybe one reason he'd had his head shaved three times was because there was nothing so calculated to keep a man out of the social whirl as a naked skull—and probably nothing so apt to cause a woman to resist his advances, if he *did* go ashore.

Anyway, Al's ideas had changed with old age. At twenty-two, it wasn't a series of casual conquests, or a dangerous affair with some married woman, he yearned for. He was ready to settle down. He was earning ninety-six plus sea pay, and he envied the guys who had wives waiting in Boston when the ship returned to home port. Except Wildoe, whose case was somehow the horrible exception. Al had a growing tendency to wish he were married; his life had a lonely present and a murky future, with no anchor, no family and home. Curly Matoli, now second class, was a married man, and Curly glowed with love and happiness, and moaned and groaned when the ship was away from Boston as much as a week. And happy as hell when the *Legume* blew for Chelsea Creek Bridge. Why should Curly be so happy? All he had was a pretty wife, love, a small apartment in Chelsea, and sex whenever he came home from the sea.

The ship was all the home, all the woman, Al Woods had.

A man, he philosophized as he brushed his teeth, is incomplete without a woman, only half of whatever he's supposed to be. The right woman, she's the other half, the better half, like they say. Together they are the complete works, a functioning unit. Right now I'm only hitting on half my cylinders, but somewhere there's a girl, the girl, *my* girl. In Boston, maybe. A hostess at the Buddies Club, or working in a bar or restaurant or office, selling tickets in a movie, going to school; maybe she walks down Tremont every day, or Boylston, or across Copley Square or Haymarket. She might even be the daughter of a Boston College or Harvard professor, God forbid. She may live way out in Newton or Brookline. The only thing I'm pretty sure about is that I won't find her in Scollay Square—unless she turns out to be a female cop or social worker, or lost. But someday I'll bump into her. I'm a fatalist, I know it's gonna happen. I'll be walking along looking at all the faces of the crowd and suddenly I'll see her and know it's her, and she'll look at me kind of stunned, and then she'll smile, and that'll be how it starts.

He even knew what she would look like, vaguely. Vaguely she would look an awful lot like an Oklahoma girl named Josephine Hill.

Al Woods was still half-asleep. He was still dreaming...

He was in the mess deck cleaning the coffee urn when Lieutenant Bennett came up the starboard passageway from the wardroom, carrying his heavy load of luggage and looking gloomy. "Mornin,' sir," Al said. "You're getting an early start, it looks like."

"Morning, Woods," Bennett gruffed. "Couldn't sleep. All set to shove off so I thought I'd do it before everybody got up. But I must admit I hoped you'd have some coffee made."

"You came to the right place," Al said eagerly. "I boiled some in the galley, it's just camp coffee but it's hot."

Bennett sighed with relief and lit a cigarette. "Woods, you saved my life," he said in his deep voice. "Join me, won't you?"

Al got two mugs from the scullery and filled them with the hot black coffee and sat across from the lieutenant at a table. "Sir," he said, "all us peasants sure hate to see you go."

Bennett raised his thick black eyebrows. "You mean you hate to see Higgins become exec, isn't that more accurate, Woods?"

Al grinned. "Both. If somebody hasta go, why not him?"

"I wish it *was* Dennis Higgins getting this command I'm stuck with," the big lieutenant said wryly. "I never was anxious for command, and now I've drawn the prize pickle, the hard-luck ship of the fleet. She's in dry dock for repairs at the moment, and guess what happened—she dropped a depth charge and blew off part of her own stern. Then the day they went into dry dock the skipper got roaring drunk, poor fellow, and walked into a truck outside the shipyard gates—the lucky stiff. Banged him up, so they need another fall guy. Personally, I think they ought to just junk the rusty old beast."

"What kind of ship is it, sir?" Al wondered. "A cutter?"

"Let's not dignify her with the title ship," Bennett said. "They call her *Snafu*, but she was commissioned as the *Algomotoc*."

"Why, hell, sir," Al exclaimed, "I got buddies on that tub."

Bennett gave him a rueful smile. "Pray for them, Woods."

"I know both the cooks," Al said. "Wildoe an' Berger. And a yeoman, Blanket-ass Christy. Lessee... Pelliteri, a bosun's mate by now, probably. And Gutsell, Brown, and Horse Flanders, and

Salter, a snagtooth quartermaster. Brownie, he's a water tender. Guts an' Flanders..."

"Water tender," Bennett sighed. "An obsolete rate in this age of Diesels, but naturally my first command would be an old steam-turbine baby. It's a great honor to be chosen to command a ship, I suppose, but I can't help wishing you'd put some arsenic in this coffee."

Al couldn't tell half the time whether Bennett was kidding or not. His usual expression was somber and his heavy-jowled face could seem very gloomy even when he was telling a joke. He had a subtle, deadpan sense of humor. Right now, Al figured, the lieutenant might be pretty much in earnest, because bossing a ship was a big responsibility. But if Bennett felt low, it could also be on account of *not* graduating to C.O. of the *Legume*. You couldn't tell about Bennett.

"Well, considerin' the screwed-up condition of the general mess, and the fact Higgins is gonna be exec," Al said, "I kinda wish I was going to the old *Motock* with you, sir."

"Come now, lad, things aren't quite that desperate here yet," Bennett chided. And added, "You haven't figured out the root of your mess problems yet, I take it?" He said it rather ambiguously, and Al looked at him quizzically and said no, it baffled hell out of him, and got up the nerve to say, "Do *you* know, Lieutenant?"

Bennett looked at his coffee, frowning. "Let's just say I've wondered about certain matters, Woods. Off the record, I suspect the general mess difficulties originate *outside* the general mess, if that's not too elaborately devious." He stood up. "So long, Woods. If it helps any, I might remark I have nothing edible in my luggage as I wend my way toward probably professional embarrassment as a C.O."

With a puckered brow, Al said, "I don't get it, sir."

"Woods, a certain fraternity obligation, despite a hearty distaste for some of my brethren, prevents me from speaking more lucidly," Bennett said ruefully. "Well ... wish me luck, and I'll reciprocate."

"I do wish you luck," Al said earnestly. "All the luck in the world, Lieutenant." And Bennett shook hands, grinning stiffly, and went off to take command of the hapless ex-Lake Michigan cutter.

There goes one of the good guys, Al thought, and he finished making coffee in the urn—for the leisure class, the people who could slumber on when better men like cooks and worried new C.O.'s were long since awake and active. One of the *few* good guys, Al added silently.

After nearly twenty-one months in the Coast Guard, he was pretty sick of it. The war which had started with such terrible sickening suddenness, with such a shivery promise of violent adventure, had now become dull and stale and seemingly endless to Alvin Woods. The *Legume* was like a man whose job it was to lime the yard stripes on a football field, but who stayed home on Saturdays and missed the excitement. The ship's job was to service and maintain aids to navigation so that other ships could get safely out into deep water where there was no safety; her job was to mark off the shipping routes for the merchant vessels that were hunted mercilessly by Axis U-boats. It seemed to Al that the *Legume* loitered on the outskirts of the war, avoiding the business section. It seemed to him this ship and her men were neutral, that the Coast Guard held a kind of noncombatant status in the war. And he knew a growing, gnawing dissatisfaction because he was here instead of where the shooting was, a Coast Guard cook instead of a buck private, or a Marine corporal, or even a Navy man.

The trouble was, nothing ever *happened* for the *Legume*, at least insofar as the headlined WAR was concerned. The periscopes of U-boats that brought her men racing topside to battle stations, all nervous and white-lipped, inevitably turned out to be only sticks floating in the ocean, or some bit of debris that resembled almost anything under the sun but a periscope. And two-thirds of the alarms turned out to be the skipper's idea of keeping his crew alert and well trained—or maybe it soothed his ego to push a button and watch ninety-odd men explode into a scrambling, wild-eyed frenzy.

"False alarm," the men would say. "Old man's ulcer actin' up."

"Nobody's mad at *us*," they said. "*We* never done nothin'."

That was the *Legume's* war, to date—nervously spontaneous false alarms and calculated false alarms. To be sure, there were U-boats in the vague general vicinity of the Bay of Boston, but no buoy tender ever caught a glimpse of any hostile craft. When the ship ran at night alone in a wilderness of black tossing seas, you slept less well than when she was in port, of course; and when the radio picked up warnings that a U-boat was believed to be operating in your neighborhood and the night was clear, you felt a sharp, insistent chill possessing your mind, and maybe your pulse accelerated. And there were sunny calm days outside when you were touched by the brief horror of floating wreckage and oily debris and shattered flotsam that might or might not have been fashioned by the warhead of a German-made torpedo; and once there had been an empty lifeboat half-awash. But the war was always over the horizon, the war was something you read about in the Boston papers, or heard about on the radio, but never expected to get within sight or sound of, otherwise. Because you were in the Coast Guard and the Coast Guard limed the yard stripes and lit the lamps and marked off the bases and defined the limits of the playing fields, but the Coast Guard was not athletically inclined or even a spectator, and took no part in the schedule of active competition.

Oh, there were exceptions—the escort cutters that made the deadly convoy runs in the North Atlantic, going as far as Murmansk, and the transports and landing vessels that put soldiers and marines ashore on enemy soil—but Al was talking about this *other* Coast Guard, this coast-bound branch of the Coast Guard, that branch of the family represented by the *Legume. That* Coast Guard was neutral, boy.

Sometimes at night during his self-imposed imprisonment aboard the ship he would uncase his typewriter and sit in a corner with the Smith-Corona on the table before him and try to write about the way *he* felt about the whole tawdry business of being a member of the human race in 1942. He believed, as all men do, that the way he felt was pretty important and probably unique in its clarity and pain, and should be recorded for posterity, should be put in a time capsule to be opened in a thousand years, so that the people of that future time might *know*, might understand at bewildered last exactly what it had been like to be a living person in 1942. And he would sit in the din of the mess deck surrounded by card games and noisy arguments, his mind and nerves assaulted by the blatant radio squawk box on the bulkhead, and he would brood over the keys, staring hopefully and angrily at the letters, willing the machine to unlock his brain and help him reveal the hard and lonely truths, the naked wisdom that dwelt so mutely in him and which was undoubtedly of such great value to mankind. He longed to write an ironic story about a cook on a ship who never smelled the acrid smoke of war or sweated the ice water of fear or felt nausea evoked by the sight of gore and torn pulpy flesh, so that all the literate

4-F's could stop feeling sorry for themselves and go happily about their business of making two hundred dollars a week. He yearned to write a satiric treatise on the military caste system, or an epic poem about the wild love of war that betrayed modern men because modern warfare was no longer glorious but only a question of who could afford to lose the most women and children and factories; he yearned to write a tender love story. Goddammit, he just wanted to *write* something. Was that asking too much? Was that unreasonable?

So once he typed: "Dear Jo—Well, a lot of water has gone under the ships, and vice versa, since I heard from you. I guess by now you are a married woman..." He tore it savagely into confetti. What brought *her* into the conversation, anyhow?

And once he wrote: "Hi, Pop—Just thought I'd drop you a few lines to say I'm O.K. and nobody is shooting at me, but if the food situation doesn't get better before it gets much worse they are liable to start doing it any day now." And that was as far as his imagination carried him. Oh, that's a brilliant piece of literature, he thought disgustedly. That's singing prose if I ever saw any. He did not know why he should feel so inhibited about writing a simple letter to his father, but it was very difficult, too difficult, and he never got it finished. And he never wrote anything else that deserved to be put in a time capsule. And there was nobody he could write letters to. So in time he acknowledged that he did not really mean to use the typewriter as a typewriter at all, but only as a guard against the brassy intrusions of his shipmates. While he sat frowning before the machine they *assumed* he was writing something, or was getting *ready* to write something, and they did not trespass on his little island of privacy in the ocean of dissonance and rude intrusive talk. He thought about a million things and killed many hard-to-kill hours with his pretense of being on the verge of writing something. But time died with agonizing slowness and he was forever bored and lonely and restless and dissatisfied in the midst of his only kinsmen, waiting for his hair to grow back so he could leave his floating Elba and go again among the land dwellers.

But finally and ultimately and inevitably the hard core of his discontent had to do with the fact that the general mess was operating in the red, and he didn't know what to do about it, or understand why it was. And in July after Lieutenant Theron

Bennett departed to become skipper of the *Algomotoc*, Al slew
legions of stubbornly, crawlingly tedious minutes trying to de-
cipher the meaning in Bennett's baffling farewell remarks. Surely he
hadn't meant the officers were somehow sacking the general mess.
Anybody knew that officers were gentlemen. They automatically
became gentlemen when they became officers.

It beats the hell out of ignorant old me, Al said to himself.

On July 7, Lieutenant Dennis Higgins became executive officer
of the Coast Guard cutter *Legume* (as well as mess officer)—and
in fact the war was going badly for the Allies everywhere. On the
eighth and ninth nothing much was heard from either Higgins or the
Axis powers, but on July 10 the Germans gloatingly announced
that the remnants of a large Arctic convoy had been attacked again
by submarines and aircraft, and the last three hapless merchant
ships were sunk. The same day, Higgins issued a summons for the
cooks and chief steward to lay aft to his stateroom for a panel discussion of the loused-up general mess situation.

The ship had left Boston with a cargo of large red buoys and
was outside the nets, making for Cape Cod and Buzzard's Bay, when
Curly Matoli awakened Al from sound sleep at nine hundred hours
and, ignoring the profanity, reported that old Ed wanted them both
in the galley right away. So Al climbed numbly out of his sack
and dressed and went to the head and then to the galley. "What's
all the panic?" he demanded irascibly, sipping some coffee straight.
"Where the hell is old Ed? What's the score? What's the latitude
and longitude, anyhow?"

"Search me," Curly said, pouring tomato puree over a panful of
mackerel fillets. A short slender handsome boy of twenty with an
olive complexion, curly black hair, liquid brown eyes, and a
definite flair for Mediterranean cuisine, Curly was from New Jersey
and a trifle cocky at times, and before enlisting had served as an
apprentice chef in an uncle's restaurant. He spoke Italian, though
not fluently, and was neat and energetic, and his brash grin covered
a sentimental Latin nature. Al liked him, and envied him his hair
and his lovely wife, whose picture Curly carried next to his navel,
in a billfold tucked into his waistband. "Search me, podner," Curly
said, and Chief Miller loomed large in the galley door and stared
at his cooks with an impassive, deadpan, sleepy expression. "Gentlemen, is this the kitchen?" he asked solemnly in his hoarse, rumbling

voice. Al said hell yes this was the goddam kitchen. "I take it you're the chef," Miller said.

"I have that crummy distinction," Al said, beginning to grin in spite of himself. Miller was an enormously rotund man in his early forties who carried himself with massive dignity and habitually wore a mask of poker-faced inscrutability, like an image of Buddha.

"And this other gentleman?" the CPO inquired gravely.

"My assistant," Al said. "Killer Matoli, the salad boy."

The chief nodded politely. "Dennis sent me," he said quietly.

"Wot's at bastridge want?" Curly demanded. "I'm busy cookin'."

"Maybe he wants to commend you on your outstanding contributions to the gastric acidity currently filtering through the ranks," Miller rumbled confidingly. "I'm to receive a plaque, too, I believe."

So they followed the trundling bulk of the chief commissary steward through the mess deck and along the starboard passageway aft past the CPO messroom and the ship's office to Higgins's stateroom, where Miller rapped lightly once and pushed the door open. They went in after him and stood there nervous and uneasy, flanking the fat, imperturbable CPO. Miller betrayed no sign of dreading the interview. Nothing ever ruffled his bland dignity. He'd been around a long time.

Lieutenant Higgins was sitting at his desk with his back to them. He did not acknowledge their presence, continuing to sit with his elbows on his desk, exercising his prerogative as a superior being by letting them chafe at the bit a while. In the months since the ship was commissioned, Higgins had put on a good deal of improperly distributed weight and his complexion had grown more florid, and his pale eyes more cold and supercilious. After a time Al had deduced, rightly, that Higgins's normal relaxed expression was a sneer and his usual tone of voice sarcastic. At the moment the new exec was ostentatiously chewing on an unlighted pipe and pretending to concentrate intently on a scatter of papers on his desk, but Al guessed that he was merely greasing his ego by rudely showing them who was the big cheese around there; he wanted to insult his visitors thoroughly and place them at a psychological disadvantage before he started chewing asses.

At long last, Higgins swung around slowly in his swivel chair, removed his pipe, put his highly polished half-Wellington boots on the monogrammed counterpane of his bunk, folded his short fat arms across his fat chest, and favored the commissary crew with his best sneer. "At ease," he said sarcastically, for nobody had been at attention. "Woods, I won't object if you wish to remove your hat as per custom."

Shrugging, Al reluctantly bared his denuded skull, and the exec's sourly amused scrutiny made him resentfully self-conscious. And abruptly Higgins snapped, "What's the matter with you people, anyhow?"

Matoli's expressive eyes went inky and wary, but Miller just gazed calmly at a pin-up girl calendar above Higgins's desk. So it was Al who answered, as it should have been. He muttered, "I didn't know there *was* anything the matter with us."

Higgins pointed his pipe stem at Al like a pistol. "Before we proceed further, let's get something squared away, Woods. Heretofore, you people have gotten away with disrespect and sloppy, undisciplined behavior. Let me say to you, those days are gone forever. Henceforth you will display a proper respect for your superiors. And when you have occasion to speak to *me*, you had damned well better say sir."

You sonofabitch, Al thought bitterly.

"Now, Woods, what is the per diem mess allowance here?"

"Eighty-some cents a day," Al said. "I'm not sure, sir."

"Eighty-SIX!" Higgins snapped, and Al thought wearily, O.K., don't get your bowels in an uproar, Dennis. "I would *think*," Higgins said, "that any competent, reasonably intelligent cook would be able to feed a man for eighty-six cents per diem, wouldn't you, Woods?"

Al sighed. You could feed say ninety men with eighty-six cents a day per man, but not one man for any goddam eighty-six cents a day—only he wasn't going to try to explain the difference to this jerk. He nodded curtly, not wanting to say sir, and Higgins pounced.

"Then why in the hell aren't you *doing* it, Woods?"

Al shrugged sullenly. He didn't know the answer to that one.

Higgins slapped the papers on his desk. "We've been getting reprimands from the district commissary officer and I don't like it one little bit, let me assure you people."

That's real tragic, Al thought sarcastically.

"Woods, you *are* aware that the general mess has a deficit?" Higgins asked insultingly, and Al nodded, refusing to speak, and the exec bawled, "You've been operating at a loss for several months now, going deeper and deeper into the red ink department every month in spite of repeated warnings and plain orders to remedy the situation."

Rave on, you sonofabitch! Al snarled in his mind.

"It must be incompetence," Higgins surmised. "Or, now, could it be sheer stupidity?" He stared at Al and Curly with a kind of malevolent solicitude. "Perhaps we expect too much of you cooks, that's a tough job you have—working every other day, getting every night liberty, sleeping until noon half of the time." He played with his pipe, letting this irony soak in, and then he shrugged, "Maybe it hasn't been altogether your fault—this has been a lax ship, where gross irregularities have been condoned and overlooked. No doubt you people felt you could safely ignore the warnings to economize, heretofore. But this is a new regime." He pointed the pipe at each of them like a pistol—bang, bang, bang, you're dead, you people— and said ominously, "You have my solemn word that from now on the holiday is over, the joy ride is ended. While I am executive officer of this vessel we are going to have an efficient ship, a *taut* ship."

Oh, you're a real big man, Higgins, Al thought disgustedly.

"This is good duty," Higgins stated. (He should know, Al thought sourly—he never served on any other ship.) "This duty beats convoy duty, or transport duty, or weathership or lightship duty," Higgins informed them with vast assurance. "This is a soft berth, and maybe that's the trouble. You don't know how lucky you are." (Oh, heavens to mercy, yes, we're the luckiest people in the world, Al jeered mutely.) "Maybe you need a taste of more rugged duty in order to appreciate this vessel," Higgins said grimly, "and I promise you, if you people don't get squared away, you'll have a chance to *try* some rugged duty."

This was the sort of thing that enraged and frustrated Al most— you had to just stand there meek and silent, swallowing your pride like broken glass, while some stupid sonofabitch that never was anybody until he got inside a uniform sat comfortably in his leather-padded chair playing the role of some minor deity. Al happened to know from yeoman gossip that in civilian life Higgins had been coproprietor of a small filling station in a one-horse town. Now he was a commissioned officer, bloated with gassy self-esteem. Drunk on authority, boy.

At this point Higgins foolishly transferred his attention to the chief, as if the CPO's detachment and owlish inattention had got under his skin. "Miller, you're supposed to be the head of the department," Higgins barked. "What have you to say for yourself?"

Without taking his bug-eyed stare from the nude on the calendar, Miller rumbled, "I understood you would deliver the sermon, Dennis."

"Watch yourself!" Higgins hissed. "Let's have no insolence!"

"You call that insolence?" Miller said deprecatingly.

"It's skating around the edge of insolence at any rate, Miller."

"Man might get transferred to shore duty for insolence," the chief murmured, and Higgins bawled, "Transferred your ass!" Forgetting, Al presumed, that he was a gentleman nowadays, by act of Congress. "This is wartime, Miller, and in case you're not familiar with the Articles of War, let me inform you that by God you could get a court-martial for insolence to a superior officer!" Higgins said furiously.

Chief Ed Miller moved his huge head slightly and favored the new exec with his impassive stare, and then he rumbled with quiet laughter and returned his avid attention to the aphrodisiac calendar, and after a moment of awful silence old Ed added a kind of absent-minded postscript to the devastating laughter—he pursed his lips and gave an impressive imitation of a horse breaking wind.

Higgins sprang out of his chair, breathing wheezily, the hot catchup-red color draining out of his face and leaving it blotchy and ugly. "Why you!" he said incredulously. "Why, I'll . . . why . . . Miller!" He seemed to strangle for a second, and then he pointed a spastic finger at the door and whispered hoarsely, "Get out of my cabin, Miller!"

With fat, unhurried dignity Miller went to the door and opened it and lumbered through, and turned before closing the door to rumble gently, "Temper, temper, Dennis." Then he was gone.

Al was afraid he was going to laugh, and saw that Curly had his eyes tight shut and his lips trembled like a man in the grip of a strong and painful emotion. For chrissakes don't laugh! Al thought. We got enough trouble with this jerk already. But nobody laughed.

Higgins had turned to his desk and was idiotically pretending to examine the papers with great interest, with fascination, pushing them around with the stem of his pipe as if looking for a particular item that would cover this situation. He reached for his humidor and slowly filled and tamped his pipe, making an interminable thing of it as the two cooks waited rigid and in torment; he lit the pipe slowly and with great concentration, making certain that it glowed evenly, like his face. And then at last he turned and perched on the corner of his desk and began to swing his foot in an attempt to seem casual and unruffled, but he kept his glance on the deck, puffing up a cloud of smoke and squinting, with his low forehead wrinkled and puckered with feigned concentration. Presently he sighed and shook his head as if with regret, and slid a wry sneer past the waiting eyewitnesses.

"That pitiful wreck of a man," he said. "For some time now I have known, of course, that Miller is unbalanced. Stir crazy. He is an example of what is wrong with most military outfits. Except in times of war, military life appeals only to misfits and outcasts and rummy idiots like Miller. He is as useless as tits on a boar hog. Either of you men, in the short time you have been cooks, could take over his duties and give a better account of yourselves than Miller ever did."

He's trying to line us up on his side against the chief, Al realized. And thought ironically, I do most of Ed's work anyhow. But he isn't nuts, he just doesn't scare worth a hoot, Dennis. If we got to have a psycho, I'll vote for you, baby, and you alone.

"I was tempted," Higgins said ruefully, "to deck him with a fast right, but I restrained myself. We don't do it that way in the Coast Guard. It would have proved nothing—although I confess I would have enjoyed it, by God. An officer has to be tough in a different way, in a nonphysical way. Tough-minded. But also fair and impartial. I'm glad that I did not fracture his jaw, for it would have made me doubt that I am a big enough man for the job I must do on this vessel. It takes a special brand of guts to accept a filthy insult without throwing a punch. Self-control is the hallmark of intestinal fortitude, as somebody once wrote. Poor old Miller, he needs to be in an institution for those whose brain cells have been rotted by alcohol."

Turn it over and let's hear the other side, Al thought wearily.

Higgins lifted a boot onto his chair and leaned over to check the high polish of the leather, and shook his head ruefully. "I was sorely tempted," he said. "But old Ed knew I wouldn't hit him. A lot of those old twenty-year rum-dums seem to think they have nothing to fear from reserve officers, and that's where they're mighty misinformed. An officer is an officer, period. And an enlisted man is an enlisted man, period. Well, one thing is certain, Miller must go. He's had it, in my book." He lifted his bulldog face and glanced swiftly from Al to Curly. "If I should decide to press charges, you are witnesses."

Haw, haw, haw, Al said to himself. Some witnesses, boy.

"Well," Higgins said, puffing up a thick cloud of smoke, "that's something else again. Now, Bennett was a good friend of mine and always will be, but let's face it," he shook his head sadly, "he was too easygoing, he wanted people to like him. Now personally I don't give a damn whether people like me or not, just so long as I know I am in the right. I intend to do my duty. If that incurs dislike, then I say the hell with it, there is a war going on and we are not here to win friends and influence people." He punched a hole in the cloud of smoke with his pipe and peered through at his audience, talking through the aperture. "Now hear this, men, and note it well. From this day forward waste, extravagance, and sloppy inefficiency will not be tolerated on this ship. I want to *emphasize* that point."

Tie up the loose ends and let's go home, Higgins, Al thought. Bastard. B as in bacon, A as in artichoke, S as in salami...

"Laxity and malingering will not be tolerated either, men."

How about ex-laxity? Al thought.

"This can be a good ship or a lousy ship, it's entirely up to you petty officers, you're expected to set the example for the rest of the men by your deportment," Higgins said rather hurriedly, as if he too were aware that the thing was beginning to drag anchor. "Now you men are cooks, your job is to cook, but never forget you are P.O.'s and the unrated men are watching you for their cues. If you have any gripes, come to me about them, don't go around crying to the other enlisted men. If you don't like the cut of my jib, speak up man to man, that's how I feel about it." (Oh, Dennis, you are really screwed down tight today, Al thought. And in closing?) And Higgins said, "Now I have said all this because I want my position clearly amplified, which brings us to one final point. I do not intend to repeat this little dramatic skit again. Because if you men can't discharge your duties efficiently, we'll just have to get some cooks on here who can. So use your heads, men, cut corners, eliminate waste, *whip* this thing. Bow your necks and lean into it." He glanced at his wrist watch and frowned. "By the way, I don't imagine Miller will be with us long—and when he goes..." he gave them a significant glance "... well, I see no reason why we should bring in an outsider to head up the department, no reason why you men shouldn't step up a rung—*contingent*, of course, on whipping this deficit, and . . ." he puffed his pipe a moment ". . . on your conduct, your attitudes, I might even say your loyalty." (Loyalty, hell! Al thought. He means our discretion, our silence. Don't spread it all over the ship how old Ed pulled the rug out from under him.) "That's all, men, dismissed," Higgins said, turning back to his desk.

Outside in the passageway Curly sighed with relief and said, "Wot did he say, Al?"

Al said, "Aw, old Dennis was just chippin' his fangs."

But Curly shook his head with mock worry. "I dunno, I got a hunch that bastringe was tryin'a say somethin'. I think he was *hintin'* at us, Al."

Al grinned. "I wasn't listenin', I was looking at his calendar." Then the pent-up anger hit him and he swore. "We're runnin' the galley like a goddam bread line already, how we gonna economize any *more?*"

"Tell you the truth, I'm worried," Curly said glumly. "You're talkin' to a guy that don't want no transfer, an' he said it plain enough. We climb outa the mess hole or we're for shippin', 'at's all."

"We're not for shippin'," Al said. "That would be too easy on us, podner. He just wants to keep us downtrodden. We're doomed to stay on this vessel twenty years, with ole Dennis chewin' our ass every day. He's got to chew somebody to show he's a real genuine officer, see. I don't know, it wouldn't be such a tragic thing to get transferred."

"You're not married," Curly pointed out. "That's different."

Different from what? Al thought. I wish I knew some answers.

CHAPTER 20

Slice It Thin, Boys

TELLING Curly not to worry was one thing, but following his own advice was quite another, Al discovered. All afternoon he kept getting a peculiar feeling of frustration about the chow situation. I'm innocent, you hear me! he said to himself wryly. I didn't do it. I don't even know what was done. I'm just a cook, I ain't supposed to trouble my pretty head about making the monthly payments, boy. That happens to be Edwin Miller's department, not mine.

So after supper he tracked down Chief Miller, who was resting in his bunk, smoking a cigar and gravely studying a movie magazine.

"You still here?" Al asked, pretending surprise.

Old Ed winked broadly. "My days are numbered, chef," he rumbled. "I put in for another transfer today. This one might get autographed."

Chief Miller had been in the Coast Guard for nearly twenty-one years, and was almost a year past the date of his anticipated retirement; now he considered himself a sort of civilian hostage, being unjustly and probably illegally detained by the Coast Guard. About once a week, to express his sentiments, he would go back to the office and have Sam Goff type him up a request for an immediate discharge, or transfer to shore duty. "Preferably near a saloon," he would say. But the skipper was not in sympathy with his plight, and refused to endorse any of the frequent requests. Unperturbed, the chief steward made it clear his internment was not going to interfere in any way with his leisure or comfort, and he refused to take his job seriously. About all he ever did was play cards in the CPO's messroom with off-duty but still-functioning chiefs, and drink beer (which he kept in the CPO's refrigerator under lock and key) or coffee laced with rum, and smoke cigars, and look at the girlie pictures in magazines, and talk about the cat house he claimed he intended to run when he got out of the Coast Guard. Sometimes he went around all day dressed in a sleazy maroon silk bathrobe, candy-striped pajamas, and bright green leather bedroom slippers. What it all amounted to was that Ed Miller had become a chief emeritus. Thwarted in his plans to retire to civilian life on a pension, he had retired anyhow, right on the *Legume*, on full pay plus longevity pay plus sea-duty pay. Back in the winter he had turned over most of the commissary department responsibilities to Al—all except the buying, inventorying, and paper work, most of which was done by the mess cooks and a storekeeper. He was a man of vast leisure.

"Edwin," Al said to him, "what's the score around here?"

"All tied up in the ninth inning, chef," Miller said gravely.

"You know what I'm talkin' about," Al said impatiently. "How come we keep goin' in the hole, Ed? I don't figure the deal."

"No sweat, chef," Miller said, waving a fat hand deprecatingly. "Dennis had some old leftover spleen he had to vent on someone, and we caught it. Don't mean a thing. Forget it. Live and let live, chef."

"In the CCC," Al said, "the mess sergeants used to sometimes get a nice kickback from the grocer. How you fixed for money, Ed?"

"I'm a poor man, chef," old Ed rumbled. "We deal with the Navy. Now if we bought from civilians, you and me could both get rich, but we don't and we can't." He held up the magazine and pointed a fat finger at a movie starlet in a revealingly skintight bathing suit. She had long black hair and wicked eyes, like Stella Wildoe. "That's the kind of debutante I plan to staff my whore house with," old Ed said solemnly.

"I'll buy a season ticket," Al told him. I got to go see Stella, he thought, feeling the old ache of desire. I got to have me a woman pretty soon now or check in my glands. "When I grow up," he told the chief, "I want to be test pilot for a white slave ring."

"A commendable goal in life," Miller rumbled approvingly.

"At the moment, though, I'm stuck with being a sensitive cook," Al said. "I'm puttin' you back in charge of the galley, Ed. Making decisions is drivin' me nuts. So just tell me what to do, that's all."

Old Ed stared at him with mock stupefaction for a moment and said owlishly, "Slice her thin, chef, slice her thin." That was about the only order he'd given the cooks in months, and it was a running joke. A long time past he stopped by the galley one day when both cooks were there and, after giving them his heavy-lidded, impassive scrutiny, he'd said, "Remember what the dying commissary steward said—slice it thin, boys, slice it thin." Now, under the circumstances, it seemed to be pretty pertinent advice, if not an order.

Al sighed. "Seriously, Ed. Don't kid about it. I'm worried."

"These mess deficits happen in the best-regulated vessels, as the saying goes, chef. Just ignore it and it'll go away. If it don't, nothing will happen—maybe. Rise above it, like I'm doing."

"Thanks," Al snarled. "You make me feel a lot better, Chief."

"I'm not through yet, chef," old Ed rumbled. "Go up the street and shack up with someone, preferably a woman. Get drunk. Raise hell. That is my advice to you, young man. You may go now."

I envy that comical old basso, Al thought as he went back to the galley. He ain't got a thing to worry about and nothing to worry with.

There were no U-boats in Buzzard's Bay, or buzzards either, as far as Al could see. "A buzzard would starve hisself to death follerin' this here poor hungerin' vessel," one of the dieting seamen said. "Unless we might thurow it one of them dadburn cooks." There was griping in Woods Hole, in Falmouth. And Al flinched when he heard it. Being a man who had a high regard for food himself, it hurt him to stint on the chow. He felt guilty about it. "You want your pancakes without bacon, or without sausage?" he would ask, but it was no joking matter. The situation preyed on his mind. He made a point of eating exactly what the men ate, although one of the traditional rewards of being a cook was free access to the larder, and he felt like griping himself.

Yeoman Sam Goff, a stocky, burr-headed man with glasses, came into the galley scowling ferociously and snarled in a fair imitation of Higgins, "You people are all washed up here. Pack your goddam sea bags an' check in your can openers an' get the hell offa this ship."

And Doc O'Neal came into the galley and said, "I'm orderin' a ton of vitamin pills. As head physician of this yacht I am worried about the health of the crew an' passengers. They ain't gettin' enough sunshine, fresh air, or food. We got an epidemic of undernourishment."

"I'm gettin' anemic right along with you other guys," Al said.

"Fix me a French-fried potato," Sam yearned, "with a side order of T-bone steaks and some pork chops for dessert."

"O.K., wise guy," Al growled. "You're the brains of this luxury liner, so tell me what the trouble is with the general mess budget."

"I figure you an' Gunner Matoli must be operatin' a black market up the street," Sam said darkly.

"Assuming we ain't," Al said. "What then, Sherlock?"

"Somebody got his hand in the cash register," Doc volunteered.

"If I was the head cook," Sam muttered in a sinister tone, "I'd try to locate the trouble before they found my nude body floatin' on the mornin' tide, that's all I got to say."

"I am innocent, boys, I just take orders from above," Al sighed. "A new cook wouldn't solve the dilemma. And it ain't the quality of the food that's lousy, it's the quantity and lack of variety."

"They still eat pretty good in the wardroom, huh?" Sam asked.

Al shrugged. "They don't have a deficit back there."

Sam said with considerable emphasis, "I'll *bet* they don't!"

They started home from Buzzard's Bay on Friday the seventeenth, while Al was asleep and dreaming a weird, elusive dream about Jo Hill. The rhythmic vibration of the ship's engines, transmitted through the bunk stanchions to Al's sensitive nervous system, ceased abruptly some time before noon, and the ship began to rock and roll a little, and he awoke from his erotic fantasy and guessed they had arrived outside the submarine nets guarding Boston Harbor. He tried to go back to sleep and finish the dream about Jo, but he couldn't, and so he got up and dressed and washed and went topside to the flying bridge, feeling sad and lonely and repressed, wishing he had a woman to come home to as about two dozen of his shipmates had. I oughta get some leave, he thought, and go back to Oklahoma and find Jo and try to break up her marriage to that dogface, old Richard what's-his-name. I wish I was a 4-F and he was gone overseas for a couple years, boy. Maybe she didn't even marry that guy, anyhow. Maybe she married somebody else. Hell, maybe she didn't marry anybody. I ought to write and find out. Or, better yet, I ought to go ashore in Boston and invest a nickel in a phone call to Stella. Or start a new romance with some Scollay Square pig.

He liked to be up on the flying bridge when the *Legume* came back to home port in daylight, especially in bright sunny weather like this. He'd found a Rand-McNally Boston guide at the Buddies Club and tried to memorize the harbor's historically significant islands listed on page twelve, and he liked to try to identify them as the ship progressed up the harbor. Some of them, according to the booklet, were cool and green, others bristling with guns. He liked the idea of anything bristling with guns, he decided, yawning and squinting against the midday sun glittering on the water. He was about to start identifying islands when his colleague found him up there. His *agitated* colleague.

"Hey, lissen," Curly said. "Buddy, we're gonna tie up around twelve hunnerd hours. Will you serve out the chow for me, buddy?"

"You got a broken arm or something?" Al asked coldly.

"I jist wanta get shaved an' cleaned up so I can make it home quicker, is all. I'm kinda worried about Maria, see wot I mean?" Al peered at an island uncertainly—the trouble was, in the guidebook they were listed in order coming *out* of Boston. "I'm a hard man, pard," he told Curly. "I'm cruel an' sadistical. Serve your own garbage." He didn't want to bear the brunt of more than his share of the gripes.

"I told you already, she's pregnant. I told you, Al."

"Not very," Al said. "It takes nine months, I heard."

"She been sick, see—vomits alla time. I'm worried, Al."

"Deer Island," Al said. "See, there's the reformatory."

Curly groaned. "Buddy, I'll make it back to you sometime."

"I'm a tourist," Al said. "I'm sight-seein', Matoli. Blow."

"You don't know what it's like," Curly pleaded. "We been out a whole complete week. You don't know wot that does to a guy, Al, not knowin' how she is or anything. Al, lissen . . ."

"They got coast artillery at Fort Warren, Fort Andrews, Fort Standish, an' some other fort," Al said. "What you shoulda done, pizon, you shoulda joined the coast artillery, not the Coast Guard."

"Somethin' mighta happened, a week that's a long time to a guy when his wife is gonna have a baby, Al. You could save me about two hours of the cold sweats, that's all I'm askin'. How 'bout it, buddy?"

"That's old Nix's Mate up yonder, unless I miss my guess," Al said, pointing. "You shoulda been a Nix's Mate, third class, Curly boy, instead of a cook. If you *are* a cook." But he felt Curly's hand plucking at his arm, and he sighed and relented. I'm just jealous because I haven't got an ever-loving wife waiting for me, he admitted. I'm being mean to Curly because he's got a beautiful female on the beach and I can't even scrounge up an elderly waitress. He's worried about his Maria, all right, but mostly he just can't wait to get his arms around her—and I'll be goddam if I'm gonna hold that against a guy.

"Stop weepin' an' go take a good hot bath," he said. "I don't want to have you claimin' I broke up your happy home, Mussolini."

Curly's face lit up. "Geez, Al, I could kiss you!" he said, and left the flying bridge in a hurry, and Al thought, I wish *somebody* would kiss me. I wish I had a girl waiting for me in Boston.

You have, boy, he thought. There's always Stella.

He took the cover off the starboard 20-millimeter Oerlikon anti-aircraft gun and examined it with a proprietary, almost paternal, feeling. It was his battle station, his weapon, his little popgun; he patted the rough, hot, gray-painted metal with affection. Hello, you worthless hunk of scrap iron, he thought. The gun had one minor flaw—it wouldn't depress far enough to be of any use in the only kind of battle the buoy tender might conceivably engage in, a fight with a U-boat. There were no enemy aircraft in the American Theater of War, and *Legume's* two high-mounted twenties wouldn't depress below the horizon. Which accounted for some of Al's wry affection for the gun; it was somehow symbolic of himself, he figured, and of the Coast Guard as he knew it, and of life in general. Baby, we're both misfits in a misfit outfit in a screwed-up world, he told the gun silently.

A trio of off-duty men came clambering up the vertical ladder to the high deck, to enjoy the view of Boston, hazy-purple in the distance; Boston, Mass., that city of sultry delights for men who had hair on their heads. When the three ratings saw Al they pretended to hold a furtive conclave, eying him over their shoulders, talking in stage whispers. How high you reckon a lousy ship's cook would bounce if he was thrown off the flying bridge? one of them asked sinisterly, and the panel discussed it at length. They reached no unanimity about a cook's bounce potential, and one man even voiced the opinion that a cook wouldn't bounce at all, but just splatter all over the well deck like a sack of ripe tomatoes.

Al grinned at them and then studiously ignored them; people were always threatening cooks with all sorts of manslaughter, from drowning at midnight to running the victim through the hamburger mill (and having a decent meat loaf for a change—one with real meat in it), but it did seem to him lately the *Legume's* crewmen were sort of unwholesomely preoccupied with how high would a cook bounce or how far could a cook swim, or how long could he stay under water.

He fitted his shoulders into the familiar padded butts of the gun and swung her around a couple of times, enjoying the feel of it, imagining himself pouring a steady merciless stream of hot tracer and armor-piercing bullets into an enemy plane.

"Secure battle stations," a rich baritone voice said behind him, and he looked over his shoulder at the handsome, grinning, cinnamon-hued face of Dave Hubert, the officers' steward. Al never saw the Negro grin without being helplessly compelled to return the grin.

"I got the bastard, Dave," he said. "It was me or him." He stepped back and made a sweeping gesture. "Would you care for the honor of knocking down the next Messerschmitt, my dear fellow?"

"Thanks awfully, old chap, that's grand of you," Dave said, buckling himself into the harness, and Al moved to the railing and started identifying landmarks again. South Boston off the port bow. Dorchester Heights. Charleston Navy Yard almost dead ahead—and the sleek, sinister, looming gray hulks of real, genuine warships: a huge cruiser, a light cruiser, destroyers, some smaller escort vessels, and an armada of cargo vessels anchored around the harbor.

"There was a sniper in that crow's nest," Dave said.

"You get him?" Al asked gravely. Old Ironsides ahead.

"I said there *was* a sniper up there, man. You *know* I got him."

There's the war, those big babies are the war, Al thought. All we do is pretend. We come strutting home from a dangerous mission in Buzzard's Bay like we really been somewhere, and Dave shoots imaginary snipers out of the crow's nests of anchored American freighters because the gun muzzle won't depress enough to mow down all those real heroes on her decks. Even those old tramp steamers are better than us, Al said to himself, because they go where the fighting and dying is—or get sunk on the way and do some dying themselves.

"I got two sea gulls with one well-aimed tracer," Dave pretended behind him. "Not only did it kill 'em, it cooked 'em too, Oscar."

"I smelled them," Al said, looking at the greasy water, seeing the pathetic drifting orange peels and banana stalks and dead fish and ship's garbage and oil patches and other ugly debris fouling the blue-green water of Boston Harbor, just as ugly questions fouled the clean emerald brain of Alvin Woods. Item: Who is doing what to the general mess? Item: I wonder if Red's ship is in port, or will

Stella be lonely and available tonight? Will I be available tonight, or just lonely and repressed? I smelled the sickeningly seared sea gulls, he said to himself. What time is it? What did the menu say for chow?

It was Friday all over the East Coast and the fishermen must have had a strong union—what do you *think* the menu says for a Friday noon chow?

The ship began to swing wide to starboard, around the bend into the Mystic River, and Al looked back at the sky line of Boston and thought wistfully of Scollay Square and all the dim, fragrant, exciting saloons, and the Common with its grass and trees and flowers and pigeons and statues and girls, its uncommon girls—all of whom were strangers to Al Woods, the lonely hunter. My true métier, gentlemen, is not really cooking at all, of course—my true métier is sex. I have a definite, unmistakable flair for the indoor sport. Ask anybody. Ask me, I'm unbiased. Ah, Stella, you and your wicked dark alluring eyes—do you think about old Al sometimes? And you, Red, do you remember your ex-colleague who gave a girl basic training and then let you take over? I got news for you, Red. We weren't really friends, we were never very close. We mostly just tolerated each other. But I was close to Stella.

And I was close to another girl once, Al bragged to himself. Don't mistake me for a rookie. Ever hear of Jo Hill, the No Please We Mustn't Girl, fellows? I'll bet when the conversation lags down yonder in the old Southwest she can always get a laugh out of Richard what's-his-name by recounting her adventures in the autumn woods with a dope named Please Alvin, or Alvin the Chickenhearted Lover, or whatever she calls me. I wish she *would* call me, boy. I wish I had just one more chance. To prove that I'm the one she cares for, de dum de dum de dum de dum dum, just one more chance. Yes Jo We Must. I am not the same simple-minded naïve yokel I once was, young lady.

"What's for chow, Onionhead?" asked Motor Mack Schwartz.

Al remembered abruptly. "Salmon loaf."

"I yi yi!" Schwartz wailed. "Feesh. Always feesh."

"Fridays are a tribulation to me," Dave said beside Al at the rail. "I got to satisfy one Jew, two Catholics, a Southern Baptist, a Methodist, and three Atheists or Infidels or something. Although it could be the chief engineer is a Presbyterian instead of a Pagan."

"He's a northern technician, Dave," Al suggested.

"Man, you must be jam-up right, cause sherbet don't shake like that," Dave said, laughing heartily at his own invention. "Well, I best lay below and see what do the people want instead of solomon loaf."

I better lay below, too, Al thought. Although, confidentially, I'm a bit weary of this eternal laying below. I would like just for the novelty of it to lay above sometime. Or lay beside, boy. I remember that telephone number, too—you think I was nuts enough to throw it away without *memorizing* it? Maybe I'll sneak over the side tonight and make a stealthy phone call, boy.

As he went down the ladder the *Legume* blew for Chelsea Creek Bridge, and he thought, I don't know how the Jews or Catholics feel about adultery, but I'm a devout Agnostic myself, without hair. And something is fishy on this vessel besides the solomon loaf.

CHAPTER 21

The Disillusioned

A L WAS on deck smoking a cigarette after chow when the new
commissary officer came aboard, although at the time he
wasn't aware he was gazing upon a new commissary officer. He
was standing at the break of the port boat deck watching Chief
Bosun's Mate Huxley and some of the deck gang carrying empty
propane cylinders across the gangplank and into the buoy jungle
of the depot yards, when movement up toward the depot gates
attracted his aimless attention. What he saw was an officer and three
enlisted men marching in step toward the ship down a cleared alleyway through the litter of buoys and cylinders and gear.

The humor of it struck Al. Here was a hot July day, and here
was a thin, gawky ensign wearing a brand-new uniform, and here
were three enlisted men with sea bag–mattress rolls on their left
shoulders and ditty bags in their right hands, marching single file
under the nervous paternal scrutiny of the ensign. "Hup toop hup
toop," the ensign was calling the cadence. He was tall and thin and
graceless, all arms and legs and long neck and pink gleaming youth
and self-consciousness. One of his three-man company was a Negro
boot, one a quartermaster, second class, and the other a plump boot
seaman whose stiff new white hat rode like an upturned bowl on
a wild nest of frizzy, mouse-colored hair. Hub toob hun toon three
forb hee fuhor, crooned the ensign, imitating some more adequate
remembered drill instructor, and he brought his motley squad smartly
to the gangplank with a rye flank hut hoo *halt!*

The ensign saluted Chief Huxley jerkily, blushed furiously, and
said, "I, ah, thought you were an officer. Are you the O.D.?" Huxley
stared at him curiously and shook his head, and the ensign said with
uncertainty that he was to report aboard the ship, as were the three
enlisted men, and Huxley spat over the rail, glanced up at Al on
the boat deck and winked, and said, "Mister Woods, would you be

so kind as to kick on the skipper's door and inform him there are people down here who want to ask permission to come aboard this vessel?"

Al grinned and walked fifteen feet to the skipper's stateroom and knocked, and the skipper yelled come in, and Al went in to see the skipper standing in his bathroom door in shorts and slippers with shaving cream on his face and a straight razor in his hand. He was a tall, gaunt, granite-faced man somewhere around fifty, with thinning black hair, icy eyes, and all his own teeth. Al told him that an ensign and three enlisted men were at the gangway wanting permission to come aboard ship and report for duty.

"Tell them I said if they have orders for this ship they may come aboard and present themselves at the ship's office," the skipper said harshly. Then he added, "Hell's bells, I'll do it myself." And he went stalking out to the boat deck in his shorts, carrying the razor, and stared bleakly down upon the new people. "I am Lieutenant Fox, commanding this vessel," he snapped. "I have been a sailor for thirty-two years and I have the reputation of being a tough captain. You'll have no holiday on this ship. Huxley, detail a guide to escort these men to the ship's office and have the master-at-arms show them where they will sleep." He turned on his heel and, as he passed Al, said wearily, "Where do they find such splendid specimens, Woods?"

Al grinned politely and wandered below to the galley.

At one-thirty there was mail call, and Al was astonished to hear his name mentioned. For a moment he had the dizzy hope it might be a letter from Josephine Hill, but it turned out to be a package from his father, containing a genuine Kaywoodie pipe and a peck of homemade cookies, with no other explanation than a scrawled note saying: "You had another birthday unless I miss my guess, Hotshot." It was signed: Your Old Man. And the gift brought a sudden lump to Al's throat; he made a mental vow to write his father a long, informative letter. But what really baffled him, aside from the unexplained cookies, was the fact that the itinerant, unstable barber who had sired him was still in the same town he'd been in a year ago last Christmas.

He was sampling the cookies with coffee when the skipper appeared in the open top half of the portside door, looking for all the world like somebody's grim old ancestor frowning out of a framed portrait. "Hubert around?" he demanded. Al said he hadn't

seen Dave recently. He could smell the skipper's generously applied
aftershave lotion, and noted that the old boy had done a messy job
of powdering his blue jowls, and had nicked his chin while shaving.
The C.O. fidgeted for a while, glancing back toward the wardroom
pantry, and finally said, "Do we still have some canned hams left
down there, Woods?"

"Yessir, I think so," Al said.

"I wonder if you'd get me one?"

I wonder what you'd say if I said no, Al thought, reaching for
the key to the stores locker, which hung on a hook beside the
door. He edged past the fragrant bachelor and headed down the
two flights of ladder to the dry stores compartment. I ain't nobody's
errand boy, he thought grouchily. But Lieutenant Fox had given
him his promotion to first class, and he was grateful. Of course,
according to the rules, the skipper could bust him back to second
class at any time without a court, for incompetence. Without even
a captain's mast. Without any particular fanfare or notice. At a
moment's whim, you might say, Al thought wryly. I got to get
along with that old boy.

There were only two of the expensive canned hams left, and he
deduced that the wardroom had been hitting them pretty heavy—
they favored the luxury items, being gentlemen and all that. I'll bet
that wardroom pantry looks like a delicatessen, he thought as he
went topside with the ham. He watched the skipper fit the rec-
tangular can into his ditty bag and zip it shut. Always room for
a ham, he thought.

Lieutenant Fox frowned thoughtfully. "Woods, how long since
you went ashore last?" he inquired sternly. Al said it had been six
or seven weeks since he went ashore in Boston. "Are you a fugitive
from the Boston cops or something?" the skipper asked gruffly.

"Nossir," Al said nervously. "I'm just waiting for my hair to grow
back." He removed his hat to demonstrate his reason for being
socially shy.

The C.O. eyed his fuzzy scalp bleakly and said, "Well, we're not
running a floating monastery here, Woods, and it's not good for a
man's morale to stay aboard for long periods of time." And he
stalked away.

Al sighed and replaced his hat and wondered who the ham was
for. Some starving, rationed civilian, probably. Most likely a dame.
Old boy would parlay that canned ham into a torrid weekend,

maybe. Al wondered idly if all the officers carried supplies to their girl friends when they went ashore. They all carried ditty bags like the skipper's, at any rate. And all civilian women were on rations now. Ordinarily, fetching up the dainties for the officers to cart up the street was Dave Hubert's job. In this case it had been Al's privilege to furnish the skipper with entree. That's the difference between an officer and an enlisted man, Al thought, grinning a little. We get it free.

When we get it at all, he amended, and stopped grinning.

Some time later, while sharing his cookies with Yeoman Sam Goff, he mentioned the canned ham and discussed at some vulgar length the notion that apparently no self-respecting woman would go to bed with an officer unless he presented himself to her bearing nine dollars' worth of boned canned ham, a rare commodity in the civilian stores. Yeoman Sam thoughtfully brushed cookie crumbs from his hands and eyed Al.

"I think you miss the full impact of that idea, Onions," Goff said. "Who antes up the nine dollars? That ham came out of the general mess stores and should now be marked up against the wardroom mess, or the skipper personally. Otherwise us peasants are stuck for it." He lifted eloquent eyebrows. "Wouldn't take many goddam nine-dollar hams to add up to a mess deficit, if you see what I am drivin' at, boy."

"All you're doin' is confusing me, Sam," Al told him. "I'm just a backward cook, I don't know how the system works. Explain me."

"The officers' steward and mess attendants—in this case, Dave an' tired, slow-movin' Moses Scales—are suppose to keep an accurate record of all the chow they take back aft," Yeoman Sam stated. "That's a weak system right there. Dave's overworked and could easy forget to jot it down every time, an' Mose is too lazy to bother. Then the mess treasurer—whichever reluctant dragon back there is stuck with the job, which usually is passed around like mess-cook duty—is supposed to keep an accurate log from Dave's list of groceries hauled aft. That's another weak link in the system. Then every month the mess treasurer is supposed to get together with ole Ed Miller and figure out how much the wardroom owes the general mess. Too much margin for error all along the way."

"You got a better system figured out, Sammy boy?" Al asked.

"Sure, I got a better system figured out for practically anything you'd care to mention," Goff grinned. "The officers each get a cash mess allowance of twenty-one rocks per month. The simple way to do it would be if they just tossed in the whole twenty-one bucks each, plus whatever their share of any possible general mess deficit was. That's the simple way. Another way would be to keep the chow locked up an' make Dave an' Mose requisition whatever they need through Ed Miller and have ole Ed keep the record alla way through the deal."

"That's the weakest idea yet," Al said. "You know ole Ed."

"Then have the cooks issue the food personally," Sam growled.

"Stop thinkin'," Al said. "The ideas just keep gettin' worse."

"The point is, I'm thinkin' and you ain't, Onionskull. I'm giving you hints but you got your brains out of the line of fire. How many nine-dollar hams can a guy buy with twenty-one bucks a month?"

Al stared at him aghast. "You just got a bull's eye, Sammy."

"The bookkeeping on this vessel is substandard," Goff said. "It's careless. It's sloppy. And I ain't eatin' so good myself, if you see what I mean. If I was the head cook an' people were plottin' against me, I'd sure start keepin' my own set of books, Alvin boy." He poured his cold coffee in the galley sink. "If you want the accurate mathematical statistics for the past few months, I'll send you Storekeeper Osborn, who keeps book on the commissary department. Ask him how much the officers been payin'."

"Send him around," Al said grimly. "Suddenly I'm curious."

"It's about time, Onionscalp," Yeoman Sam said, and went out.

Al started preparations for supper. Country Boy Bagley, the cook's helper, traditionally called the Jack-o'-the-dust, appeared in the doorway grinning; he always grinned, with his small black possum eyes buried in puckers of squinting flesh. His brown beardless face gleamed with cleanliness and his lank black hair fell over his forehead in a Hitler bang, and he had the sunniest nature of anybody Al had ever known. He was as strong as a young bull, but docile and gentle; he didn't drink, smoke, swear, or fool around with girls. A farm boy from Missouri, he was probably the only unanimously well-liked member of the ship's crew. "Need ary thing, Mister Woods?" he inquired, and guffawed. The "mister" was a standard joke with him.

"I need a plump, sanitary, hot-natured blonde," Al told him.

Country Boy guffawed again. "Cain't hep you none thar."

"Then peel me about a ton of spuds," Al said.

The two other mess cooks—who unlike Bagley were transients,

serving their month in the mess deck and then gladly quitting the commissary department—began cleaning off the tables in the crew's mess compartment, plodding like somnambulists through their hated chores. Fireman Kafferhamp and Seaman Smith, the July mess cooks, were no exceptions to the rule that nobody wanted galley duty in the summer. Firemen hated it any month of the year, but when cold winter winds began knifing across the decks the seamen all wanted to strike for cook and serve in the snug mess deck. But now the duty was an endless sweaty grind, seven days a week, and Al didn't blame the mess cooks for always being sullen and troublesome. The only one who really had a soft racket was Schlemmer, the CPO's permanent mess cook, who was supposed to get a dollar a month extra from each of the chiefs, but seldom did because his easy job depended on the indulgence and good will of his customers, and it was poor policy to dun a delinquent chief.

The supper menu called for potato pancakes, and Al was running raw potatoes through the meat grinder when Storekeeper Osborn appeared in the galley door, blinking through his bifocals. "Goff said you wanted to see me, Woods," he said politely. He was a plump, stolid, humorless man of twenty-six who seemed much older, who had a wife and four children living in two rooms in Malden, and who yearned constantly for duty on the West Coast where his parents and in-laws lived. For some time now Al had been in the habit of slipping Osborn a little butter to take to his kids whenever the ship came back to Boston. There was something pathetic and gallant about Osborn keeping his cumbersome family with him, and Al paid tribute to his stolid heroism with hard-to-get butter. As a result, something vaguely resembling friendship had developed between the two of them, although Al felt somehow ill at ease in the presence of the unsmiling storekeeper.

"I just want to know how much the wardroom has been payin' for chow lately," Al said. "Say, for the last three or four months."

Osborn removed his glasses and polished them, gnawing his lip. "I couldn't say, offhand, Woods. It varies. Higgins says they buy a lot of their food ashore."

"The hell they do!" Al snarled. "Is he the treasurer now?"

"Well, he's *been* the mess treasurer for several months," Osborn said nervously. "Nobody else wants the job, I guess." He put his glasses on again. "I have off-axis astigmatism," he volunteered stolidly. "You read a lot, Woods. Don't your eyes ever bother you?"

"I see good," Al said. But maybe I'm stupid, he thought grimly. "I still want to know how much the gold braid pays for chow, Osborn."

Osborn sighed. "I don't know if I could tell you that, Woods—without proper authorization, I mean."

"Authorization my ass!" Al said. "Look, I'm the senior cook, I got a right to know. You *act* like there's something funny goin' on."

"It's . . . well, a matter of ethics," Osborn said, grimacing.

"Ethics," Al snorted. "That's a pretty word. It ain't ethical for me to give you ship's chow to take to your kids, Osborn, if you want to get moralistical about it. I want some information, boy."

Osborn looked very troubled. "Let me think it over."

"What the hell is there to think over?" Al demanded to know.

Osborn squirmed. "If I get Higgins sore at me I'll *never* get a transfer to California. My transfer depends on him now, see."

"The rest of us ain't gettin' transfers to California," Al said coldly. "We're gonna stay here and keep gettin' screwed. The chow is chinchy an' Higgins keeps yellin' cut down on expenses, but you won't be here to suffer malnutrition like the rest, huh? O.K., boy. I get it."

"I'll think about it," Osborn fretted. "Hafta look it up."

"Think fast," Al snarled. "And look it up soon, buddy."

The troubled storekeeper trudged out of the galley and Al started frying potato pancakes, snarling irritably at the hot grease that splattered from the electric grill onto his bare arms.

Three times a day the mess deck was invaded prematurely by a clamorous group of starvelings the galley crew sarcastically referred to as the Goddam Sea Gulls. They always showed up fifteen minutes before chow time and began squawking and cackling like their namesakes. Us eat! they would cackle. Bring onna goddam muckin' chow! And they had prodigious appetites and always got first grabs on the platters and bowls of food. Time after time Al was reminded of the words of the plump widow who had cooked for a girls' dorm back at the University of Oklahoma where he'd washed a million dishes for his meals. "You'll notice it's always the girls with no breeding or background who complain about the food," she had said, or words to that effect, which Al translated into sea-going parlance to read: "It's always the bastards from the bread lines who bitch about the chow." The Sea Gulls complained forever about the quality and quantity of the food, the slowness of the mess cooks, and so forth. They found soap streaks on the silverware and blood in the joints of fried chicken, and nobody could fry an egg to suit a member of that morbid group. There was always some flaw in the chow to spoil their happy lives. Al theorized that they were neurotic eaters suffering from a kind of paranoid gluttony; down deep in their shadowy psyches they shared a group obsession, a subconscious terror of drowning which their middle minds distorted into a fear of being too skinny to float well. Food was their sex and opium and whisky, but there was no joy in it for them. They were incorrigible malcontents.

Al stood over the electric grill cooking potato pancakes, and the warm grease fumes rising around his face, thick and fragrant, made him drowsy; his skull felt stuffed with cotton and his eyelids were heavy. He was weary now, but he knew that as soon as he secured the galley and could go hit his sack he would no longer be sleepy. He always reached his peak of wakefulness at night. I got a neurosis about sleep, myself, he thought, yawning. I'm a compulsive sleeper but my timer is out of whack, I'm compelled to sleep in the daytime instead of at night. Maybe I'm afraid of the dark. I sure envy those goddam pancakes—they're all layin' down. They're takin' it easy, boy.

His mind drooped and melted and ran down inside his spine like hot wax, and then the clamor from the Sea Gulls congealed his mind and sent it spiraling and coiling back into his skull like a snake into a gallon jar. He removed thirty pancakes from the grill, stacking them in a pan, and began pouring more cakes, plop, plip, pleep, plup, along the sizzling, glistening black surface of the grill. Why is that? he wondered. I can pour them babies so they're all the same size, but they all sound different hittin' the griddle. Somebody oughta do some scientific research about the acoustical tonality of potato pancakes.

"Mister Woods, I'd like you to meet my new boy, Oliver White."

It was grinning Dave Hubert and the new mess attendant, black, slim, clean, shy, and self-conscious. Al felt a groggy sympathy for the boy, seeing what a frightening thing it must be for boot mess attendants like Oliver White, coming aboard a ship that scared him and would be sailing on a very deep ocean that would scare him, while he served a hard-to-please bunch of officers that would scare anybody.

"Pleased to make your acquaintance, Oliver," he said. Oliver bowed his head humbly. "Yassuh," he said. "Thank you, suh."

"Don't call me sir, I'm just a cook," Al told him.

"Yassuh," Oliver said, and smiled helplessly. "Scuse me."

"Call me Al. Or even Onionhead, if you prefer."

"Yassuh," Oliver said meekly, ducking his head.

Dave broke into pleased laughter. "That's my boy," he gloated. "When I gander this sharp cat and think of that long, lean, lustful square known as Mose, I am tempted to rejoice mightily, good people, because no more will I toil in solitary grandulation on account of I can't locate me no Mose when I need one. I have me a real staff now, cats. This here is a real do-something boy I got now. Right, Ollie?"

"Yassuh, I sure gonna try," Oliver said humbly.

"Where you from, Oliver?" Al asked sleepily.

"Alabama, suh," the new boy said, and Dave, who for months had carried most of the wardroom load without any help from lanky, double-jointed, slack-mouthed, tired Moses Scales, laughed happily. "Alabama, hog ham an' hominy heaven." And Al reflected that it would take a boy from Alabama quite a while to shed the habit of calling all white men "suh."

"Well, Oliver, you're lucky," he said sourly. "I hear they eat pretty good back in the wardroom these days."

Dave pretended alarm. "Somebody done blabbed," he said. "Who let de cat out de satchel, Alvino? We tried to keep that hushed up."

Al squinted at him. "Dave, you keep a record of all the chow you take back there?" Dave nodded. "An honest record?" Al persisted. Honest as God, but subject to minor errors, Dave said. "I write it all down, man," he said earnestly, "and when the sun goes down Lieutenant Higgins gathers up the day's record and logs it in his little book."

"Dave, do the officers carry much chow up the street?"

"Some do, some don't, far as I know," Dave said.

"Just for the hell of it, from now on I'd like to know who takes what up the street, Dave," Al said. "I never stuck my big nose in your business, an' you don't have to do it, but I'd appreciate it, buddy."

"I'll slip you the news when, if, and whomsoever," Dave said. "Right now me and my assistant headwaiter better go aft and start putting the gold napkin rings on the velvet tablecloth. What do the

menu say tonight, Alvino?" Al told him potato pancakes, powdered-
egg omelette, breaded tomatoes, and applesauce. "Man," Dave
sighed, "I see I'm gonna do some culinary cooking myself this fine
evening."

The M.A., a bosun's mate known as Chicken Hawk, blew chow
down and Al went on turning out pancakes in a kind of trance while
the mess cooks plodded in and out, refilling the platters. His body
went about its tasks automatically while his mind walked the narrow
spine of time between sleep and wakefulness, reeling through briers
of nebulous thought, stumbling over half-hidden, shadowy ideas.
And presently Storekeeper Osborn, a fast eater, cleared his throat
in the doorway, causing Al's mind to skid down the jagged slope
and crash awake. He looked at the storekeeper stupidly.

"Woods," Osborn said worriedly, "don't let Higgins know, huh?"

Al got half a pound of butter out of the reefer and wrapped it in
newspaper and gave it to Osborn. "For the kids," he said, and
stood there eying the storekeeper and waiting, and Osborn looked
furtively up and down the passageway and leaned in the door and
said rapidly, "April, May, and June. April, eleven-fifty per officer.
May, ten dollars and eighty cents. June, ten dollars and fifty cents."

Al stood rooted in his tracks long after Osborn had gone. He
heard the rattle and clink and clatter and loud voices in the mess
deck, the overriding music from the squawk box, and the closer
sizzling and popping of grease on the grill.

I don't believe it, he thought, stunned. Ten dollars and fifty cents
last month—barely enough to pay for one canned ham. Thirty cents
a day—maybe thirty-five cents a day—and I couldn't feed an enlisted man half as well on eighty-six cents a day while going in the
hole again in June. Officers and gentlemen, wartime leaders, patriots,
and as miserable a bunch of petty thieves as the world has ever
known, boys.

Well, he thought with sudden grief, now I know, don't I?

Isn't anybody in this goddam lousy world fit to be trusted?

CHAPTER 22

J'ai Accusé

IT WAS dark on the flying bridge and a cool breeze soothed the fevered brow of Al Woods, a man who had opened Pandora's box and was inclined to wish to hell he hadn't. He sat on the starboard ready box, shivering a little from the cold knowledge of a July night, staring across the inky shimmer of water toward blacked-out Boston. He was the center of a wilderness of ebony nothingness, and the throb of his heart was like a punishment. He felt again the old pang of homelessness, but also a germinating sense of mission, a growing feeling that he had to Do Something. Something Drastic.

All right, he said to himself, I'm onto your little game, so knock it off, felons. Come down off those pedestals of rank and stand hitched, because on tonight's agenda we have got the case of the decent element, the enlisteds and cooks, versus the wardroom mob that is turning this ship into a goddam rogues' galley. You are charged with misappropriation of foods, holding out on the dough, pilfering, duplicity, moral turpitude, stealing, robbing the poor, cheating, and corrupt practices. (The officers materialized before him in imagination on the black page of the night, eying him warily. They were nervous, boy.) This is unofficial, he told them, so you guys can be honest for a change.

He thought it wryly, humorously, but he did not feel wry or humorous. He felt like a lonely outsider, a misfit, who had jealously watched other men gorging on ample bedtime snacks; he was again somehow the forlorn victim of a cruel status quo, a rebel wincing with the old stabbing ache of betrayal. It wounded him and grieved him to learn that six of the seven officers (whom he so badly wanted to admire and respect and trust) were either implicated in a dark plot to starve the lowly enlisteds into abject submission and truckling obedience, or were anxious to pocket an extra ten dollars a month at the cost of the crew's collective stomach, or else were just so appallingly stupid that they felt ten dollars and fifty cents was a fair board bill for the three square meals a day plus between-chow snacks they got.

So he said to the ghostly images of the six suspects, Gentlemen— and I use the term loosely, in jest, mockingly—gentlemen, as I call your names, step forward and plead guilty. I will begin at the foot of the class, with the least likely crooks. Ensign Fineberg!

Ensign Fineberg, Nathan Fineberg, twenty-five, good-looking, athletic (Nobody would ever guess, from looking at him, that he was a Jew, the crewmen always said. He was blond, sun-tanned, and had a short, football-flattened nose.), a graduate of N.Y.U., and not "stuck up" like so many officers. A real nice guy—or was he, now?

"I'll tell you how it is, Al," Fineberg's wraith seemed to say with an easy shrug, "I found this little out-of-the-way eating place called the wardroom, where the food is tasty and abundant and so reasonable you wouldn't believe it. Not guilty. I just *eat* here."

Al sighed. How could you call Fineberg a crook?

Halfway Hathaway, creep forward! Al said sternly. Go on, alibi.

Ensign Hathaway was an erstwhile junior-high-school principal; there was something chalky and bookish and pedantic about him, even in dress uniform. He was, unfortunately, nothing much; unimportant. Because he could look no man square in the eye. The enlisteds had discovered this flaw in Hathaway inside a week of his coming aboard, and they were without mercy. Whenever they met him they would deliberately and cruelly stare him down. Once he had started up the passageway from the wardroom while the crew were at chow, and somebody said *psst!*, and all those at the inboard ends of the tables turned to stare at the approaching ensign —whose immediate agitation and distress were sickening to see, his glance darting about like a trapped animal climbing the walls of its cage. He couldn't face those unswerving stares, his courage swerved instead, and he pivoted, as if suddenly remembering some neglected chore aft, and hurried back the way he had come. From that day on he was Halfway. Ensign Halfway, haunted by his visibility, reduced to insignificance by a barrage of unwinking blank stares. He may have been a good junior-high-school teacher, but the slender, pale ensign was not even a propped-up imitation of an officer.

"I mind my own business," Halfway's spook said defensively. "I obey orders. Higgins tells us how much we owe. Don't pick on *me*."

Ensign Hathaway was no thief of food—he only robbed men of their faith in the System, the Service, and other men.

Chief Warrant Machinist McFarland, if you please, Al said.

The gangling, spare, gray-haired, bushy-browed, dark Scotsman moved forward distractedly, his hand cupped behind his inclined ear, listening to the heartbeat of the ship, his whole body a stethoscope recording the pulse of his beloved Diesel engines. Of him Dave had said, "He eats anything we give him, gulps some coffee, an' hurries back to the engine room. Won't stay for dessert. Never talks much." But a Scotsman, according to humor's legends, knew a bargain when he saw one. Ten dollars and fifty cents a month was the sort of board bill that would please the dour heart of a canny clansman. But goddammit, McFarland loved his engines and his spotless, antiseptic engine room, and his solitary spare-time reading of technical journals; he was not dour with his engine-room gang— down there he was stern but genial, they said, and always just and fair.

"The port mainstem bearing bushings sound a little tickety," the Scot worried. "We best to regrind the ring-pin valve eccentric rods and put jusssst a bit of oil on the axillary crankshaft gears."

Al sighed again. O.K., Mac, go love your engines. No jury would convict you of anything but a one-track mind. Cupper, you're next.

The grotesque spirit of Ensign "Hog" Cupper slouched forward, grinning loosely, a big shaggy squat-bodied lumpy-faced brutish man with a braying laugh and a halfwit's slack-mouthed leer. It was difficult to understand how he had got in the Coast Guard, although Sam Goff suggested he might have joined at night and nobody got a good look at him until the next morning when it was too late. It was even more difficult to understand just exactly what he *did* in the Coast Guard. Every three or four days he caught O.D. duty, but that appeared to be his only function on the ship. "I figure he's the morale officer," Doc O'Neal had quipped, but Cupper headed no department, like Fineberg, officially gunnery officer, Higgins, exec and commissary officer, or even Halfway, who was nominally the signal officer. Cupper's main interests in life were food, women, poker, and hillbilly music, not necessarily in that order. He never took over the bridge at sea—the skipper seldom ever turned the ship over to any of the junior officers, but sometimes reluctantly vouchsafed the *Legume* to Higgins or Fineberg on long wearying voyages. Higgins and Fineberg also split the job of navigation officer between them, so Cupper wasn't that either. And it didn't seem at all likely that he was from Intelligence. Cupper may have been the gluttony officer, according to Dave Hubert. One Sunday the skipper had said tartly, "Mister Hubert, see if you can urge Mister Cupper to have some more chicken, he has only eaten twenty-five or thirty pieces and I don't want him to leave the table hungry."

The ectoplasmic oaf said tolerantly, "I take what I can get, cook. So what? But I'm not the wardroom mess treasurer either. I'm not the misappropriation officer. I'm just ole laughin' easygoin' woman-chasin' lusty gusty fun-lovin' food-lovin' Austin G. Cupper from down yonder in Texas, where I went an' lettered in pigskin at A. & M. an' where me an' my pappy got the world's biggest small hog ranch. I feed the kitty whatever ole Dennis asks. I ante up what the dealer says."

Now only the wraiths of Higgins and the skipper remained on the breeze-fanned flying bridge with baffled Alvin Woods. So he said bitterly, Dealer Higgins, you the guy stacked the deck in this game, you the bastard slitherin' the aces off the bottom. Speak up.

"Let's have a little more damned reverence there, Woods," the sneering ghost of Higgins said sarcastically. "If you don't like to play the game, let somebody else have your seat. You're not indispensable, you're easy to replace. I've known for some time that you were mentally insane, of course, poor incompetent wastrel. What you need is some rugged duty elsewhere. I'll arrange a North Atlantic cruise for you, and maybe I'll deck you with a fast left in parting. An officer is an officer, period, and an enlisted is an enlisted, semicolon, and you've had this easy duty too long. Pack your goddam sea bag, get a short arm, pick up your papers, and get the hell offa our vessel. We deal summarily with insolent sea lawyers and I might add you're damn lucky you don't get a general court-martial. Good-by."

That's what I figured, Al said to himself in glum frustration.

And the skipper's eerie likeness said stonily, "I promoted you to first class and I can demote you for incompetence at any moment, Woods, and this is that moment. Remove that third stripe from your uniforms as you pack your sea bag. In the Coast Guard a mere ship's cook does not impugn the honor of any officer, least of all accuse his commanding officer of smuggling hams ashore and

aiding and abetting a gradual robbing of the general mess. Your
charges are in thuddingly bad taste and shockingly bad judgment,
and rank has its privileges and this is my ship, I'm entitled to take
anything I want whenever and whatever . . ."

Aw, shut up, you dishonorable old goat! Al thought, defeated.
Because there was nothing he could do about it. Anyway, nothing
but lay his silly-looking head on the chopping block and yell thief
as the sharp ax of authority decapitated one more rebellious sea
lawyer.

He stayed on the flying bridge a while longer, slumped in dull
resignation, while the fading images of the invulnerable wardroom
gang gibbered with echoing laughter in his mind. Calf rope, Al
said to himself. Uncle! Let me up, I'm whipped, felons.

His knowledge of their cheating was a boomerang, and in defeat
he lost his assurance and began to doubt himself, began to dis-
believe the facts of the matter. Maybe Osborn made a mistake—
maybe Osborn was a psychopath, maybe he'd worried so much
about his family that he had blown his stack and was trying with
maniac cunning to pull down the officers who wouldn't buy him a
ticket to California's sunny clime. Maybe Osborn was the real
culprit, even. He had access to the stores, and he needed money to
support his wife and four kids, didn't he? Maybe Osborn and Chief
Miller had a juicy black market thing going, with no telling who
else helping smuggle chow up the street.

Maybe I'm nuts, Al said to himself wearily.

But nuts or not, he still felt the heat of outrage in his mind, still
felt the soreness of shocked sensibilities. It was just that he was
helpless, the gun was aimed at his own head. The smart thing to do
was ask for a transfer, meanwhile keeping his mouth shut. Fold my
tent and steal away in the night—if they don't steal my tent first,
he sighed, and climbed down from his high retreat, where justice
had gone terribly awry so that the judge, jury, prosecutor, and chief
state's witness had been sentenced to hang for knowing too much.

He was getting ready to lock up the galley for the night when
the new ensign appeared in the doorway and stood there smiling
and blinking his boyish blue eyes. "Hello there," he said, and Al
said hello. "I am Ensign Scraggs, and I believe they said your name
is Woods, isn't that right?" Right, Al said. (Somehow he didn't
feel able to say sir to anybody tonight.) The ensign smiled his

aching smile and tugged at his earlobe and said, "I am to be commissary officer."

"Well, now, that's wonderful," Al said with irony. "Let me be the first cook to offer you congratulations."

"Thank you," said the ensign uncertainly, as if not sure Al wasn't attempting to fraternize with him. "Well," he said. "So this is the galley." Al said, "Ayep." It seemed rather small, the ensign remarked. Or should he say *compact?* "Starkly functional," Al said.

The boy ensign batted his eyes and smiled like it hurt to smile but was the least he could do for his country, and Al studied him, seeing a lanky, awkward, almost delicately frail youth with pink beardless cheeks, a taffy-colored cowlick, thin wrists dangling from his sleeves, huge feet, an earnestly innocent expression, and a self-consciousness and diffidence that made him seem even more undeveloped and immature than he naturally was. This is an officer, Al reminded himself. A leader of men, steadfast and unswerving in his duty to God and country. When he grows up he might even get to be skipper of a vessel, who knows?

"I understand the enlisted men's mess is having some difficulty in balancing the budget," the new commissary officer said in a pure, well-modulated tenor voice. Oh, Al said airily, we have our fiscal problems. "It offers a challenge, sort of," the ensign said eagerly. Yeah, Al said, a challenge. "Well, ah, Woods, I'm glad to have met you," Ensign Scraggs said. "We shall probably get much better acquainted in the future. Tomorrow I would like you to show me around the department, I wish to familiarize myself with the general perimeters of the..." he smiled furiously "... department. What hour would be most convenient?"

"Around nine o'clock is a slack time," Al said, and the ensign blinked and pulled his ear and smiled brilliantly and said roger, nine hundred hours then. And he wheeled gawkily and went marching out of the galley like a tin soldier that needed oiling, and Al said to himself, Hup toob threeb forb. Well, I can sure relax my vigilance now, boys, I can pack away all my worries and anxieties and suspicions, old trouble-shootin' emergency specialist Scraggs is on the job.

Doc O'Neal, wearing a towel and wooden shower sandals, came clomping into the galley with his enviable mane of hair plastered wetly to his head. He manipulated his two-tooth bridge forward and grinned at Al hideously, like a drowned squirrel. "Me an'

Yeoman Sam are goin' to a sayloon an' chugalug a couple barrels of suds, Onionskin. Why don't you slip on a wig an' join us?"

"Give me twenty minutes to put on my drinkin' clothes," Al said.

He locked the galley and went below to change into dress whites, his mind still numbed by shock and disbelief and frustrated anger. He thought, I'll ask for a transfer. But he didn't really want a transfer. The problem would still exist for the crew, for Doc and Sam and all the other guys, and for whoever replaced him. And his heart sank at the thought of being uprooted again and running away from unpleasantness again in the old pointless quest for a place to fit in. If I could be the captain of a ship and then do the cooking, too, I could run an honest commissary department, he thought bitterly.

"Hey, Onions, what's for breakfast inna mornin'?" somebody yelled at him sarcastically. "French toast or pancakes?"

He stopped dressing, arrested by a sudden inspiration. Now that he knew what the problem was, he'd be a dirty yellow dog if he went on playing patsy for the wardroom gang. What can I lose except my epaulets? he thought. By God I'll use it up before they get a chance to steal it. Somebody on this vessel oughta act like a man and try to live up to his duties and responsibilities.

"We're gonna have ham an' eggs," he said clearly and distinctly. There was a hoot of bitter mocking laughter.

"Tell your friends," Al said angrily. "Ole Al's cafeteria is featurin' free ham an' eggs for everybody tomorrow morning. With hot biscuits, by God! And pineapple juice!"

"Get the nets, men, Onionhead has went nuts!" somebody laughed.

They got a right to laugh, Al said to himself. But I'm through aiding and abetting a bunch of sneaky petty thieves. I won't ask for a transfer, I'll just cook myself into getting one.

He finished dressing and went up the street with Doc and Sam and had a few beers and felt restless. He felt pretty insecure, and whenever he felt insecure he was lonelier than usual and dwelt more than usual on the pleasant oblivion that was one of the less publicized aspects of amorous pursuit. He had told Doc and Sam the shocking news, and they were shocked, and indignant, and said they ought to get up a petition or something, and they drank moodily and without much pleasure, and Al grew more and more restless. He didn't want to get very drunk—he had to bake biscuits in the morning. Doc and Sam were unrealistic dreamers, they couldn't do anything to rectify the goddam lousy situation. But Al Woods was the head cook, and he could at least ease the plight of the crew a little by throwing caution to the winds and beginning to serve decent chows again. While I last, he thought, I'm the only one in a position to do anything constructive about it.

Around ten o'clock, while on his way to the men's room, he detoured into a phone booth. He called Stella Wildoe's number, and got a busy signal. Fifteen minutes later he tried again and nobody answered the phone. Somebody beat me to her this time, he thought, and felt a curious mixture of regret and relief. That was close, he thought. He drank some more beer and thought about Jo Hill, and about how yearning for usually available Stella always reminded him of the distant and lost Josephine. He stared dreamily into his beer and imagined how it would be if he were married to Jo and they had an apartment, like Red and Stella, or Curly and his wife. He'd be there now, all this disillusioning betrayal forgotten for a while.

"Oh, hell, boys," he sighed. "Let's go back to the lousy ship."

But they wanted to get drunk, so he went back alone, trudging through the hot July night, very lonely and deeply troubled.

CHAPTER 23

Incubation

HAVING got off to a depressing start, July never recovered. All over the world and in the wardroom the enemies of Democracy seemed to be getting all the best of the war. Lieutenant Higgins was ominously quiet, and the scuttlebutt was that the new exec kept busy back in his cabin drawing up blueprints for a stern new daily routine for the crew. And there was dissension in the galley, when Al told his colleague to forget all that old crap about economizing.

"Our legal and moral duty is to feed the guys well," Al said. "Under the circumstances it's even more so, pizon."

"Yeah, but jeez, we just be gettin' our ass in a jam, Al."

"Look, I told you what's the matter, Curly. It ain't us and it never was. They're robbin' us blind. We could go along a while trying to plug the hole, but they'd just keep unpluggin' it. We can't win, so we're just gonna ignore the mess deficit and feed right, see."

"You just fixin' to get us shipped to Siberia," Curly groaned.

"Personally I just ain't smart enough to figure out how we can feed officers for thirty-five cents a day and not be able to feed enlisteds on eighty-six cents a day," Al said grimly. "So the hell with it, I'm not worrying about the money part any more, I'm goin' back to feedin' like we used to do. I got some pride and self-respect left."

"So have I," Curly bristled, "but that don't mean I want a transfer to Greenland or some place. I got a pregnant wife, in case you forgot about it. We get ole Higgins riled up any more an' I might not see my kid until he's in high school, boy."

"You married guys signed the same contracts us bachelors signed," Al said sarcastically. "It didn't call for weekends at home, boy."

Anger glittered in Curly's liquid brown eyes. "I got married after I joined up, just for your smart goddam information. Anybody but you, he'd know how a guy wants to get home once in a while. But that ain't the point anyways. The point is we got orders to economize, an' we s'pose to obey orders from Lieutenant Higgins. That's the point."

"Look, Curly," Al said. "I happen to be the senior cook here, an' you take your cookin' orders from me, an' I'm ordering you to start feedin' the guys better, including desserts, an' fruit juice an' bacon an' stuff for breakfast. I'll give you menus to follow an' you just follow 'em an don't worry about goin' home nights."

"Aw, go to hell!" Curly yelled, and went stalking out of the galley in a Latin rage, convinced that Al Woods was trying to throw a monkey wrench into his marital happiness, convinced that Al had chosen a suicidal course that would scuttle them both.

But Al restored the general mess to full rations, and began keeping a record of the food items carried ashore by the skipper, Higgins, and Cupper, as reported to him by discreet Dave Hubert.

In July, Al waited impatiently for his hair to grow, and read anything he could find to read, and played checkers with Doc or Sam, and quite often thought of Stella Wildoe with wrenching desire, and of Josephine Hill with wrenching nostalgia. And a couple of nights after he got the Kaywoodie pipe and cookies in the mail, Al wrote a letter to his father. It was the only real letter he ever wrote his father, and it was the last.

The new seaman who had come aboard with Ensign Scraggs, plump and frizzy-haired and unhappy, watched Al type with arrogant interest. His name was Franklyn P. Scott, III, and—according to Yeoman Sam, who read everybody's service record sooner or later—he was a Harvard man.

"Can you do formal business letters?" he asked Al.

Al shrugged. "I guess I could if I took a notion, Harvard."

"I'll pay you to do some for me," Harvard said eagerly.

"I might do it," Al said, yawning. "For a dollar a page."

"Very well," Harvard said. And that same evening Al earned ten dollars typing business letters, and got to know a good deal more about Franklyn Peabody Scott, III. The Harvard law student had been busted out of cadet school at the last minute because he was "not officer material." Which meant, he confessed, that he had argued endlessly with the instructors. He had brought up the theory of relativity in celestial navigation class, to the intense annoyance of the tutor, who regarded his teachings as traditionally and officially pure and unsusceptible to error. Scott was also a snob, and a very brilliant fellow with an amazingly encyclopedic mind who enjoyed astounding peasants like Al with his infallible memory.

During the course of considerable letter-writing, trying to trap Harvard off his mental base got to be a game that Al enjoyed playing, with no notable success. You couldn't catch him short with any question involving history, poetry, authors past and present, classical music, military leaders, or anything else. Yeoman Sam got in the game and browsed through an unabridged dictionary in search of obscure definitions, but no definition was obscure to Franklyn Peabody Scott the Third. "What's a dugong?" Sam asked. Harvard yawned, "A cousin to the manatee." Sam had to look up manatee to check; Harvard was right. "What's thaumaturgy?" Sam inquired hopefully. "Magic," Harvard sighed wearily, and Sam said, "You're a little off, it's the performance of miracles."

You had to admire the guy, even if he was supercilious and superior, and he paid off for stenography like a rigged slot machine. The letters were inevitably to public figures, politicians, military bigwigs, high governmental figures, and other men of influence, most of them names Al had seen somewhere or other in print, and all of whom apparently had one remarkable distinction in common: They had all been close friends at Harvard or elsewhere with F. P. Scott the Second. All Harvard wanted of them was help and influence in getting the officer's commission he felt his education and social position rated. "Dear General Schlemp," he would declaim unctuously, "my father often speaks of you with great admiration and affection . . ."

Four or five nights a week Al would uncase his typewriter and bang out eight or twelve persuasive applications for assistance, shrewdly leaving wide margins. He liked the idea of being paid to stay aboard ship for a change, and liked to think of all the money he wasn't spending, and involving himself with Harvard's expensive campaign to get off the vulgar buoy tender and into a sinecure ashore served to keep Al from dwelling at morbid length on his own problems. He was unaware of the hidden peril in acquiring an easy, coherent facility for writing letters to important personages he didn't know; he did not realize until too late that he was being indoctrinated with the insidious philosophy that if you didn't like the way things were you could write to people who might change the course of human events. And although he considered himself a resigned fatalist whose whole life had been somehow concerned with food problems, the truth was that Al hardly ever felt the elbow of destiny nudging him onto a new course.

He was aware that five nights a week an angry radio commentator named Winfrey Fugate went on the air in New York to issue blanket indictments against all the tyrannical, corrupt, brutal, despotic, unpatriotic, sadistical military leaders and lousy rats who made life miserable for enlisted men like Al. Two or three nights a week the program was tuned in on the radio in the wardroom and piped into the mess deck through the amplifying squawk box, and Al listened with one ear while earning his pay as a part-time private stenographer. Apparently the fact that he only half-heard and half-registered the program was what saved him for a time from the folly germinating in the hot, dark, fertile rebellion of his soul. As long as he was earning more money than the skipper, the wild seed of sedition did not begin to sprout.

And the griping of the crew had abated; although the truth about the general mess trouble was now common knowledge, the men of the *Legume* were curiously inert about it, apathetic regarding the brigands in the back room. But this inertia was largely attributable to Al's restoring the crew to full rations again. Sometimes Al thought about it, and having known both aching hunger and repletion he was cognizant of this curious human frailty that made it difficult for a man to register moral indignation on a full stomach. But he was also aware that the clock hands were moving inexorably toward a deadline. He was enabled temporarily to banish famine simply because gullible Ensign Scraggs had replaced Higgins as mess officer. While he sank the deficit shaft deeper, Al managed to give the impression he was driving a lateral tunnel upward toward the sunlight of a stable economy. But it couldn't last, and there would be a hairy explosion when Higgins wised up, and sometimes Al worried with dread and foreboding, although that was against the rules for a confirmed fatalist.

A cook exiled for incorrigible honesty might wind up in Greenland, where rumor had it the galleys were converted igloos with whale oil for fuel, where all foods were powdered or dehydrated, and all women—outnumbered ninety-to-one in the first place—used cod-liver oil for cologne and were sewed into their sealskin skivvies. But there were moments when Al would snarl to himself, in a mutinous mood, that any place was better than a place where all the officers were petty thieves. And it was all Coast Guard, whatever that might imply.

Sometimes he felt pretty sensitive about being in the Coast Guard. He wasn't exactly ashamed of it, just self-conscious. He had duty on a noncombatant, virtually neutral vessel whose officers were little fellows preoccupied with gluttony and the social life their uniforms made possible, and who believed rank was a splendid protection against being caught pilfering. It often seemed to Al that the entire Coast Guard was a little embarrassed about being Coast Guardsmen—except maybe the cocky bearded men off the convoy cutters, who needed to apologize to no man because of any lack of battle stars. But in general, Army and Navy guys looked down on Hooligans.

How's the war goin' at the USO, Hoolie? they might ask. How'sa ole bathtub navy these days? How'sa ole knee-deep sailor, Hooligan?

And no matter how you reacted at the moment, the sting of truth seemed to fester in your mind forever after, and you weren't happy about being a Coast Guardsman, you had no pride of service.

Coast Guard? people would say with insulting bewilderment. What's that? What does the Coast Guard do, guard the coast?

We keep a sharp watch for German U-boats in Buzzard's Bay, Al thought sourly, and made excuses for himself in his mind. I didn't know what the hell I was joining, back there in Oklahoma City. I just saw a poster with a clean white ship slicing the sapphire seas and I couldn't see me wearing the red pants of a Marine or the heel blisters of a soldier. Maybe I joined like all the others joined— maybe we were all cowed by the Leathernecks, awed by the Army, unnerved by the Navy, and that left us very little choice in the matter.

He saw the *Legume* as the epitome of the Coast Guard and her officers as prototypes and her humble duties and ugly problems as being representative of the whole service. Somehow he had come to believe it was all buoy tenders controlled by officers who wounded their knuckles dipping into the general mess petty-cash drawer.

Thus, in tense and troubled July, he was torn between a desire to stay on the *Legume* at some cost to his self-respect and a yearning to leave the ship and deny he'd ever been her senior cook. Whatever happened, it didn't seem to matter a great deal, did it?

But there was adventure in July, when the *Legume* made a run down east to Rockland, Maine, in nasty weather. The C.O., who knew every mile of the rock-bound coast, went hook-happy for a week, anchoring each night in a different small rocky harbor of some small rocky fishing village. And two nights in a row the skipper took Bosun's Mate Hawk and Motor Mack Galkowski on lobster-trap raids in the Monimor, and Al happened to be the seafood chef on the *Legume*. He was persuaded to preside at the last rites for some two-hundred-odd lobsters, mostly under the legal size. He didn't particularly mind the work involved, and the skipper generously shared his poachings with any crewman who cared for lobster, but Al was squeamish about dropping live lobsters into boiling sea water. Sometimes they screamed sibilantly at contact, and although he figured they probably died immediately and without too much agony, there was something reproachful and betrayed about that last whisper of shocked surprise and chagrin, and it unnerved him and preyed on his mind a little afterward. And he thought, The skipper has no qualms about stealing other people's food, that's clear enough.

July ended, with the whimper of crucified crustaceans, on a note of tense, ominous waiting, and no matter how you analyzed it, July had not been a good month, although it *had* been profitable to Al Woods.

Curly Matoli lived in dread, in waning July, of not being home nights in August or November, or especially January when he was to become a father. And the War Shipping Administration announced bleakly that during the week of July 12 (which by sinister coincidence had been the first week of Higgins's tenure as exec) Allied losses at sea had reached the highest level since the beginning of the war, and in the future ships under its jurisdiction would be limited to hauling only cargoes essential to the war. In foul July a U-boat torpedoed an American passenger ship with 372 persons aboard—nine lives lost. And Berlin announced that the four days previous to July 21, while the U.S.C.G. Cutter *Legume* dawdled in Chelsea Creek with hooded guns, U-boats had sunk sixteen Allied ships, seven in the Eastern Atlantic, three in the St. Lawrence River, and six in "American" waters. President Roosevelt told newsmen there were four million men in the United States Armed Forces, and Al wondered how many were married men, and how many of those got to sleep with their wives as often as Red Wildoe of the *Algomotoc* and Curly Matoli of the *Legume*, both cooks. And he wondered how many of the four million were stealing food from the rest.

On July 31, just to twist the rusty blade of guilt in the heart of any Hooligan, Berlin announced the sinking of another thirty-five Allied ships off the American coast and in the Mediterranean— twenty-four cargo ships, ten sailing vessels, one convoy escort ship.

The Allies were taking a beating everywhere: in the Pacific, Atlantic, Gulf of Mexico, Mediterranean, Gulf of St. Lawrence, and Chelsea Creek. Al totted up his notes. Lost for the last half of July: At least three American canned hams, ten pounds of Allied beef, one sugar-cured ham, seven cans of asparagus, three cans of fruit cocktail, eleven pounds of butter (not counting Storekeeper Osborn's kids), three pounds of sugar, four pounds of coffee. These were positive losses, but it was believed there were other losses that could not accurately be estimated. Al wondered if maybe the July losses had reached the highest level of the war, locally; he wondered how badly the budget had been torpedoed in July.

But still, for Al Woods personally, July had been a huge fiscal success and not without encouragement in the hair department. It seemed to him his hair was coming in thicker; at any rate in another couple of weeks he would look like a minor convict instead of a Prussian general. And he had earned seventy-one dollars with his typewriter writing circulars for a strategist called Harvard, who said haughtily, "One letter, to the right person, can accomplish miracles."

"Thaumaturgy," Al said brightly, listening with one ear and a segment of his brain to a radio commentator named Winfrey Fugate.

CHAPTER 24

The New Regime

AUGUST started with a thud. The thud was Higgins closing the thick book of Navy Regulations, which had not been revised to any great degree since the days of John Paul Jones. The grand new program for improving morale, efficiency, discipline—and in fact everything else except the food situation—was ready. Tacitly abetted by the skipper, whose custom it had always been to leave personnel matters to the discretion of his executive, Higgins caused the master-at-arms to blow his bosun's pipe and tell all hands to lay aft to the quarter-deck at thirteen hundred hours. Exchanging looks of alarm and foreboding, all hands laid aft. The skipper did not attend the forum, since he was in his stateroom drinking milk and eating pills for his ulcer.

Now hear this! Higgins bawled.

Quote: Henceforth there would be calisthenics every day at thirteen hundred hours except Sundays and during heavy weather, to be immediately followed by semaphore drill. For *all* hands. Henceforth the evening report muster would be held according to the book and men required to muster would do so in clean undress uniforms and watch caps or white hats. CPO's would wear khaki overseas caps or other suitable covering. Henceforth the use of obscenity would be forbidden; there would be a tapering-off period of one week, after which the guilty would be placed on report and severe punishment would befall the more flagrant offenders. Henceforth (and it should be the sole responsibility of the O.D. to enforce this regulation) the lights in the crew's mess deck would be doused at twenty-two hundred and thirty hours except Saturdays when in port. Henceforth the cook with the duty would secure the galley as soon as possible after evening chow and turn in the keys to the O.D. at evening muster. If for some reason the galley was not secured by report time the cook would report to the O.D. at muster that the galley was not secured, and give a suitable explanation. Henceforth the rules of etiquette applying to the custom of saluting superior officers and of standing at attention whenever a superior officer entered a compartment would be observed. Henceforth all men would maintain a tidy appearance when off duty, keep their gear, bunks, and uniforms neat, and shave each and every day.

And henceforth, Higgins added as if he'd almost forgotten, all hands would receive one hour of artificial resuscitation drill each week, and these new orders of the day would become effective as of this moment, and Ensign Scraggs would now take over for calisthenics.

Ensign Scraggs took over smiling fiercely. Let us begin with a few deep knee-bends to loosen up, men, he said. Ready? Hunh, toop, hup, doo, huh, hoo, hut two. Scraggs had found his niche in the service.

Sweating in the hot sunshine, Al gave himself up to disgust. The mess deck was half-cleaned and here were the mess cooks toning up their ligaments. The galley was a mess and here was Country Boy and the two cooks wearing themselves out and getting their hands all dirty from the gritty deck doing push-ups. In fact Al Woods wanted to take loud exception to every henceforth in Higgins's proclamation. Semaphore drill your aspirin! Why should a first-class cook learn to send a message by waving his hands and arms around like a moron? And evening reports, for chrissakes! What did a cook have to report—that in spite of the earnest efforts of the wardroom mob there was still a little food left in the stores locker? And what was the big idea turning out the mess deck lights at ten-thirty every night? Where the hell would an off-duty cook go to do his necessary reading until one or two in the goddam morning? Listen, Higgins, Al thought heatedly as he touched his knees without bending his toes, I'll lock up that goddam galley when I get good and goddam ready. Who the hell do you think you are?

But Higgins had gone below. The calisthenics wasn't for officers, of course. They were all fine physical specimens to begin with, and stayed in shape by decking snotty enlisteds with fast rights, by carrying heavy loads of enlisteds' chow ashore, by pulling themselves up to the table, and by diligent social climbing.

The mess cooks for August were Seaman Sonnichson, a slender, pale, burning-eyed blond youth who had the worst inferiority com-

plex Al had ever heard of, and Fireman Grannell, a fat boy from
Nebraska who was terribly self-conscious about taking showers because he had breasts like a teen-aged girl. They always send me their
best men, Al thought sarcastically. The main trouble with Sonnichson was that the only time he stopped feeling inadequate was when
he got drunk, which he regularly did by drinking three highballs
or five bottles of beer. When he got drunk he felt very adequate,
but wasn't, and most of the time he had at least one black eye.

Hut, hoot, hub, hoo, Ensign Scraggs insisted under the broiling
August sun. My *gawd!* Harvard moaned. This is unspeakably
vulgar! Seaman Preacher Carter unslung his long jaw and said
audibly, "Relly, now, old bean, this is rawthuh absurd, doncha
think?" Bastard! Curly muttered, but Al wasn't sure if he referred
to Higgins, Ensign Scraggs, or the senior cook. Doc O'Neal whispered loudly, "This is good practice for shackin' pigs, Okie." And
Sam Goff puffed, "I'm a yeoman with drag at the D.O. and this is
the last time I do this crap."

"O.K., fellows," Scraggs beamed. "Now for the semaphore drill."

The Hooligans groaned in cadence. Some deal, boy. Some ship.
Some weird outfit, boy. Some goddam way to fight a war.

In August rebellion smoldered in the breast of Al Woods, and
Germany referred to Russia as "the beaten enemy," and U.S. planes
dropped three and one half tons of bombs on Fuchow, and the
cutter *Legume* cruised intrepidly on the dangerous waters of
Buzzard's Bay, and the new commissary officer had a parley with
the head cook.

"Ah, Woods, they tell me you make up the menus," he blinked.
Al nodded. He just couldn't force himself to sir this kid. "Ah, the
exec feels that perhaps in the future I should sort of countercheck
the menus, Woods," Scraggs smiled painfully, holding his ear. "In
rough draft form, before they are typed up in final shape."

"Chief is suppose to make up menus," Al said. He didn't want this
boy editing his scripts. Let him go parley with old Ed.

"Well, you know the saying, Woods," beamed the ensign known
thereabouts as Skinny Scraggs. "Two heads are better than one."

Al nodded, grinning a little. If the crew's head was crowded, a
guy could always use the CPO's head, he thought. But, since that
was not the type of head Skinny referred to, maybe he meant he
had two heads that were better than Al's one. One Onionhead, was,

however, vastly superior to a pair of Officerheads. So, Al told himself, stop kidding yourself that he don't mean his head and Higgins's head.

"Look, Ensign Scraggs," Al said. "This drill stuff, it sure fouls up the galley work. How about fixin' it so the cook on duty an' the mess cooks wouldn't hafta do it? Anyway, why should cooks hafta do wigwag? They don't make the signalmen learn how to cook, do they?"

Smiling his blazing smile, rearranging his earlobe, Skinny said he was afraid there was nothing he could personally do about the daily all-hands routines of the ship. "You'd have to discuss that with Lieutenant Higgins, I'm afraid," he regretted. "Incidentally, when we return to Boston I shall go with Chief Miller to the Navy Commissary Warehouse and, ah, assist in purchasing the food stores."

What a relief! Al said to himself. Now I can stop frettin'.

"I, ah, I'm rather concerned about the deficit, Woods."

"That makes two of us," Al said, fraternizing brazenly.

The *Legume* tied up in New Bedford and an Army private called Seaman Sonnichson a USO admiral, and Sonnichson, who had consumed five beers and was feeling adequate, took a swing at the dogface. In the ensuing brawl, which swept through the bar like a prairie fire and inflamed all the male patrons and a couple of female patrons, Al got a fist in the eye while trying to shield the prostrate form of his inadequate mess cook. The fist released some of his stored-up violence, and he had polished off a drunken soldier and an undersized but scrappy civilian when the Shore Patrol arrived, and was currently slugging it out with a huge Coast Guardsman from the local base who had got all confused about which side he was on. Pretending each opponent was old Dennis Higgins had added considerable zest to the thing for Al, and had given him an unfair advantage. After a great deal of bellicosity and whistle-blowing, the Shore Patrol got the melee stopped and the *Legume* boys were herded back to the ship and turned over to the O.D., who happened to be Ensign Nathan Fineberg.

"Well, you guys look like you had fun," he observed. "A fight?"

"Yessir," Motor Mack Galkowski said indignantly. "Some civilian hit a woman with a shot glass an' somebody hit him an' then everybody started pickin' on us Coasting Guards." Everybody else had a different version. Nobody but Al, it seemed, knew that Sonnichson had fired the first salvo, and Al kept his mouth shut. But Sonnichson didn't. Having revived, he wanted to fight somebody. "I'll knocka goddam block offa any subbabish at smarts off at me," he offered, and Al said firmly, "Get your ass downstairs and climb in your crib, baby. You didn't look like no light-heavyweight champ when that doggie pushed the switch."

"Few wasn' a peddy osser you cudden tawka me li kat," the mess cook said, reeling around pugnaciously, and Ensign Fineberg grinned and said, "Lay below, fellows. Sorry, this has to go in the log."

So they went down to the mess deck and sat around until midnight drinking coffee with the lights burning brightly. Because Fineberg was a good guy and didn't consider it his mission in life to save on the electric bill (or the food bill? Al asked himself) or to deprive the enlisteds of visibility after ten-thirty, as did Cupper and Skinny Scraggs and Ensign Halfway when they had the O.D. duty. But the names of the men involved in the brawl ashore had been logged, and the next morning Higgins hailed them up before the skipper, for a captain's mast. Galkowski, deciding to be spokesman for the accused, said very earnestly that the Coast Guardsmen had only defended themselves, which could hardly be called precision reporting. The skipper was still having trouble with his ulcer, and he stared at them stonily and in a wintry voice passed sentence. Five days' restriction to ship. Al felt like laughing. Restriction to ship was a punishment that held no terror for him. On the other hand, nowadays he had to do his reading in the crew's head after 10:30 P.M., and the light in there was hard on a man's eyes while the traffic was hard on his concentration.

No matter how you looked at it, Al was getting pretty fed up with the way things were going on the ship. It didn't help matters much when on August 7 the Office of War Information in its first statement to the nation on the state of the war said, in part: ". . . but as a nation we are only ankle deep in the war. We can win it . . . but we are not winning it yet." Amen, brother, Al said. On this neuter-gender buoy tender we ain't even got our feet wet yet. When they sandbag the USO and issue gas masks to the hostesses, then maybe the old Sleepy Lagoon will get the news there's a war going on.

Oh, he wasn't infallible, he wasn't *always* right, and his crystal ball was sometimes a little smudged and murky. But the main thing was a lack of hot-off-the-war information. The U-boats were bad that spring and summer, thicker than flies. In 1942 the Axis powers concentrated the main fury of their submarine warfare in the western approaches of the Atlantic. They sank Allied merchantmen in sight of New England's coast, in the St. Lawrence, off Sandy Hook and Cape Hatteras, off the white beaches of Florida. These things were not publicized, and a cook on a buoy tender got only fragments of news from a radio controlled by hands in the wardroom—usually Cupper's hand dialing around in search of hillbilly music. The deadly torpedoes wrought havoc and death at the mouth of the Mississippi, and in the Caribbean; and in the Gulf of Mexico a U-boat sank a rescue vessel that was loaded with exhausted survivors of an earlier sinking. The beaches of America's Atlantic Coast from Newfoundland to the Florida Keys were foul with the oil and refuse and washed-up cargoes and sometimes the soggy corpses from merchant ships sunk close offshore. And there were the macabre gothic touches: the empty, bloody, bullet-ripped lifeboats drifting ashore on the tide; the charred, hideously bloated bodies of crewmen from coastal tankers that had been shelled to fiery oblivion in sight of stunned watchers ashore. There were grisly, horrid things bumping and rolling in the surf of America's beaches in 1942, reminders that the Axis was playing for keeps. But these things were not played up in the newspapers or on the radio, and a cook on a buoy tender wasn't well informed on current events.

Al Woods did not know that in May the wolf packs and loner U-boats had made one hundred and two acknowledged kills, mostly along the east coast of America. He was unaware that in June the toll was one hundred and eleven Allied ships, a new world's record kill, or that in July, that calamitous season of Higgins's rise to power, the bag dropped to a scant fifty-one sinkings, largely because the Allies had developed effective countermeasures against the U-boat packs that harassed the Atlantic convoy lanes. The Allies had pretty well destroyed the effectiveness of the wolf-pack type of submarine warfare, but in so doing they had caused the U-boats to scatter and begin to concentrate on easier victims—the lone ship seen through a scouting periscope, the careless, the unwary, the slow, and the helpless. Some ships had enjoyed the immunity of comparative unimportance, heretofore, but now the subs were becoming less particular. A target was a target.

And a poorly armed Coast Guard vessel was a target.

Perhaps one reason the skipper's ulcer bothered him so much

lately was because he knew a lot of dark things that a ship's cook would never know until he read the pages of history after the war was over. Maybe it wasn't only pure cussedness in August that caused the skipper to have more and longer general quarters drills, and to send the men to battle stations at gray dawn and purple dusk when even a fat waddling old scrubwoman of a buoy tender offered a temptingly easy silhouette against the horizon.

"Report any object in the water you're not absolutely *sure* of," the skipper told the men at quarters. "I don't care what you think it *might* be, or what you *suppose* it is, or what it *resembles*. It's better to mistake a broken spar or stick for a periscope than mistake a periscope for a broken spar or stick. Report anything not instantly identifiable, and we'll blow it out of the water!"

Brave, foolish, hollow words. The *Legume* with her one 3-inch gun compete with a U-boat? With her flying-bridge twenties you couldn't depress sufficiently to fire below the horizon? The skipper was suffering from delusions of grandeur, boy. He thought he was commanding a fighting ship, but the *Legume* was like Mess Cook Sonnichson, inadequate.

Al Woods applied his inner eye to his jaundiced mental telescope and surveyed the world situation, and he could see nobody who was mad at the Coasting Guard. Why, everybody tolerated the silly old Hooligan Navy, because it was so obviously neutral. But maybe Al was looking into the wrong end of his viewing instrument, maybe he couldn't see any lurking menace of U-boats because his vision was impeded by the lurking menace of larcenous ship's officers, and by sinister Dennis Higgins, who was trying to turn the goddam vessel into a floating boot camp. And maybe Al's eye was dimmed by his own irresolution.

August was a good growing season for kernels of insurrection, helped by the rich fertilizing voice of a slightly jingoish patriot named Winfrey Fugate, who unctuously despised all who abused the privileges of rank. And really, in August, all a cook needed in order to flare into crackling rebellion was a slight nudge or two.

And he got them in August.

No decent place to read after ten-thirty was a nudge.

And having to relinquish the galley keys at night was a rude elbow in a cook's touchy pride—it almost implied that Higgins was insinuating that the cooks were the real culprits, hoodlums who embezzled at night when honest felons were asleep.

And Ensign Skinny Scraggs's enthusiastic shopping for bargains
at the Navy Commissary was more than a nudge, it was a kick in
the belly. He came back beaming brilliant self-assurance, followed
by a trundling, enigmatic, blandly unconcerned chief steward, followed by a truckload of marked-down specials and remainders. Old
Ed came to the galley and gave Al his bulge-eyed, hooded Buddha
stare.

"Would you be the chef?" he rumbled soberly. I am he, Al replied.
"Then I wonder if you'd be so kind as to turn out the mess cooks
and help the commoff get the stores aboard, chef?" Miller wondered.
Al shrugged; might be interesting. "I knew you would co-operate,
chef," the chief emeritus said courteously, and went to his bunk to
rest as was his long-time custom and prerogative.

Scraggs gave Al the manifest and asked if he would check the
chow aboard, to be sure the trucker hadn't mistakenly left anything
at the warehouse. Al checked the manifest, and soon realized that
the trucker's mistake was not in leaving practically all of it at the
warehouse. Skinny was a lousy purchasing agent. There was an
item listed as "Overseas Hams." Not Swift, not Armour, but Overseas. And as Country Boy started across the well deck with a crate
Al said hold the deal, and he broke open the crate, and swore
pungently. "Ensign," he said disgustedly, "these things aren't fit to
eat. They were invented for emergency use in tropical climates,
they're so salty they'd keep forever in hot damp jungles, they were
intended for use by the Army. They can't spoil because they are
already unfit to eat."

"Surely you exaggerate," the commoff said hopefully.

"Well," Al said, "I guess they'd keep a man alive, if he drank
twenty gallons of water with each slice of ham."

The ensign looked a little hurt and bewildered. He had been so
proud of the shrewd business deal he had consummated with the
Navy. He had bought six crates of the wonderfully inexpensive
hams. He had also bought a lifetime supply of Overseas bacon. Al
hoped he hadn't bought any salt—they weren't going to need any
salt for ten years.

"All right," Al snarled at the mess cooks. "Take that crap below."

But there were other bargains. Six boxes of hamburger, as the
Navy optimistically labeled the stuff. Four boxes of "stewing and
boiling" beef, which defied description, and could scarcely be
graded. Al knew there was U.S. Choice, Good, and Commercial

beef. This was none of those, this was Stewing and Boiling beef. But it was better than the gray hamburger that bled a colorless ooze when thawed out. "On this so-called hamburger," he explained wearily to the chagrined ensign, "they use a short-cut process. Usually you raise barley and oats an' feed it to cattle an' make hamburger outa the cow, but on this deal they just abolish the cow's role an' make the hamburger outa barley, oatmeal, an' some kind of artificial meat that is 90 per cent suet. I don't know where they get the suet. Not off the boilin' beef, because it has all of its own suet an' somebody else's to boot."

"Well, you have bought those items before, Woods," the gloomy rookie economist pointed out defensively.

"We *had* to take a box of hamburger an' a box of stewin' meat with every box of 'roastin' an' fryin' ' meat, or else," Al explained grimly. "Did you get any of the roastin' an' fryin' beef, Ensign?"

"Why, yes, I purchased two boxes of that," Skinny said warily.

Al sighed. Well, send a kid to do a man's job, whatta you expect? There was one crate of pork loins, four boxes of obscene gray link sausages that shrank in a skillet. There were two crates of chickens and a crate of turkeys; not good but the best frozen fowl available at the warehouse. I got to look at the bright side of things, Al said to himself. In one fell swoop here ole Skinny the commoff may have put a termination on the stealin' of hams aboard this vessel.

He checked the rest of the stuff aboard, thinking what he'd like to do to Higgins with each and every one of the sausages, and then beat him into a state of cowering sanity with an Overseas ham. Here he'd figured his main grievances had to do with stuff the higher castes were carting *ashore*. Now he had to start logging it both ways, the stuff Skinny was bringing *aboard* was the worst crime yet.

"Hold the deal!" Al said. He had come to a line that read: Beef loins, 1, U.S. Choice. "How come you only got one slab of T-bones?"

"Oh, that ... it's for the party," Ensign Scraggs said brightly. What party? Al demanded. "The uh party for uh the commanding officer," Skinny blinked nervously. "His birthday is Saturday the fifteenth, you know." Well I'll be dadblamed, Al said as if stupefied. He's a sly one, never told me he was havin' a birthday, or a party either. "Yes, on August fifteen," Al's departmental superior said. "Next Saturday night."

"Oh, that'll be nice," Al murmured, silently adding his favorite four-letter obscenity. "A T-bone an' sirloin party," he said bitterly.

Unaware, or not fully grasping the fact, that it would also be a final-nudge party. A Last Straw party. And as he supervised the caching of the loot shrewd Scraggs had swindled the Navy out of, he thought about the new menus, blue-pencil specials on which Higgins exercised his authority to cut, revise, and substitute; and he meditated about the changing-rapidly-back-again attitude of the crew, who were feeling the pinch of not-enough once more. They couldn't adjust with equanimity from Al's recent generous splurging to the suddenly renewed stinginess since Higgins decided it was up to him personally to take over the general mess problem. And the men knew who to blame, too, for Al thoughtfully displayed the marked-up and crossed-out and written-in menus on the bulletin board in the mess deck. Remembering the growing volume of protests as the guys read the menus for August, Al grinned to himself. The natives are growing mighty restless, they're beating tom-toms in the swamp again, sahib.

Bread pudding, rice pudding, stewed prunes, applesauce—no upside-down cakes, no more lemon meringue pies, no cream pies. Baked beans with just a whisper of bacon three times in one week already. Boiled carrots and boiled potatoes and fried potatoes and potato salad and mashed potatoes and baked potatoes and boiled cabbage and navy beans, kidney beans, lima beans. Oatmeal and cornmeal mush and hot cakes, pancakes, griddlecakes, hoecakes, French toast. Bean soup, fish chowder, brown bean soup, vegetable soup without beef, split pea soup without ham hocks, creamed celery soup with very little cream. Butter served in flat inch-square patties. No bacon, no ham, no sausage for breakfast, not even creamed chipped beef for breakfast. But cornbread and biscuits and bran muffins forever, and pancakes and French toast into eternity. No fruit juice to tonic up the old digestive tracks, boy, just stewed dried apples, stewed dried apricots, stewed prunes, stewed raisins. And they knew to blame Higgins for the new abridged editions of Al's old standard menus. Breaded tomatoes and cole slaw and fried potatoes and no seconds on the chicken-fried stewin' meat for the crew, but the blueblood-bluebeards aft were allergic to canned tomatoes and fried potatoes, they broke out in an unsightly rash if they didn't have seconds and thirds and fourths on the chicken-fried "roasting and frying" beef, and some orr-durves to

whip up an appetite ahead of time, and some canned creamed mush-
room soup to hold their appetites in check until Dave Hubert arrived
with that therapeutic chow of shoestring potatoes, creamed corn,
asparagus, lean steaks, creamed gravy (this out of the common pot,
for pete's sake), and Waldorf Salad (which was the cole slaw with
diced apples, raisins, and nuts added) and a hot apple pie with
sliced cheese.

In the pastoral peace of the green hills of the Atlantic, the old
plantation aristocrats et out of the same youall kitchen as them
happy-go-lucky illiterut ole deck hands. But not the same pots, suh.

Well, at night, down in the fetid sheds where the sullen-eyed
natives slept after totin' that barge all day, there was hex talk, and
whispered rumors of conjure and thaumaturgy, and the voodoo
drums of the hoodoo Hooligans throbbed menacingly in August—
or was that only the throb and beat and rhythm of the Diesel
engines? Gittin' restless, gittin' notional an' fool-minded, yassuh.
Frettin' away the days, and listenin' to rogue minds, heedin'—with
a kind of lassitude, but baleful-eyed—renegade tongues that uttered
wild gore-tinted exhortations about Writin' to the President of the
Goddam United States in Person. Or Gettin' Up a Petition an'
Sendin' It to the District Commander. Or Goin' Back There an' All
of Us Askin' for Transfers.

July's dietary abandon and prodigality had sucked the general
mess deeper into the quicksands of deficit spending. Even the fellows
back aft, who usually were awfully picky and delicate about their
eating, had each bought eleven dollars and thirty cents worth of
groceries from Ed Miller's Cut-Rate Market—according to their
treasurer.

They overspent the hell out of *their* budget, too, Al thought
sardonically, feeling himself the pivot and focus of a new epidemic
of tension and storm warnings and scandalous talk. Sometimes
his busy mind balked, refusing to paw and prod and poke at the
dilemma any longer, and he could only utter Anglo-Saxon oaths
of frustration.

And by one of those quirks of timing, the tapering-off period,
the amnesty week for users of obscenity, had ended the day before
the pink-cheeked new commissary officer went on his shopping
spree. Right away several articulate crewmen ran afoul of the new
foul-mouth ukase. Lanky, lugubrious Moses Scales had already
drawn a week's confinement to ship for inability to refrain from

using a particularly obnoxious expression in the pantry. Chief Huxley had been severely tongue-lashed by Higgins for mentioning certain organic indelicacies when addressing the deck gang. Motor Mack Galkowski had been threatened, and had switched to Polish expletives.

But Al had been too preoccupied with his massive reveries of revenge, and with massaging his scalp, to pay particular attention to the oral trend, and although he didn't like the eternal dreary obscenity that had been basic prior to the executive ultimatum, he had one pet monosyllable that he was wont to mutter in times of stress. When he had finished putting away the grotesque results of Skinny's first venture into commodity buying, he was wrought up and under considerable stress, and when he got up to the galley he forced his clenched teeth apart and released this loud, gutturally eloquent exclamation. Unaware, of course, that the executive officer was only just then pussyfooting into the mess deck. Higgins poked his florid features into the starboard door and favored the cook with a triumphant scowl.

"I heard that," he sneered. "The rule applies to even you, Woods. You petty officers, dammit, should try to set the example. Any more filthy language and you'll find yourself on report."

And with a final threatening sneer he plunged aft on his stealthy crepe soles. Al sighed and shook his head wearily and moved to the door. The mess deck and the passageway were empty, and he made the mistake of supposing Higgins had gone into the office, and he turned back into the galley and inhaled and, in tones of brave defiance, repeated the forbidden epithet. Immediately, like a genie summoned, Higgins stuck his ruddy avenging face around the edge of the *other* door. He had ducked into the thwart alleyway and crossed over to the port passageway to set a trap, and now his thin sarcastic smile showed how well he had succeeded.

"I expected that, Woods," he said witheringly. "You're one of those wise lads that are insolent behind the backs of your superiors, and it's just exactly lads like you we intend to crack down on around here. This means a captain's mast. You'll learn someday. You'll learn."

The wheels of discipline spun faster nowadays; Al was summoned topside by an amused Chicken Hawk, the master-at-arms whose glistening baldness used to haunt Al, and whose sense of humor was cruel at best. "Onionhead, my heart bleeds for ya, sweetheart, let's go topside," he said. "You come peaceful an' I won't hafta use no ropes or chains."

The thought-control dragnet had snared other victims of bad diction, and Al was only one of five glum offenders fidgeting in the skipper's stateroom—but he was the only petty officer. A big, blond, arrogantly handsome, swashbuckling seaman named Peter Irvin, who had the mentality of a retarded ten-year-old delinquent and a limited vocabulary consisting mostly of chilling obscenities usually prefaced by squalid superlatives, drew a five-day restriction and grim warning. The other three were first offenders and lost only one liberty each, after stern lectures. Al, who was charged with insolence as well as smut-mongering, and was also a pace-setting petty officer, got a ten-day restriction to ship. And it wounded Al to draw double the penalty of scum-tongued Peter Irvin, who happened to be the loudest, profanest troublemaker among the Sea Gulls, and a bullier of mess cooks as well. Besides, Al still had two days to serve for the New Bedford skirmish.

There was, he had learned, a vast difference between voluntarily remaining aboard ship and doing so by mandate. The former situation could be terminated at any time, but the latter had to be sweated out.

Getting restricted to ship for ten more days was another nudge. Another push toward the slippery slide. Events were goading him toward some extreme act of retribution, some feverishly immoderate retaliation.

Guys like Higgins caused all the trouble in the world. Hitler was a guy like Higgins. And Mussolini, and Tojo. They were all power-mad greedy ambitious coldhearted vicious egomaniacs, misanthropes, and dictators who abused enlisted men and took what they wanted, protected by a dirty intangible known as authority.

He's been picking on me since the first day I saw this vessel, Al said to himself bitterly. I spotted him right off, I knew his type.

Oh, the insensate perfidy of all officers.

His anger flared higher, guttered, sputtered, and then purred like an oil-blower galley range. And the potent hybrid seed of mutiny kept swelling in the fever of his soul, in the mulch of his hot indignation and betrayal.

CHAPTER 25

Dear Mr. Fugate

PHLEGMATIC, taciturn, cynical Al Woods marked time, brooding, and as the week wore on Dave reported more gastronomical dereliction on the plateau of administration, and the gaunt enlisteds complained of their frugal, Spartan fare. But the *Legume* went her way, the work routine unaffected by the social ruptures and dissensions and the defections of her officers, the mutterings of her men. People would come and people would go, but the good ship *Legume* would continue to plod through her life span as imperturbably as Chief Ed Miller, obeying any master, responding to the ministering hands of whatever fragile human machines were charged with her operation. It made little if any real difference to a buoy tender if her officers were eccentric, if they had certain monetary idiosyncrasies, if they were not consistently honorable and steadfastly conscientious. Just so they knew something of seamanship—and the skipper was a giant on the bridge. It didn't make any difference to the lumbering vessel if Curly Matoli locked his face and shuttered his eyes when he encountered his senior, or if the senior spoke to his colleague only when necessary. The *Legume* didn't even care that Lieutenant Thomas Fox was having a birthday. But the skipper's table-fellows cared enormously, because it meant a gay festive night. And Al Woods cared enormously, too, because he would have to cater the affair. And the crew cared, because they felt the older Old Tom got the more likelihood he might succumb to his ulcer and leave the ship, although that could be a very complicated sort of blessing, since Higgins might succeed to the throne.

All the good wide wallowing buoy tender knew was that she had a load of scraped and painted buoys for Buzzard's Bay. And it seemed to the senior cook that the locale was extremely appropriate. There was nothing in the newspapers or on the radio about Saturday, August 15, being the anniversary of Thomas Fox, although it might conceivably have influenced the entire course of the war. The fabulous occasion was duly celebrated by ninety American enlisteds first, with an early evening chow consisting chiefly of scalloped potatoes au gratin, although ordinarily the presence of baked ham would have been newsworthy. Meat not hidden in a casserole, drowned in a stew, or ground into a dubious and diluted meat loaf, was rare for the crew these days. But this was not the delicately sweet-pungent ham of Armour or Swift or Cudahy or Hormel, redolent of hickory smoke and honey and peppery curing. It was Overseas ham, redolent of brine. Al had soaked five hams for three days in the stock pot, changing water half a dozen times a day in an effort to draw some of the puckery harshness out of the meat, and had parboiled them twice before boning, then boiled them a while in a further fruitless attempt to extract some of the entombed salt, finally baking the gritty petrified pork with pineapple and brown sugar. But still the peasants were ungrateful. Let them eat scalloped potatoes au gratin then. Well, Al thought, dismally regarding all the leftover ham, I can use some of it in meat loaf—maybe it'll give the lousy hamburger some flavor.

"Our guests have guests coming," Al informed Country Boy, who grinned a puckery grin. "They will eat dirty ole T-bones and sirloins come sundown," Al announced. Country Boy refused to grin about that.

With the anguished reproach of his fellow men ringing in his ears, Al commenced the job of fixing goodies for the thieves' carnival. Technically, he often reminded himself, and according to authoritative books on the subject, ship's cooks were supposed to cook only for the general mess, and officers' stewards were supposed to cook for the wardroom. But any regulation that could be broken or ignored in favor of the gold braid was doomed and long since obsolete. Anyhow Dave seldom had any free time for cooking. He was too busy as waiter, bus boy, bellhop, bartender, chambermaid, custodian, and valet—those guys back there all wishing to live in the pampered lap of luxury like before they were pulled bodily out of their Cadillacs and urged into uniform.

But that was digressing somewhat from the point. The point was it had become a shipwide custom for Al to cater these fiestas they held at regular intervals, and ordinarily he wouldn't mind, knowing his friend Dave would have his hands full in the pantry supervising

inexperienced Oliver and untrustworthy Moses. Ordinarily. But
somehow this wild rejoicing on August 15 because the scrawny old
C.O. had grown a little more decrepit, and probably senile too, was
just pushing a good thing a little too goddam far, boys.

I will give them the best chow I know how to fix, Al said to
himself, because I have a stern code of culinary ethics, I have certain
undeviating standards of excellence that I must observe. I can't
stand to see good food mistreated, and I will say here and now it is
lucky for some people that I have integrity and scruples and a
nagging sense of honor that prevents me from spitting in the salad
and rubbing the steaks on the deck and a few little pranks like that.
Besides, I understand from usually unreliable sources—from the
officers, I mean by that crack—that women will be present at this
function, as they have inevitably been at all wardroom social
functions, and I happen to have deep respect for women, although
I mistrust them each and every little one of them, and cannot think
of anything particularly nice to say about any girl, woman, or whore
who would associate with the likes of Dennis Higgins, Hogpuncher
Cupper, et cetera.

Whenever he thought of women he generally sooner or later got
around to brooding momentarily about Stella Wildoe, and now he
thought, I wonder if she is sleeping with everybody in town—and
half of the boys from the country. But that is neither here nor
there—or, to be accurate, it's *there*, and I can't do anything about
it because I'm here on the flagship of the Hooligan Navy fixing an
abundant feast for poltroons who have no ethics or scruples—well,
except Fineberg, and McFarland, and Halfway who is just a meaningless bystander, and of course Skinny, who is a naïve, gullible
child. But Hog Cupper looted the wardroom pantry when he went
grunting ashore in a rutting condition, and Higgins made regular
forays, and the skipper did some intermittent ditty bag requisition-
ing. Personally, Al said to himself, I can understand a guy stealing
chow if he's hungry—I did it myself when I was a student and my
stomach kept gnawing on my backbone. What continually beats
me to my sensitive moral knees is the idea of those jerks paying for
about half of the food they eat and then stealing some more to carry
to their doxies in the village.

He studied the party menu. Hot rolls—he had the dough rising
under a damp cloth in the warming oven. French-fried potatoes,
steaks, onion-tomato-green-pepper kabobs... *kabobs?* Who were

those ruffians trying to kid? They probably didn't even know for sure what a kabob was, for chrissakes. Any more than I ever cooked one before, Al thought ruefully. Chef's salad. Well, I'm the chef, I'll invent something. Cold asparagus—those guys sure got a fetish about asparagus. Fruit cups, and "chilled" turtle soup, both items to be handled in the pantry by Dave and his crew. Ten guests, Skinny said—sixteen people in all, if the O.D. was excluded, or if he wasn't, but McFarland shied away from the shindig. Anyway seventeen steaks. But where the hell did they find ten guests in Buzzard's Bay? Did they import some from Boston?

Al started heating salad oil in the deep-fat fryer for French fries, and turned on the grill to low heat, and checked his dough, and lit a cigarette. Presently Dave came up to leave the stack of huge silver platters with U.S.C.G. *Legume* engraved on them. "Man," Dave said, "you oughta get a gander at all the whisky back there. I got to watch ole Mose all the time, he's droolin' like a camel."

"Whisky an' sirloins, ten-fifty a month," Al said. "That's the way to live, Dave. We all ought to go in for that kind of livin'."

"Those cats know how to jive it up," Dave agreed.

There wasn't anything much to do for a while, so Al took a stroll onto the well deck. The sky was overcast, but the clouds were thin, and the water was a kind of olive green. He leaned on the edge of the open buoy port and watched the glassy swells slide under the ship, lifting her and rolling her gently on her taut anchor chain. The shore was a good quarter of a mile away and the town was around a curve of the shore, and as he looked he saw the Monimor coming around the headland. Bright colors in the motor launch would be women in summer party dresses. Oh, how romantic, he thought sourly, throwing his cigarette over the side and remembering, vaguely, what women were like. They always smell so good, like a flower shop, he recalled wistfully. And he had to admire the officers' strategy out here on the bay where if the gals didn't co-operate you could say, O.K., swim home.

A few minutes later Doc O'Neal came clogging into the galley and wiggled his hips. "Dearie, I just hadda come tell you how much I enjoyed that divine ham we had for supper," he said, pushing his dental repairs out about half an inch and leering gappily. But although he grinned a little, Al was having solemn thoughts, and he said, "Doc, that guy on the radio, ole Winfrey Fugate, he says if a guy knows about some dirty ole officers abusin' the privileges of rank ..." He left the thought unspoken, to complete itself by implication.

"Look," Doc said. "I don't mind bein' seen around socially with a cook, but I wouldn't want to run around with a seaman *ex*-cook. What we oughta do, you an' Sam an' me oughta put in for transfers."

The idea hardly deserved comment, so Al said, "Look at all this high-class chow. We're buyin' them people a high standard of livin'."

"I'll have mine medium rare," Doc said. "Listen, have you seen them debutanties yet? Did you squint at all that talent that just come aboard?" He sighed. "The gold braid located a whole covey of wimmin."

"I didn't see 'em, I ain't interested," Al said sourly.

"Cape Cod heiresses," Doc said lasciviously. "Thrill hunters."

"They oughta get plenty thrills tonight," Al said, and Doc gave him a squirrel-toothed leer and said, "I'm goin' tompeekin' around at all them ripe tomatoes, baby. Happy birthday, dear Onionhead, to you."

Making the rolls, Al indulged in whimsical fancies. What if a sub sneaked through the canal and threw a tin fish into old Lagoon's round fanny while the party was at its peak? It would sure astonish the newspaper readers to see where among the survivors they listed Miss Mabel Roundheels, Miss Bessie Willing, and several unidentified young ladies who were nude when rescued. The officers were all naked, too, and they explained the blast had blown off their clothes. One of the undraped beauties was rescued by a ship's cook and was last seen disappearing into the woods saying, Oh No Al We Mustn't.

He heard girlish laughter in the passageway. Women! *Fee*males!

Higgins was showing some of the guests around the ship, and they appeared in the open top half of the doorway, and Al wished the bottom part was open too so he could see their legs. With Higgins were two girls and an Army officer. The procurer? Al wondered. The girls were quite young and rather pretty. The Army officer was neither, being ruddy and pouchy-eyed, with a black toothbrush mustache. A real rounder, Al thought, and a drinker of much whisky. I wonder how much he pays for chow at his post. I wonder if Army officers are able to swindle their daily bread from the regimental mess allowance.

"This," Higgins said eloquently, "is the galley."

"Oh, isn't it adorable?" the blonde girl said. She was carrying a highball—those lechers weren't wasting any time priming the victims, Al thought enviously. The Army captain leaned into the galley and gave it a brief, asinine scrutiny. "Nice compact little unit," he said.

"It's cute," the black-haired girl said crisply. "I think I'm going to do my kitchen over like a galley. You know, nautical style."

"Oh, you nautical girl," the pouch-eyed captain said coyly.

The exec said self-consciously, "That would make a charmingly original *décor*, Miss Tyler." And Al thought, Incidentally, Miss Tyler, this object all in white is the cook. Say something penetrating about the chef. Isn't he a nice compact unit? Isn't he adorable?

"It's all electric," the exec said smugly. "Everything in there."

Including the cook. My friends and constituents, if I am electric by your volts, I promise you nickel beer and free sex...

"But how conveenient," mooed blondy, sipping her aphrodisiac, and the captain said defensively, "Well in the Army naturally we must settle for mobility and simple functionalism in our kitchens..."

I know ole Simple Functionalism, from Mobility, Alabama, Al said to himself. Did he make corporal yet, General Baggy-eyes?

"Electric range, grill, stock pot, oven, coffee urn," Higgins elaborated. "Reefer." And even electric lights, Al supplied silently, and Miss Tyler said in her brisk, no-nonsense way, "I want something electric for Christmas." Plug me in, baby, Al thought, I'm five hunnert watts myself. And the captain said lecherously, "Are you AC or DC, honey lamb?"

"Now, Chester, cut that out." Miss Tyler giggled.

Chester, Al said to himself. Chester the Jester, from Kokomo, Montana, come to help eat up the poor folks' rations.

"Who is your *current* boy friend?" Chester inquired wittily, old life-of-the-party himself, and the girls laughed, but Higgins glanced at Al and frowned his displeasure. Al looked at the clock and then looked back at the guests and found the cute blonde gazing at him over the rim of her highball glass; she widened her eyes at him and he grinned and thought, Thanks for noticing I'm alive, baby.

"Come along, people," Higgins said, taking the blonde's arm. I would like to take her arm and work down from there, Al thought, and the captain winked at him and asked, "How you doin', bub?"

"Not as good as you're doin', General," Al said, and old Pouch-eyes chuckled vulgarly and said, "That remains to be seen, bub." Don't call me bub, you jerk, Al told him mentally. And then, as

the captain convoyed Miss Tyler forward along the passageway
Al moved to the door and watched, noting her fine long legs and
the provocative swaying of her svelte hips. He shaped his mouth in
a silent whistle and lifted his gaze to find that she had glanced over
her shoulder and caught him window-shopping, and she gave him a
swift, veiled, inviting smile as she moved around the corner. She's
nuts about me, Al daydreamed.

A sudden ear-splitting cacophony erupted from the squawk box
in the mess compartment and then it went squeeawkwowoweewooeek!
as an unseen hand back in the wardroom twirled the dial, and then
it subsided to noisy but organized dance music. May I have this
dance, Miss Tyler? Al thought with a warm tingling appreciation
of all women.

There were more voices in the passageway and Ensign Fineberg
came along with another girl, and Al's heart thumped violently when
he first saw her, because she was small and neat and had a short
tilted nose and light, silvery-gray eyes, and at first look she had been
like a ghost of the past. But Al saw that she didn't really favor
Josephine Hill of Oklahoma, but she was some little queen just the
same, boy.

"This is the kitchen," Fineberg told her, "and that handsome rascal
is our chef, whose unsurpassed product you will shortly enjoy." The
girl smiled amiably and said, "Hi, chef."

"Hello," Al said.

"Miss Arranfeldt," Fineberg said graciously, "Mr. Woods."

The girl grinned at Al. "I know from cooks," she said. "I sling
hash for a living." She pointed at the pile of steaks. "Are those for
us?" Al nodded, and she sighed happily. "Make mine real well done,
pal."

"O.K.," Al said, envying Fineberg. "Where do you sling hash?"

"The Silver Spoon Grill," she said. "Come try *our* chow."

"Sure, if I ever get a parole," Al said, feeling bewitched.

"Hey, have a heart, man," Fineberg said ruefully. "What will the
boys at the gourmet's club say if I lose my girl to a mere enlisted?"

The girl studied Al with smiling speculation. "Ensign," she said,
"you may have something there. After all, can *you* cook?"

Fineberg groaned and began pushing her away from the door,
and gave Al a friendly wink as he left. This is wink-at-the-cook
week, Al said to himself. But that was pretty affable of the socialites
to josh with the servants like that. And that Arranfeldt beauty, she

was a free agent and probably not too snooty to go out with a cook. I better get a fix on this anchorage and mark it on my charts, Al thought. Maybe when my hair gets long and slinky I'll look that little doll baby up. We could make beautiful breakfasts together.

Chief Bordeau, a machinist who liked to think he had a French accent, stopped by the galley to comment. "See dem gals, ma leetle bull?" he inquired. "She is very beautifool, no?"

"Wee, wee," Al said. "Bot she is not for CPO, ma fran."

"Is moch too monyafeek for man lak, say, skeeper, exec, or mos' of dem back in de shaft alley, huh?" Frenchy said wistfully. "Well, I go play cards with ole Ed an' theenk about sax, no?"

"Yes," Al said. "I'll stay here an' help you theenk about sax."

After a while Dave brought Al a drink, compliments of the C.O., and Al accepted the highball but rejected the compliments. The old bastard was just showing off, he thought. Impressing the company with a democratic gesture. "How many girls back there, Dave?" Al asked.

"Eight ladies, two Army joes," Dave said. "I guess this is a big thrill to those ladies, havin' dinner on a battleship, man."

"It's a big thrill to the general mess to pay for it, too," Al said sarcastically. "We're all happy to defray the costs. *Happy*, man."

Dave snapped his fingers. "Glad you reminded me, old chap. While I was servin' a round of drinks one of those Army cats said wow, man, this little shindig must be settin' the wardroom mess back plenty. And ole Higgins kinda prooned his feathers an' says, why nossir, as a matter of fact this here little snack was no strain a-tall, as they had managed to build up a tidy little surplus in the mess kitty." Seeing Al's amazement, he chuckled. "That's what the man said, Alvin. He said why General suh, it don't cost us a red penny out of our own pockets *beee*cause they had done gone and bought all that goofus juice an' little *dee*leckacies with a *surplus* they had a*koo*mulated in the righteous wardroom mess kitty. That's what the man said."

"God *dayum!*" Al said hoarsely. "That sonofabitch!"

"Yes lord, but there's more," Dave said. "The Army cat looked astoundished an' says, quoth, how in the livin' world did you manage to do a splendid thing like that, sir? You must have one helluva sharp mess treasurer. An' ole Higgins *pree*ooned hisself some more an' says, I am the cat that hannels the kitty back here, General, an' the how come of it is I am a little too hep to human nature to let the chief commissary steward cheat us. You got to watch them chiefs like a hawk or the general mess would have us officers payin' for *twice* what we actually *get*. Al, I wouldn't snow you, that's what the man *said*."

Something broke inside Al, something sprouted and grew. He sighed. "Well, that does it," he said quietly. "That tears it, Dave." He lit a cigarette and blew smoke angrily. "I'm gonna write a letter. We didn't take those bastards to raise. I'm gonna write me a letter." He looked at Dave narrowly. "Dave, you hafta pass your bunk when you go below after chow for the wardroom. From now on keep *two* records, one under your mattress, one in the pantry. Will you do that?"

Dave sighed. "Man, make it an order so I'll *hafta*." Al said it was an order. Dave grinned weakly. "I got to obey them orders, Al."

The seed had sprouted and grew apace, and when the banquet was all removed to the rumpus room Al broke out his typewriter and wrote the letter. He'd always known someday he would *need* that typewriter, to strike a blow for the rights of the common, or enlisted, man. It was an instrument of fate, this sure must be the shining hour.

Al wrote an indignant letter to Winfrey Fugate, champion of the enlisted man. He told how little the wardroom had paid for chow for April, May, June, and July, how much the general mess had gone into debt over the same period, and accused the officers of carrying more food ashore than they paid for in a month. He mentioned the party and the "surplus" Higgins had gloated about. And finally he accused the officers of robbing the general mess without remorse, without pity.

Doc and Yeoman Sam were playing checkers and insulting each other two tables away, and when he finished the letter Al put it before them without comment. "This is dynamite," Sam worried. But Al had it all figured out. This man Fugate would break the scandal over the air, without mentioning actual names and places (he always promised to protect his sources) and the officers would blanch and start sweating, and also start paying for the food. Once they knew some powerful guy like Fugate had the goods on them, they wouldn't dare steal any longer.

Al put another sheet in the typewriter and wrote a line to the effect that the undersigned were endorsing Al's sincerity, sanity, and honesty, but were not otherwise involved. "I accept full responsibility for the charges made herein," Al typed heroically.

In grim silence Sam and Doc signed the voucher. And so did five other petty officers and four seamen. And that was that. The un-American atrays and ouslays were about to be exposed to the shocked world.

CHAPTER 26

The Mountain to Mohammed

THE reaction hit him and shook him, and he felt weak and sick and apprehensive and very lonely. He was on the foc'sle, staring down at the glittering ebony water, trying to close his mind against the clamoring alarm and dread of what his letter might do. They'll know I did it, he thought. They'll transfer my ass to Greenland.

He had thought of using the threat of the letter, not actually sending it, but letting Higgins and the other officers know of its existence, holding it over their heads as a dire warning that unless they changed their corrupt habits immediately . . .

But it wouldn't work. Somehow they would doctor up the books, cleverly hide their complicity and duplicity, and he himself would be court-martialed for some monstrous fabricated charge—blackmail, most likely, threatening officers. Hell, the most heinous charge of all—conspiracy to mutiny.

It would be a despicable thing now *not* to mail the letter, it would be an act of shoddy cowardice. But he wished he'd never written it.

He sat a while in the mess deck drinking the coffee and listening to the music and hearing the laughter and glee back in the wardroom, and steeled his mind and courage, committing himself to his course. Restlessly he paced, and with turbulent mind he wandered the black decks of the ship, and found himself in time leaning wearily against the depth charge rack almost directly above the merriment. He put his feverish face on his crossed arms and swore at his own weakness.

The *Legume* placidly chewed at her anchor chain in the dark overcast night, rising and falling ponderously on the swells as if breathing deeply, and from the ventilator Al heard muffled laughter and the music and the clink of ice cubes down in the wardroom,

277

and Al could not remember a time when he'd felt more utterly alone, or had felt more excluded from the normal living routine of the human race.

You never really understood the appalling difference between an enlisted man and an officer until there was a wardroom party that included women guests. A cook couldn't bring a woman aboard. Not even a CPO could bring a woman aboard. And the inequity seemed painfully magnified now, with the ship anchored out so that you couldn't go ashore and find a woman of your own. The eagle-hats and the crow-arms, Al thought. The commissioned vultures and the enlisted sparrows. The buzzards of Buzzard's Bay, feasting on the putrescent, rotting corpse of the general mess. They were not like other men. Yet the women, who were also officers' prey in a sense, bridged the difference easily—they could drink and make love with men of any rank.

Al yearned for somewhere to go, and he thought of the CPO's snug little mess room with its closed door that shut out everybody who hadn't reached that peculiar in-between status of chief. The CPO's jealously guarded the narrow chasm separating themselves from a PO first class—they shut themselves in to play cards, shutting you out.

There were times when a cook did not seem to belong anywhere at all, not even on the goddam ship, and this was such a time.

He heard the women laughing and felt a dumb misery, the lonely misery of nowhere to go, nobody to go to. This was the old and constant wound; never in his life had he had anywhere to go, anyone to go to. This was the dull pain that kept him awake late at night, and the quick pang he felt now hearing a woman laugh the easy, calm, assured laugh only a woman can laugh—because she knows she belongs anywhere and everywhere, and can shape her soft body and soft mind into any reasonable situation or circumstance. Women were pliable, compatible, adaptable. But a man had hard unbending edges and had to find his right place, or not fit in. A man's mind and heart were set in a mold, so that he hurt himself trying to fit in where he did not belong; bruised himself with futile anger and lonely hunger when he had no place to go, nobody to go to, and could only wonder in outer darkness listening emptily to women laughing in another world. And maybe a cook had the roughest, most abrasive edges of anybody, a stoniness of mind that kept him awake when his fellows had gone below to their beds, seeking the balm of sleep for their strangely injured pride that winced at the sound of alien women laughing with the officers who robbed their plates. But Al's hardness was like scar hardness over a sensitive wound that he kept bumping on the hard realities. In pain he had revolted and written a letter to the vague unknown world beyond the ship's rarefied atmosphere, not hoping for much, dreading a good deal, but not really looking beyond the myopic fact of having translated the pain into words on paper—and knowing that he would mail it, that he couldn't stop now. He'd had the final outraging push. The letter was like a crumbling clod thrown into darkness toward a pin point of light—you couldn't be sure it would hit anybody, or know if it did, but only hope someone would be concerned to find out why it was thrown.

He leaned on the rail and looked down, seeing the black soft water arching and sighing against the gray hardness of the ship, and he thought that the sea must be female instead of the ship, because the sea was malleable, reconciled to time and place and circumstance, stormy of mood sometimes but sometimes warm and inviting—and stronger in the end than the ships, as women were less destructible than men.

He believed that women had a higher anguish threshold than men, and shallower sensibilities; were less lonely, less sad, less morbid—and by the same token less happy, less delighted with living. A woman might weep, alone in the night, because of some particular man, or some minor tragedy in her life, or some passing unrelated sorrow, but having wept, having staged her own private drama, she was done with it. She would not know how a man could be desolately lonely in the night and feel grievously betrayed, hearing the taunting sound of women laughing with predatory officers. She would not understand, unless you told her she was the woman who laughed, which to her would therefore explain and justify your deep and solitary despair.

This night was familiar to Al. He remembered ruefully prowling the nights at OU, foraging for food like a stray dog (or an officer on his way to his girl friend's apartment), watching wives and daughters bare their tantalizing bodies behind careless half-drawn shades, and watching obese men gobbling bedtime snacks of unimaginable richness while he, Al Woods, the exiled outcast, fed his stomach on tomatoes and hard green pears and sour apples, and fed his lonely discontent by profanely and covetously scrutinizing the ripe warm naked wealth that belonged to other men. As a ship's cook, first class, Al had all the money he needed to spend, or his remembered hungering would let him spend, but he was still afflicted with this other, greater poverty.

He heard the women laughing tipsily and temptingly below, but nearer at hand he heard another voice, calling with husky vehemence, "Scales! Goddam you, answer me, Mose!"

"Is that you, Dave?" Al asked the darkness.

"Yes, man." Dave sighed.

"You seen that no-good Mose?"

"No," Al said.

"That bastrid." Dave groaned, his white uniform ghostly on the quarter-deck. "I'll slay him, man. I'll murder him dead." Al asked what Moses Scales had done, and Dave said disgustedly, "He copped a fifth of Scotch. Kept sneakin' up on the whusky all evenin', beltin' it when my back was turned, an' he got higher than a catfish. So I made him lay below before he got hisself some bad bad trouble. Only he musta slithered back into the pantry whilst I was fetchin' drinks to the people an' Ollie was handin' around the blue cheese an' crackers. Oh, man. There was a whole great big wonderful unopened fifth of Black and White, an' it's gone an' the other flagon of Scotch is most nearly empty, an' what am I gonna tell the lady when she asks for Scotch on the rocks an' all I got is rocks, man?"

"The robbers got robbed, huh?" Al said with malicious pleasure. "Hell, Dave, just give the lady bourbon—I'll bet five bucks she won't know the difference. She's probably higher'n a kite already, huh?"

"They all gettin' up altitude, man. They all glowin' with a righteous, tighteous glow." Dave chuckled. "Feelin' no miseries. Those cats really lappin' up the catnip, an' the joint is jumpin' with jive. They havin' the *nicest* time." Then he sobered suddenly. "Oh-wee! I got to find that Moses an' whang the tar outa him an' regoblinate that ever lovin' Black and White. That lady cat won't drink nothin' else but."

"No rush, man," Al said. "Tell me all the dirty, lewd details."

Dave laughed softly in the night. "Well, the main head host took a lady to see his etchin' collection about an hour ago, an' they were still in his cabin when I come Scotch huntin'. A lady has got Skinny cornered an' he's tight but puttin' up a real good resistance. Al, I wish I had a movie cammer so I could *ree*cord that love scene.

Lady keeps callin' him her bashful lil virgin an' astin' him to take her to his cabin an' show her *his* water colors, but he ain't gubblible as yet. He afraid the lady gonna make him do somethin' naughty. Hot dog! That boy gonna lose his chastastity 'fore long. Al, I gotta go down.''

"Don't stop now, tell me more, Dave," Al said eagerly.

Dave groaned worriedly, but lingered. "Them others dancin' an' prancin' an' rubbydubby, huggymuggy romancin',," he said. "Ole Higby Higgins ain't doin' so good, I figure—his charm gits negative when he's gulpin' an' his dancin' got room for improvin'. Mostly he likes to stand still an' kinda rotate an' revolve, like, an' if I'm any judge the lady cat don't pleasure up much from that dipsy-doodiddle stuff."

"How the other fraternity brothers makin' out?" Al asked.

"Cupper got the tallest, least-lookin' lady outa there a long time hence an' locked his cabin door. They havin' a good long chat in there about Texas razorback hogs, I surmise. Ole Halfway, now there's a cat knows how to *dis*interest a lady quick, man. He already blowed his opportunities, I expect—he's one of them sad, pitiful drunks. Last seen he was all broody moody in a corner, anguishin' hisself. Fineberg is a cat can handle his ladies an' his likker both. He's doin' all right, but he acts like he's thinkin' of the future, tryin' to line up a long-time program. Man, I gotta shove off an' officiate."

"Quite a night down there," Al said with wistful envy.

"Oh," Dave said airily, "just average, man, just average. If you see, hear, or smell that Scotchified Mose, lemmee know, will you? I gotta scat, Ollie don't know how to mix them drinks yet an' them folks the thirstiest cats in town. Owooo, owooo, owooo."

When the steward had hurried away, Al went Scotch-hunting. I'd take a drink without somebody twisting my arm, he said to himself. And it occurred to him that Moses would most likely have staggered out onto the well deck and lost himself among the tangle of buoys and gear. So he started forward along the starboard boat deck, and he was passing the Number 2 lifeboat when he heard a strangling adenoidal snore. Moving stealthily, he found the loosened tarpaulin, felt around in the boat, and found dog-drunk Moses Scales sprawled there. And Dave had underestimated the loss, because Moses was hugging *two* bottles to his bony chest. The fifth of Scotch was still unopened.

"Much obliged, Moses," Al murmured. "It's what the doctor ordered."

He climbed carefully to the high breezy flying bridge, found it uninhabited, and got comfortable on the ready box by his useless old 20-millimeter gun. The Scotch was very good, very quick, and he thought about rousting out old Yeoman Sam and Doctor Harry O'Neal and sharing the booty with them, but he didn't really want anybody up there with him. He wanted to be alone with his bottle of dreams, feeling the gentle soaring lift and sensual roll of the ship. This was fate, boy. Fate had rewarded him for his courageous insurrection. Old Moses didn't look like an instrument of destiny, but he was.

Fate, destiny, whatever you're called, Al said to the black skies, thank you for the whisky, but you didn't send me a girl. He could not hear the music and gaiety of the party up here, and the Scotch warmed the cockles of his rebel heart and eased the tension in his mind, and it was very peaceful surrounded by the hushed soft murmur of the August night in his own private high world. For the moment, for an hour or two, he had found his place to go.

Somewhere off yonder a town slept with its lights extinguished in uneasy compliance with the wartime rules. Or maybe it didn't sleep but lay restlessly listening to ghostly music and far thin laughter across the water, wondering what the hell was going on out there. Al drank a toast to the uninformed village. To you, torpid town, for sending us your plump wanton daughters for the lusty pleasure of our fine gallant officers, while a poor old reckless cook with no home town, no family to speak of, no place to go and nobody to be with, can't even chase one of them down ashore. But don't sweat about it, for I have this flagon of solace and my own exclusive party. Listen, town, I'm happy up here. For a little while the hell with everything. Feel that cool ocean breeze? Smell that salty subtle complicated pre-aroma of golden autumn promised on the night air? Feel the living buoyant motion of the ship? Nobody up here but me and my 20-millimeter and her sister, a pair of stiff-backed girls that can't curtsy worth a damn. You are deceived if you think I am a mere cook, town. As your plump long-legged daughters study with panting intentness the ceilings of our leaders' plush staterooms in the gritty, shoddy, vulgar, carnal world below, I just happen to be a renegade correspondent, a rebel leader, and the best combination cook-gunner in captivity, that's all.

But even here on the summit of the night there was no privacy, for somebody was furtively scraping shoe leather on the rungs of the steel ladder, breathing badly, climbing slowly. If it is Moses come for the Scotch I will throw him into Buzzard's Bay, Al thought, and he stashed the bottle under the canvas cover of the big searchlight mounted between the guns, and held his breath, listening. The invader of his aerie was making slow work of it. The leathery scuffing stopped and he heard only the panting, sibilant gasps. The climber was resting, and Al moved silently to the rail wondering who but an officer could be in such poor physical condition as all that. Leaning over the rail with its canvas windscreen, he made out a blob of ghostly pallor, and he said gruffly, "Who's that on the ladder?" His reply was a startled gasp, and a meek voice saying, "It's only meeee. Help."

Al was incredulous. A woman! She'd break her ignorant little neck climbing around a ship in the dark like that. A woman who said, "I can't go up or down, and I can't hold on much longer. Please . . ."

So Al reached into the pool of blackness, risking his own neck with Scotch disregard, and found the girl's wrists and helped her up the ladder and onto the flying bridge, where she collapsed against him trembling and breathing with difficulty. One of the party girls.

"Me and my big fat impulses," she panted. "I was beginning to think that ladder went all the way to Mars." Al couldn't tell from her voice whether she was one of the girls he'd seen. Or her height either. She wasn't tall or short, and felt slender and shapely when she leaned against him like that. She didn't seem to be especially drunk. "Please," she said wistfully, "get me a nice chair to collapse on, huh?"

"We have no chairs," he said. "I'll get you a cloud to sit on."

"A cloud would be fine," she said. "A drink would be nice, too."

"I might be able to locate some whisky," Al said, and she said gee whiz, he wouldn't happen to have Scotch on the rocks? This must be the lady Dave spoke of, Al thought. "No rocks," he said, "but I do have some fine smoky old Black and White." He led her to the ready box and seated her, and got the bottle and sat beside her. "No glasses either," he said, and put his arm around her in a perfectly friendly manner. He had a proprietary feeling about this girl. Hadn't he saved her beautiful, supple bones from any number of compound fractures? It wasn't every night he had a girl up here on the flying bridge, and he wasn't going to dawdle around about it.

"Love this Scotch," the girl said. "It was sheer fate that sent me up here to you and this beautiful stuff. They ran out down there."

Sheer fate, Al thought dreamily. How right she was. He sure had the right connections tonight. Send me a girl, he'd prayed to fate, and here she was. He couldn't see her, but he knew she was beautiful. She smelled like a high-priced flower shop and good Scotch whisky.

"When I was guided around the ship before dark," the beautiful girl said, "I wanted to come up here. I was outvoted. But here I am."

"They're liable to be worrying about you," Al said. That was his main worry, that someone would come looking for her any minute.

"Let them worry," she said scornfully. "They didn't worry when I was in that room being attacked by that sloppy sex-fiend."

Suddenly unhappy, Al muttered, "Who raped you? I'll kill him."

"Nobody did, don't worry," she said, touching him in the dark, her finger tips exploring his face. "But old slobberin' Dennis Higgins sure gave it an all-out try." She giggled. "*He'll* have a lump or two." Her breath was warm and intimate against his face, and he wanted to kiss her, now that she hadn't really been raped after all. "He just kept after me with his big lies about having some more Scotch in his cabin," the girl said. "So finally I went with him, and he locked the door and started grabbing. I detest the grabby kind. Especially when they are blind drunk." Her sweet Scotchy breath was on his face and it bothered him, it made him feel like the grabby kind himself. "Why couldn't the stupid thing just come right out and say will you or won't you?" the girl said indignantly. "Then I could just say no thanks, and nobody would have got hurt." She giggled again and tilted the bottle. "He was roaring drunk, and in the mad scramble I shoved him over a swivel chair and he hit his head on the desk or else just plain passed out. Saved me the trouble of decking him with an ash tray or something. Anyway, I closed the door behind me, and here I am, and my dear friends no doubt think I'm being seduced by a drunk lieutenant, if they bother thinking about me at all. Who are you, chum?"

"I'm the guy who cooked the dinner," Al said.

"Loved that dinner," she said. "It was the only nice part of the evening—until now. The steaks were wonderful, cook."

"Thanks," Al said. "Look, I'm gonna be forced to kiss you."

"All right," she said. "Maybe I'll like that, too."

Her mouth was warm and clinging and a little experimental, and she liked the kiss. "Nice," she breathed. "So you're the genius who fixed the chow. Kiss me again, genius." He kissed her again, sensing her slightly analytical response. Then she snuggled against him and sighed and said, "I don't really know what made me come up here, but I'm glad I did. Are you married, genius?" Al said he wasn't. "Not that I suppose it matters," she said. He took a drink and she took a drink, and he kissed her, longer this time, and she said, "Genius, do they have those wild wild parties very often?" Not often, Al said, but too often at that. "I think I know what you mean," she confided. "Why don't they just hire prostitutes in the first place, instead of depending on whisky and steaks and sheer brute strength, I wonder?"

"An officer wants everything to be free," Al said.

"Well, it's my first sea party. And oh, brother, my last."

"You're nice," Al said impulsively. "You sound nice. I can tell you're pretty, too. From your voice, and kissin' you. You're just *nice*."

"I like you too, genius," she laughed. "Can I buy you a drink?"

Al laughed quietly, happily, and accepted the bottle and tilted it, not needing the Scotch any more, intoxicated by the girl's presence and the crazy unbelievable situation. The ship lifted and rolled in gentle slow motion, and the flying bridge was a square small world with a powerful hooded searchlight and two crazy incompetent guns, hidden in the velvet fog of the night. It was a kind of enchanting thing, being up here with a girl he couldn't see and hadn't ever seen and probably never would see, a girl he could only taste and hear and feel and smell. She tasted, sounded, felt, and smelled wonderful.

"I'm enjoying our party, genius," the girl said. "You smell nice and sirloinish and French-friedish—you make me hungry all over."

"You read my mind," Al said. "I was just thinking you smell pretty yummy yourself, like a pretty girl should—as near as I recall. It has been a long time since I was this close to a pretty girl."

She looked up, her face bumping him softly, and he kissed her, feeling the old remembered warmth flooding his belly and loins, and she said, "Why *haven't* you been close to any pretty girls, genius?"

So he told her about his restriction, making it sound worse than it was, and at all the sad inhuman places she punctuated his woeful

tale with compassionate kisses that grew longer and more abandoned each time. "If I'd known what a sadistical louse Dennis was
I would have kicked him in the teeth when I had the chance," she
said. She was a sensible girl, sympathetic, warm-blooded, and
sensually responsive under the stimulation of Scotch and Al. And
now she said softly against Al's cheek, "We're all alone, there's
nobody in the whole world right now but us—and nobody will
come up here. Right?" Al said that was right. "Give me a kiss and
a drink," she said, "and then let me quarrel with my puritan conscience for a minute, genius."

A little confused, Al followed instructions, and she sat very still
in his arms for a while as the ship lifted and rolled lazily. "How
long has it been since you were with a girl?" she whispered.

"A million years," Al said.

"Hmmm," she said, dreamily. "A girl gets that lonesome urge
sometimes, too. And gee, this is a funny thing, how you happened
to be up here with some Scotch, feeling lonely, and I came up here
because I . . . well, I don't *know* why. It's kind of like a dream, a nice
dream so far. It almost seems this was meant to happen, huh?"

"Yeah," Al said huskily. "Maybe we shouldn't fight it."

"That's what I mean," she whispered a little breathlessly. "That's
how I feel too." And she came to him, sighing, warm and eager and
passionate. Al yanked the canvas cover off the searchlight and
spread it on the deck and pulled her down into his arms, a girl he
couldn't see but didn't need to see, and they lost themselves in the
blind reeling night as the *Legume* rose and fell and swayed and
rolled gently on the black voluptuous water. And the delight of it
was in no wise lessened by the knowledge that Higgins had tried
and failed. They stayed in each other's arms afterward, silent and
content, unmindful of the Spartan couch, dreamy and distracted by
the hushed peace of the August night, lost in a sense of unreality and
enchantment. Al felt that if he moved he would find it was only a
lonely sailor's dream after all; he wanted the moment to endure
forever, touched by the magic and mystery and Scotch and warm
human intimacy.

The girl moved at last, breaking the spell, her soft body gently
protesting the weight and hard edges of Al, and they got off the
rough canvas pallet and drank some more of the Scotch, and talked
in hushed voices about nothing much that he would remember for
long afterward. He introduced her to his useless old 20-millimeter

Oerlikon antiaircraft gun, with which he had chalked up two box kites on the firing range in April—two vicious enemy box-kite targets sent aloft from the ship's bow. He explained about the gun's short-comings to his unseen lover, in spite of which it was a great little gun. He told her about the endless battle drills and dry runs and live-ammo firing at towed sleeve targets. He strapped her into the harness and showed her how to swivel and train the gun, how your body became a part of the gun and it was a very intricate business, like dancing, requiring rhythm and a sense of balance and muscular co-ordination and precise timing, so that the more you became one with the gun the more instinctive became its operation. Being a very sensible, intelligent, sweet, passionate, well-built girl, she was immensely interested in Al's gun, intrigued by it, and there was no hurry about anything, really.

The second time was better. The second time was always better. Al did not know the hour, or care; it was NOW and he was king of the flying bridge and emperor of the night, sharing it with this mysterious but undoubtedly beautiful, eagerly passionate girl whom fate had sent him, and who had come so unerringly by instinct through the darkness to Al and the fifth of Scotch. He didn't try to learn who she was, it sufficed that she had found him in his high private soaring hideaway, it was enough that for a brief time of thundering heartbeats she had belonged to him. He sensed in her careful anonymity that there would be no sequel to this unbeliev-able night of half-drunk enchantment. She had given herself to him *because* he didn't know her and wouldn't recognize her if they ever met again. And she knew he was the cook who had done the ban-quet, she could find him again if she wanted to. At the end she made it clear she wouldn't try to find him again.

"But if we did meet, I think I'd know you," she murmured sadly.

"I'd smell like onions an' grease," Al said.

"And I'd smell like Scotch, if I could," she said. "Genius, please don't remember me as just a tramp who came to the wild party."

"I couldn't," Al said, touched with sadness because he knew he would probably remember almost that way. The girl Higgins tried to rape. He wouldn't try to find her, because he'd always wonder how nearly successful Higgins had really been, and whether maybe she would have given herself to Higgins if he'd been a little less drunk and brutish. And whether she'd given herself to other officers at other parties.

"I want to go down now, please," she said softly. "Back to earth."
He helped her down the ladder and guided her to the starboard
hatchway where a ladder led down to the main deck. He kissed her
for the last time, sorely tempted to strike a match and save himself
the trouble of wondering forever afterward what she looked like,
but he didn't. She might be hauntingly beautiful, so that he'd never
be able to forget her face, or that she was a party guest who may
have come to him on the flying bridge only because Higgins passed
out too soon.

"Good-by," she murmured. "I'll never, never forget tonight."
And he let her go into the black maw of the hatch, turning away
before she slipped through the blackout curtain. He went below
and put the rest of the Scotch in his locker and hit his sack, and fell
asleep with the scent of her clinging to him. Sinking into slumber,
he thought, Thank you, baby. And you, too, fate. And even you,
slobberin' Dennis.

That's how it had always been with him. Feast and famine. Go
hungry forever and then gorge himself briefly and then go back to
short rations. And in the morning he did not feel very well, or very
happy, wanting something more than infrequent quickie romances
—but he felt much better after he saw the lumpy bruise on Higgins's
forehead, sustained in attempting, in his curt authoritative fashion,
to seduce a girl. Old slobberin' Dennis was so accustomed to taking
whatever he wanted that he'd forgotten how to handle the tricky
spadework. I wish he knew how the story finally ended, Al thought,
grinning to himself.

All the officers except McFarland and the skipper had hang-
overs, and Yeoman Sam relayed tidbits of gossip to Al throughout
the long weary morning. The skipper had awakened in a foul
mood, and bawled out the other officers at breakfast. They had, he
accused, acted like a bunch of juvenile delinquents on their first
binge. You were a fine bunch of alcoholic bums last night, he told
the penitent wardroom crew. And to Higgins he said with bleak
disgust, "Just look at yourself, mister. And you're the *second*
officer of this floating whore's nest!"

Al felt a little dubious about the skipper's disapproval. If the
party got out of control, it was probably because the commanding
officer wasn't there to inhibit his juniors with a sense of decorum
and caste protocol. The truant skipper had been amazing one of
the lady guests in quarters, demonstrating how remarkably young

he was for a man as old as he was. And if McFarland and the skipper were the only officers not badly hungover, it was because McFarland simply didn't drink, and the skipper was coddling his ulcer. Old Tom hadn't abstained prudently because of his high station in life, that was certain.

Only McFarland and resilient Ensign Fineberg took solid food for breakfast, one because he needed it and the other because he *thought* he needed it. And when Dave came to the galley to get soft-boiled eggs for the ensign, he said sleepily, "Say, by George, old chap, you owe me five quid. Remember the lady who *pree-ferred* Scotch on the rocks? I oozed some bourbon into her glass and she sure knew the difference. When that lady say Scotch, she mean Scotch. So you owe me five, man."

"O.K.," Al said, interrupting his work to smile dreamily at the bulkhead. "It was worth it," he sighed.

CHAPTER 27

Death of a Barber

AUGUST wore stormily on, leaving the shambles of a Hooligan birthday ritual strewn in its turbulent wake. For a few days after the drunken brawl the general alarms became more frequent, reflecting the skipper's angry mood, and the officers were quiet and chastened. Al remembered less and less vividly the flying bridge episode, and began to wonder where his next girl was coming from. He mailed the letter to Winfrey Fugate on August 17, sneaking it ashore with Doc, and gingerly sat back to await results. The results were to be maddeningly slow in coming. The grist mill of Hooligan justice ground exceedingly sluggishly and rather coarsely in August.

Al could not do twenty push-ups without stopping on the swaying quarter-deck, and he had also learned to send a few forbidden obscenities to Doc O'Neal, his partner in the semaphore drills.

Then, on August 22, with the ship just through the Cape Cod Canal on the return trip to Boston, laboring in heavy seas, Chicken Hawk awakened the senior cook at nine hundred hours and solemnly informed him that the skipper wished to see him on the bridge at once. Al felt a clammy hand of dread clutch at his heart. The letter! he thought, crawling groggily out of his bunk and fumbling for his pants. It couldn't be the letter so soon, he thought.

It wasn't the letter. He got dressed, his eyes sore and his tonsils swollen and prickly, his body tired and stiff, cheated out of three hours of scheduled sleep. What's the deal? he asked, but Chicken Hawk only shrugged and said he didn't know, and went away.

Al dragged his protesting body up the steep ladder and splashed cold water on his face in the crew's head and looked at his hair, which was an inch long and somewhat shaggy. But his head felt great. No more itchiness, no dandruff. Stop stalling, he told himself, when he calls a man up to the bridge at sea, it's something big. He left his towel in the galley, ignoring Curly Matoli and being ignored in return, and climbed to the boat-deck hatchway, where a wet mist was slanting against the rolling ship, and on up the wet outside ladder to the wing of the bridge, shivering in the penetrating breeze. It was going to be autumn any minute now, he reflected worriedly, and pulled aside the storm curtain apprehensively and went into the bridge.

The skipper was sitting on his stool, his skinny legs crossed with the toe of one shiny shoe hooked behind the calf of the other leg, arms folded, staring bleakly through the windshield, stony-eyed, forbidding, grim creases beside his mouth, lumpy jaw muscles tight-bunched, the very prototype of every Captain Bligh who ever ruled a ship. Seaman Mike Kelly was helmsman, his eyes glued to the compass needle; Ensign Fineberg stood quietly by the other hatch curtain; Signalman Heatly lounged near the chartroom door. Al never did like audiences when he was getting chewed out. Goddammit, he thought.

"You sent for me, sir?" he asked, a bit breathless.

"Yes," the skipper said, and he handed Al a sheet of yellow paper. "Radio message from the D.O., Woods. Copy of original telegram." And then the skipper, the helmsman, the ensign, and the signalman looked considerately away while Al learned that his father was dead.

The message did not say when or how Windy Woods died, but only that he was dead and the funeral was set for Monday, 1 P.M., August 24. The original telegram, as best Al could determine in the shock of the moment, had been signed by a person named Lester Potts. Dumbly Al read the message again, feeling no immediate pain but only dull shock, dismay, weariness and sleepiness, and desperate need for some hot coffee to awaken him and anesthetize his sore throat. All right, he thought dismally. O.K. He's dead, then.

"We'll be in Boston tonight," the skipper said. "You can have six days' emergency leave, Woods."

Al shook his head. "I won't be goin', sir," he said. He didn't know why he felt that way about it, but that was the way he felt. He couldn't go home if he had no home, goddammit?

"As you wish," the skipper said. "You have my condolences."

Al felt required to explain his reaction to the message. "It's just, well . . . he's dead," he muttered. "I can't do anything for him now. I'd just rather remember him like he was the last time I saw him, sir." Oh, hell yes, remember him talking into your face with a beer breath, remember him telling everybody ole Hotshot was gonna be a big shot.

"As you wish, of course," the skipper said in his normal chill tones, but somehow the words reproached Al, and he felt a quick sense of shame and guilt and compunction. But he just didn't want to go back to Oklahoma for his father's funeral. The idea was utterly repugnant to him, although his feelings probably didn't make any goddam sense.

"Well," Al said. "Thanks, sir, for... well, thanks." And he turned and shoved the heavy storm curtain aside and left the bridge, going down the wet ladder and inside, away from the wet pelting rain, and on down to the main deck, and the galley, and the hot black coffee he needed so badly. He sat in the mess deck drinking the coffee and smoking a cigarette and staring blindly at nothing, feeling nothing, thinking nothing, no longer sleepy but still tired, still sore-eyed and sore-throated. Ought to get my tonsils out, he thought dully.

Alvin Woods, Senior, was dead. Windy Woods was dead. Impossible. That was absurd. I am now Alvin Woods, Senior, by royal ascendency, Al thought bitterly, and I don't want to be Alvin Woods, Senior, at all.

He felt a gentle hand on his shoulder. It was Sam Goff. "I'm damn sorry, Al," he said.

"Thanks," Al said dully.

"I'll get your leave papers ready," Sam told him.

"No," Al said. "I'm not going."

"Oh," Sam said uneasily, "well... can I do anything, Al?"

"No," Al said. "Thanks."

He stared blindly at the bulletin board, not seeing it, and he drank the coffee without tasting it. Everybody died some day. Hell fire.

The news got around and Al's friends found him staring blindly at nothing and thought it was numb grief and shock, and tried awkwardly, as men must do by custom and tradition, to say the miraculous words that would lighten the burdened heart. "Goddam, Al, I'm sorry," Doc said helplessly. Thanks, Al said stolidly. Some of them gave him useless information about how he could catch a ride on an Army cargo plane. ATC, they said. Get an ATC outa East Boston, Al. Get another ATC outa Jersey. ATC, ATC, ATC, they kept saying, not believing that any son could not want to attend his father's funeral. Thanks, Al said dully, staring blindly at nothing, feeling nothing, but knowing it was easy to want not to attend his father's funeral.

"If you need any money," old Ed Miller rumbled solemnly, and Al shook his head. No, thanks, Ed. Enigmatic Alvin Woods, Senior, staring enigmatically and inscrutably at empty nothing, saying thanks, thanks, thanks, thanks. Thanks for what, goddammit? Thanks for nothing. "We got to set the tables," Mess Cook Sonnichson said apologetically, and Al said dully, "Set them, then." And stayed seated. So they put the guard rails around the tables to keep the plates from sliding off when the ship rolled, working around Al, and he drank the tasteless coffee and smoked the pleasureless cigarettes and scowled at nothing. But when the men began to come into the mess deck, staring at him curiously as men stare at men who are related intimately, by blood or marriage, to inscrutable pitiless death, Al stirred and came out of his blank trance and left the mess deck, and as he went they said sorry Al, sorry Al, sorry Al, and he said thanks, thanks, thanks. Thanks? To whom and for what? To nobody for not a goddam thing. Couldn't they see he was only distressed because he had suddenly become the star attraction, the flesh and blood son of a man who had just died somewhere in Oklahoma? A notorious cook who henceforth could sign documents and petitions and letters to patriotic commentators with the name Alvin Woods, Senior, because that aristocratic title had just been vacated forever. Because Windy Woods, the barber, was dead.

He went back to the quarter-deck and the faceless man on duty at the can racks said sorry, Al, and he said dully thanks and fled forward and as he passed the three-inch gun tub a stranger said too bad, Al, you got my sympathy, I know how you feel, and he said thanks and he thought angrily, You dumb bastard, you don't even begin to know how I feel because I don't feel any way at all except pretty goddam sick of having people like you extend their phony heartfelt sympathies. He stood for a long time at the fore end of the boat deck where the superstructure rose sheer and high and gray and wet above the well deck, feeling the thin rain in his face and the ship rolling and pitching, and he stared at the gray seas climbing, climbing, climbing, and then falling back again, and that was how he felt too, somehow—just futile and frustrated, like what's it all about, what's the big idea?

He went below and got into dry whites, and the strangers looked at him pityingly in the gloom of the berth deck, and he hated their pity because he didn't want it or deserve it or need it, and he said thanks and thanks and thanks, sardonically sometimes and dully sometimes and sometimes raspingly or sarcastically or ironically, trapped on a ship in the futile lunging seas with all these stubbornly persistently pitying strangers. Didn't they know his father was a nobody, a weak, childish man who brought shame and disgrace to his son in every town he could before the son escaped finally and went away? Didn't they know that Windy Woods had been a verbose, semi-illiterate, drunken nonentity and that the only real honest emotion his death could possibly bring to anybody who knew him well was the guilty, shamed, regrettable emotion of numb relief?

Stop saying you're sorry! he wanted to yell at them. What have *you* got to be sorry about? And what in God's name have *I* got to be sorry about? I'll tell you what. I'm the only one now. I'm alone now. I always *wanted* somebody, a father, a brother, a mother, a sister—I *still* want somebody, I'll *always* want somebody—but all I ever had in memory was a vain strutting little man who had thick hair and an irritating, perpetual voice and a lame sense of humor and a filthy habit of pissing in all the beds in all the crummy cheap rooms in all the small stupid scandalized towns in Oklahoma where he was known as Windy Woods the beer-swilling barber on the back chair. If I grieve it's not because I lost a father, it's because I never *had* a father.

He climbed the ladder out of the stale air and stale pity of the crew's quarters and entered the galley, not looking at anybody, for fear they would be sorry about something, and Curly was in the galley and you could depend on him not to say a word because he was a sullen little bastard who would be willing to feed the men stale bread and sea water if it meant he could be home tonight rolling on a bed, engaged in the pleasures he rated more vital than honor and decency and loyalty. But then you never could really *depend* on Curly. "I'll take your watch if you want," he said gruffly. "I don't mind workin' your shift, Al. I ain't tired. I'll work it, Al."

"I'll work it," Al said dully.

"Well," Curly said awkwardly. "Wot can a guy say? I'm sorry."

The seas worsened in the afternoon and there was no question of

having anything but soup and sandwiches for evening chow, and
Al had the mess cooks stack the tables and benches and secure them
when the *Legume* altered course in midafternoon and began to take
the pounding seas almost full on her starboard beam so that she
rolled far over in the troughs. Usually when it was rough Al hung
a greasy piece of pork in the mess deck because it was supposed to
separate the men from the boys, the iron stomachs from the queasy
ones, and he would appreciate a few less customers to feed. But in
fact, he had yet to see a seasick man who didn't think he owed it
to his stomach to force some food down there. As Doc said, you had
to load her before you could fire her. And today it didn't seem to
Al the men would appreciate any such rough humor from the cook
whose sire had just kicked the bucket. It would be in thuddingly
bad taste, as they said.

He made sandwiches and stowed them in a cardboard box, and
made the rich soup that was more like stew, and made coffee without scalding himself, timing his movements to the lurching, careening gyrations of the fat, round-bottomed ship, and all the time he
felt nothing but bleak discomfort with never the sudden piercing
grief or pang of regret. Thousands of men died daily. And there
was no barber shortage.

Who'll bury him? Al wondered abruptly, thinking of nothing.
Will they toss him in a hole in potter's field and scrape clods over
him and call him buried? Does he have insurance or belong to a
burial association? He sent me a genuine Kaywoodie pipe and a
peck of cookies from that town. Will there be anybody at his
funeral who gives a damn one way or the other? Lester Potts must
be the undertaker. Will anybody pay Lester Potts? (Drop your old
man a line sometimes, Hotshot.)

Does anybody anywhere care that Windy Woods is dead—except
insofar as it concerns them commercially? The other barbers, they'll
close shop for an hour and go look in the coffin and say doesn't he
look natural? And then they'll go back and open the shop and tell
the customers, Amazing what embalmers can do these days, they
fixed old Windy so you'd never think he took a drink in his life.

(Unless I'm badly mistaken you had a birthday recently, Hotshot.)

They'll talk about him like he was nothing, Al thought, staring
blindly at the bulkhead. They'll say nasty true things about him. A
mediocre barber, they'll grade him posthumously. Just so-so. And
he bored people to death, yakkity yakkity alla time he was cuttin'

your hair or shavin' you, and when he was drinkin'—when *wasn't* he, ha ha?—his breath would knock a mule down. Heard old lady what's-her-name kicked him outa her roomin' house—kept wettin' the bed at night, ho ho ho! Kinfolks? they would say. Naw. Jist a boy somewhere in service he was always braggin' about. Didn't come back for the funeral. Maybe couldn't, but most likely wouldn't. Can't say I blame him none. Old Windy wasn't anything to be proud of as a father, they'd say.

What would *you* say, Hotshot? Al asked himself, staring blindly at the rocking bulkheads, ignoring the soup splashing onto the deck tiles where he'd poured salt to make it less slippery. Somebody ought to see he gets a decent burial. Funerals are primitive, macabre goddam ceremonies, but they're even worse when there is nobody there to pay respects to the natural-looking corpse in the high-priced casket.

When supper was over he climbed all the dry ladders and the wet ladders again and found the skipper still sitting gauntly on his stool like a thin bird humped on its perch, scowling stonily through the tear-wet windscreen into the gathering sorrow of stormy dusk, his skinny legs crossed and one foot twisted awkwardly behind the other calf.

"Sir," Al said dully. "I changed my mind. I want to go."

"All right," the skipper said. "We'll be in Chelsea in four hours."

"O.K. if I tell Goff to get the papers ready, sir?"

"The papers are already signed, Woods," the skipper said bleakly.

Gray dawn was seeping into the East Boston Airport warehouse when Al awakened from cramped, chilled sleep. The corporal was tapping his shoulder, telling him the ceiling had lifted and the ATC plane would be leaving pretty soon, and he could get on board. Al got off the hard crate, yawning and shivering, and went out to the plane. He had never flown, and he felt nervous and tense, but the other hitchhiking servicemen in the bucket seats were very calm. One morning like this, about this hour, he took me duck hunting, Al thought. I was just a kid, but I remember he got a couple ducks, and it was raining.

The plane left East Boston in the thin rain and climbed above the slate-gray clouds into sunshine and flew toward New Jersey, but it soon went down through the clouds again and landed at an airport, and all of the servicemen were nervous, watching the cargo loading and unloading, and Al learned about the facts of ATC free-riding. Cargo had priority and he might get bumped by a crate at any airport along the way. After that, when the plane hit turbulence among the wreaths of gray cloud, he only worried about getting to Oklahoma in time.

In New Jersey he sweated and fidgeted on a bench for a couple of hours and at the last minute got a seat on a St. Louis flight. On the ground he was hot and itchy, but in the air he would grow numb with cold in the uninsulated plane, and couldn't sleep while flying. The St. Louis flight stopped at every pasture airport along the route it seemed, and he got panicky in Cincinnati, Doc's home town, when all the riders were ordered out to sit in a waiting room until they got the freight juggled and the weight figured. Al told a woman behind the grill that he was trying to get home for his father's funeral, and she said she'd try to get him on the plane again. He sat on a bench in the hot, sticky blue dress uniform that regulations required a sailor to wear while traveling on leave, even in August. He was very tired and sleepy and uncomfortable, and then the lady smiled and said his luck was holding and he was still on the St. Louis flight.

He was still aboard when it arrived in St. Louis around ten that night. He got off, carrying his bag, and began hounding laconic pessimists about a plane to Tinker Field, near Oklahoma City. Before daylight he got an ATC flight to Kansas City, and had some breakfast there and bought more cigarettes, but wasn't able to find any planes going to Oklahoma City. He began to get a little panicky—it was much too late to think of trains or buses. But he finally learned of a charter flight going to Wiley Post Airport, and they had room for him, and he had the thirty dollars they asked.

It was almost ten o'clock when he got downtown in Oklahoma City, with three scant hours to cover the last one hundred and thirty some miles in time for the funeral. The next bus would not run until ten-forty-five and there were no railroad connections. But the last bus had been gone only a few minutes, and so Al got in a taxi and told the driver to catch that bus, and the cabby stuck his foot in it and caught up with the bus forty miles east of the city. Al gave him twenty dollars and got on the bus, and arrived at three minutes of one. It never did occur to him that he could have telephoned ahead and had Lester Potts delay the services until his arrival. He was so regimented and used to accepting rigid schedules that he just assumed the funeral *had* to be at thirteen hundred hours.

The town was bigger than he had supposed, big enough so that the bus station people did not know Lester Potts, and Al walked rather aimlessly along the tree-shaded sidewalk of the main street. It was a clean town, attractive, with wide streets and lots of trees, and quite a number of people in evidence, all of them curious about the sailor boy hurrying so uncertainly along. Feeling lost in the small city, Al went into a drugstore and asked the girl soda jerk if she knew Lester Potts, and she said Les Potts was a barber, and worked at the Domino Barber Shop, on down about a block. Al went on down to the Domino and found it closed, with a small black wreath on the door. This is where he worked, he thought, staring through the plate-glass window at the neat modern shop with only three chairs. There were two big shade trees in front, and a bench for loafers to sit on. And there was a clock that told Al the funeral had started a minute ago.

He was dirty and whiskery and itchy and groggy from loss of sleep, and his uniform was rumpled and smelled of sweat, and he just wanted to turn around and go back, leave the town behind. It was just miserably hot, a typical August day in Oklahoma, and he had no time for a bath or a shave, a change into a fresh uniform. The funeral had started somewhere in this town and he didn't know where, and he wanted to just forget it and go back to Boston. And he started running along the street wildly, filled with panic. Where *is* somebody? he wondered miserably. He hurried into a café and got the attention of a waitress and asked her if she knew where the funeral of Woods the barber was happening at. All the faces of all the customers turned toward Al, munching, then not munching as they saw it was a sailor, a Hooligan so far from salt water. The waitress called to a woman named Opal, and Opal said Shannon Funeral Home was where Mister Woods's funeral was being held. The first waitress, too tall, too tired, too thin to be pretty, told Al in a monotonous voice how to get there, and then said, "You his boy?" Al nodded dumbly, very tired and discouraged. "He ate here," she said awkwardly. "Sometimes. We were sure all sorry to hear he had passed away." Al nodded and thanked her and hurried out.

Two blocks. One over. He dogtrotted along the streets, seeing heat shimmering above the concrete, avoiding little knots of people in the shady places, dodging playing children. He cut across the street diagonally and side-stepped a pickup with some squealing pigs in the back, and came to the corner and saw the high white funeral mansion ahead in a big grassy yard with a big neon sign. There were cars, which he did not associate with the funeral, and he ran faster, his breath sobbing through clenched teeth he hadn't been able to brush since Saturday, and as he neared the wide lawn he heard the high thin wavering dirge, "Rock of Ages," rendered by scratchy female voices. He pounded across the street and across the lawn, past the neon sign, and then he stopped and leaned on one of the big white porch pillars.

I can't, he thought in despair. I can't go in like this, all dirty and sweaty and needing a shave. I'm too late anyway. You can't just go busting into the middle of a funeral. I don't *want* to go in.

But he went in. Here was an empty, ornate reception room, and the awful singing was louder now and more horrible. A man came tiptoeing through a door to his left, eyebrows lifted questioningly. A bald man, short, dressed in a dark suit, an utterly antiseptic sort of man with a look of false professional solicitude on his bland face. "Are you the son?" he whispered. Al nodded, panting, and the man shook hands, seemingly deaf to the terrible screeching voices in there, and Al knew by the feel of the obscenely soft hand that this was Shannon, and that Shannon had personally embalmed Windy Woods and was now linking death and life by touching Al's cringing flesh. Al shivered and wanted to wipe his hand on something, at the same time embarrassed by his own disreputable appearance, and the embalmer smiled his affably pitying reassuring smile and said apologetically, "We didn't think you'd make it."

"That's O.K.," Al said, and the two appalling witch voices were now launching unconfidently into "Nearer My God to Thee," in two-part harmony, like two cats yowling, and Al heard discreet chords from a piano backing the hideous duet but not attempting to compete with it. Shannon urged Al with soft insistent fingers on his sleeve, and Al dropped his ditty bag and followed the undertaker through another door into the front of the dim air-conditioned chapel, his nostrils immediately assailed by the cloying sick-sweet fragrance of flowers which were probably meant to conceal any unfortunate aroma of decay but only managed somehow to intensify the sense of moldering death in the place.

Al took one horrified look at a swimming blur of faces as he removed his soiled white hat, and then he looked down at the floor, embarrassed, surprised, and chagrined that so many spectators had come; he felt like a seedy bum, and resented these morbid creatures, these ghouls who thrived obscenely on secondhand grief. Why did Shannon let those fake mourners in, damn him? The reedy, quavering old sopranos caterwauled "Nearer My God to Thee," and the flowers overwhelmed him with their clogging perfume, and Shannon ushered him to a vacant front bench, the family pew. And Al slumped there abruptly stunned, twisting his dirty white hat, staring with horror at the white waxen tip of his father's long nose jutting above the edge of the pearly gray coffin. His heart hammered painfully, stiflingly, and he thought he was going to faint—from loss of sleep, from the heat and everything—and he tore his shocked and fascinated stare away from the ugly casket and discovered the two wrinkled old ladies half-concealed in a flowery alcove, wearing rusty black and gripping songbooks in their worn hands and wailing forlornly and desolately that Windy Woods was "Nearer My God to Thee." Why did I come here? Al thought with anguish, and behind him he heard snuffles and sobs and was furious. None of those free-lance mourners had any right here. They were intruders.

The dreadful dirge continued interminably and he sat there numb and miserable, his thoughts desolate and melancholy. (He sent me a ten-dollar genuine Kaywoodie pipe for my birthday, and some cookies.) Aware he was the focus of curious, probably censuring eyes behind him, very conscious of his dirty, rumpled appearance, hating the ugly hiccuping sobs back there in the room, and wanting to take his tired dirty body and heavy-lidded eyes and shocked mind somewhere and sleep until this pagan nightmare ended.

The weird threnody ceased at last and the preacher spoke gently of God's compassion for mortal sinners and of the beautiful peace of the hereafter, and Al stared blearily and with dulling horror at the waxen tip of Windy Woods's dead nose poking inquisitively into view as if he wished he could sit up for a second and see whoall had come to his send-off, his shipping-out party. He'd put in his long hitch as an earth-bound barber and now he was being transferred and given an honorable discharge. Al's groggy, incoherent mind must have napped a little, or else it was a very brief eulogy, because suddenly it was over and the pussyfooting embalmer was there grimacing with that rare and unreassuring solicitude, asking in sepulchral tones if Al would care to view the deceased. Don't touch me, Al thought, but he stumbled to his feet resignedly, stiff and aching and groggy, and moved without volition toward the open coffin, accepting this one more mandate of society which made it compulsory to view the deceased. As if, at the very end, to make certain of the cadaver's identity so that they would not bury the wrong man. The pallid sculptured-marble features came fully into view and he stopped and stared warily at Windy Woods, phlegmatic now, taciturn in death, silent at last. And somehow gauntly dignified and distinguished in death. And then abruptly all of the emotion he had so long scorned and repudiated found a chink in Al's tired and sleepy armor and ganged up on him.

He was stricken with a terrible shame and remorse and guilt, knowing here at last that although he had not admired or respected or worshiped his father, and had been scornfully intolerant of his father's human frailty and inadequacies and defensive egotism, he had loved him. Nevertheless he had loved him; despite his cruel young disapproval he had loved his father. And now, physically exhausted, tired unto death himself, tense and embarrassed and uneasy and stunned, Al was at last vulnerable, his defenses were down. He felt his face twisting uncontrollably and his chest muscles drawing hard and tight, felt the scalding pressure behind his eyelids, and he clamped his teeth hard and fought it savagely. But he was still less man than boy, and the violent spasm of sorrow and remorse shook him and hot tears poured down his contorted face and an anguished moaning sob broke past his clenched teeth as he stood helplessly stricken by the casket of his father, who had not been much of a father, perhaps, but had been the only father Alvin Woods would ever have; whose death left Al completely alone in the world of men, isolated, with no ties and no bonds of love and nobody to care if he had a birthday; with nothing but this sudden crushing burden of unspeakable woe that shook and wrenched him. And even in his agony he thought it was unmanly, unseemly; he hated it but could not help himself, and he thought with bitter self-loathing, I could have written, I could have tried . . .

It was over quickly and he stood limp and exhausted, wiping at his tear-streaked face with the wrinkled sleeve of his hot wool blouse and gazing with yearning and sorrow at the face of his father, redeemed in death; committing the dead face to memory. At the last he extended his strong living hand and touched the cool marble hand of his lost father, and that was all. I'm sorry, Pop, he thought. I was a worse son than you were father. I'm sorry I didn't try harder.

He turned away from the coffin and saw the woman who had been sobbing and was sobbing yet, and the man supporting her whose face was set in glum, disconsolate lines. The man sadly announced that he was Lester Potts. "I was his best friend, I reckon," he said. And then he gently drew the weeping woman forward. "This is Mrs. Webb. Arline Webb, a friend of your daddy." Al shook their hands, confused, not knowing why the woman should be so inconsolable. And he was self-conscious about his own tear-dampened face and ashamed of the way he looked. Arline Webb was a woman of middle age, still pretty in a worn fashion. Lester Potts was a lanky man with thin black hair combed over a wide bald spot, and a mustache, and sad brown eyes. But they were strangers, people he had never seen before or known about. He couldn't understand why they were so grieved and disconsolate—he was the one who should weep, not strangers; he was the one staggered by guilty remorse and regret and sorrow. He was embarrassed and a little angry because a middle-aged woman named Arline Webb should indulge in this ugly exhibition of melodramatics, as if her life henceforth would be dark and joyless forever. He stood there looking warily and helplessly at the sad strangers, mute and dumb and embarrassed, entirely miserable, feeling as if some terrible and stupid mistake had been made—either they had come to the wrong funeral, or he had. He didn't know what to do, and there was nobody to turn to for help, nobody except the somehow repellent undertaker who was only superficially involved, who earned his good living from the misery of inexorable death.

Somebody do something, Al thought, his trapped helpless glance avoiding the two embarrassing strangers before him, supplicating all the other strangers in the horrible place, begging for help.

And then he felt his sluggish heart soar with relief and surprise, because Josephine Hill stood at the side of the chapel watching him with shy, soft concern and compassion, her gray eyes sorrowing for him. It was impossible, he thought wildly; it was a trick of his exhausted mind, a figment of his anguished imagination.

But as he stared in disbelief, the well-remembered face was coming toward him, the gray eyes searching his face. She took his grimy, trembling hand in both of hers and said softly, "Hello, Al."

And he sighed with wrenching relief. He wasn't alone in a gray bleak sorrowing world of strangers after all. Jo was here.

CHAPTER 28

A Room in Tulsa

WHEN the four of them returned to Arline Webb's big, old rooming house after the pitiless hot ordeal of the cemetery, Les Potts sighed heavily and said by godfrey he didn't think a good strong drink would be out of order, and he got a bottle from his car and went with Arline to the kitchen for ice, leaving Al alone with Jo for the first time.

"I'm filthy," he apologized, very self-conscious.

"You look fine," she said, but he sensed a shyness in her, and perhaps an uneasiness. He couldn't get over the wonder of her being here, lovelier than he remembered, fuller of body and more poised. She would be twenty-one now, he thought. She had matured since he saw her last. But she had the same oddly vulnerable smile that touched him with some nameless pang, the same generous mouth and faint freckles and tiny spaces between her teeth, the boyishly square shoulders and small sturdy feminine body, which seemed more alluringly desirable to him than ever before. And the same cute bowlegs.

"Jo," he stammered, "I just...I can't get over you being here."

She had told him in the car about seeing the notice of his father's death in the paper. She was still with the news-clipping service, having transferred to the Tulsa bureau, and it was part of her job to read all the regional dailies and weeklies. At first, she said, she had been terribly stunned, reading that Alvin Woods had died. Then she read the rest of the small item and realized that it must be Al's father, for it said an only son was in the Coast Guard. "I don't really know why I came," she said. "But I'm glad I did, Al. I guess I just wanted to see you."

She had come, that was all that mattered. She had eased the worst of the lost misery for him.

Lester Potts brought the drinks and said that Arline was freshen-

303

ing up, and he took the opportunity to enlighten Al. Windy Woods had lived here in this rooming house and, Al deduced from his carefully ambiguous manner, had been having an affair with Arline. They planned to get married, Les said. All of the people at the funeral had been friends or regular customers of Windy's, he said. Everybody *liked* old Windy. The two elderly ladies who had done the singing lived upstairs, and often played pitch with Arline and Windy last winter. Windy was a great one for kidding the old ladies, Les Potts said nostalgically.

Arline came back with the ravages of her grief hidden by fresh make-up, and Al knew a rush of feeling for her—she might have become his stepmother, if things had been different.

"Now you're to stay here as long as your leave lasts," Arline told him. "And Josephine must stay too, if she possibly can." Jo was looking at Al uncertainly, and he begged her with his eyes to stay, and she smiled a bit wryly and said she could stay the night, at least. So Arline took them back to see the rooms. Which, she said, were her guest rooms, never rented but kept available for relatives and friends. The two rooms were in the rear, on the ground floor, and connected by a bathroom. The idea of Jo being so near, with only the bathroom between, bothered Al. I won't sleep much, thinking about her being in there, he thought. They returned to Arline's private sitting room, and Les had mixed fresh drinks. Arline took hers and said if they would excuse her she would like to go lie down for a while.

So Les enlightened them some more, including Jo matter-of-factly, as if she were a member of the family. Al's father had died of a heart attack in the shop while cutting a man's hair and listening to a St. Louis Cardinal baseball game. It was, Les said gravely, as if every small detail were very important, the bottom of the ninth inning and Marty Marion was at bat. Windy was a loyal Cardinal fan, Les said.

And presently he stood up and said, "Well, I'll leave the bottle with you kids. How long can you stay around, Alvin?"

"I'll have to start back tomorrow," Al said, because he didn't want to stay here in this house where his father had lived, with these good people who had known his father better than he ever had. Les said doggone, if Al could of stuck around a while they'd go fishing, and Al recalled with a heavy heart that his father had said almost the same thing the last time he'd seen him alive.

Potts left, and he was alone with Jo again, and he wanted to touch her, to put his arms around her. He sighed. "Jo, I sure need a bath and a shave and a fresh uniform. Reckon Arline would have an iron handy so I could press my whites?" Jo volunteered for the job, and he gave her his folded dress whites and went to the bathroom. He took a shower and shaved quickly, and when Jo brought his uniform they began to talk, without self-consciousness, about the old days at OU. He felt presentable now, and her wifely pressing of his uniform seemed to have formed an easy, comfortable bond between them now. She told him that Beulah Flachtter, who used to buy Al beer and read her short stories to him, had married her thirty-year-old writer of westerns and had a baby now, and wasn't doing much writing herself. Al brushed his teeth, listening to her through the bathroom door which was ajar, and tried to comb his hair, which was an impossibility. He was glad it was an inch long, at any rate. He would have hated for Jo to see him a month earlier. "Come on in," he said. "I'm presentable, I guess."

She came through the bathroom into his room and looked at him, smiling quizzically. "Right handsome," she commented. "You look real nice, Al." She was carrying her drink, which she'd barely tasted, and he looked at her with his heart thumping in his chest, and took the drink from her hand and said, "Jo, would you mind if I kissed you?"

"No," she said breathlessly. "Shucks, no, Al."

He took her in his arms and kissed her, and felt the old rush of blood to his head and the pleasant dizziness that kissing Jo had always given him. Presently she pushed him away, a little breathless, and said fiercely, "Why didn't you answer my last letter, Alvin?"

He remembered something then, and said, "My God, Jo, was I kissing a married woman? Did you marry that character?"

"I wouldn't be here if I had, darn you."

"You still engaged to him?"

She frowned. "I told you all about it in that last letter, Al."

He picked up the drink from the dresser and shook the ice around and started to lie to her, but then he didn't. "Jo, I burned it. I was afraid to read it. Afraid it would say you were married already or something." He grinned. "You broke my heart, woman."

She sighed with exasperation. "Never burn letters unread, boy. I told you Richard had gone in the Army and we'd broken our silly engagement and the whole thing had been a mistake." Al sat down on the bed and closed his eyes and sighed with enormous relief. "When I heard no more from one Alvin Woods, I just decided you had a new girl . . ."

"Jo, I'm a one-woman man," he said reproachfully. He put the glass on the dresser again and took her in his arms, more confidently this time. She was here. That meant something, didn't it? "Jo," he said earnestly, "don't get engaged any more, please?"

She grinned her strangely wistful grin. "I'll try not to."

So he kissed her again, and she came up on tiptoe and hugged him fiercely, and he thought, We've got to get the hell out of here. That bed is so handy, I'm afraid I'll spoil everything. But Jo saved him the trouble of making a decision. "We'd better get out of here," she said grimly, and laughed shakily. "Nobody affects me like you do."

They went to the kitchen and made fresh drinks and talked, but he kept her close, his arm around her, and kissed her tentatively now and then. He felt a little guilty about being so pleasantly preoccupied so soon after his father's funeral, but it did not occur to him that in dying, his father had brought Jo back into his life. He told her about his feeling of remorse, how he kept thinking if only—if he'd only been friendlier, if he'd written oftener, if, if, if. And she said wisely that everybody tortured themselves that way when somebody died, thinking of all the ways they could have been kinder, more devoted, more attentive, more understanding. When she was a little girl, she said, her older brother was killed in an auto crash, and for a long time she punished herself unforgivingly because she'd had a quarrel with him the last time they were together.

She sighed. "Al, we don't need to be so gloomy. I've got an old beat-up automobile. Let's go for a drive."

Al took the fifth along. It was still better than half-full. He kept remembering the last time he and Jo had been together, and he wondered, with a quickening pulse, if she was remembering too. They drove out into the August countryside. This was a part of Oklahoma not well known to Al, a region of rolling hills and woods, ranches and dairy herds and hay meadows and inviting streams. He felt a clutch of homesickness for this Southwest country, and told Jo what Boston was like, and what New England winters were like, and about the ship, his special friends Doc and Yeoman Sam and Dave Hubert.

It was much too hot for driving, and in time they stopped at a tavern in a grove of trees, and discovered there was a juke box and a small dance floor and air conditioning, and nobody there but the barmaid. They danced, and tried some beer, but it was sour and offensive to Al after the rich and potent brews of Boston, so they ordered cokes and ice and mixed sweet inoffensive highballs that were better. And in between dances, in the privacy of the high-backed booth, they kissed.

At sundown they went back to the rooming house to see if Arline would go to dinner with them, but she was crying again and said she couldn't eat a bite. Al thought of the raw new grave in the cemetery and felt guiltier than ever, because he could not be sad with Jo, the way he felt he should. He was a little moody then, and during dinner of broiled steaks in a café, but it was no use. He talked about it to Jo and she held his hand and insisted that it was unnecessary to go around in mourning for the benefit of others, and useless to reproach himself if he didn't *feel* awful. "I guess that's why I'm here," she said softly. "To keep you from feeling so bad about everything."

They went back to the rooming house and found that Arline had gone to bed. So they took some ice and ginger ale and went back to Jo's room, farthest from Arline's, where their talking would be least apt to disturb her. Al had a pounding anticipation in his blood, and he sensed that Jo was conscious of the tension. It was warm in the room and Al took off his neckerchief and blouse and kicked off his shoes, and removed her shoes and kissed her small feet in a rush of sudden tenderness. She looked at him a little uncertainly, and he pulled her to her feet and began to kiss her, and their mouths became bruisingly urgent. They had been far along this recklessly thrilling road before, and knew the way.

He said against her fragrant black hair, "Is that the only dress you've got with you?"

She nodded, and he said, "You'll get it all rumpled, you ought to take it off."

"Don't be silly," she said breathlessly.

And he said, "Take it off, sweet Jo; you're wearing a slip, aren't you, dopey?" She sighed resignedly and got out of the dress and stood before him shyly in the clinging pink slip.

"You make me nervous," she said darkly.

He kissed her and lifted her in his arms and put her on the bed and lay with her snuggled close, kissing her, feeling her tremulous response. And when he began to remove the slip she just sighed with resignation and said thickly, "Turn off the light."

"No," Al murmured, "I want to see you, darling Jo." He felt very emotional and excited. And she just closed her eyes and bit her lip and let him have his wish. He gazed in delight and wonder at her small, curved, satin-sleek body, all golden pink perfection, her flimsy garments more revealing than concealing. He crushed her in his arms and kissed her with mounting passion and insistence, and she groaned helplessly when he began to unfasten her brassière, and caught her breath when his mouth fastened to a small firm naked breast.

"Oh, darn you," she wailed. "Turn out the light."

He got off the bed and turned out the light and got undressed, and she moaned again in helpless protest when she felt his feverish nakedness against her, but he stopped her with his mouth, and her body moved against him sensually, voluptuously. He began to remove the last flimsy barrier and she only sighed and raised her hips to help him, completely resigned to the inevitable. At the last, when he moved over her in trembling blind urgency and pushed her legs apart, she gasped and said, "Al!" and then only groaned in that completely hopeless way, surrendering herself to him passionately.

Afterward he held her and kissed her tenderly, with a great feeling of love and pride, caressing her warm satin stomach and softly firm breasts, and she said glumly, "I knew what to expect. I was scared to death this would happen, Alvin." But then she whispered confidingly, "I wanted it to happen, I think. Did you know that?"

"I wasn't sure," Al said, and kissed her, and because he was exhausted and content, he fell asleep holding her in his arms with her head on his shoulder and their legs entwined. It was gray daylight when he awoke, but she was still in his arms, her breath warm against his neck, sleeping as sweetly as a child. He kissed her awake and she squirmed lazily and then clung to him, sighing contentedly—and then she said, "My gawd, it's morning!" He began to nuzzle her small vibrant breasts, and she whispered, "Stop that, for heaven's sake! You didn't sleep in your bed—what will Arline think of us?" She groaned in dismay.

"She'll think I slept in my bed, don't worry," Al said, and he picked her up in his arms, kicking feebly, protesting softly, and carried her through the bathroom to his neat unslept-in bed, yanking the top sheet back. She looked at him gravely, then smiled, and he put her in the bed and made love to her again, without haste, sustaining it to the point of torment, and at the end her body was almost frantic, her breath caught on a gasp, and she cried out softly, incoherently. And then they were limp and spent and unmoving for a long time, and he thought of nothing, wanting nothing more than this but wanting it forever. "Jo," he said. "Jo, darling, let's get married."

She touched his chin with a tentative finger. "No," she said.

"Why not?" he asked. "Don't you know we belong together?"

"Oh, yessss!" she sighed. "I never dreamed it could be so . . . so . . ."

"That's how it is with the *right* person," he said.

"You're the right person," she whispered. "You were always the right person, Alvin." And she said tenderly, "Maybe after the war . . ."

"After the war hell! Right away, baby! Now! Today!"

"You're sweet," she murmured lazily. "But I don't want to be a lonely war wife, Al darling." She turned serious abruptly. "Alvin, we've shared something more wonderful than I dreamed it could ever be, but that doesn't mean we're in love. Maybe part of the sweetness was knowing it wouldn't last, that it was just an episode in our lives."

"I love you, dammit," Al said with frustration. "And you love me or you wouldn't be here with no clothes on letting me do impertinent things to you—like this." He demonstrated his impertinence.

"You stop that," she said with mock severity, and seemed suddenly conscious of her nakedness in the growing light. But she didn't try to hide it, or stop him from taking fresh liberties. "Al, I don't really know if I love you or not," she said. "You always kind of fascinated me, but it might be just infatuation, you know. And for all *you* know, I may be just a shameless, immoral hussy." She grinned.

"That's how I want you to be, with me," Al said unsteadily.

"You're just noble, anyhow. You want to make an honest hussy out of me," she accused. "You don't *have* to marry me, honest."

"Jo," he said. "Look, I've got four days to get back to Boston. Couldn't we be together, like this, until I hafta go back? Please?"

She stared at him soberly for a moment. "Well, why not?" she said. "I'm already a scarlet woman, a bad immoral girl. So I might as well enjoy it. And," she added softly, "I think I *will* enjoy it."

"Let's go to Tulsa and get the bridal suite," Al said eagerly. "We

can pick up some of your clothes—but you won't *need* any clothes."
She chuckled, and he had to kiss her all dizzy and squirming, but
there was no use overdoing it, and presently he said, "As soon as
we can decently scram, we'll go." And she nodded and said wistfully, "Al, I know I should have girlish regrets, but I'll never
regret this, never."

They had breakfast with Arline and she said she would be glad
to look after Windy's things until Al came "home" from the war,
and she hugged Al in parting and said she hoped he would come
back and live here, in this town, in this house, because she had
almost been his mother, in a way. And Al, deeply touched, thinking
that his father had been happy with her the way he had been with
Jo, said he would come back.

Jo waited in the Ford while he went to say good-by to Lester
Potts, and Les stopped shaving a customer and got Windy Woods's
barber tools in their kit, and said Windy always said he wanted Al
to have the electric vibrator if he died. "But," Les said, lifting Al's
white hat and rubbing Al's bristly hair, "you don't need it yet,
feller." So Al took the vibrator but asked Les to leave the other
things with Arline. Then he shook hands and hurried out to Jo.

They registered brazenly in a first-class hotel as Mr. and Mrs.
Alvin Woods, and they had a wonderful two days and two nights,
and Al wanted desperately to marry Jo, to be sure of having her
always, and he pleaded with her sometimes to go back to Boston
with him. But she was stubbornly adamant about the idea. She
simply did not see any wisdom or logic in getting married in
wartime—and besides, she kept insisting, she wasn't sure in her heart
that this was true love. It was romance, it was thrilling, it was
wonderful, but was it *love?* she asked distractedly. Let's wait, please,
Al, she said. The war can't last forever, and I'll wait, and we'll write
real often, and then . . .

Ah, yes, someday. But meanwhile . . .

Sometimes they would lie silent and wide-awake in each other's
arms, each with his own thoughts but still with that perfect, calm,
easy, warm communication between them. Sometimes they talked
and talked, and they had meals sent up to the room, and listened
to music and soap operas and baseball games on the radio, and
laughed at Bob Hope. And Jo gave him scalp treatments with the
vibrator, and also toned up his back muscles, which needed it
worse. They seldom left the room, and it was true that Jo did not

need any clothes. They were happy, unashamed nudists, completely unself-conscious, and they made love very often, and it seemed to Al there could be no two people more perfectly mated, and why in the hell couldn't she see it too? And always, under the surface of his mind, he was conscious of the swift passage of this brief respite from the ship and the Hooligan Navy and the trouble, the big trouble.

"My lips are swollen and bruised, darn you," Jo would say. "Stop kissing so hard. Just kiss me real easy and gentle, darling." But when he tried to kiss her easy and gentle, Jo would be the one who became bruisingly urgent. She was not insatiable, she was only generous and loving and fiercely compassionate, conscious that Al would soon be leaving, and she never refused Al or stinted in giving of herself.

"My golly," she said with consternation. "What will the girls at the office say when they see my Ubangi lips?"

The idyl cost Al a lot of money, but he had saved a lot of money by staying so long aboard ship. And what he got of warm loving delight and tender rapture couldn't be measured in terms of money. Jo, he would think with wonder, hearing her soft breathing beside him in the dark of night, and he would be a little sad, wanting her beside him all the years of his life. But she was unwavering about that, and worst of all she wouldn't say, without hedging cautiously, without qualifying it in her painfully honest, overly reasonable way, that she was in love with him. I love you, yes, she said. I am very happy now. You're all I want in the world, darling Al—at the moment. But people change, and the war may be long and we may be separated for a terrible eternity—which is why people do crazy things in wartime. You might meet somebody else. Or I might. And anyway, I just want to think about it away from your disastrously attractive presence, you lug. I want to calm down and not make any important decision under duress.

It was useless to plead, to argue. She had a will of iron.

He hated like fury to leave her, and in the end he overstayed, deciding to risk the uncertain ATC connections going back instead of a slowpoke train. But he had to go, finally. He put on his freshly dry-cleaned blues and his snow-white hat, squaring it saltily, and Jo sat cross-legged on the bed, wearing clothes for a change, watching him with tender brooding sadness. "You're sorta handsome," she said.

"I know it," Al grinned. "But you! Baby, you're beautiful!"

"Don't lie, I'm not beautiful," she sighed. "You're just a poor lonely sailor, and any old girl would look beautiful to you."

"You're nuts," Al said, aching inside, and he kissed her with great tenderness and yearning, and held her for a long time, and then they left the hotel and said a last good-by on the street. He didn't want her to go to the airport, he wanted to get it over with fast and not drag it out. "Baby, don't be sorry. Don't regret it."

"Never!" she said fiercely. "I couldn't! Oh, Al . . ."

He turned and walked away, not looking back, and his heart was lead in his chest. And he was eight hours AWOL getting back to Boston. But the *Legume* didn't return to Chelsea Depot until the next day, and nothing was ever said about his tardiness. Maybe that was because the officers had other things to fret them, maybe they were a trifle wary of further offending Alvin Woods, the busy typist. Because there was a letter awaiting Al's return, a stupid letter that drove him to drink.

It was from Winfrey Fugate's secretary, and it was brief and shocking. It read: "Mr. Fugate has asked me to notify you that your letter has been received, and has been turned over to the proper authorities, and to say that he commends your courageous action." That was all, but gawd almighty wasn't that *enough?* Didn't that dumb sonofabitch know that all mail to servicemen was *censored?* Didn't he know his stupid letter would be read by one of the *Legume's* officers? And that casual reference to the proper authorities—did he mean the FBI, the Treasury Department, or (God forbid!) the Boston District Office?

August was almost finished now, and soon the black Atlantic gales would begin. Already there was a sting in the wind and an ache in the lonely, bereft heart of a ship's cook, and thorny worries in his mind. Jo, he thought at night, write me that you know now, that you love me and want to marry me for always. And days he watched the officers for signs of nervous apprehension, but he seemed to be the one suffering from the whips and jingles, constantly assailed by fears and dreads, and lovesick thoughts of Jo, utterly necessary Jo Hill. Sometimes he felt cold anger, too, and disgust, and he was bitter.

I'll never write to *that* dumb bastard again, he vowed.

CHAPTER 29

The Waiting

SEPTEMBER was a pain in the neck, a time of waiting for something to happen about the letter. And nothing at all happened about the letter except that it was pretty apparent the officers, most of them, knew a letter had been written, and were nervous and curious, and suspicious, and coldly, aloofly resentful about the whole thing.

Other things happened, things unrelated to the letter. Seaman Peter Irvin was off restriction two whole days before his loud and obscene mouth got him right back on again. Chicken Hawk, the sour master-at-arms, got himself a new set of very white false teeth, and began to smile oftener. Curly's mother-in-law came to Boston to stay with her pregnant daughter, but that didn't improve Curly's disposition; he was no friendlier with Al. And the officers were chill of manner.

The big war in which the Hooligan Navy took no part continued. American GI's were stoned in Ireland and told to go home, and a German spy was sentenced in Newark, and seventy hostage Frenchmen were executed in Vichy, and there was heavy fighting in Egypt, Russia, the Solomons, and sometimes in Scollay Square. But nothing about the letter happened except that the officers eyed Al in a rather unsociable fashion.

There was a correction of a mistake in battle station assignments in September, when the exec informed Al sarcastically that he was no longer a 20-millimeter gun captain. "Cooks," Higgins said, "are by long tradition supposed to serve in the ammo magazine during GQ drills, and in the future that will be your station."

"I've been on that twenty since the ship was commissioned, sir," Al protested heatedly, and Higgins sneered and said, "I can't imagine why, and we won't argue about it. I believe I made myself clear."

Then, by way of adding insult to injury, Higgins appointed

Seaman Peter Irvin to replace Al on the starboard 20-mm. Of all the enlisted men on the *Legume*, the blond swashbuckling Sea Gull with the sewer mind was the only one Al genuinely and utterly detested. But all that of the gunnery had no bearing on the letter— or, now, *had* it?

There were transfers in the second week of September. Store-keeper George Osborn, who had done the books for the commissary department, came by the galley to say good-by. He was happy, at long last that much-yearned-for transfer to California had come through; now his kids would not face the bleak New England winter with their asthma. And by way of parting gesture, Osborn informed Al that for August the officers paid thirteen dollars and seventy cents per head for chow. Which was startling and somehow a bit ominous, as if the wardroom guessed what the letter had been about. But of course Osborn's transfer was in no way even obscurely connected with the business of a foolish letter.

In September there were wild gales and towering seas, and the ship loaded her well deck with bagged coal and freighted it to the lighthouses and isolated surfboat stations along the rough New England coast, but as for letters, there were only the tender despair-ing ones Al wrote to Jo Hill, and her brief, wary, noncommittal, and exasperatingly *friendly* answers. He dwelt a great deal in his mind on the lovely short idyl with Jo, and missed her with a constant melancholy ache, and felt sick with love of her. And to over-compensate the anguish, he became resentful sometimes, and cynical. O.K., the Tulsa thing had only been a fling for Jo, as she had hinted. Maybe illicit episodes in hotels were rather commonplace for her. Certainly it had not touched her deeply and lastingly as it had him; and obviously if she didn't love him now she would never love him. Maybe he had only imagined her innocence and inexperience in the beginning, and he tormented himself with jealous doubts about her virtue. She hadn't been hard to get. And hell, to be realistic about it, a man would sure get tired of her after a while. The world was full of beautiful women who wanted to marry men with hair and be true and warmly devoted forever after—and really, to be quite sensible about the matter, his primary trouble was just all this strain of waiting.

The officers were watching him warily, coldly, and Hog Cupper tried to pump Yeoman Sam about the mysterious letter, oafishly and without sublety. Aw, come on, Goff, don't pretend you don't know all about it—what was it *about*, Goffy? Was it about that party we had for the skipper? But Sam expressed ignorance and surprise, and indignation that something had occurred on the ship without anybody letting him in on the secret. And when he sardonically relayed the news to Al, it only worried the worrier more, because why would they think it might have been about the party? Were they that sanguine about the condition of their mess records? Al groaned with anxiety.

Well, it was an anxious period everywhere, for that matter. The Navy disclosed that more than 2,301 officers and men of the merchant marine were dead or missing as a result of enemy action at sea up to August 1, and it might be assumed the score was higher now. And in Berlin, Adolf Hitler ranted, "For this year we have a very simple plan!" The gist of which was kill, destroy, slaughter the enemy—including, perhaps, even a few unfortunate members of the Hooligan Navy, whose motto was *Semper Paratus*—which the men of the *Legume* ironically translated to Simple Paralysis.

When there was a GQ drill, Al would descend glumly to the magazine hatch in the crew's quarters (if it was night, he wouldn't bother to dress, since the hatch was twenty-two feet from his bunk) with the nervous mess boys and Dave and Curly and the fireman and seaman ammo passers, and then he would stand down in the close airless place with its racks of three-inch shells, sweating and tense, and think with jealous longing of the clean cold air of the flying bridge and his darling useless 20-mm. being defiled by foul-mouthed Seaman Peter Irvin, who bragged forever of the debasing, degenerate submission he forced upon any woman who captured his fancy ashore. ("You kin make a goddam slut of a woman do anythin' yuh want—or anyways I kin.") And down in the grisly light and sweating tension of the deadly hold, Al would think of Jo and say to himself, If a torpedo hit this goddam magazine I wouldn't have any more goddam troubles, boy. But if I got to die I'd rather do it up on the flying bridge. Goddam that Higgins!

Something had to give under the terrible strain of September, and sometimes Al was afraid it would be his tormented mind—and he wondered how it would be to get a Section Eight, a psycho discharge.

Transfers in September. But certainly. First Osborn. And then a chief emeritus, a trundling mountain of a man named Edwin Miller. The exec had persuaded the skipper to "get rid" of the pathetic old liability, Yeoman Goff reported. And Ed in person came to confirm the scuttlebutt. Inserting his huge bulk in the port doorway he stared imperturbably at Al with his hooded eyes and rumbled with quiet laughter and said, "I take it you're the chef?" Al nodded, sensing that this time it was different, and old Ed said gravely, "You're talking to a civilian, my boy, so beware—the slip of a lip may sink a ship. They gave old Edwin another physical and the admiral has decided to mothball me." And then he said blandly, "For which I thank *you*, chef."

"You're welcome," Al said. Then, belatedly, "Why thank me, Ed?"

"For putting the heat on, chef. For making it advisable for certain parties to get rid of what might be called material witnesses."

"I halfway figured you were one of the mob," Al said wearily.

"I was an intimidated underling, chef. They coerced me."

"Ed," Al said unhappily, "why did you let it keep happening?"

Old Ed jabbed a fat blunt finger at the gold hash marks on his sleeve. "The gold is for good conduct, chef," he rumbled softly. "I got them for saying yessir and nossir, not for arguing with superiors. Gold braid says black is white, the answer is yessir. If he happens to be a poor civilian temporary wartime substitute of an officer with a shortage of scruples, the answer is still yessir." He studied Al's pained features for a moment and added in an almost gentle manner, "You can't buck the system, chef, and you shouldn't ever try to. If you don't like your ship, ask for another ship, don't try to change the one you're on. Never do anything, chef, that might hurt your outfit. The rules you lived by outside don't always apply in a branch of the military. There are some good officers on this tub. The skipper is a good officer, and some others *will be* good officers. And there are a couple of bad apples who taint the whole barrel, but you got to bear in mind they're not *real* Coast Guard, they're *reserves*, without any pride of tradition. They couldn't get in the Coast Guard except for the war and the lowered standards and the big hurry-scurry expansion. When the war ends they'll be civilians again, and the Coast Guard will still be the Coast Guard. An angry man trying to change things is in danger of doing more harm than good, chef. I know about the letter—I imagine everybody on the ship except the skipper knows about the letter. If he knew he'd have you on the rug talking your head off. If you had to mail a letter, you should have sent it direct to the D.O., not some dirt-shoveling outsider. But, then, you shouldn't have sent any letter in the first place. You should have gone to the skipper."

"The skipper," Al said scornfully. "He's a crook, too, Ed."

"Maybe not, chef, maybe not," old Ed rumbled. "Well, you've done what you thought you had to do, and no telling how far the bad smell will spread. It could hurt the service, chef. People outside wouldn't stop to consider these aren't real Coast Guard officers, they will just assume all Coast Guard officers are corrupt." Old Ed laughed again, without humor. "All CPO's aren't gourmets, either. You'll pardon me, I trust, I did not intend to make a speech. Civilian's got no right lecturing servicemen. But one thing more, chef. You're not proud of being a Coast Guardsman, are you?"

"A Hooligan," Al said bleakly. "I can't say I am, Ed."

"Maybe you don't know much about the Coast Guard," Ed suggested. "Someday somebody's bound to ask me if I was a Hooligan, chef, and I'm gonna look him in the eye and say, quote: You're mighty goddam right I was a Hooligan, and I'm proud I was. Unquote." Old Ed stared owlishly at his audience, and his audience felt uneasy, troubled, and wished the interview would end. "Now as I go to my life of loafing leisure," old Ed said, "I leave you something to think about, chef." He held out a small key. "I won't need this any more. Maybe it'll explain why I never got awful indignant about certain matters." Al took the key, puzzled, and Chief Miller rumbled with laughter one last time and said, "Remember what the retiring chief commissary steward said, chef. Slice her thin, boys, slice her thin."

And he left the ship as Osborn had done. Or, to put it another way, he dropped out of the case, as Osborn had done.

And along with all the tension and worry and dread, Al had to cope with a bewildering sense of guilt, of having burned a house to get rid of an annoying mouse in the pantry. But he pocketed the key and forgot, for a while, that he had it.

That was the first half of September, two weeks of tense and crouching dread, of ominous worried nail-biting apprehension. A time bomb with a nerve-rackingly slow fizzling fuse that un-manned Al Woods. And the scream in his mind kept pushing nearer and nearer the surface.

What could a man do? A man could get drunk.

He was trying to get drunk, the night Ed left, in a Scollay Square dive, when abruptly a pair of uncouth, sinister-looking Hooligans surrounded him and eyed him with evil intensity. One had a villainous black beard and a heavy pirate's ring in his ear, and a manner arrogant as sin. The other was swarthy and slim, with a blue-black spade beard and carefully waxed longhorn mustaches. And they were both vaguely familiar.

"Leave us git this cookie drunk an' shanghai him back to the ole schooner," the arrogant one said arrogantly. And Al knocked his drink over lunging to his feet. "Gutsell!" he shouted. "And Blanket-ass, the quill-pusher! Well I be goddam, ain't you got no razors?"

Gutsell was a coxswain now, and the part-Choctaw yeoman was a first-class feather merchant. They were still on the *Algomotoc*, they said. They had been on the Boston-to-Halifax convoy run, they told him between drinks, but now the old tub was going to patrol the Bay of Massachusetts. "Because we got a tough reputation," Gutsell said arrogantly. "Ain't 'at right, Quilt-bottom? Ain't we rugged?"

"We have seen an oil slick or two," the yeoman admitted. "We have burned some powder an' dropped a few dozen cans."

They put money in the kitty and drank, and told Al what a great old bastard of a ship the *Motock* was, and what a great skipper old Theron Bennett was. "But we could use a cook or two," Blanket-ass said. "Red Wildoe hasn't improved a bit. He gets worse, if anything. And that boot camp buddy of yours, Charley Berger, is even worse than Red. Why don't you transfer to the *Tomock*, Alvino? We need you, man."

"I'll do it," Al said thickly, touched. "By God I'll do it."

They told him their new sub-chasing duty covered an area from Monomoy Point, at the lower tip of Cape Cod, to Pigeon Cove, up near Gloucester. They said they didn't, in truth, much relish the idea of hacking it all alone, but what the hell. "C'est lay gurr," Guts shrugged.

The conversation grew more disjointedly general, and Gutsell said, "Ole Red is fat as a pig. Not on his cookin', 'at's for sure. On sex, I figure. His wife don't allow him to grow a beard like us other Hoolies." Guts elbowed Al and winked and whistled lewdly, but Al wasn't sure he got it, or that Guts knew what he meant himself. Anyway, he didn't want to talk about Stella Wildoe. Or even think about her. She was an awful temptation sometimes, now that his hair had grown out again and Jo's letters were so pen-palish and everything.

"What about ole Pelliteri an' Brownie an' Snag Salter an' Horse Flanders?" he asked nostalgically. "They still with you?"

"Can't run 'em off with a shotgun," Blanket-ass said. "Outside the food, we like that ship. We got a good deal. Outside the chow."

"I figure Red, he's too pooped to cook good any more," Gutsell leered. "Love has slowed him down an' put dark circles unner his eyes."

Stop talking about Stella, for chrissakes! Al thought. And he thought wistfully and drunkenly of Jo Hill with no clothes on—and of Stella with no clothes on. And he filed the information that the *Algomotoc* would be out for a week starting the next morning, while the *Legume* was slated to stay in for two or three more days, this trip.

In September, with the wind cold off the North Atlantic and dread cold in a cook's mind, a guy was apt to dwell at some length on creature comforts, on snug and feverish pleasures.

And so, the next night, Al remembered a telephone number and got in touch with Stella, and met her in a bar in East Boston, and devoured her with his eyes while they drank, and was in turn consumed by her darkly wickedly languorous eyes and knowing Mona Lisa smile that hid her sharp little teeth. She had put on a little weight, just enough to make her look more voluptuously desirable, and presently they got into a taxicab and went back to Stella's apartment in Everett. Al refused to consider the moral aspects of the situation; he flatly refused to think of Red, and especially of Jo Hill. This didn't concern anybody but Alvin Woods and Stella Pappharonis Wildoe, boy.

But when they got inside the small untidy apartment, the very first thing he noticed was the large tinted portrait of Red Wildoe, looking as stiffly wooden-faced and pompous as if it were Red in the living flesh, and suddenly Al was sick of himself, sick of Stella.

"What's wrong, honey?" she asked, seeing his sick stare, and she came to him, alarm in her eyes, and pressed against him and kissed him, but his lips did not respond, although his body wanted to. "I'm sorry, Stella," he said. And thought, I keep seeing all the other guys.

"Please, Al," she said without pride or shame. She threw her coat on the chair and began to wriggle out of her sweater and skirt, and he watched with sick fascination, unable to go. She tore off her slip and stood before him, inviting with her dark wicked eyes, pleading with her ripe mouth as she unfastened her brassière, freeing her large and beautiful and maddening breasts, and presently she was entirely naked and warm and dizzily tempting. He touched her breasts, so large but firm and outthrust, and he groaned and picked her up in his arms and kissed her hungry mouth, and carried her to the bed and put her down. She lay there stretching her olive-skinned body lazily like a cat, sinuously and maddeningly, commanding him. He walked to the bookcase and turned the picture of Red to face the wall, and looked at Stella like a starving man looks at food. But he didn't go back to the bed. He was on a diet; it took all of his will power, but he was through with Stella for good. And he heard her dismayed wail as he hurried out the door.

He ran two blocks before he felt safe from his awful tendency to go back. He caught a bus and then a trolley and then the subway, and got off at Scollay Square, where he meant to get blind drunk. But after one drink he was too restless to sit at the bar, and he went out into the darkened city and walked to the Common and aimlessly entered the Buddies Club. But once inside he was no longer aimless. He got ten dollars changed into dimes and quarters and nickels, and got in a phone booth and put in a call to Tulsa, Oklahoma.

"Keep trying," he told the operator when Jo did not answer, and he smoked up all his cigarettes and paced back and forth outside the booth, and bummed smokes off a soldier and a marine, and another soldier, and checked to be sure the operator was still trying and that he'd given her the right number to call back, and paced and fidgeted until twenty minutes of twelve o'clock, when the phone finally rang in the booth. He was very angry now, shaking with nerves—probably out with some guy, necking up a big storm, no telling what all, he thought.

"Jo?" he said. "Where the hell have you been?"

She didn't answer immediately. Then, "Are you drunk, Al?"

"I am not drunk," Al said coldly. "I have only been tryin' to reach you for two hours. It's almost *midnight*."

"It may be midnight in Boston," she said, "but we happen to be on Central Standard Time here, my dear fellow. I've been to a movie."

And Al collapsed like a punctured balloon. "Jo," he said miserably, "Jo, baby—I hadda talk to you, I hadda hear your voice. Jo, I need you, I love you. I'm cold sober, an' I'm so lonesome I could shoot myself, an' I want you to come out here an' marry me, please. I need you bad, Jo baby. Please marry me."

"O.K.," Jo said very matter-of-factly.

"You will? You mean it? You're not kiddin' me, baby?"

"It'll take a few days to get organized," she said.

"Aw, baby!" Al said, going all to pieces. "Jo, honey, I'm so ... goddammit, hurry up and get out here, will you? Hurry, sweetheart."

"Yup," she said. "Listen, I'll write you a letter, a long one, and I'll know when I can get ready to make the trip and everything."

"I'll wire you some money," Al said eagerly. "Aw, baby ..."

"I've got some money," she said. "I'll sell my car, too. But for heaven's sake, Alvin, let's not waste our money on cross-country phone calls. We've got to start economizing." (Al winced at the word.) "Now, Alvin, you really want me to come? You do *really* love me?"

Al groaned. "What the hell have I been sayin' all evenin'—you *know* that, honey. I *told* you. I love you more than ... than anything."

"O.K., that's fine, darling," she said. "That's all I want to know. I suspect the feeling is mutual—I've missed you something awful, darling. I love you, too—I'd *better* love you if I'm gonna marry you." She laughed a trifle wildly. "Well, look, hang up now, darling, and I'll write. And you behave yourself, you hear? Bye, darling Alvin."

Al hung up and slumped against the wall of the phone booth until he regained his shattered composure. Oh, man! he thought. It's O.K. now. Everything is gonna be all right now. Jo's coming. Oh, *man!* And he staggered away from the booth thinking, Now why the hell didn't I call her a long time ago? That's all it took, boy. One phone call.

Next morning the *Legume* loaded bright new buoys, huge bell and whistle buoys, lashing them snug, securing them to rings in the well deck. And on the next day she unmoored at six hundred hours and headed for outer Cape Cod, to swap the new buoys for old, barnacled, rusty ones. Outside Boston Harbor, outside the nets, the skipper set course for the upper tip of the Cape and had a GQ drill to tauten up the crew. Which was how it happened that they discovered Seaman Peter Irvin had taken French leave; had jumped the ship; had gone AWOL. There was no gunner for the starboard twenty, but only a loader and a third crewman known locally as a "utility infielder." The irate skipper summoned Fineberg, the gunnery officer, and Higgins, the exec, to the bridge. Al, who was sweating down in the magazine at the time, learned of the interview later.

"Who is gunner on that starboard twenty?" the skipper growled.

Fineberg, grimly: "The exec should answer that, sir."

Exec: "Seaman Peter Irvin is supposed to captain that gun."

Skipper: "Then why in God's name isn't he doing so, Mr. Higgins?"

Exec: "It appears he, ah, jumped ship, sir. He isn't aboard."

Skipper: "Why was that muck-up put on a gun in the first place?"

Gun Officer: "Mr. Higgins assigned him, over my protest."

Skipper: "How long have you been assigning gun crews, Higgins?"

Exec: "It was just temporary, sir...until Fineberg could find..."

Skipper, harshly: "Who was formerly on that gun, Mr. Fineberg?"

Fineberg: "Woods, the cook, sir. Since the beginning. When we first made up the gun crews I checked everybody for the guns, sir, and Woods had better reflexes and co-ordination for the twenties than anybody on the ship. He's a good gunner, sir. I've seen him up there in his spare time practicing, tracking imaginary targets, acquiring the skill that was evident on the firing range. He's a good gunner, sir."

Higgins: "But, sir, traditionally cooks don't serve in gun..."

Skipper, bluntly: "Get Woods back up there. And, Mr. Higgins, may I suggest you confine your brilliant inspirations to your own department in the future? Mr. Fineberg is the gunnery officer, is that clear?"

Higgins: "Well, but Woods...yes, sir."

So Al went racing up all the ladders, delighted to escape from the sinister airless tomb of the magazine, and strapped himself into the familiar harness and patted the useless 20-mm. affectionately. "Old Al's back, baby," he said, and grinned fiercely at his loader, grinning Country Boy Bagley, and the utility loader, Seaman Smith. They hadn't liked old Sea Gull Irvin worth a hoot, Country Boy said, guffawing.

It was great to be back on the high clean windy flying bridge, but after GQ was secured, Al started to change into clean white pants and found the key in his watch pocket. The key old Ed had given him. And just like that he knew what the key opened. So when he got dressed and ready for the galley, he went into the CPO's mess compartment, where Huxley and a chief electrician named Dixon were drinking coffee. Al put the key in the padlock on the CPO's private refrigerator. It fit, and he opened the refrigerator, and felt a little sick.

Canned ham, a pitcher of milk, tomato juice, grapefruit juice, salami, several pounds of butter, canned fruits, fresh fruits—he went to the door and yelled at the mess cooks. And he looked at the chiefs with disgust. Huxley said rather lamely, "What the hella yuh think you're doin', Onionhead?" and Al said bitterly, "I'm puttin' you goddam aristocrats back on straight rations. You get the same eighty-six cents a day chow allowance as any other enlisted man, and by God you're not gonna get any more goddam chow than the crew gets from now on. I'm taking the padlock offa your reefer. You can throw away your keys. From now on any extras in it better be stuff you can prove you bought ashore."

The mess cooks stood in the doorway, questioningly, and Al said angrily, "Clean out that reefer and take that stuff to the galley. It belongs to the general mess."

Huxley reared up. "Just a goddam minute, Woods!" he bawled. "Who the hell do you think you are? Get out of our private mess room!"

"Sit down, goddam you!" Al yelled. "Old Ed's gone now, can't you get that through your thick head? I'm acting commissary steward now, and you just fell off your dirty little gravy train, Huxley."

Huxley stood there fuming, but he made no effort to stop the mess cooks. They cleaned out the reefer and departed, and Al took the padlock and looked at Huxley and Dixon scornfully. "And *you* bastards had the goddam gall to complain about the chow situation!" he snarled, and stalked out. He knew what old Ed had meant, now. The key had been the answer to something that had long puzzled Al. Chief Miller had held still for the wardroom's ridiculous underpayments because he was tarred by the same brush. If he hadn't played dead for Higgins the reefer might have been taken away from the greedy chiefs.

They had a gentleman's agreement, Al thought, feeling sick. Old Ed and Higgins. The pot and the kettle. Honor among thieves.

Dave Hubert was in the galley when Al came raging in, and he backed away, pretending to be afraid of scowling, muttering Al. "Don't beat me no mo' wid dat hawse chain," he begged, and Al had to grin a little, and he said disgustedly, "Dave, sometimes I think you an' me are the only decent, honest guys left in the whole wide world—an' I ain't so sure about myself any more."

But that was only half of September, and food problems weren't life-and-death problems. The U-boats didn't care about the honesty or decency of the Americans they blew up and drowned. They were wary nowadays of the convoys, and preferred to track down the loners, the weak sisters, the slowpokes, the careless and reckless, the lame and the luckless. They didn't care if a cook was happy or sad, a scoundrel or a cuckold, competent or inadequate. They didn't ask questions at all, but fired whenever they got a target in the periscope.

The Coast Guard Cutter *Algomotoc*, originally a proud white sweet-water ship but lately a notoriously ill-starred salt-water vessel, was patrolling the perimeter of the Bay of Massachusetts; and on the fat, waddling old buoy tender *Legume* the men of the Hooligan Navy laughed about being inoffensively neutral and safe from harm.

"Nobody mad at us," they said scornfully, self-effacingly. "And anyway the battleship *Algomotoc* is protectin' us noncombatants, boys."

But all that, even including the duplicity of the CPO's who wanted to live like officers, was somewhat beside the point as far as Al Woods was concerned. Once he simmered down, he wasn't too mad at the naughty chiefs. He wasn't much worried about the letter, even. His agony of mind had been assuaged by a telephone call, and Jo was coming soon to Boston, and that was the biggest news of the war, boy. Jo guessed she loved him. Anyway she was going to marry him.

CHAPTER 30

The Sinking

FOR three rough days the *Legume* hoisted rusty, barnacled buoys out of the breaking seas and patiently maneuvered under the skipper's gentling hands so that she could put the new buoys over the side precisely where they were supposed to go. Sometimes she cruised in circles and laid down oil slicks in order to approach buoys whose bells jangled with agitation, or whose air whistles—which worked somewhat on the same principle as a tin whistle—sounded like a frantic jug player in a washboard band. It was slow and dangerous work, and another skipper might have chosen to lay to in the harbor of Orleans and await a break in the glowering weather, but Lieutenant Fox took the view that the seas might only worsen. And they got the work done, slowly and with great patience and caution. The new buoys were all placed and the old weathered and crusted buoys were got aboard and lashed down on the well deck, and she finished her risky chores off Monomoy Point by early afternoon of Saturday, the nineteenth of September. That night she ran into the harbor of Orleans and anchored, ready to shove off at dawn for Chelsea Creek. But long before daybreak she was under way on another course, lumbering north and east into peril—at twelve knots.

Al was in the crew's head reading newspapers when the running and shouting occurred outside in the passageways. Then he heard the muffled thunder of the Diesels coming to life, and the bosun's pipe eerily calling, and he left the litter of newspapers and hurried below to get his windbreaker and watch cap and life jacket. Then he went racing topside to find out what was happening.

It was after midnight when he went scrambling up the sheer ladder to the flying bridge, hearing the water whisper along the flanks of the ship as her engines moved her forward on the slackening tether of her anchor chain, hearing the voices of men on the laden well deck and forward on the foc'sle. He leaned over the rail, just above the starboard bridge wing, and heard the skipper there under him snapping orders, and the foc'sle winch whining, and the chain rattling in through the hawser hole. Al was squinting in the gloom of cloud-filtered moonlight, watching the dark movements of men on the foc'sle, when he heard Higgins's worried voice right under him.

"What's up, Captain?" the exec panted, and Al noted that Higgins was the only man aboard who affected to call the skipper "Captain."

"Theron Bennett's ship is sinking out there!" the skipper said harshly. "Torpedoed! We can be there by daylight, but I pray God somebody faster heard the SOS and gets to him a lot sooner."

Al Woods felt the blood grow cold in his veins, and suddenly it was unbearably lonely there in the dark on the flying bridge, and he went back down the ladders to get the keys from the O.D. They would need strong black coffee tonight, and sandwiches.

The skipper seldom bothered to let the crew know what was going on, but this time he did, this time he passed the word. It was a rescue mission. The *Algomotoc* was sinking or had sunk out there somewhere in the Atlantic night, and they were going after survivors. All hands must be fully dressed and wearing life jackets. He ordered lookouts posted in the bow, the stern, bridge wings, flying bridge, and in the crow's nest. Look sharp! he told them. He ordered full crews on the depth charges, the Y-gun, and the three-incher. The crew's mess was to be readied for emergency first aid, the CPO's quarters would be used as a sick bay for survivors. The smoking lamp was out, except in the mess deck and below decks. Carry on, the skipper said.

Al made an urn of coffee, stronger than usual, and put salami and liverwurst and bread and mustard and canned cream in the scullery. Doc O'Neal and Yeoman Sam Goff were helping stack the mess tables, and Doc looked at Al and said heavily, "I keep rememberin' New Orleans, Al. Remember how ole Hamburger always wanted to go to a cat house as soon as we crossed the river? He's tough, Al, he'll make it, huh?"

Al nodded, but he was thinking of others, too. Red Wildoe, who talked without moving a muscle of his face, who walked like a fat man ice-skating, and who had married a Milwaukee nymphomaniac after Al gave her basic training; he was thinking of Blanket-ass, who was part-Choctaw and had blue-black handlebar mustaches and a spade beard now; of tough, arrogant Gutsell, a coxswain now but once a contemptuous pot-walloper who had forced Al to try on his new PO authority for size, back on peaceful Lake Michigan; and Quartermaster Snag Salter, eternally twisting and braiding his forelock and staring into his watch cap as if he might find the answer to his private, obsessive problem there, and who had taught Al how to fire off an oil-blower range. Al was remembering Pelliteri, too, a handsome Catholic boy with brooding dark eyes, who had been carnally susceptible to big, buxom Nordic girls in Milwaukee. And Water Tender Brown—old Brownie who bought a girl one drink, felt of her leg, and said let's go to a hotel; whose rate was obsolete in this Diesel age, Lieutenant Bennett had said wryly. And big, loudmouth Horse Flanders, homely as a mud fence, who would give you his last dollar, who would sleep with women homelier than he was and twice as old. And Al thought of Lieutenant Bennett, big and brusque, kindly and humorous, a cigar-smoking extrovert who had made a fine executive officer until he got his own ship, a ship that had once blown off her own stern with a depth charge, and now was sinking or had already gone down in the cruel Atlantic night.

Al thought with dumb sorrow of all those men he had known on the *Skedeelia;* he could not bear to think that they might be drowning at this very moment, crying out for help with strangling words no one could heed. Around him in the mess deck off-duty men huddled, as if cold, and gazed wide-eyed at nothing while they drank coffee and smoked.

He went back up to the flying bridge and stared into the darkness where the pitching and rocking ship was going as fast as her heavy cargo would let her, seeing the phosphorescent glint and shimmer on the crests of the long glittering black swells, and the distinct line of horizon where the ebony Atlantic rose tumid against the slate gray of the overcast. Clouds scudded westward before a cold thin wind, and sometimes the moon's full, treacherously bright face peered down through breaks and rents in the scuff, and he thought, with a shiver, that men called it a "hunter's moon," because this was the kind of night when U-boats liked to prowl on the surface looking for easy silhouetted targets. It was also the kind of unnerving night when the creamy crests of the long swells looked like torpedo trails, and torpedo trails looked like creamy breaking wave crests. Or so he had heard. This ship did not often run at night, and *never* went northeast at night into the wide, endless, ominous Atlantic like this. He thought of men in lifeboats in the grim cold September seas, or in life rafts, or in soggy life vests, or even half-naked and without jackets, swimming desperately for their lives in the numbing water, waiting for this slow and wallowing buoy tender, made slower by her load of buoys.

He stood over the starboard wing of the bridge and knew that the hatch was fastened open, because he could hear the measured *pinnng!* of the sounding gear in the wheelhouse over the splash and murmuring rush of water along the ship's flank and the thin singing of the wind in the taut rigging overhead, and he wondered how it was going to feel when they got wherever they were going. How would it feel?

He could see Coxswain Kritikos's shadow against the forward rail, and Signalman Heatly's motionless bulk against the uncovered searchlight, and as he passed them he said, "I'm gonna put on my long johns." Heatly laughed nervously, his teeth chattering a bit in the ghostly night, and Al went down the ladder and through the dark hatch and blackout curtain and on down to the passageway, illumined faintly now by the red battle lights low on the bulkhead. Why do I keep yawning when I'm not sleepy? he wondered. And went down the last ladder quietly, when he'd always gone down clattering noisily before.

He thought a man could have carried the tension out of the crew's quarters in buckets, it was that thick. Men were lying wide-eyed and fully dressed on their bunks, wordless, preoccupied. As if they were listening, Al thought, waiting for a particular sound, like a cry for help, maybe, the strangling, gasping plea of a drowning man.

Think of something else, for chrissakes! Al told himself, and he thought, This is all wrong, the Hooligan Navy is neutral. Somebody made a bad mistake. And we're making a worse mistake now.

He stripped to his goose-bumpy skin, shivering, and put on his itchy woolen long johns and dungarees and turtleneck sweater, and there wasn't anything else to think about, after all. He got his windbreaker on and stuck his arm through an armhole of his life jacket and lit a cigarette and concentrated on Jo Hill. But this had nothing to do with Jo. This had nothing to do with anybody ashore. There wasn't anything to think about—except Red Wildoe, and Guts and Blanket-ass and Sticker Pelliteri and Horse and Snag and Charley

Berger and Lieutenant Bennett out there floundering and dying in the cold bottomless Atlantic in the grisly bone-colored moonlight, choking and coughing, struggling, cramping, growing numb, aching with the cold, and knowing only hopeless, stunned despair. We're so slow! Al thought. We're so goddam slow! And he thought, Brownie, I forgot to mention Brownie. It seemed to him that forgetting to include all of them was terribly wrong, as if he would care less if this one or that one died. Nine guys, he thought. Nine friends of mine out there, nine good guys. God, I hope they make it, I hope they *make* it, I hope none of them . . .

"Hey, Bob," a quiet voice said. *Yeah?* Bob said. "You 'sleep?" *Oh, sure, naturally*, Bob said tartly. "Know any guys on that ship besides Bennett?" *Yeah*, Bob said. *Seaman named Orbin Daniels.* "Oh," the first voice said. (The voices were strange, altered by the thick insulating tension; Al wasn't sure who spoke.) *A good guy*, Bob said. (There are three guys named Bob sleep down here, Al thought.) This Bob said, "You hear about White? Oliver White, the colored mess boy?" (All mess boys are colored, Al thought.) "He's got a brother on the *Motock*," Bob said with dull wonder. Al stared at the tip of his cigarette and listened to the rhythmic mumbling of the Diesels through the steel bulkhead, feeling their pulsing beat through the soles of his shoes. Somebody had said—who *was* it said—they couldn't do better than twelve knots, loaded with the buoys and all. How fast is twelve knots? Al wondered. A little more than twelve miles an hour—not as fast as a man can trot. Not anything like fast enough.

He looked around the bank of lockers toward the bunk he used to sleep in, the one he had given up to Oliver White because Higgins said he wanted the Negroes all together. Ollie wasn't in the bunk. Ollie still couldn't remember not to say "yessuh" to petty officers. Ollie had a brother on the *Algomotoc*. Had had? Not *on* it any more.

"Reckon we'll git there by daylight?" a voice asked nervously.

"Yeah, if we get there at all," a sullen voice answered. "If we don't get our ass blowed outa the water."

"What are you, the voice of gloom or something?" That sounded like inadequate Sonnichson. "Nobody talkin' to you anyway, mack."

"I was voicin' an opinion," the sullen voice said. "My opinion is we ain't got no business goin' out on no hero routines like a big fat-assed sittin' duck. This rust bucket couldn't fight a rowboat."

"You know anybody on the *Motock?*" It was Sonnichson, all right.

"No, an' I don't wanta know anybody on it."

"Well shut your goddam mouth then," Sonnichson said furiously.

"There's plenty other ships could get there faster'n us, an' probly doin' it, too. We just wastin' our time, an' I just hope we don't get a torpedo shoved up our bucket like the *Motock* done, at's all."

The new man, the new quartermaster, Al thought coldly. The one nobody likes and likes nobody. Somebody oughta feed him some teeth.

Then the voice of Franklyn Peabody Scott the Third floated condescendingly down from his upper bunk (naturally an upper bunk, Al thought, grinning), saying, "A torpedo is really an intricate small speedboat that travels at forty knots just under the surface, and is filled with cordite. And," Harvard added with haughty disapproval, "it is perfectly absurd to expect anybody to sleep while wearing one of these incredible and preposterous kapok cummerbunds."

Al grinned suddenly and got his dictionary out of his locker and opened it at random. "What's a *lithotrity*, Harvard?" he asked.

"Spell it," Harvard ordered. Al spelled it. "It's surgical," Harvard said. "I never interested myself in surgery, it repels me."

"Aha!" Al crowed. "Got you, huh?"

"Not quite," Harvard said oh so wearily. "I believe it has to do with gall stones—no, bladder stones."

Al threw the dictionary at the bulkhead. "At's close enough."

Chicken Hawk, the ex-surfman M.A., growled, "I wish you dern bastringes would hush so I could sleep a little. At my age I got to have my beauty rest or I'm liable to come down with bladder stones."

"Chickie," Radioman Levine said falsetto, "can I go to the USO?"

And Seaman Smith suddenly began chanting from the shadows, "Geeve a beeg sub-stan-chul cheer for de good old you-hess-ho, for dat is de place all de Hooligans love to go, raw, raw, raw."

Al grinned and crushed out his cigarette with his heel, hearing the low laughter travel around the berth deck, and he got a folded blanket off his bunk and went up the ladder. Seaman Mike Kelly was in the scullery making a sandwich. "Where's the onion?" he demanded. "You know liverwurst ain't fitten to eat without onions on it, gut-robber."

Al unlocked the galley and got four large Bermuda onions and threw them into the scullery sink, and then he got some coffee for himself and sat down, and saw Doc and Yeoman Sam sitting on the stacked tables eating sandwiches in the scarlet gloom of the battle lights. He thought about joining them, but he knew Doc would be brooding about Lieutenant Bennett and Charley Berger. Everybody was so gloomy. He gulped his coffee and went on up to the flying bridge and sprawled out on his blanket against the starboard railing, just above the open hatch of the wheelhouse. He heard the skipper's voice down there.

"They must have abandoned right away. In the water hours already."

In the water hours already. Al lay on his back on the swaying deck staring numbly up at the clabbery cloud deck that hid but did not entirely subdue the brilliant traitor moon, and he listened to the regular measured *pinnngs!* of the sound gear below, and the whine of the wind up in the taut wires of the rigging. He shivered and pulled the blanket around him, yawning constantly but not sleepy, wishing he could sleep, wanting to sleep away the next few dragging hours. He heard Heatly and Kritikos talking in low voices, uneasy and furtive voices, and after an eternity of listening to the *pinnng-ing* of the ranging sound gear and the thin keening of the wind and the constant splashing mutter of the ocean, he fell into a restless, uncomfortable dozing. To awaken some time later to find a thin rain falling on his face, and turn on his side and pull the blanket over his head and doze again, his senses lulled by the pendulum motion of the high bridge and the soothing wash of the seas and the monotonous *pinnnngs* in the wheelhouse. But he was very uncomfortable, sleeping fitfully, his sleeping mind full of woe and fragments of disturbing dreams, and finally he came awake and got up, stiff and sore and chilled, and climbed heavily down the ladder again.

Doc was sleeping wedged in a corner of the mess deck, and Sam was sitting owl-eyed with a cup of coffee and a cigarette on the tables, and half a dozen other men sprawled on the linoleum deck sleeping. It was very depressing, and Sam asked hollowly, "Did you know Ollie White has a brother on the *Motock*, Al?" Did have, Al thought grimly, nodding. "I know nine guys on the *Motock*, Sam," he said dully, and Sam stared at him speechlessly. The clock said it was four-twenty-two—the only thing slower than a ship, Al thought, is a ship's clock. He checked the coffee—there was some left but it was strong and oily, so he cleaned out the urn and made fresh coffee, and fixed himself a sandwich with a lot of mustard to kill the taste of the cheap salami Skinny had tricked the Navy out of. When the coffee was ready Sam came stiff-legged across the rocking deck and filled his cup. One of the men on the tilting deck was snoring adenoidally, like a man strangling, and Al went back to the flying bridge.

It was almost morning now, after four-thirty now. In Oklahoma four-thirty was a good time for a kid to get up and eat peppery fried eggs and hot biscuits cooked by a barber, and go down into the river bottom pecan groves to hunt squirrels in the shivery dawn—before the barber lost interest in hunting squirrels in September. He must have eased up on the beer drinking in that town, Al thought. Maybe all he ever needed was a nice-looking landlady to sleep with. He heard the thin sad rain on the steel deck and the canvas cover of the starboard twenty, and the mournful wind stronger now in the rigging. A man without a woman is a pushover for alcohol, he thought. No good to himself at all.

It was a curious, unreal thing to be awake in the rain on the flying bridge of a ship far out at sea with morning coming. It was a cold, uncomfortable, itchy, and ominous thing, too. He thought of the skipper down there on the dark and silent bridge sitting on his stool with his skinny legs crossed, staring stonily and patiently through the windscreen into the murky dregs of darkness. Is he worrying? Al wondered. Does he dread what we will find out here? Is he sick with thinking how slow this ship is and how fast it would need to be?

I wonder what Jo is doing right this second—sleeping all soft and warm. I can almost feel her breath on my neck, and how it was to wake up and find her really there in my arms, sleeping so trustingly, like a baby but not looking like a baby. I hope she is dreaming about her Alvin, about coming to Boston and marrying a cook. Married! Imagine that, boy. I'll never let her be unhappy. I'll compel her to be happy.

He dozed again, cramped and itchy under the wet blanket, and he didn't know what woke him, but heard the scuffing and scurrying and the curt voices, and sat wedged where he was, orienting himself, the dream of Jo overlapping into harsh reality. And then he heard the new sound from the bridge, the excited *pinnng-ping!*

pinnng-ping! of the sound gear, and he came fully and coldly awake, throwing off the blanket. The sound gear was getting a bounce, an echo; it had made contact with some solid object in the water—maybe the *Algomotoc*, Al hoped, stumbling to his feet. He found his flak helmet and removed the cover from his gun and got a heavy clip of shells out of the ready box, and attached the lanyard, and had the starboard 20-millimeter aircraft gun ready for firing when Country Boy and Seaman Smith came scrambling sleepily over the railing in answer to the GQ alarm that had awakened him. It wasn't daybreak yet, but there was a grayness in the world, and you could see the horizon, as the ship changed course so the seas began to break heavily against her side, causing her to wallow far over. Al swung the gun outboard a little, figuring maybe if there was anything to shoot at the ship's rolling list would depress the muzzle far enough to get in a few rounds. Faintly below he heard the chilling *pinng-ping!* that meant the unknown object was closer; he strained to hear over the whine of wind and the splashing rushing seas and the rhythmic muted thunder of the big engines that formed the beating heart of the ship.

"Wot's happenin'?" Seaman Smith panted, and Al said he didn't know, and the ship came on around, so that the seas broke against her stern, and held a steady course, and the sound gear was going: *Ping-Ping! Ping-Ping! Ping-Ping!* The ship quivered from the strain on her great Diesel heart, shuddering forward, and the echo was louder and louder and quicker and quicker: *Ping-Ping! PingPing! PINGPING!* And Al froze, tense and hollow, and thought, So this is how it feels.

He heard the shouted orders and repeats and the initial *blap* of the Y-gun on the quarter-deck, but still the explosions startled him and shocked him and he winced, seeing Country Boy's white face framed by his helmet set in a meaningless, paralyzed grin. The heavy ship shuddered from stem to stern as the sea tore open behind her and off both quarters, and then the rest of the diamond pattern let go in the creamy wake and the white ghostly waterspout rose high against the gray darkness and the ship shook again from the impact as the depth charges exploded deep in the ocean. The skipper brought her around again and made another run with the sound gear for his guide and laid down another pattern of destruction, and the ocean erupted again in great blossoming fountains. This time the light was stronger and Al could see the waterspouts more clearly in the bleak Atlantic daybreak. A third time the *Legume* attacked her unseen adversary hiding in the depths, tearing the ocean apart. But when she completed the second loop of her figure-eight course and came down the foaming lane again there was only the steady, regular *pinnng* again, and no echo at all. And there was a great greasy bubbling spread of black oil on the gray water, and enough dead fish to feed the crew for a week, it appeared. A fifth time the ship swung over the spot with no echo on the detection gear, and Chief Bosun's Mate Huxley was ready to shove a red nun buoy overside to mark the spot. And the men were ready to cheer shakily and triumphantly, because now they could claim title to an oil slick in the Atlantic that might, just possibly, mean there was a dead U-boat down there in the muck. We got it! they shouted. But they had no real proof. Oil slicks without wreckage and bodies meant little any more, for the krauts had learned to release oil so their enemies topside would think they were badly damaged and would stop blasting their eardrums with those goddam explosion shock waves while they sank to the bottom to wait it out. But all you could be certain of was that the detection gear had lost contact and there was some oil on the ocean, and a lot of mullet going to waste in the ship's back trail.

It was daylight now, gray and gloomy, and the thin rain fell coldly into the endless gray-green wastes of the Atlantic, and there was another red nun buoy staking another dubious claim, and the *Legume* resumed her original course. Up in the crow's nest it was pretty rough going for Waxey Franks, and the seaman was seasick. But he considerately waited until the nest was suspended far out over the churning seas to do his vomiting. And when he wasn't busy vomiting he was an efficient, sharp-eyed lookout in the best vantage point on the ship for scanning the desert of tumultuous brine. It was Waxey who spotted the men first.

"On the bridge!" he howled, forgetting his phone, and the C.O. lunged onto the bridge wing and looked up, and Waxey bawled, "Objects in the water twenty degrees off the port bow, sir!"

It was a life raft, and men in the water, and they were from the *Algomotoc.* There had been seventy-two men and officers on the *Motock;* there were forty here all told, clinging to the raft or scattered in the area in their soggy life jackets. Of these forty only twenty-three still lived. Forty-nine men of the ill-starred *Algomotoc* were dead or missing, and it was a good guess their murderers were

back there under an oil slick and a nun buoy, maybe dead themselves but more than likely still alive and still deadly.

Al got out of his gun harness and stood at the rail with a heavy
heart, trying to identify the sodden, oily, pitiful objects being
hauled aboard through the buoy port. There were two bedraggled
men in officer's watch coats, and Huxley and Ensign Hathaway,
supporting a limp heavy figure between them, looked up at the
bridge, Hathaway calling in his reedy voice, "It's Theron Bennett,
sir ... he's alive but hurt." And Al thanked somebody for Bennett,
and stared until his eyeballs ached trying to see something familiar
about each of the other survivors as they were dragged aboard by
willing hands.

There was one man in a life jacket farther out, alone and limp
and drifting away from the ship. Abruptly Al saw Ensign Hathaway taking off his clothes—stripped to his white skin and baggy
shorts, he dived into the heaving green water and swam to the
waterlogged man whose head was half-submerged. Hathaway (who
couldn't look anybody in the eye) lifted the head and towed the
limp body strongly back to the ship, a hand gripping the thick black
oily hair. And as they brought him over the break of the deck Al
saw the upturned face, the spade beard and drooping handlebar
mustaches and the big homely nose, and his heart stopped for a
moment and then thumped painfully against his ribs. That was
Blanket-ass Christy, but was he alive or already dead?

Hathaway came aboard, his wet white body shivering, and yelled
at the men to get Blanket-ass inside and start artificial respiration.
"Get the lead out!" Halfway yelled with new confidence, with
angry new self-assurance, shivering in the cold September rain.
"Get moving!"

The *Legume* made a juicy target, moving slowly, sometimes
almost stopping dead in the water; and the skipper kept shouting
for the lookouts to keep a sharp watch, dammit, and never mind
what was going on down there on the well deck! But Al was on a
gun that wouldn't depress below the horizon, and there were no
aircraft out here in this lost world of leaden sky and jade-green
water and bone-white foam, so he stood frozen at the rail, numb in
the cold rain, staring down at the cluttered well deck and the cleared
space around the buoy port where survivors were coming aboard
along with the soggy corpses of those who hadn't survived. Each
time Doc O'Neal knelt and checked for pulse and heartbeat, Al

held his breath. But it didn't help. Two officer survivors and twenty-one enlisted men went aft, including the doubtful Blanket-ass, and seventeen more, all enlisted, were put forward under the foc'sle—the known dead of the *Algomotoc*. Some of the dead were put inside the foc'sle housing, but five or six rigid, sodden corpses were visible from the flying bridge, and Al stared down at them with sick dread. Who *are* they? Do I *know* them?

When Doc started inside Al yelled down to him in despair, and Doc turned his white glum face upward and saw Al and called, "Berger made it." He didn't know any of the others Al wanted to know about, and Al thought sickly, What about Red, Gutsell, Pelliteri, Flanders, Salter, Brownie? What about Oliver White's brother, too? Most of the survivors had been so oily you couldn't tell if they were whites or Negroes.

The skipper scoured the area for an hour, risking eternity, but the two more men they found were dead, making nineteen under the foc'sle. And finally, reluctantly, the skipper abandoned the hunt and set course for Provincetown. The *Legume* got the seas on her tail for a change and made better time in the cold melancholy September wind and rain, but the skipper ordered the men to remain at their battle stations.

"We're not home yet by a hell of a lot," the skipper advised.

He was right. Shortly after nine-hundred-hours, Waxey Franks, still ill in the high crow's nest, began to bawl and squall wildly, and pointed a trembling finger off to port. "SSSS . . .!" he stuttered, and finally got it out in a scream, "SUBMARINE!"

The skipper saw the pointing hand and gave a sharp order and the helmsman brought the ship around to port, going at full speed, and the *Legume* laid far over to starboard in a deep slippery trough until Al thought with sudden panic that she was going to turn turtle; there was a loud rumbling crashing booming racket down on the well deck, and the ship rose and shook herself and labored out of the trough, answering her helm, but when she had come around to her new bearing she still listed far over on her starboard beam. "The buoys broke loose!" Kritikos said from the forward rail of the flying bridge. "They're all shifted against the starboard side!" The deep roll had caught Al by surprise and thrown him off balance, swinging down in an arc in the gun harness, and he had dragged the gun around so that it was aimed at the sky. Now he was clawing back up the slippery wet tilted deck to get the gun aimed forward, and feeling the hair stiff on his neck and his mind still chill with fright, because he had thought all that racket must be a torpedo slamming into the buoy tender's vitals.

He got the gun around and planted his feet on the slanting deck and suddenly froze in icy astonishment and horror. He was staring between the flat gun shields directly at the long, ugly, black, wet nightmare lying awash in the cold gray rain and the cold gray-green seas no more than three hundred yards away. Al had never seen a submarine before—except a half-built American sub in shipyard—but he was seeing one now with men in its conning tower and its stern under water and its ugly shark-snout bow thrusting up out of the waves. He was shaken by the sight, unmanned, chilled to his marrow, his knees weak and rubbery. But most incredible fact of all, he was seeing it through the gun's sight, right on target, zeroed in, dead in the cross hairs. He didn't believe it, the twenty wouldn't depress that far; then he realized it was only because of the ship's deep starboard list. And he just braced there on the slanting deck with his muscles quivering and his mouth open to yell but no strength to yell with, and watched the submarine wallow there.

Somebody down on the bridge wing could yell. "It's our sub, the one we ash-canned! She's crippled, we hit it good, sir!"

"God Almighty," Al whispered fervently, staring at the crippled U-boat rolling helplessly in his cross-haired gun sight, making no apparent effort to come about so the torpedo tubes would bear on the advancing Coast Guard ship, seeming in fact to be drifting helplessly without power in the chopping seas. Men were yelling below, some with alarm, some with vehemence, and some even with purpose and logic, but Al continued to watch with rigid hollow fascination in that brief but endless span of time, seeing the sub coming nearer just off the starboard bow, and seeing dark figures spill over the edge of the conning tower and scurry onto the sub's gun platform, working with the sea-tight cover, bringing the gun around to bear on the laboring *Legume*. Abruptly a machine gun began to hammer down on the bridge wing, and almost at the same instant it was answered from the sub's conning tower, and over the loud racket of firing Al heard the bloodcurdling scream of steel-jacketed slugs ricocheting off the hull of the cutter and smashing into flat surfaces with loud sledge-hammer blows. Suddenly the glass of the huge searchlight lens exploded, spraying glass all over the flying bridge, and Al came out of his catatonic shock.

He swung the twenty and got the sub's deck gun in the sights and saw its muzzle blossom flame and heard the ear-splitting *wham!* of the gun itself and almost immediately, far aft, the explosion of the shell that had missed the plunging *Legume*. And he started firing the twenty.

He was aware, vaguely, without opinion, that the rest of the men on the flying bridge had thrown themselves flat on the deck, except for Country Boy who clung frantically to the right-hand gun shield and grinned with horror. Al saw that the molten-pink tracer bullets were a little low and he walked them up the side of the U-boat until they began to splash off the deck gun like sparks, and the deck gun bloomed fire again, but the sub was rolling so that the gun fired high. And when it wallowed back again the glowing tracers stitched a tight arc across the gun platform as Al instinctively and automatically and without volition adjusted delicately for the rolling and plunging of the *Legume*, not thinking about it but only doing it from long practice, a mindlessly integral part of the gun. He didn't believe this was real, but the cold rain on his face was real, and the acrid fumes were real.

And the deathly silence when the drum went empty was real, too.

"Reload!" Al yelled, and Country Boy clung to the gun shield and grinned his ghastly, uncomprehending, horrified grin. "Reload, goddammit, reload!" Al screamed, kicking his loader on the shins, and Country Boy unfroze and got a fresh clip out of the ready box and climbed back up the steep incline like a somnambulist. "Move!" Al yelled, and then, logically enough, the gunnery officer was there on the flying bridge, briskly removing the empty drum as Al pulled the release, slapping the full heavy one into place, helping Al cock the twenty again. Fineberg's face was bloodless under his gray flak helmet, but he had control of himself, and he slapped Al on the back and pointed at the sub, now scarcely a hundred yards away, and Al began firing.

There were hoarse yells below and the constant banging of the machine gun on the bridge wing, but the three-inch gun aft couldn't fire—it covered a range from dead abeam around the stern to dead abeam, the ship's superstructure barring it forward. And dimly Al realized that the port twenty was thudding away and saw from the corner of his eye Ensign Fineberg firing the gun alone. His own tracer bullets and the winking trajectories from the port twenty converged on the sub's deck gun and conning tower, and he saw the dark figures on the U-boat jerking from impact and crumpling and one, trying to run to the conning tower, stumbling and falling into the sluicing seas. And then the wallowing, silent U-boat was sliding below his cross-hairs as the distance dwindled to nothing and Fineberg shouted, "Hang on, men, we're going to ram her!"

The machine gun on the wing below kept firing short stuttering bursts after the twenties quit, and men were yelling everywhere to stand by for collision; at the last minute the skipper called for stop engines and reverse engines and the twin screws under the cutter's stern churned in reverse. When the cutter's heavily reinforced ice-breaker bow smashed into the sub's pressure hull between the conning tower and the snout-like bow with a grinding, rending, jarring crash, the jumble of buoys and gear on the well deck surged forward rumbling and banging, and it sounded to Al like the end of the world. He was braced stiffly but the impact hurled him bruisingly against the gun butts and twisted him around, sliding down the tilted deck, and he hung groggily in the harness, numb and resigned as the *Legume*'s bow plunged and then rode high, grinding and ripping, and the ear-rupturing cacophony continued as the sturdy bow slid down again with a screech of sundered metal in the deep wound it had chopped in the U-boat, the powerful Diesels shaking the ship like ague, shuddering her free of the rammed U-boat and backing away, rolling and pitching in the turmoil the collision had created.

The machine gun spoke again in short bursts as the buoy tender backed away, coming about to face the seas and beginning to move ahead past the stern of the mortally wounded submarine, which was listing to starboard so that you could see the dead men in her conning tower, and Al Woods climbed the wet gritty deck again, bringing his twenty around and down again to bear on the target, and emptied the drum of visible tracers interspersed with invisible armor-piercing shells at the enemy. When the *Legume* was barely fifty yards distant her three-inch gun aft began to slam ear-splitting rounds into the disabled sub, and the conning tower was ripped and blasted and laid waste. This time there was no room for doubt as the U-boat slid lower and lower, her snout rising briefly then wallowing under. The Hooligan Navy had got an Axis hearse for sure—but the skipper was a methodical man, and he sent some ashcans down to insure the workmanship of the job.

The men yelled themselves hoarse with delirious triumph, until

they remembered all the dead and missing of the *Algomotoc*, and
then they shouted hoarse blasphemies and obscenities after the plum-
meting enemy craft, and swore to take vengeance on others like it.

The skipper got the seas on her stern again and the damage control
party found only a minor rip and a lot of indentations in the sturdy
bow; they stuffed a collision mat in the rip and closed off the
forward watertight holds. And down in the engine room the men
who had sweated out the fight and collision unable to see or know
what was going on babied the Diesels into giving a little extra speed,
and the old Hooligan Battleship *Legume* ran for home with lopsided,
canted arrogance and pride. But with nineteen dead men lying under
the foc'sle, some of them now under the clutter of her cargo, and
with a deep list to starboard that made her skipper uneasy. There
might be healthy subs around.

At ten hundred and zero five hours an old U.S. four-stacker de-
stroyer, now property of the British Admiralty, came over the misty
horizon under a long smutty pennant of coal smoke, and patrolled
around the *Legume* while she slowed to a walk in the pelting rain
to tidy her cargo and trim ship and get everything battened down
in Hooligan fashion again. The limey ship had a doctor aboard and
hove to upwind to send him in a bobbing boat to look after the
injured survivors. And when a sleek lean lethal-looking Coast Guard
patrol cutter with *North Atlantic* written all over her came out of
the gray rain and joined up around noon, the skipper finally secured
battle stations. Let the limeys and the U.S. Coast Guard worry now,
the tired old Hooligan Navy needed a rest and dry gear, and something to eat.

Al got out of his gunner's harness and lay down on the deck of
the flying bridge and cried like a baby from reaction. Not because
he had stinging cuts on his left leg and left cheek from flying glass,
and aching ribs and raw shoulders from being slung around in the
harness of his gun, but because he was all torn up in his mind and
soul. He was mourning the dead of the *Algomotoc*, but he was
also grieving for the faceless, nameless human beings he had stitched
with the thread of winking death from his gun, watching them jerk
and sag and crumple with cold horror in his mind. Grotesque rag
dolls with smoke curling from them when the ghastly rose petals
of death showered them, with Al Woods watching, withdrawn,
through his gun sights as the pink phosphorus drew macabre designs
across dark living human shapes. Ramming a U-boat was impersonal

and vitally necessary, but he had *personally* killed men, had *intimately* slaughtered Germans. And he was heartsick and stunned.

"You did what you had to do, Al," Fineberg said. Fineberg knew how it felt too, Al thought, wiping his face on his wet jacket sleeve. "Come on down out of the rain," Ensign Fineberg said. "It was kill or be killed, friend—and personally I'd rather do a little killing than get it." And he added bitterly, "The Germans don't mind killing—they slaughter women and babies and old men in Germany, Woods."

"I know it," Al sniffled, and thought of the helpless Jews in Germany, and the helpless men of the *Algomotoc*, dead in the deep ocean, dead forever in the cold bleak September seas. But the Germans on that sub had been people, guys with wives and girls and kids and parents; living, breathing, feeling, thinking *men*, with yearnings and fears and joys and problems. Just like us, Al thought with terrible aching guilt.

"Maybe I'm a rare bastard," Fineberg said calmly, "but I enjoyed using that twenty, Woods. I loved every blessed minute of it, friend." Then he said gently, "Come down out of the rain, old buddy."

"All right," Al said, sniffling. "I'm all right. It's O.K."

He went down to his bunk, ignoring the excited dissonance of everybody loudly and exuberantly retelling his vital part in the big battle of the Atlantic. He got out of his wet itchy clothes and went up to the showers naked and washed the stink of fear and cold sweat and horror off of him, and then he went dripping back down into the odorous crew's quarters and toweled himself and got into cook whites. Poor Curly and Dave, he thought, down in that goddam magazine all that time. He went up to the galley and unlocked it and began dumping canned vegetables into the electric stock pot. It was good to be a cook again instead of a killer. A box of "roasting and frying beef" was in the sink, left there since yesterday evening to thaw, and he hacked the slippery stuff into rough chunks and dumped it into the electric pot. There'll be some *meat* in this stew, he thought.

He made a fresh urn of coffee while the mess cooks cleaned up the mess deck and started putting up the tables again. He sent Country Boy down to the storeroom for canned fruit and more canned milk, and more salami and some cheese to dull the crew's hunger until the stew could get done. He mixed up a great pan of biscuit dough, and chopped up celery for the stew, and peeled potatoes for the stew.

And then he had run out of things to help him procrastinate, and couldn't stall any longer, and so he went back to the chiefs' quarters where the survivors had been put to bed. He found Blanket-ass, revived and cleaned up and pale under his dark skin, staring blankly at the springs of the bunk above him. "Hello, buddy," Al said, and the yeoman turned dark, beady, dead eyes on him and saw him, like buttons would see him, and the lips moved soundlessly, and that was all. Al patted him awkwardly, not knowing what else to do, and turned away, dreading to look further. But he found Gutsell immediately. Tough, cocky Gutsell who had once given him a rough time when he was a green rookie cook. Guts looked at him with hurt, questioning eyes, pale under his beard.

"Hello, cooksie," he croaked raggedly. "Where we headed?"

"I guess we're goin' on to Boston," Al said, having heard that.

"I figured Boston," Guts said. And he shut his eyes tight and said, "We wasn't tough enough wen it come time." And tears ran down his cheeks into his fierce, matted beard. "We got it good," he said.

Al located Berger, fatter than he remembered, but his face hard and cynical under the fat; the pale blue eyes were like windows with dead winter behind them. "Hello, Charley boy," Al said, and Berger's tough Cicero, Illinois, face came around, bleak and doughy, and he said, "Okie, ya jerk, wotta youse doin' here?"

"This is my ship," Al said, feeling a strange pride in the words. "This is the old Lagoon," he said. And abruptly the glass shattered in the wintry eyes and Berger looked around at the double bunks, and Al followed his aching glance and saw that almost none of the upper bunks were occupied. And Berger said pleadingly, "Where'd youse take all dem others? Where's all the guys? Scattered around, huh? In other compartments, huh, Okie?" And then a little wildly, "Some other ship picked 'em up, maybe. *Tell* me sumpin, ya dumb jerk! Where's all de other *Motock* guys at?"

"Some other ship," Al said thickly, and turned away.

He saw the young Negro, and when he did not find Red or Brownie or Salter or Flanders or Pelliteri in any of the other CPO bunks, he stopped by the Negro. "Are you White?" Al said, realizing how silly it sounded, but the Negro only looked at him forlornly and said, "Yessuh."

"You're Ollie's brother," Al said, thinking about the foc's'le.

"Yessuh," the Negro sorrowed. "Ollie, he my bruthuh, suh."

Don't sir me, I'm just the murdering cook, Al thought, wanting to go now, feeling clumsy. "You get to see him yet?" he inquired.

"Yessuh, thank you, I done seen Ollie," the Negro boy mourned.

Al left the CPO's quarters and found a weary Dave Hubert in the galley, and Al thought, There are five more of them somewhere. But he knew they were dead, five unlucky dead ex-friends of his, and he said, "Skipper had anything to eat since we left Cape Cod last night, Dave?"

Dave shook his head. "Just coffee, far's I know, Al."

"He oughta eat something," Al said. "Milk toast, maybe."

"I'll fix some," Dave said tiredly. "He rates something special, don't he, Al? He's the head tomcat in my book from here on in."

Al nodded, he knew that now. Old Tom Fox, forty-nine years old and with a duodenal ulcer and a bad habit of taking nine-dollar hams to his mistresses, a man of vast icy scorn and intolerance for stupidity and incompetence, who could sit forever on a bridge stool with his skinny legs crossed, like a stony-eyed old hawk sitting on a fence post, grim and bleak and kind of inhuman—old Tom Fox had more goddam guts and knowledge and ability than any man alive. He didn't have to live by the petty rules of others— hell, let him have all the hams he wanted. After today, let him take the whole ship up the street, boy.

"How was it topside?" Dave asked carefully—having heard already.

"I had a good view," Al said. "I saw it all, Dave."

"I truly don't love that magazine detail," Dave said ruefully. "A man just plain don't know what's goin' on down there."

A man never knows what's going on anywhere, Al thought, staring at his hands. And he knew he wouldn't go up forward and look under the foc'sle. It might be that he would find them there, or some of them, or one of them, or maybe none of them at all, but he didn't want to go look at the dead. If I was dead, he thought bleakly, I wouldn't want anybody looking at me. And I don't want to know. I know too much already.

CHAPTER 31

Hero

OLE ONIONS, they insisted, was a real, genuine, bona fide hero. But Al Woods knew better. He was a fool and a murderer. In the days immediately following the great fight, he was sick and appalled to find that the unanimous heroes of the U-boat sinking were Lieutenant Thomas Fox (for unhesitatingly turning his lumbering inadequate ship to attack the sub—with either incredible courage or incredible foolhardiness) and Cook-gunner Alvin Woods (whose coolness under fire, and quick unerring deadliness with the 20-millimeter gun, had kept the sub's lethal deck weapon from being effective) and Ensign Hog Cupper (who stood on the bridge wing with a hot, heavy machine gun cradled in his arms, firing and yelling Texas war cries that unnerved the enemy) and Ensign Fineberg (for manning the port twenty when he realized the ship's deep starboard list had made the usually ineffective antiaircraft guns murderously effective for once).

Old Tom was also hailed for taking the laden vessel out on the rescue mission in the first place. And there were lesser heroes. Ensign Halfway Hathaway, who had dived into the bitter Atlantic to rescue a drowning Blanket-ass, and in so doing had rescued himself, and become, at last, an officer. And Chief Gunner's Mate Riley, who had prevented the three-inch gun crew from firing at the U-boat at point-blank range and possibly killing a few Hooligans with flying metal from the explosions. In fact, everybody had been heroic except, perhaps, immature Ensign Scraggs, who had thrown up several times down with the magazine detail (for which nobody much blamed him), and Executive Officer Higgins, who was rumored to have (1) huddled in a corner of the wheelhouse as white as a sheet, (2) disappeared into the after gear locker during the skirmish, (3) tried to launch Number 3 lifeboat singlehandedly, or (4) had been busy in his stateroom confessing all his many sins and asking forgiveness. If he had personally won the battle, hardly anybody would have wanted to admit he was a hero. Higgins was not the hero type.

Al Woods was not the hero type, either. The mantle of notoriety hung uneasily from his slumped shoulders, and his haunted heart rejected all the kudos. Fate had played a grotesque trick on him at last, making his useless old twenty briefly and traumatically useful, like handing an ax to a crazed dope addict or something. He had acted automatically, while scared out of his wits. And the night after the big battle he was host to one incubus after another, tortured by nightmares of the agitated rag-doll Germans, half-obscured by puffs of greasy smoke and glowing pink dots, jerking and wincing and sprawling. He couldn't shake off the gray clinging horror of having killed flesh-and-blood men, and he moved under a monstrous burden of guilt and remorse.

The others, who had made no living puppets dance at the end of lacing, fiery threads, held jubilant victory celebrations for several nights in a row, consumed by a hot and swelling pride and a new sense of self-esteem a man can know only after running the gauntlet of terror. But Al sat among his fellows like a deaf-mute, lonely and heartsick.

He couldn't even get decently drunk...

After the grim business of unloading the *Algomotoc's* survivors and dead, and her cargo of battered buoys, the *Legume* had laid alongside an ammunition barge to unload her explosives, and then had gone directly to dry dock for repairs. That first night, on orders from the D.O., nobody was allowed to go up the street, and in the morning a high-ranking official came aboard and spoke gravely to the ship's personnel at a special muster. He commended them, but then he spoke of the vital need for complete silence and secrecy. They mustn't mention the *Algomotoc*, or the U-boat. And the skipper drew a nervous laugh by stating that nobody would ever believe such a wild story anyhow. And then *he* commended the men. He told them he was just tremendously proud of every man aboard. "We were very lucky," he said, "but when we got a few breaks, we exploited them efficiently, I thought."

He was cheered lustily by the Hooligans. Great ole Tom Fox.

Afterward everybody got liberty, and nearly everybody got drunk, but although Al's body and tongue became almost helpless, his mind remained starkly sober and his conscience refused to give him any respite.

The letter from Jo should have helped. Maybe it helped a little. He got it that morning, and it was a fine letter. She wrote: "My dear darling Alvin: I can hardly wait, I simply ache to be with you, sweet Alvin, but I must let common sense rule my palpitating little old heart for once. The boss said if I'd stay on long enough to train a new girl he would give me a month's wages as a wedding bonus, and I've found a buyer for my Ford—six hundred dollars! We'll be rich!!! I must spend a week or so with Mom and Dad, poor things, who are horrified about the whole business, but resigned and pathetically sweet. I keep telling them they aren't losing me, they're gaining *you*. Meanwhile, dearest Al, you be finding us a cozy nest in dear old Boston, and I'll write more in a few days with statistics, time of arrival, et cetera. I am simply giddy with happiness, out of my mind to see you again. Love, Jo." It was the best letter *she* ever wrote, and maybe it helped. Ordinarily it would have had him walking around in a happy trance, but now he just wanted Jo in person with a despairing urgency. She could help him now, she could help him forget for a while. A while at least.

In a way her letter kind of canceled out, because it reminded him forcefully of the other letter, and along with feeling like a cold-blooded killer, he had this other older dread to contend with. I don't want anything to happen about the letter! he thought with dismay. Not now. Not after what we all went through together. That isn't important any more, it's beside the point now. I hope nothing *happens*.

I wish I'd never learned to run a goddam typewriter!

I wish the officers would suddenly see the error of their ways and pay off the deficit they caused, and reform for all time. But wishing was foolish. He was helpless on the tracks of destiny and a train was either coming or it wasn't coming. Somebody else would have to throw the switch and derail the choo-choo, he realized unhappily.

"Doc," he said, "did I happen to mention I'm gettin' married?"

"Not lately," Doc said. "Go ahead, mention it, Alvinhead."

"I'll meet this train," Al said moodily, "and she will get off, and the sun will shine in the world again an' forever. I'll be O.K. I got a letter from 'er s'morning." He shook his head sadly. "Doc, I wish

I hadn' wrote 'at goddam letter. Doc, you think I'm a bloody murderer? Tell me the hones' to God truth."

"I think you saved the ole homestead," Doc said affectionately.
"I think you saved my life, Al, an' I wanta thank you in person."

Al shrugged forlornly. "S'all right. Glad to do it, baby."

"You an' ole Cupper an' ole Nate saved the immigrant train, Al."

Al shook his head and stared with distaste at his twitching hands.
"Can't stop the train now, Doc. Mail train. Got the U.S. free mail on
it an' ole Sleepy Lagoon stalled on the crossin'. S'all my stupid fault."
He couldn't stop shaking his head sadly. "I'm all bloody," he
mourned.

There were half a dozen *Legume* men drinking around the table
of the East Boston tavern, and the others, unhaunted, smug, jubilant, had reached that stage where they wanted the world to know
what the humble Coast Guard Cutter *Legume* had accomplished
lately, but being sworn to secrecy they only skirted indiscreetly
around the edges of the subject. "Here's to the ole Lagoonie,"
Kritikos winked. "Ole hit'n run Hooligan yachit went down 'at ole
torpedo alley an'... well, boys, nobody would ever b'lieve what
happen, would they?"

"I'd believe it, Kritikos," Ensign Fineberg said, drifting over from
his quiet place at the bar, looking amiable. If Al had been less preoccupied he might have suspected the ensign's presence was not
sheer coincidence; the skipper might have assigned his officers to keep
an ear on the more volatile crewmen. But Al only thought that
Fineberg was a vital cog in the terrible confused dilemma, so he got
unsteadily to his feet and bowed and said politely, "Won't you join
us, Ensign?"

"I'm honored," Fineberg said, and pulled up a chair. "Now, men,
what is your considered opinion of the current football picture?"

"Didn' see it, sir," Al said thickly. "May I assa quest-shun?"

"Shoot," Fineberg said, and winced. "Sorry, Woods. Ask away."

"Sir," Al said politely, "don't you sometimes feel 'at you *ossers*
have too mucha va good thing inna *chow* depar'ment sometimes?"

Fineberg lifted his handsome brows. "How do you mean,
Woods?"

"Doncha think," Al said distinctly, "you oughta pay more
money?"

Fineberg looked puzzled. "Why, I dunno, chum. Hadn't given it much thought. But twenty-one dollars seems fairly reasonable to me."

Al blinked at him. "*Who* pays twenny-one dollars, Ensign?"

"Why," Fineberg said slowly, "we all do, Woods. At least *I* do, and I naturally assume the other officers do too." He eyed Al curiously.

And Al gaped at him in perplexity. Wrong answers, he thought. This man keeps givin' me wrong answers alla time. "Then how come," he wondered aloud, "the general mess don't get but half of it?"

Fineberg's eyebrows went up again, and he shaped his lips in a silent whistle. "Oho. The crux of the mysterious letter, eh, chum?"

"Assolutely," Al said. "April, May, June, July, Augus' . . . mos' the wardroom paid was thirteen somepin', lease was ten somepin', an' Higgins hollerin' at us cooks we gotta cut down. Cut down cut down! Ole slobberin' Dennis say get outa hole or else. Clean up 'at deffisint or we gonna get cooks know how to economize. He say cook oughta be able feed a man on eighty-six centsa day—'cept ossers, spose be able feed ossers for ten dollars an' fiffy centsa month, huh?"

Fineberg whistled out loud this time. "Bless my soul," he said. "Well, well. We . . . we have a thrifty mess treasurer, do we not?"

"Cheap lil ressurant named wardroom," Al said wearily. "Food good, service excellen', no tippin' allowed, all osser can eat thirty forty centsa day. Seaman get eighty-six, goes inna hole." He shrugged elaborately. "Well, ho hum. At's life, hey? Rich get richer, poor get poorer, cook gets chewed out. Shod any good moose lately, Ensign?"

"So you wrote a bitter billet doux," Fineberg said wryly. "And who could blame you? Who can say you didn't have sufficient provocation?"

"Can't stoppa train now," Al said with sorrow. "Not after *your* ass, sir. Ever'body likes *you*, b'lieve me. Like Skipper. Like McFarland. Might decide we like Halfway. Got nothin' 'gainst Skinny. Tella truth, wish I hant rode it now. Wish I hant done it, Ensign. Wish I hant shod any moose lately, too. Feel like a bloody hangman, Ensign."

"Let's not go into that, chum," Fineberg said with firm kindness.

"Sorry," Al mourned. "Keeb my big mouse shud now on, sir."

"It's late," Fineberg said. "Why don't we go back to the ship, gentlemen? That's a long, limber ladder we've got to scale tonight."

"Jus' leavin'," Al said with dignity. "Me'n Doc jus' leavin', sir."

"Just left," Doc grinned. "Been gone for some time already."

"Carry on, gents," Fineberg said. "I'll finish my drink."

But he didn't fool Al, boy. Al knew he didn't *have* a drink, boy. Outside, he nudged Doc. "Din' *have* a drink," he confided shrewdly.

"Had too dern many, if you ast me," Doc said, grinning. And he hooked his fingers in the back of Al's waistband and they started home.

On the street to the shipyard there was a small old Catholic church, and as they were about to pass it, Al suddenly balked. "Doc," he said solemnly, "at'sa church, right?" Doc nodded. "Catholic, right?" Al asked. Doc nodded again. "Jus' Catholics allowed to go in there?" Al wanted to know. Doc said he guessed anybody could go in.

"Even a murderin' cook?" Al asked with sudden choking grief. "Even a lousy killer like me, Doc?"

Doc, who was not drunk at all, looked at his friend with sad wonder and pity. "Even you and me, Al," he said.

Al leaned against the dingy brick wall and rubbed his forehead. "You know your way around in there," he said. "You go alla time, huh?"

Doc said ruefully, "Not as often as I should, buddy."

Al sighed raggedly. "Doc," he moaned, "take me in there. I'm not really drunk. Can't *get* drunk. Can't sleep, Doc. Can't think."

Doc looked at him silently for a long moment. "All right, Al."

They went up the worn steps, worn by the hurrying tread of humble people seeking solace and reassurance, and into the small old church that was a sanctuary from pain for those who knew how to use it. There were dim lights down by the altar to guide those whose troubles became unbearable at night, and moonlight came feebly through the panes on one side. Al groped for a bench and sat down, and after a moment Doc sat down beside him. Physically, the place was dank and cold. And Al didn't feel anything. He had hoped wistfully to feel something. He sat there waiting for something and nothing happened. It was only a dark dank-cold strange place, and no sudden relief warmed him.

"Doc," he said in a hushed voice, "do you ever pray?"

"Sometimes," Doc admitted. "Yesterday I prayed a little, Al."

"Can a guy ... get somebody else ... to do his prayin'?" Al asked with embarrassment. "If a guy don't know how, or don't figure he's got the right, could he ... could somebody else ... ?" He sighed heavily. "Doc, you know the score, you know how. Would you do it for me?"

Doc was silent a moment. "Pray for who, Al?"

"All the people I killed," Al said miserably, thick-throated. "I don't know how many. All the poor helpless guys I killed."

"All right," Doc said, and he slid off the bench and knelt, and after a second Al followed his example, leaning his feverish brow against the hard cool back of the pew. He didn't hear Doc praying, but he figured Doc was praying silently. It didn't have to be out loud, necessarily. (I wish I'd asked him to try to do something about the letter, Al thought.) He stayed on his knees, hoping to feel some quick miraculous alleviation of his torment, some abrupt easement of his burdened mind and soul, but he felt nothing, except gratitude toward Doc, who was trying to help him. And when Doc crossed himself and got back on the seat he said, "Tomorrow I'll ask the priest to pray, too, Al. For the Jerries, I mean. He'll be glad to do it." So you could see Doc was working on it. He was thinking about it.

"Thanks," Al muttered. He didn't feel any easing of the load, but maybe it didn't happen all at once. Or maybe being physically drunk made him ineligible. "Let's go," he said, feeling a little disappointed.

When they got to the dry dock he looked at the great bulk of the ship, high and dry in her cradling timbers, and he looked at the long, limber ladder going up to the buoy port and felt a little dubious. Oh, well, he thought glumly. If I fall off maybe it'll end my worries. But he didn't fall off, because his body was sober now, too. Tomorrow I'll try to get drunk again, he thought. I just *got* to get drunk.

He had the nightmares again that night. Little men twitching and crumpling in the mushrooming puffs of smoke and wound-pink tracers. He was haggard the next morning, and Doc looked at him with concern and said, "Tonight I'll fix you up with a needle, Al."

But the others said, Ole Bull's Eye. Ole Onions the Gunnions.

That day Al toyed with the idea of destroying all the evidence he'd been accumulating. It seemed to his hungover, depressed mind that if he tore up the ugly evidence it would somehow cancel out the ugly, reprehensible cheating. He believed Fineberg. He was

ready to declare McFarland, Scraggs, Fineberg, and Hathaway innocent—they just ran with the wrong gang. But in checking his data
Al realized that Higgins, Cupper, and the skipper had carried ashore
food worth more than they had paid the general mess for regular
meals. Also, it seemed, the C.O. was sort of faithful in his looting—
that gaunt and craggy bachelor only carted food ashore in Boston.
Higgins and Cupper apparently had lean-bellied friends on Cape
Cod and in Maine, as well as Boston.

And there was always the possibility the other officers raided the
wardroom pantry on their way ashore. Al put his incriminating
statistics away, shaking his head despairingly. He was torn between
his new pride for the ship and her officers and men, and his ancient
hatred of injustice and the abuse of privilege. He didn't know what
to do. Maybe, he kept thinking, if I just talked plain English to the
skipper, he would see what a terrible thing they're doing. They
could repent and atone, they could make restitution. Boy, I wish to
hell they would.

He went ashore alone that evening. He didn't want to be with
the happy arrogant Hooligans, or even Doc or Yeoman Sam. He
had a few drinks and went to a movie, but he couldn't sit still, and
he went to the Buddies Club and danced a couple of times, but the
girls were not Jo, and eventually he tried again to get drunk. About
all he accomplished was to grow drawlingly, earnestly philosophical.

In a bar, a Navy gunner's mate said, "Coast Guard." Tentatively.

"Coast Guard," Al informed him solemnly, "is just a category.
You're a gunner's mate, but you probably don't actually pull the
trigger of a gun, you strawboss the job. I'm a cook, but I operate a
20-millimeter Oerlikon in my spare time, as a hobby. So if you want
to be technical about it, I am probably as much a gunner's mate as
you are. On the other hand, mack, since the start of the war the
Coast Guard has been a subsidiary of the Navy, so for the duration
I am a Navy cook. Which illustrates the fallacy of trying to put
people into a category. That bartender might have lost a brother
or a son in the war already, so he's more involved than you or me,
it's more personal to him. My idea is, there ain't any Coast Guard
or Navy or Army or Civilians when you look at it a certain way.
There's just us, people. Just people."

"You're a little too deep for me, cook," the gunner's mate said.

"I'm deep, all right," Al admitted. "Clear up to my chin, boy."

"What do you shoot at with your little old twenty, cook?"

"Kites," Al said. "Towed targets. Sea gulls. Ghosts."

"Well," the Navy man said, "the twenty ain't a bad little gun."

"It's a very bad little gun," Al said grimly. "A deadly bastard."
And he got up and left the bar and found another where nobody
wanted to talk about shooting guns at things. But all of the strangers
were more strange than ever, they were not citizens of a world of
horror as he was, they did not even imagine what he *knew*. So
finally he got a flat bottle and stuck it under his waistband and
went back to the ship. He got undressed and lay in his bunk in the
darkness and drank from the bottle and tried to make his mind
blank. But it was like trying to put the lid on a can of worms when
the can had a dozen holes in it. Thoughts kept squirming out. The
skipper, he said to himself, would at least try to clean up that mess
before somebody comes poking around. Maybe he doesn't know
about the letter even yet. I ought to warn old Tom.

He got up and dressed in his cook whites, including his apron
and white hat, and took another fortifying drink from the bottle,
and went up the ladders to the boat deck and banged on the C.O.'s
stateroom. He did not know that it was three o'clock in the morning. He hadn't given it any thought. Besides, there was a light in
the skipper's cabin, as if he had just got out of a warm bed and come
home. I will talk turkey to that old boy, Al told himself drunkenly.
Cold turkey. I will lay it on the line for that gutty, unshrinking old
genius of a skipper, boys.

The skipper shouted, "Come in," and Al went in. The skipper was
sitting at his desk in robe and slippers and black-rimmed glasses, with
a book and a bottle in front of him and his hair awry as if he'd just
got out of bed. His face was drawn, stonier and craggier than ever.

Al removed his hat. "Sir, I would like to speak to you alone."

"We're quite alone, I assure you," the skipper said ironically. "At
three o'clock in the morning, I doubt if anybody else is awake."

"I can't sleep," Al explained glumly. "I don't *want* to sleep."

The skipper examined him through the glasses, then removed them
and wearily rubbed his eyes. "I believe I know what you mean,
Woods."

Al slumped into a chair, then staggered to his feet again.

"Go on, sit down," the skipper said. "At ease, Woods."

Al sat down again and stared at his hat. What am I doing here?
he wondered. He glanced warily at the skipper and noticed the
bottle and jigger, and the book. The book was a Bible. And the

skipper *never*, under *any* circumstances, drank whisky *straight*. He had an ulcer.

"What's your problem, Woods?" the skipper asked tiredly.

Misunderstanding, Al sighed and said glumly, "Nightmares, sir."

"Yes." The skipper nodded stonily. "Would a drink help, Woods?"

"Nossir," Al said. "I tried it. Doesn't get the job done, sir."

The skipper turned his Bible face down and rubbed his eyes again, slowly and abstractedly. "Yes, I believe I am conversant with your ailment, Woods," he said sternly. "A man is required by nature to be a bit sensitive before he is entitled to a duodenal ulcer, you know. A duodenal ulcer is not the worst thing that can happen to a man, but commanding a ship in wartime is probably the worst thing that can happen to a duodenal ulcer." He grinned a rather ghastly grin.

Al didn't know whether to smile or not, so he didn't.

"We're celebrities now, Woods," the skipper said with a bitter smirk. "We'll certainly get a unit citation, and some of us may even get individual citations. This ship performed a remarkable feat, and the people up at the District Office regard us with stupefied awe."

They call me Onions the Gunnions, Al thought. Ole Bull's Eye.

"We'll never live it down," the skipper sighed. "Would you care for a drink, Woods? Excellent Scotch. Gift from an admiring superior."

"All right, sir," Al sighed. He drank from the bottle. "That's mighty smooth stuff, sir," he said glumly. "That's fine whisky."

The skipper poured himself a jigger full and studied it coldly. "The exigencies of war," he murmured. "We do incredibly brutal, inhuman things almost casually, or in anger, or in fear—and fear can be more vicious than anger. But afterward we are shocked by what we have done. It seems decent men have a perverse compulsion to feel guilty, and to punish themselves. We have not been schooled to accept brutality. In wars, the enemy is always a cold-blooded sadist, and it seems to me the decent man becomes a relentless masochist, Woods."

He's really lettin' his hair down, Al thought, surprised at the skipper's erudition. I never guessed he was a thinker, Al thought.

The skipper shook his gray head and sighed, and hit the desk with the flat of his hand. "Everybody knows they always run in packs, there's always another one somewhere nearby. It's folly to assume anything else. *That's* why I did it the way I did it. *That's* why I rammed it and then ripped it apart with the three-inch gun. I had to choose the safe and sane way, the quickest way. It had undoubtedly radioed its condition to a sister ship, and we certainly had no damn business loitering in that area. *They* don't spare any pity for their victims, why the hell should they expect any mercy?" He glared fiercely at Al.

Al shook his head, feeling confused. Feeling a bit awed.

"But there it was, Woods. Dead in the water. Helpless. I could have come alongside with that three-incher staring down their throats and they would have been glad to surrender, I imagine. But they are treacherous, I didn't trust them. We could have salvaged some humanity out of that wrecked U-boat, and come home with prisoners. But then *we* would have been dead in the water, we would have loitered in the danger area. I wanted to get out of there fast, before another of the slimy bastards showed up and blew *us* out of the water." He poured himself another drink, the bottle tinkling against the shot glass because his hands shook a little. "I had to make a split-second decision, a choice which once made would mean total commitment." He drank off the Scotch, his face constricting briefly. "I made it!" he said harshly.

And he said wearily, "It was the only sensible, logical, safe, practical, reasonable, rational, intelligent decision possible."

For a while the cabin was utterly quiet, the skipper staring flint-eyed at the bulkhead. Then he said quietly, "But the truth is, I didn't *want* any of those people to live." He turned and handed the bottle to Al, and Al drank and handed it back. "That's the awful *truth*," the skipper said. "I was vengefully angry, I had just seen their brutal handiwork, I had just picked up what was left of the *Algomotoc*. I knew the officers on that ship, all of the officers who died. So I sentenced the U-boat's officers and men to death, and executed them. I was the sheriff and the judge and jury and the firing squad." He snapped his fingers, and sat scowling terribly at nothing at all, or at ghosts.

Al was shocked. Even woozy from whisky, he was shocked.

"The trouble with Americans," the skipper complained, "is that we have no talent for sustained hatred, Woods. Our flaw is that we do not hate efficiently. We're a neurotic tribe full of pity and compassion and mercy and remorse, and we don't see hate as a virtue, but as a sin."

I didn't hate, I was scared to death, Al thought. Scared stiff.

For a long time the skipper only sat rigidly, unblinking, as if listening tensely for some faint and distant sound, and then he sighed and turned his swivel chair around so that he faced Al. "Now, I believe I know what your problem is, Woods. I know what you did up there, I saw it very clearly. We needed every ounce of fire-power we could summon, and you did a fine job. But you had no choice, it was not your decision, it was mine. You may have wounded a few Germans, but I killed them. If you have the silly, insubordinate idea that you are in any way responsible, get it out of your head right now. I am in command of this vessel, I alone am totally responsible, Woods."

"Yessir," Al mumbled uneasily, and struggled to his feet.

"Was there anything else troubling you, Woods?"

Al remembered that he'd intended to cold turkey the skipper about the mess situation. Now he didn't want to say it right out, yet he still felt he ought to subtly warn the skipper to protect himself. He didn't want the skipper losing the Congressional Medal of Honor or something just because the damn government didn't pay him enough and he had to cheat a little on the board bill. Al straightened to attention and slapped his hat on his head and looked the skipper in the eye.

"Sir, do you happen to know how much a canned ham costs?"

"Seven dollars and fifty cents," the skipper promptly replied. He grinned his ghastly grin again and poured another drink. "Of course I imagine Higgins has seen fit to make me a special price on them, Woods. He is quite a toady, you know. He curries favor. As a special concession to my rank and position, and the fact that I am solely responsible for this ship at all times, and have to make decisions only God has any right to make, why I just imagine Higgins has given me a tidy discount on the canned hams."

"That's all I wanted to know," Al said confusedly.

"Stop feeling guilty and remorseful, Woods. That's an order." The skipper put his glasses on again and peered through them at Al, and he suddenly looked small and tired and defenseless, a mere man and not much of a man at that. "Any guilt accruing to this vessel is all mine," he said. "Any blame or shame is mine. Anything any man or officer of this ship does, I am responsible, Woods. If you have problems, bring them to me. My hobby is collecting problems. Will you please just kindly inform me of one thing that puzzles me and confounds me, Woods?"

Apprehensively, suddenly suspicious, Al croaked, "Yessir."

"Why in God's name does any man want to command a ship?"
Al sighed with relief. "I dunno, sir," he said. "Good night, sir."

He went below, carefully navigating the ladders, and got into
his sack with his clothes on. He felt a great pity and affection for
the skipper, who had told him he was not a killer after all. Maybe
someday he'd even get so he could believe it.

Stretched out on his mattress, Al thought about the skipper's
terrible burden of command and decision. Jo would like the skipper,
he thought. She would know what a fine man the skipper was. I
want her to meet him. Sweet Jo ... she'll be here soon ... few
days ... got to find us an apartment in Boston, maybe Chelsea. Gee
I hope nothing happens about the letter, I hope it all just blows over.
Sweet Jo, sweet gray eyes, wistful vulnerable warm sweet mouth ...

Sleeping, he dreamed quite a lot about Jo, and not as much about
dying Germans, not as much about killing people. Already he was
in the process of breaking out of his traumatic shock. Time was a
cure for everything, for the deepest wounds to a man's spirit.

But time wouldn't gradually bury the letter, and it wouldn't just
blow over and be forgotten. The train was coming.

CHAPTER 32

Whitewash

THE ship was in dry dock three days while her bow was repaired. On the fourth morning the dry dock slid down its tracks and the ship floated free, and the skipper took her to a dock in the Navy yard and moored her. Nobody knew why, until the delegation of officers from the D.O. came aboard, and at first it was rumored the *Legume* was to be given a unit citation at a special muster.

But it was in reality a Board of Inquiry.

And it seemed to have nothing at all to do with the letter.

Al was on duty in the galley when the three officers and two enlisted men came aboard and marched back to the wardroom, and he had a sick, queasy, loose feeling in his guts. Here they are, he thought shakily. Here's where we destroy a proud ship, boys. Here's where we cancel out in a few short words all the honor and fame and glory.

But when they started calling the men back to the wardroom in alphabetical order, and a seaman named Arrington returned along the passageway pretending to wipe cold sweat off his brow, the big gusty relief set in. "It's about Pete Irvin," he said. "They picked him up AWOL an' he said he jumped ship because this here's a goddam slave ship, or somethin'. They're investigatin' about him desertin', that's all."

Machinist Red Baker reported the same thing.

Seaman Dusak reiterated. "They tryna fin' out about Irvin."

Seaman Peter Irvin, the foul-mouthed Sea Gull, the one who would have killed Germans with a 20-millimeter gun if he hadn't gone over the hill, jumped ship, taken French leave, gone AWOL; Irvin was in the brig, the Shore Patrol had picked him up. And in truth, this inquiry progressed with great rapidity, with much speed and dispatch.

Brewer, Bordeau, Boskwitz. And Burns, a radioman who had signed the letter. Burns was a little pale when he came back. He got coffee and looked at Al and grinned. "Whew!" he said. "Well, relax, Onions. It ain't got a thing to do with the letter, but only Pete Irvin."

"Then how come Country Boy didn't get called back yet?" Al asked. Bagley should come before Brewer, Bordeau, Boskwitz, or Burns. Maybe it was an oversight. Or because Bagley was busy. Busy B for Bagley. Al went down to his locker and got the Manila envelope.

Kafferhamp, Kelly, Kritikos . . .

Lang, Lewis, Lofton; Marsh, Melchamin, McCafferty . . .

They didn't call Curly Matoli! Al thought with a growing sense of doom and inner panic. Who's kiddin' who about this deal, boys?

Naylor, who had signed the endorsement to the letter, came back shaking with relief. "All about one Peter Irvin, deserter," he said.

They didn't call Miller, either, Al said to himself. Because old Ed by strange coincidence is no longer on active duty. And they won't call Osborn, because George is in sunny California.

Phillips, Potter, Qualls, Quinn, Rabinsohn, Radovich . . .

Salo, Sadwick, Schlemmer—and Schlemmer was gone longer than anybody else, wasn't he? When Schlemmer returned he said evasively that it was because him and ole Pete Irvin had been pig-chasin' buddies.

Seaman Sonnichson went aft on call, looking angry. He had nothing at stake, he was just angry because of the strain of waiting. But he was pathetically relieved coming back. "Not about nothin' but Irvin."

Sparlin, Steuben, Sullivan, Sweet, Tanner, Tate . . .

Ubbevale, Ulowitz, Vann, Vestings . . .

Hear that drum beating? Al asked himself. That's your heart, your waxen, frightened heart, boy. You're really sweatin', hero.

Vickers, Ward, Webbley . . .

Al felt like yelling. He was all knotted up inside.

Wheeler, White, Whittle, Wollaker . . . (Now! Al thought sickly.) Yates, Yellowhorse, Zane, Zellin. All right, Al thought resignedly. I guess that's plain enough. They skipped old Al Woods, boy. They're savin' the best for the last. I'm gonna be the dessert. Soon, too, because they have run out of alphabet soup.

There was a considerable lag in the proceedings, and Al busied himself in the galley. It was almost eleven, time to start getting ready for the early watch-standers. He tried to breathe normally, but it seemed to him normal breathing lately was panting.

MATOLI! said the bailiff of the inquisition.

Al listened to the sodden clamor of his heart. Go ahead, you guys, lie some more, tell me this isn't about that goddam letter!

Curly didn't come back to the mess deck at all, and Al's summons caught him unprepared, not ready yet, not steeled to it. *WOODS!* howled the foghorn trumpets of judgment. *LAY AFT TO THE WARDROOM!*

I'm the blue cheese and coffee, he thought, walking stiffly along the passageway with panic in his mind, without confidence, with jitters and stage fright. I'm the Jello with whipped cream, boys.

His face felt hot and his hands were damp and clammy—he kept wiping them on his dirty pants under the clean apron. His guts were in a knot he'd never in this world get untied. The wardroom door was shut and he rapped and gritted his teeth and took a deep breath, but he wouldn't get ready if he had ten years, he'd never get ready to go in there. He waited, his knees like water. The door was opened by Dave Hubert, and Dave's eyes tried to send him a swift message, but Al didn't read it at all. He stepped inside, very conscious of the Manila envelope under his waistband, under the apron. He removed his hat.

The Board of Inquiry people were at his left, the officers in casual, relaxed poses in the leather chairs, the yeomen straight and non-committal and efficient over their shorthand pad and typewriter.

The *Legume's* officers were arranged to his right as if sitting for a group portrait, arranged so that he could see—and be seen by— each of the seven. They gave the impression of being a jury; their faces wore varying degrees of the same closed, aloof, curious, watch-ful inscrutability. Except for Higgins. Higgins hated him openly.

Al saw that he was expected to stand there on unsteady legs during the interview. His face felt hot and his throat felt raw and itchy, and he knew his voice was going to be bad, unsteady, weak.

"State your name and rank," a visiting officer said briskly.

"Alvin Woods, ship's cook, first class, sir."

"How long have you been on this ship, Woods?"

"Since before it was commissioned, sir." His voice *was* bad. He tried to ignore the fourteen reproachful or whatever-they-were eyes to his right, tried to meet unswervingly the stare of the questioner. He hoped they would somehow like him a little bit, feel a little pity and sympathy for him, consider his youth and ignorance. Couldn't they see he was repentant about that letter, very remorseful?

They asked a great many curious questions. How long had he been rated? Where else had he cooked? Had he gotten his promotion to first class on this ship? (They'll take care of *that* before they hang me!)

The Board officers were too casual. One tapped his palm with a pencil. One examined his fingernails carefully, finding mild fault with them. The third officer had his legs crossed and was watching his foot move from side to side with a fascinated stare. The yeomen scratched, wrote, yawned, and would have looked out the window if there had been one. But the ship's officers were not bored. Heavens, no; not *bored*.

Do you know a Seaman Peter Irvin? Yessir. Did you know he had gone AWOL? Yessir. Did you know why he went AWOL? Nossir. Don't you even have a theory about it? Nossir.

"Irvin claims the food was very bad sometimes, Woods."

"He always griped about everything," Al said gruffly.

"Then you mean the food was never bad, is that it?"

"We got some bad buys from the Navy Commissary Warehouse," Al said evasively. "They sold us some pretty sorry junk sometimes, sir." I'm quibbling, he thought. I'm mealy-mouthed. How come, boy? Why don't I just hand these guys my little compendium of notes? he wondered. Why don't I give them straight cold turkey answers? I know it's because I'm scared sick, but scared sick of *what?*

"Would you expand that a bit, Woods? Sorry junk, you say."

Al found himself deeply involved in a rather asinine discussion of Overseas hams and bacon, foul link sausages, gray hamburger meat, too much too-fat "stewing and boiling" beef. He glanced at Skinny Scraggs and saw the ensign's miserable blush of embarrassment, and threw him a straw of pride to clutch at. "Sir, if it's not out of line, I just like to say I think we'd be a lot better off buyin' from Army Commissaries, gettin' beef by the carcass an' stuff like that."

"Then, as I understand it, you attribute the former bad chow on this ship to the quality of foods purchased from the Navy, is that it?"

"That's some of it," Al said. "We had to cut down on expenses."

"Why was that, Woods?" the obtuse officer inquired.

"The general mess was in the hole, sir."

The obtuse officer backed away from that. "This Irvin," he said. "Did he complain about the *quality* of the cooking, Woods?"

"He complained about everything, sir."

"Would you say the cooks were ever at fault, Woods?"

Al saw the opening, but he ignored it. He was beginning to catch on, all right. If anybody mentioned any letters, it was up to him. If anybody said anything about the officers' cheating, it was his big line of dialogue, all they intended to do was feed him cues. He said in regard to the possibility of cooks having been at fault, "Any cook has a bad day now and then, turns out a poor chow, sir."

"Then would you say the cooking was often poorly done, Woods?"

These guys were getting him pretty annoyed. "Sir," he said stiffly, "you talked to everybody else on the ship before you got around to me. If they said my cookin' was lousy, I'll go along with that."

The questioner eyed him reprovingly, but only nibbled on his pencil, showing his white, even teeth. All three of the officers were pretty nice-looking joes, Al thought. They looked like decent guys. Why didn't they stop beating around the bush and get down to business?

"Then would you say the general chow picture was improved now?"

"Not necessarily," Al said. "We've still got plenty of those Overseas hams an' bacon left. An' a lot of that other stuff, sir."

The officer let his breath out slowly. "How do you prepare your menus on this ship, Woods?" he wondered. "Who plans the menus?"

"Ordinarily, sir, the chief steward does it," Al said. "Or the senior cook. An' then the commissary officer checks it an' O.K.'s it."

This led into a rather involved and, Al felt, pointless discussion of balanced diet, variety, and other technical stuff. He was beginning to feel a little steadier now; his knees had firmed up some, and his voice wasn't as bad as at the start. All they had to do was ask him, frankly, about the letter. That's all they had to do.

"Now, Woods," the moderator said suavely, "would you say the food *formerly* was bad enough to justify Irvin's going AWOL?"

"Sir, I don't think anything justifies anybody goin' AWOL," Al said virtuously, and the officer looked faintly baffled for a moment.

He tapped his pencil against his teeth and studied the yeoman's typewriter, a quiet and inoffensive machine. "As a first-class cook, are you familiar with all the, err, various workings of the commissary department—inventories, purchasing, per diem allowances, et cetera?"

"Nossir," Al said. "My rating wasn't required to know all that." And he thought with exasperation, *They can end all this pussyfooting around with one or two simple questions. Why are they stalling?*

Finally the officer said carefully, "Could there have been, err, other factors involved in the, ah, lower standard of chow here, Woods?"

They want me to just bust out and accuse the officers, Al said to himself. *They're making it as hard for me as possible, leaving it right in my lap, boy. Birds of a feather, boy. They had to come here because of the letter, but they don't necessarily want to find out anything on the wardroom gang. They'd lots rather find out I'm a mutinous, insubordinate crackpot and the letter was a big lie—only they're afraid I'm not and it wasn't. Why are they so damn stealthy?*

And then it came to him. *This ship is a symbol now, some kind of proud symbol, a dungaree Navy vessel that killed a submarine, and proved the Coast Guard had guts and that Americans can whip Germans just by sheer courage and aggressiveness, or something. After last Sunday the old* Legume *is a legend, and these guys don't want to be disillusioned about her, they don't want to know it if she has a blot on her escutcheon. They want to protect her from scandal.*

And so do I, goddammit! he thought with sudden anguish. *I don't want to hurt this ship, or any of the officers. Except Higgins, damn him. He's all that's really wrong with this ship. We got a great old vessel here except for Higgins, and I don't want to foul her up. If they ask me, I'm gonna blame the whole thing on slobberin' Dennis.*

But a question, a very dangerous question, had been asked, and he looked at the Board officers and somehow got the feeling they were holding their collective breath, not wanting him to utter the harsh, ugly, tragic, disillusioning truths. *By God!* Al thought. *I'll play it their way, I'll pretend I think it's all about Pete Irvin.*

"Nossir," he said. "Not that I know of, sir."

And the ship's officers stirred, like men reprieved might stir.

"Do you believe he deserted because of the food situation, Woods?"

"Nobody else did, sir," Al said gruffly.

After that they seemed a little at a loss. The three of them leaned close and murmured and shook their heads and studied their notes, letting Al fidget, and shook their heads again.

"Well, then, Woods, I guess that's all. You may go. Thank you."

Don't thank me, Al thought grimly, turning toward the door.

But it wasn't really over yet. "Oh, one moment, Woods!" the spokesman, the head inquisitor, said brisky. And Al's blood chilled as he swung around. "Perhaps we overlooked some, ah, aspect of the general mess situation," the conscientious officer said, frowning at the deck. "Is there anything you'd like to volunteer about... anything?"

Until that moment, Al wasn't really sure they knew about the letter. It could have been Irvin blabbing about a letter he'd heard rumors of but hadn't actually seen. There was no certainty the letter had been turned over to the D.O. But now Al knew with cold reason that these officers had the letter with them, knew all about it, and in conscience had had to ask this last open-door question.

Al looked at the *Legume's* officers. The skipper, old stone face in person, his flinty eyes betraying no nervousness, no emotion. The engineer, Warrant McFarland, puzzled, uncomprehending, thinking about his Diesels, completely uninvolved with any of this. Fineberg, with mild regret on his handsome face, knowing what he knew, maybe wondering to what extent he must consider himself guilty. Skinny, a nice boy shoved into a nasty situation, doubting his ability to perform his officer job adequately, not sure what this was all about. Cupper, somehow less oafish since the big battle, his heavy features trying to look detached and curious but looking a little trapped. Hathaway, who had grown to manhood overnight, meeting Al's questing glance steadily. And Executive Officer Dennis Higgins, whose normally beet-hued face was the color of cream of tomato soup, whose eyes were splintery with hatred and menace, glittering at Al, but whose whole body was frightened. Higgins was scared silly, and the reddish-brown bristle of a mustache he'd started growing seemed to quiver, and sparkle with jewels of sweat. Higgins repeatedly smoothed back his thinning red-brown hair; he couldn't sit still.

All they need to do is look at him, Al thought, and felt a hot surge of heady triumph. I've got that bastard where I always wanted him! Ever since the first day I came aboard this ship I've hated his supercilious, overbearing, stupid guts. He's had me and Curly in a tight squeeze for months, but now I got *him* in the vise, boy.

Al got the Manila envelope from under his apron. And suddenly saw the flicker of the skipper's eyes, the fleeting, mercurial sadness. Wait a minute! Al thought, looking at the skipper (who had made a split-second decision last Sunday and would wonder forever if he'd made the right one) and feeling suddenly sick at heart. I don't want to hurt *him*. Maybe he's done a little cheating himself. And even if he hasn't, it'll hurt him; he's responsible for the actions of his officers, he'd be splattered by the tar; it's his ship, if I break this off in Higgins it'll reflect on the skipper who let him get away with his cheating. I don't even want to hurt Cupper, not after Sunday, him down there on the wing firing a hot, blistering machine gun and yelling Texas war cries at the U-boat. Cupper cheated, but I don't want to get him for it. Hell, I don't even want to cut Higgins down this way. I'd love to deck him with a fast right, but I don't want to expose him as a dirty crook.

I can't hurt one without hurting them all!

The silence in the wardroom was like a crashing of thunder, it was like the end of the world, and the tension was gut-wrenching; they all stared with dread at Al's menacing Manila envelope. And he thought, But if I don't go through with it now I'll be in real trouble, maybe. They'll have to do something about me. They'll surely bust me down to second-class, and ship my ass to hell-and-gone—and Jo due any day.

He looked once more at Higgins, whose eyes were sick and desperate on the Manila envelope, whose career as an officer and gentleman was ready to fall in ruins around him. Crawl, you snake, Al thought. Faint with fright, goddam you! But, strangely, he felt pity, too.

Sighing, Al Woods walked over to the *Legume's* officers, sitting there like a jury, or like a group of dishonored men about to be photographed for the dishonor files. Al looked at the skipper's bleak face and thought that his own must be equally bleak, and he handed the envelope to Lieutenant Thomas Fox, a great man whether he paid for his canned hams or not. The skipper took it, his eyes stony and unreadable on Al's face. Nobody spoke. It seemed

to Al that ten minutes had gone by since anybody spoke in the
charged atmosphere of the wardroom. His own throat felt raw and
thick, and his voice was bad, scratchy, not at all suited to the
sacrificial role he was playing.

"Nossir," he told the Board of Inquiry and its yeomen and the
seven worried officers of a heroic, foolhardy, waddling, inadequate
buoy tender that had had the incredible effrontery to attack a
U-boat head on.

"Nossir," Al said scratchily, "I don't have anything to volunteer
that I know of, offhand." And the die was cast.

He turned and left the wardroom, the hushed wardroom, and he
took with him a premonition of disaster and professional ruin.
They'll put it in my record that I made wild, false charges against
the ship's officers, he thought dully. I better wire Jo and tell her to
stay where she is, because I've fouled it up good for us. I don't want
her to marry a second-class cook on the Murmansk run.

In the mess deck they stared at his haggard, ashen features and
asked questions, but he only shook his head mutely and went into
the galley to get out the noon chow. He was busy frying pork
chops when the three officers and two yeomen from the D.O. went
forward in the port passageway, leaving the ship. And he was frying
the same pork chops when Yeoman Sam Goff came into the galley
looking confounded.

"Pack your sea bag, Al," he said gloomily. "You can get your
savings out of the office safe an' pick up your transfer papers."

Al shrugged ruefully. "They don't waste time, do they?"

"It *was* about the letter, wasn't it?"

"Yeah," Al said. "That's what it was all about, Sam."

Goff frowned. "But I thought you had proof, Al. I thought..."

"I had a bomb," Al said, "that would have blown this ship all to
hell, Yeoman Sam. Anyway, I was getting tired of this luxury liner,
I need a change of scenery. Same old faces day after day. You
know."

He went below and started emptying his locker, and Doc came
clattering down the ladder, his handsome face angry. "Al, they
tricked us," he said. "They had me fooled good—I thought it was
just a routine investigation into Pete Irvin's desertion."

"I knew better," Al said wearily. "They didn't fool me, baby."

Some of the others came while he packed, attempting to explain
in angry bafflement how they'd been taken in by the inquiry, and

Al kept grinning and saying, "I been wantin' a transfer a long time, I don't like these Boston winters, this vessel ain't big enough for me an' slobberin' Dennis both, I'm glad to sign off this luxury craft, boys."

Ole Onionhead the head gunnion, they said. Goddam. Sure sorry you're leavin' us. You can't cook, but you ain't a bad guy when you're asleep! Now maybe we'll get a decent chow once in a while, they said, and Al thought, They'll get decent chow from now on, I'll bet a million bucks.

"Al, buddy, I'm puttin' in for a transfer," Doc snarled.

"You talk like a man with holes in his head," Al said gruffly.

Wearing his dress blues, Al stopped by the galley to see that Curly had taken over. "Well," he said awkwardly, "I'll sell you my share of this here all-electric kitchen, Curly." Matoli stopped frying pork chops and came to the door, reaching embarrassedly for Al's hand.

"Goddam, Al," he said gloomily. "They railroadin' you."

Al grinned and gave a deprecating shrug. What the hell. Getting railroaded was better than being tied to the tracks. "It's gonna be O.K. from now on, podner," he said. "You won't have to worry about the budget. They'll go straight."

"Lissen," Matoli said worriedly, "how it was with me, Al . . ."

"I know how it was," Al said, thinking wistfully of Jo. "Well, I hope I don't get a goddam oil-blower range, wherever I'm goin'."

He went back to the ship's office and pushed the door open, and Higgins was waiting for him, vengeful and furious. "If you weren't departing in such haste," he grated, "I'd invite you onto the dock."

"Well, I'm not in any big hurry," Al bristled.

"I oughta deck you right here and now," Higgins raged. "You pathetic incompetent useless excuse for an imitation cook!"

"That's enough!" said the skipper, coming through the door, and Higgins stiffened, his splintery eyes hot on Al. "Lock the door, Goff," the skipper said, and Yeoman Sam, the only other man in the compartment, got up and clicked the lock. And the skipper stood there staring icily at Higgins with the Manila envelope in his hands. "There is some very enlightening material in this envelope, Mr. Higgins," he said.

"Captain, this man is a congenital liar!" Higgins snarled.

"Mr. Higgins, how much money is in the wardroom treasury?"

Higgins swallowed hard. "Around three hundred dollars, Captain."

"Turn it over immediately to the general mess fund."

Higgins deflated a little. "Captain, don't believe this man . . ."

"Mr. Higgins, you may go now," the skipper said very coldly.

Higgins nodded, tight-lipped, and started to leave. But as he passed Al he was seized again by the glassy-eyed rage. "You cheap punk, I've made it my business to personally censor your mail lately," he said viciously. "If marrying that bag is a shotgun necessity . . ."

That's when Al Woods made it his business to deck Higgins with a fast right to the sneer. He swung with a wild and wonderful sense of reckless abandonment, and it was enormously satisfying to watch Higgins bounce off a filing cabinet, ricochet off a desk, go plunging over a chair, and sprawl ludicrously on the deck. If I don't get more than twenty years at hard labor for that, it's worth it, Al thought.

Higgins scrambled to his feet, clutching his bleeding nose, and squawled, "Striking an officer! You saw it, Captain! Now by God we'll see! Striking a commissioned officer! You're under arrest, Woods!"

"Stop shouting, Mr. Higgins," the skipper said disgustedly. "You fell down. I saw you fall down. Goff saw you fall down. Go to your cabin, Mr. Higgins, and clean up. Your nose seems to be bleeding."

Looking stunned and unbelieving, eyes rolling wildly, Higgins gaped at the C.O. for a long incredulous moment, and then went stalking indignantly from the office. Goff locked the door again, grinning.

"Noisy fellow," the skipper growled. "Now, Woods, I've checked this stuff you gave me. Cupper is going to pay for every article you have marked against him. Likewise Higgins. I ask you to believe that I have paid monthly for every canned ham, or whatever, I've taken ashore. If I'm not entirely honest, at least I'm too smart to take chances."

"I believe you, sir," Al said. What about hitting Higgins?

"You had an excusable grievance, Woods, but you should never have gone to a civilian gossip-peddler with it. As captain of this ship I'm responsible for the conduct of my officers. You should have laid your complaint before me. However, that's second-guessing now. Do you realize what would have happened if you'd spoken up back there a while ago? If you'd turned this envelope over to the Board of Inquiry?"

"I think so," Al said. Hitting Higgins was a major offense.

"Whatever your reasons, I appreciate the fact that when the chips were down, you elected to protect your ship from scandal, Woods. But I wonder if you understand what your silence may get you?"

Al shrugged. "I expected to get busted to second-class an' shipped out, at least, sir," he said. What *about* Higgins? he thought.

"You won't be demoted, don't worry," the skipper growled. "But you're to report to the receiving station, and undoubtedly they will reassign you to a pretty rugged kind of duty, Woods. Now, I'm fully aware that you've made yourself the goat of this affair, but it isn't too late. Say the word and I will go with you to the District Office and explain this situation as I now understand it, Woods. I believe you're entitled to clear your name. You may have acted impulsively."

"Nossir," Al said stubbornly. "I thought it out, I knew what I was doin'." He shrugged. "After last Sunday—well, everybody's proud of this ship, sir. That goes for me especially, I guess. If it got around that some of the officers . . . well, I made my choice, sir."

The skipper nodded bleakly. "One thing I *can* do for you," he muttered. "You'll leave this ship with a 4.0 in conduct, Woods."

Good conduct means gold hash marks someday, Al thought wryly. Maybe I'll get a good conduct medal, even. I can hardly wait, boy.

The skipper came around his desk and shook Al's hand. "Good luck, Woods," he said. "Next time, have faith in your C.O., eh?"

Al nodded, feeling a little overcome, and took his envelope of savings and his orders, and shook hands with glum Sam Goff. "I'm gonna miss this old bucket, Yeoman Sam," he said. "How about droppin' me a line sometimes, boy?" Yeoman Sam nodded. Sure, Al. Sure.

When Al got out to the well deck with his mattress roll and sea bag, a dozen shipmates waited there with angry, apologetic faces, and he shook hands all around, making facetious remarks and inane remarks, and then he was leaving the *Legume* forever. He was crossing the gangplank when Doc O'Neal yelled for him to wait. "You forgot your goddam typewriter, Hemingway," Doc said with a lame grin, bringing it to Al.

"Throw that dirty double-crosser over the side," Al said, but he accepted the cased Smith-Corona, and stood looking at Doc. "Well, maybe we'll bump into each other again somewhere, some time, barber."

"I told you, I'm puttin' in for a transfer," Doc said firmly. "You watch, boy. Goff will, too. An' plenty other guys."

"Don't be silly," Al said gruffly. "Well, *bon voyage*, podner."

A truck was waiting to take him to the receiving station, and he loaded his gear in the back and started to climb into the cab. And behind him he heard the bosun's pipe of M.A. Hawk, and heard the powerful Diesels rumble to life. He turned and watched, seeing the skipper appear on the bridge wing, feeling the skipper's stony eyes on him briefly, hearing the skipper's curt orders. "Cast off the bow lines!" Huxley echoed in his hoarse bawl. "Cast off breast lines!" The *Legume* began to ease away from the dock, and then the stern lines went snaking aboard and the Diesels hummed and the great gray buoy tender was moving faster. Maybe I'll never see her again, Al thought, with a lump in his throat. Her starboard side was shoreward, and he looked up at the high flying bridge, seeing the tarp-covered twenty with its muzzle tilted skyward, threatening the gulls and the clouds. Al sighed a shuddering sigh, and saw the men on the deck waving, and waved, and saw the skipper still there on the bridge wing, small and erect, a man who had a duodenal ulcer and could have asked for easier duty ashore, or even a discharge; a man who had guts and pride and a bleak arctic dignity that hid the essential kindness inside.

"Let's go, mack," the truck driver said impatiently.

"You're gettin' paid by the hour, sonny," Al said. "Relax."

She was out into the greasy harbor now, and then disappearing behind other ships, but he could still see her rigging and the flying bridge and the covered twenties up there, gliding away. Old Hooligan bastridge, he thought sadly. He sighed. Well, here I go again.

CHAPTER 33

The Greenland Pool

A T THE receiving station Al handed his papers to a yeoman
third who was extremely cocky, but who had a ribbon on
his chest with battle stars on it, and therefore was entitled to his
cockiness.

"Another SC for the GP," the yeoman said. What's GP? Al
asked. "Greenland Pool," the yeoman said. Al's heart sank. Wait
for me, Jo, he thought. I'll be back in a couple years, little darling.
When does the Greenland Pool ship out? he asked, and the yeoman
shrugged and said, "No tellin', mack. Couple weeks maybe, give or
take a few days." But then, leafing through the papers, he said
abruptly, "*Legume*, huh?" And he looked at Al with sudden interest.
"Is it true, what they say?"

Al had a right to be cocky too. "Yeah," he said. "Anything anybody says about the Lagoon is bound to be true, quill-pusher."

"O.K., gut-robber," the yeoman grinned. "You'll be port watch."

All transients at the receiving station, a hotel that had joined the
Coast Guard for the duration, were divided into port and starboard
watches. At morning muster the master-at-arms would bawl, "Port
watch got the duty. Starboard watch fall in over that side." So Al
would fall in with whichever group *didn't* have the duty. Then the
M.A. would assign cleaning details and various chores to the duty
watch, and the off-duty guys could loaf. On the second morning the
M.A. asked for volunteer blood donors, and Al stepped forward, not
so much motivated by patriotism as by the M.A.'s statement the
donors would have liberty after finishing at the Marine Hospital.
He gave a pint of blood, got a free lunch (which wasn't fit for a
Hooligan, he thought), rode back into Boston, and did some lonely
drinking, which was good for his sore tonsils, and some lonely
thinking that didn't lead much of anywhere.

I got to beat this Greenland rap, he kept thinking, or I won't be with Jo for a long long time, boy. I got to figure me something.

He went to the Buddies Club and wrote her a long letter, explaining the situation, and urging her to drop everything and get on out to Boston, so they could at least get married and have a few days before he went off to live in an igloo. He sent it to her address in Tulsa, because he didn't know her home address, except for the town, and he figured it would get to her about as soon by being forwarded by her Tulsa landlady. Anyway, she might still be in Tulsa. He thought about calling her, but he was afraid the sound of her voice across the miles would undo him. He was emotionally a little unstable. And he could explain better in a letter. He sent it airmail. . . .

He cultivated the cocky yeoman at the receiving station. "Look, buddy," he said. "Can you find out any details about when and where this Greenland detail is gonna be goin'?" The yeoman said they had a big quota to fill, and everything was pretty indefinite. "You got two weeks at least, is my guess," he said. "Drink fast an' lay 'em often."

Al drank some, but he was a one-woman man from now on.

It was on the fourth morning that he saw Higgins among the officers at muster. Al eased into the rear ranks, out of Higgins's view. What's he doin' here? he wondered uneasily, and after that his main object was to avoid bumping into Higgins. I guess life wasn't happy for him on the *Legume* after the Board of Inquiry, Al reflected. Maybe he couldn't stand everybody knowin' who bloodied his pointed nose.

Al kept volunteering as a blood donor, just to get out of the hotel. He'd go to the Marine Hospital with the rest and then tell the technician, who never seemed to remember him, that he'd had an operation two months before, and the technician would say well, you better not give any blood, then. Or he'd say he was drunk the night before, and the technician would say they wanted blood, not alcohol.

As the weather got colder, his tonsils were sorer oftener. A pharmacist's mate third at the station gave him some salt water to gargle, but Al could get better temporary results with bourbon, or even beer.

He kept worrying about why didn't Jo write. He kept ducking the cleanup details, and volunteering as a blood donor. There were so many transients milling around that nobody ever caught on, and he didn't care if they did. What could they do to him? Being shipped to Greenland was about the worst punishment he could think of, and he was already lined up for that long cold exile. He knew he was supposed to be reporting to the galley every second day, but what the hell.

"You get anything definite about the Greenland bunch yet?" he would ask the yeomen. They would shrug. "Big dark secret," they said. And the cocky one would say, "Nobody seems to know anything definite."

So on the sixth morning Al went to the sick bay and said, "I got a sore throat, Chief." The CPM was always on duty at morning sick call, and he pried Al's mouth open with a wooden spatula and peered with interest into his throat, and clucked disapprovingly.

"If you're slated for Greenland, you got to have them out, son," he said. "You're goin' to the Brighton Marine Hospital today."

Al knew the way, all right. He'd been there before.

At the hospital they looked, and clucked. "That's about as pretty a set of long-infected tonsils as I've ever laid eyes on," the doctor said. "That's going to be quite an undertaking, sailor."

On the second day they gave Al a needle and a pretty young nurse insisted he get into a wheelchair, although he felt like a fool, and she pushed him down the long corridor and around to a room, and the doctor put him in a chair like a dentist's chair, or barber-shop chair, and used a little novocaine around the main area of trouble. And then he went in there and started to work. Immediately Al was spewing blood all over the doctor's clean white smock and his own hospital gown, very embarrassed and dismayed and trying to apologize between gagging and spraying torrents of crimson. The doctor's expression was very grim and concerned, but he didn't quit until he was through in there, and he told the nurse to nevermind the wheelchair, get a cart, and they took Al back to his bed in the big ward flat on his back, still gagging and spewing. He'd had no idea it would be such a messy deal; he'd always heard people talk about running down and having their tonsils extracted and then going back home.

"Don't clear your throat," the nurse said sternly. "If you'd stop trying to clear your throat you wouldn't bleed so much. Every time it begins to coagulate in there, you tear it loose again."

"I'm sorry," Al strangled. And he tried not to clear his throat, but when it would feel as if he were about to choke to death, he just couldn't help himself, and he would clear his throat. And here she'd come again, the blood—and the impatient nurse, whose impatience turned into frowning worry. She kept emptying the pan and Al kept filling it. Along toward evening another nurse came, with a coat-hanger deal and a bottle of some clear liquid, and they taped a needle into Al's vein and transfused the liquid into him. But he kept filling the pan.

He kept apologizing, too, but that didn't help either.

Around ten o'clock that night they pushed his bed down the corridor and into the operating room, and the doctor sewed up the right tonsil, which was causing all the trouble. Al lay on his back with the catgut or whatever it was laced into his throat, and every time the doctor tugged it to draw the seams tight, Al felt like a catfish that had just swallowed a baited hook.

Around midnight he began hemorrhaging again, and the night nurse went scurrying, and pretty soon he was back in the operating room again, having the left tonsil stitched shut. "You're a contrary cuss," the sleepy doctor said. "You make a fountain out of a mole hill."

"I feel like a catfish," Al husked weakly. "Listen, I gave a pint of blood a few days ago, if it's important or anything."

"Oh, hell," the doctor said. They transfused him that night with plasma and a pint of whole blood, and the technician called him an Indian giver. He was pleasantly weak and blank of mind.

They tried to bully him into eating breakfast, but there just wasn't any passage between his mouth and his stomach. He asked for coffee, but they refused. They're sore at me, he thought, and I don't blame them. But they gave him some Aspirgum to chew, so he could at least swallow saliva when he had to. His throat felt like he had a roll of barbed wire jammed in it. He couldn't eat, that's all. Anything as big as a match head wouldn't go down.

They fed him intravenously that night, and the friendly night nurse said he was one of her best patients because he wasn't always ringing his buzzer and wanting something. I just don't happen to want anything, except out of here, Al thought weakly.

Every morning he demanded his freedom. "I got to get back to the receiving station," he'd tell them urgently. "I'm expecting some important mail. It might be there already. I'm strong, let me out."

You're a physical wreck, they said. You're so weak you couldn't

get a dime out of your pocket for carfare, chum. We've got to
build you up a little before we turn you loose.

But on the sixth morning the nurse said, "If you eat every bit of
your breakfast, the doctor says he'll parole you."

So Al forced all of the food down, including the toast that was
sheer torment to his throat, and they brought him his clothes, and
the doctor signed him out on a three-day convalescence leave.
"You're an outpatient, check back with us once a day," the doctor
said sternly.

Al headed for the receiving station, tense and worried. There must
be a letter from Jo somewhere, dammit.

The first person he saw when he entered the hotel was a short,
stocky, glum, bespectacled yeoman named Sam Goff, who stopped
a cigarette halfway to his mouth and stared at Al in disbelief. "You
must be a ghost," he protested. "You're suppose to be long gone for
Greenland."

"What the hella you doin' here, Yeoman Sam?" Al demanded.

"Me an' the ship's surgeon put in for transfers," Goff said. "Al,
they said you shipped out in the Greenland Pool, buddy."

Al explained the situation, not fully grasping the fact that the
Greenland Pool had departed without him. They can always ship
me to Greenland as a one-man pool, he thought. He didn't know
whether he approved of Doc and Sam resigning from the *Legume*
or not. Right now, he wanted to find out if there was any mail from
Oklahoma.

"Doc's in the sick bay," Goff said. "You wanta go see him, Al?"

"Later," Al said. "Look, Sammy, I'm anxious to see if I got any
mail. Where do they keep the mail, buddy?"

Goff was checking mail back of the desk when the cocky yeoman
third with the battle stars sauntered out of the office and saw Al.
He looked surprised. "Hey, *Legume*, I thought you went north
like a high-flyin' goose," he said. "You s'pose to be Greenland bound,
boy."

Al explained about his operation, without going into detail, and
the cocky yeoman looked a little rueful or something and said,
"There was a girl come in while I had the duty lookin' for you, pal.
I told her you had shipped out with the Greenland Pool. You better
call her."

Al's heart was thumping like a bass drum. "What she look like?"

The yeoman shrugged. "Small, like. Black hair. Good-lookin'."

Jo! Al thought wildly, and Sam was handing him a letter, and it was from Jo. He ripped it open with shaking hands and read it. "I'll arrive at three-ten, October first," she wrote. "That's a Thursday. If you can't get off to meet me, Alvin dear, I will go to the Copley Plaza and register as Miss Josephine Hill, temporarily." There was more, but Al's stunned brain refused to register it. This was Monday, October fifth. And Jo thought he had gone to Greenland.

"No kiddin', I thought you'd shipped for Greenland, pal."

"No," Al said, his thoughts going off in all directions. "No."

"I hope I didn't louse up anything for you, Woods," the yeoman said worriedly, seeing Al's white-faced panic.

"I gotta find her," Al said. "If she didn't already go back."

He left the receiving station at a run and wildly flagged down a passing cab. But there was no use hurrying. When he got to the Copley Plaza he learned that Jo had checked out Saturday, the third. Day before yesterday. She's gone back to Oklahoma, Al thought with anguish. He went to South Station and asked all sorts of questions, but they were unable to help him. They didn't remember any particular small square-shouldered girl with crow-black hair and gray eyes and a wistful smile and slightly bowed legs. During their passionate interlude in Tulsa, Jo had mentioned idly that she had a college chum and sorority sister who lived in Massachusetts, but Al couldn't remember where in Massachusetts. She might be there, he thought. But his leaden heart told him where she was. On her way back to Tulsa.

Al took a fast cab back to the receiving station and hunted up Yeoman Sam. "I got to have some emergency leave," he panted. "She must of gone back to Tulsa, Sam. She thinks I'm headed for the North Pole." Sympathetic Sam took him to see the chief yeoman, a warm personal friend of Goff's, it seemed, and the chief patiently got all the details and said judicially, "Right now you're on convalescence leave, Woods. You got to check back to the hospital once a day, it says on your pass. But Thursday morning, if you're cleared by the hospital, we'll fix you up with thirteen days' regular leave. You got a lot of accumulated leave time on your record. Thursday come see me. Right?"

Doc and Sam finagled liberty that afternoon and the three of them sat in a dim bar drinking moderately and listening to the juke box play songs that tore Al's heart into confetti, and Doc, trying to cheer up the poor old cook, said, "Hey, Alvinhead, did Sammy tell you what he's got cookin' for us three musket-eaters, buddy?"

Al shook his head, sighing despondently.

"Him an' the chief yeoman are ole friends," Doc said. "Sam's fixin' it up for us to get assigned to a crew together. They're gonna start poolin' for sub-chaser school in Miami. That's in Florida, in case you never heard of it." There is a Miami in Oklahoma, Al thought sadly, not far from Tulsa. "Land of eternal sunshine," Doc enthused, "an' citrus fruities an' flowers, especially the Spanish fly an' other well-known aphrodisiacs. The poop is them sub-killers carry one surgeon, one stenographer, an' one short-order cook. That'll be us, baby."

"Boy," Al said listlessly. "That's great," he moaned.

Goff built it up a little. "The chief thinks he can fix it so we'll get a home base in Florida somewhere. I tell you, us *Legume* graduates are treated with southern courtesy. That Florida stuff, fish an' swim, lay around in the sun, drink rum collins. Those chasers got twin-forty-millimeters, I heard, Al. They're fast babies."

Al had a vagrant thought. "What happened with slobberin' Dennis?"

They hooted with laughter. "When the skipper put the arm on him to pay for the chow he smuggled up the alley, he got real indignant an' demanded an immediate transfer," Yeoman Sam related. "He got it—just in time to latch onto the Greenland Pool."

"He'll probly open him a blubber black market up there," Doc said. Then he groaned at Sam Goff. "This cook is a real eager beaver today, Sam. You know what I think? I think he's in love."

Jo, baby, where the hell *are* you? Al thought with dumb misery.

He slept at the hospital that night so he could check in with the doctor in the morning and have done with it for the day, and then he rode the streetcar and subway into Boston and wandered around like a lost soul. It was a sunny, crisp, poignant autumn day, and October was when he had first started falling helplessly in love with Jo; he was consumed by a bittersweet nostalgia for Oklahoma in October. Season of mists and mellow fruitfulness. Season of the anguish and the searching, season of smoke and crimson flame and the lonely pathos of wind-blown leaves. On Boston Common there was gold and scarlet and the dry dead cackle of drifted leaves underfoot, and Al had all of life condensed into one great leaden counterweight suspended in his chest.

He sat on a bench by a pool, chewing Aspirgum and brooding at the leaves skimming across the water like elfin ships, brooding at the mirrored loveliness of sky and trees. Jo would have loved it here, he thought. She always loved October best of all. And me best of all, too.

A scatter of people strolled along the paths and he looked at them fiercely, envying the couples and feeling compassion for the lone ones, knowing how it was to be desperately alone. Like that girl coming through the trees, wearing a yellow polo coat, hands jammed into the pockets, her dark head bent, kicking at the leaves. Kicking leaves is no cure for anything, Al told her mutely. Kicking trees or rocks is no help, either. The hard truth is that nothing helps, madam.

Suddenly there was something throat-clutchingly familiar about that girl, the polo coat, that dark head, that leaf-kicking routine. Al got unsteadily to his feet, staring with his heart in his eyes as she came on along the path. Don't trick me now, you crazy mind, Al begged. Don't cut me to ribbons every time a girl with black hair goes by.

She lifted her head to look at the sky and her face was sad, pensive, wistful, and terribly vulnerable. Al choked and started toward her like a sleepwalker, unsure, fearful, and she saw him and stopped, the stunned disbelief clear on her sweet face, a hand going to her throat. And then they were running, arms reaching out.

She was warm and real, weeping in his arms, kissing him. "Jo," he said huskily. "Jo, baby. I thought you'd gone back home."

He'd never seen her cry before. She cried beautifully, her arms clinging desperately around his neck, crying and covering his face with tearful kisses. "They sssaid you'd bbbeen sssent..." She choked up. "They sssaid you'd gggone to Greenland!"

"I missed by the skin of my teeth," Al said. "Aw, baby doll."

"I didn't know what to do," she sobbed. "I didn't want to go back—this was closer to Greenland than Tulsa. I thought maybe they'd need civilian government employees there, and maybe I could go too..."

"Hush, honey, don't talk about it," Al said. "Nobody is goin' to Greenland. We're goin' to Florida, baby. You wanta go to Florida?"

"Oh, Alvin," she said, leaning back in his arms and giving him a tremulous, damp, lopsided smile. "Anywhere, just so *you're* there."

That's all he wanted to know or would ever want to know or

need to know. Thanks, he said a little self-consciously in his mind. Thanks for everything—especially the tonsils. I don't know why I go on worrying about everything when everything always turns out O.K. in the end. From now on I'm through worrying, boy. I got it made.

"Hey!" he croaked. "Let's go see about gettin' married, Jo."

"O.K.," she said, sniffling. "I don't mind if I do, Alvin."